RIDE
FOR ME

The North Shore Crew—Book One

-VR BAUCKE-

Copyright © VR Baucke, 2017.
Published by VR Baucke, 2019.
All rights reserved.

Cover image from Shutterstock © FXQuadro

All rights reserved. No part of this publication may be reproduced or transmitted in any form or by any means, electronic or mechanical, including photocopying, recording, or any other information storage retrieval system without the written permission of the author, except for brief quotations in a review.
Thank you for respecting the hard work of this author.

This novel is entirely a work of fiction.
Names, characters, businesses, places, events, locales, and incidents are the products of the author's imagination. Any resemblance to actual persons, living or dead, or actual events is purely coincidental.

This novel is intended for those 18 years and over.

Paperback ISBN-13: 978-0-473-47803-2
E-book ISBN-13: 978-0-473-47804-9

DEDICATION

To everyone who wanted to try something new,
but feared doing it.
This is proof that you can do anything!

BRACE YOURSELVES

You're about to meet The North Shore Crew!!!
Lil, Gage, Mace, Trav, Mickey (Josh), Kimmie and Nico are waiting for you, and are about to take you on one hell of a journey.

AUTHOR'S NOTE

This book is written using UK English, and down here in Aotearoa (New Zealand) we also use some random-ass slang that you may not have come across before. Just roll with it. In the words of Trav; "It's all gravy, baby."

"Even the darkest night will end and the sun will rise."
-Victor Hugo.

PROLOGUE
GAGE

~Four months from now~

I CAME HERE today to say goodbye to her, a proper goodbye this time, and it killed me that I couldn't look her in the eyes and ask for the forgiveness I knew she would willingly give.

I wanted her to stare back at me through the tears and tell me it would all be okay.

But she wouldn't - she *couldn't*.

I longed for her to tell me I was making the right decision, that she forgave me, even though the unexpected turn of events that had brought me here today had nothing, yet *everything*, to do with her. I needed her to slap me for it, to wake me from this dream that I didn't want woken from.

But still, she *couldn't*.

Instead, I settled on the grass beside her while trying to collect the appropriate words. I took my time to organise them in my head, internalise them, repeating them over and over until they sounded just right.

She didn't acknowledge my presence, though, I knew she would already be aware of why I was here after months away without visiting her once.

For that I was incredibly guilty.

It wasn't my intention to be gone for so long.

I'm such a shit human.

I clung to the big bouquet of dark purple roses like they were my only life line. Realising I had all but destroyed the stems by squeezing them nervously, I slid them into the large vase beside me, buying a few extra moments.

Turning my attention back to Lotte, I growled roughly to clear the wad of dread from my throat.

"Babe, I..."

Fuck, this sucks. So fucking much!

Placing my hand on the grass next to her, I decided to speak straight from my heart.

"I'm sorry I haven't been back for months. I intended to but was hurting and didn't want to face this shit reality again. You have always been my world and this whole situation is… well, it sucks. I let you down. I failed you, and now I'm here asking, *begging,* for forgiveness because I've found someone when I least expected to. I never wanted to love a woman again like I love—loved—*love* you."

Ah, fuck!

"You will always be special to me. *Always*. And you will always own a part of me that I can never give to anyone else. For some reason, in this fucked up universe, there is this ray of sunshine who is dragging me kicking and screaming out of the darkness that's surrounded me for too long. And as much as I've tried, I don't I want to fight it anymore."

The feeling of defeat was immense. I hung my head between my knees while raking my hands through my hair. I definitely felt like the bad guy - even though I shouldn't. Technically I hadn't done anything wrong.

"I love you," I whispered so only she could hear.

Despite the day being perfectly still with only the low hum of bees and the songs of the birds to disturb us, I felt the ghost of a cool breeze ripple across the back of my neck. As per usual, everyone else around us was peacefully quiet. I smiled as the goose bumps prickled over my neck then wove across my shoulders. I was unable to suppress the shudder that followed.

"Stop that, it's creepy as fuck," I chuckled, pulling some grass and tossing it her way.

But my words and actions were met with silence and stillness.

"Lotte, I don't expect you to forgive me for everything, and I can live with that. Just... just know that you'll always be my first and nothing can change that. I know you would want me to be happy, and if I'm honest to us both, it's been a long time coming. But now I can finally say I truly am happy again. And I want to be."

I closed my eyes and swallowed heavily. I knew she could hear me.

"Goodbye, baby cakes. I'll visit again soon."

Giving the grass between us one final pat, I rose before whispering, "Sleep tight, babe."

Pressing a kiss to the end of two fingers, I aimed them her way then turned to leave. On my way down the path to where my truck was parked, I tried to shrug off the feeling of eyes boring into my back.

LIL

~Present day~

MICKEY SWERVED AND pulled in at the curb. My body lurched forward before being thrown back into the seat of his ute.

"Jeez, Mickey, what the hell!"

"Look," he threw an arm close to my face and pointed at the house. "They started the fucking fire without me."

"Well that's what you get for making us late!" I sassed, already opening the door and stepping onto the footpath.

Sure enough, the smell of burning wood tainted the late afternoon air and the remaining ghosts of smoke dissipated into the sky beyond the roof of the house. We approached the backyard where laughter rose, combining with the music. The crew came into view when we rounded the corner of the house.

"Whatup, bitches! Lil 'n' Mickey in the hooouuse!" I whooped with my hands raised above my head.

My brother and I were welcomed by various greetings hurled from our group of mates sitting around the firepit. The crew were well into their first few rounds of drinks, and Mace was the only one to stand after snapping his head our way.

"About bloody time!" He stalked over to us and engulfed me in a bear hug, just like always. "Nice of you both to finally join us."

I scoffed. "Blame Mickey. *I* was running on time."

"What the fuck ever," Mickey mumbled and headed for the chilly bin.

Mace ducked his head to be closer to my ear. "Bad day at the office?"

"Yup. He's not saying much though, as per usual." I pursed my lips.

"Hey," Mace lightly tapped me on the ass, "you drinking tonight?"

I raised my brows and met his pretty blue eyes. "Do bears shit in the woods?"

"Oh crap," he guffawed. "It's gonna be one of *those* nights, isn't it, Lil Bean?"

Linking arms with my best male friend, I fell into step with him. "You'd better brace yourself, because shiz is about to get real."

Mace rumbled a chuckle until I gave his bulging bicep a quick squeeze.

"Don't touch what you can't afford," he drawled.

I snorted. "Says the guy who just touched my ass!"

"Oh, I can afford it."

"Whatever, keep telling yourself that, love," I teased.

Mace simply rolled his eyes then propelled me towards one of the worn outdoor couches. "Just go sit down while I find you a drink."

"Thanks, Macey-poo. You're the best."

"Hey!" Kimmie exclaimed through Mace's growl—he hated that nickname.

I threw my ass into the space beside Kimmie and whooped when she bounced a couple of times, almost landing on my lap.

Regaining her seating, Kimmie dropped her voice low and asked, "Is Mickey okay? He seems a little uptight."

Possessing the hearing of a bat, my brother whipped his head around and glared at Kimmie.

"He's fine," I reassured her while flipping him off.

Mickey simply flared his nostrils then resumed talking to Trav. My eyes snagged with Trav's across the flames and he raised his beer in greeting. His dimpled grin always made my own smile appear, and tonight was no exception. However, the smile slipped from my face a second later when I realised I was still empty handed.

"Mace!"

He spun, immediately halting the conversation between him and Nico. I threw up my arms to emphasise my lack of vessel.

"I'm getting it," Mace shouted over the music. "And I definitely didn't forget."

I laughed through my exclamation. "You totally forgot, didn't you!"

Nico man-giggled. "He totally forgot, Lil. Sorry for distracting him," he grinned.

There was no way I could hold it against the gentle giant. "All good, Neek, you know how Mace is; sees something shiny and can't maintain focus."

"Oh, ha ha, cut a man when he's down," Mace bitched as he dug out my drink.

He lobbed a bottle of alcoholic ginger beer my way and it sailed through the air in slow motion. I moved on instinct, hurling myself from the couch and diving for the bottle. The air was knocked from my lungs when I landed, and damn did it hurt my boobs! However, satisfaction reigned when the bottle neatly landed in my hands before hitting the grass. I lay prone for a few beats while my friends pissed themselves laughing.

"Jeez, Mace!" I sat back on my heels and flicked the lawn clippings from my jeans and top.

"Just keeping you on your toes, Lil Bean," he chuckled and popped the cap off his beer.

Trav's voice rose above everyone else's. "Lil! That was epic! That's gotta be your best dive yet."

I stumbled to my feet and brushed off again. "Thanks, Travie. That one hurt the most too." I held up the bottle and frowned. "Dammit. I can't drink this now that it's shaken."

Trav flicked his hand. "I'll take care of that. Chuck it here."

Our Travis was never one for wastage; especially when it came to an alcoholic beverage, and it was most definitely the reason why he frequently ended up in trouble.

I handed him the shaken bottle on my way to get a fresh one, and he immediately flipped his hat backwards, dropped to one knee and chugged it back.

Kimmie stood and clapped her hands. "And this is where we need to get some food cooking!"

She was the mother hen of the group, always making sure the crew was taken care of—especially while on the rarks.

Nico nodded and headed for the barbecue without a word.

"Not without me, you won't," Mickey called and jumped to his feet. He was at the barbecue and lighting a match before Neek had the chance.

Trav chuckled from beside me and tilted the empty bottle toward the boys.

"Between the two of them, they have enough knowledge and skills to blow up the entire neighbourhood. I'd better supervise."

I laughed hard. "I really don't think your powers of supervision will *decrease* the chances of something getting blown up."

Trav turned and continued to walk backwards as he threw his arms wide. "Seriously, Lil, what could go wrong?"

"No, Trav!" I exclaimed and pointed at him. "Every time you say that, something *always* happens. You're a trouble magnet!"

His grin widened. "It's all gravy, baby."

"Oh my God," I snickered and waved him off. "Just don't burn the food this time, *please!* I don't like my sausage burnt!"

Mace sniggered from behind me. "Neither do I, Lil. Neither do I."

I twisted and found him sitting on the couch where Kimmie and I had been. Without giving too much thought of where I was sitting, I blindly collapsed beside him and apparently squashed the edge of his thigh.

"Ouch! Fuck, Lil Bean. Watch where your goddamn ass is going!" He then slung his arm around my shoulders and pulled me close.

I scoffed. "As if your rock-hard thighs can't handle it."

"I wasn't fucking tensing," he growled against my forehead.

"That's what they all say."

Mace scoffed and raised his bottle. Clinking it with mine, we both took a swig in silence while watching the guys. A couple of beats passed before Mace bent his head towards mine again.

"How have you been, Lil? Like, *really* been?"

I met his eyes and let the façade drop for a moment. "In all honesty, I've been great lately."

"I hope so." He tapped his forefinger against the tip my bottle. "Go easy tonight, yeah?"

"Always."

With a raise of his brows, he gave me the *yeah right* look I'd received countless times throughout the years.

Mace and I (and Mickey) went way back; almost as far as Kimmie and I did. He knew things about me no other living soul did. And likewise, I'd seen Mace through his darkest days. We'd battled through a lot over the years, and were always there for one another; it was simply what we did.

"I mean it, Missy. Last time we got on the piss, you tried to molest me with a goddamn bottle."

I threw back my head and laughed at the dimming sky.

"Oh, c'mon, don't pretend you didn't like it. It would be right up your alley."

Mace's expression darkened. "I can assure you that I do not enjoy being the recipient of ass play."

"So, you've dabbled?" I countered without missing a beat.

Mace ran a hand over his face. "Fuck me," he muttered. "You're dirty, Lil Bean, and I don't want you to say another word about it."

I shrugged nonchalantly. "Don't knock it till you've tried it, is all I'm sayin'."

Mace threw his hands up and pushed to his feet. "Nup, I'm outies."

"Love you, Macey-poo," I called as he made a swift getaway.

He waved me off and headed for the guys without giving me the satisfaction of replying to my bullshit.

I loved winding him up. It was too easy and totally hilarious. Plus, the sadistic side of me was convinced he actually *enjoyed* me annoying the hell out of him.

LIL

ALCOHOL WAS THE devil on my shoulder. Him and I went way back, and some of our history wasn't pretty; there was a sickness lurking at the bottom of every bottle, a disease I was susceptible to. It hadn't been an issue in quite some time and thankfully Mace had relaxed his constant vigil over my consumption.

The few hours that slipped past saw all of us in various states of disarray. I half-listened to Kimmie talk smack with Neek while I danced a little to the music. Lifting a drink to my mouth, I frowned when no liquid passed my lips.

<*Damn, my drink's empty.*>

Reading my mind, Mickey leaned over the arm of the couch and dug through the chilly bin. His irritation grew with each bottle he pulled out then put back. Finally making eye contact with me, he gave me the bad news.

"You're out. There's more in the house."

"Dammit!" I stood and yelled over the music. "Hey, does anyone need anything from the inside fridge?"

"Oh," Kimmie waved her arm. "Another bag of chips please, Lil. Trav's such a hungus."

"The fuck!" Trav, exclaimed indignantly, somehow raising his voice an entire octave.

"You totally are, Trav! Be right back. No one take my seat," I warned with a savage finger point across the crew.

Jogging across the lawn and leaving the music and laughter behind me—as well as Trav yelling, "Yeah, get some!"—I took the steps in a single bound. Entering the familiar kitchen without slowing my pace, I made a beeline for the fridge and yanked it open. This place felt like home and I treated it as such. Kimmie had moved back home a couple of months ago before her parents took off on a year-long overseas holiday. The Davis residence was designed for entertaining, and the crew planned to make the most of her parent's absence.

I shoved various condiments out of the way until I found the ginger beer stash. Quietly celebrating to myself, I moved a few to the bench and danced to the beat of the outside music.

I had my head in the fridge again when an unfamiliar growl of a motorbike caught my attention. It pulled up to the house then cut out, and it wasn't long before a new voice rumbled in conversation with Mace close to the back door. Mickey invaded my mind at that precise moment.

<Stay inside, we need to talk before you meet this guy.>

With the fear of missing out getting the better of me, I tightly clasped three bottles in each hand then drunkenly ran through the kitchen and across the deck. In my haste, I utterly failed to see where the last step ended and the lawn began.

One moment I was on my feet, the next I had lost all contact with the ground. One leg folded at an awkward angle, my arms flailed and sent bottles in all directions, and my long hair whipped wildly around my face before I landed on my ass with a mortified shriek.

"Shit the bed! My ankle!" I growled and clutched the throbbing joint.

Despite the pain, I still had the sense to glance around to ensure I wasn't surrounded by broken glass.

Mace's booming laughter commandeered my attention until a deep, cynical voice spoke.

"Who are you and what the fuck does that even mean?"

I snapped my head skyward to see a large silhouette of a man standing between me and the fire.

"It *means,* I just smashed up my ankle. I'm fine by the way, thanks for asking," I deadpanned.

The newcomer may have chuckled, though it sounded more like a scoff. He did, however, offer me his hand

After a moment's hesitation, I slapped both my hands in his and hopped slightly as he hauled me to my feet. I was about to release his grasp when a tingling sensation prickled through my palm, causing my fingers to involuntary squeeze against the unexpected feeling.

Judging by the stranger's explosive reaction, he felt something too; he dropped my hands, reared back and drew to full height then eyed me cautiously.

I raked my gaze up and down the entire length of his body, automatically assessing and drawing conclusions.

He was tall and muscular, long, straight nose, dark eyes and dishevelled hair. And, to complete his hostile demeanour, a dark beard surrounded the scowl on his mouth.

Black. Black everything; motorcycle boots, jeans, leather jacket hanging from one hand and t-shirt that revealed the barest hint of ink at the bottom of one sleeve.

I swear to God my ovaries swooned as every last hint of moisture left my mouth.

What an... an...

ASSHOLE!

A shadow seemed to shroud his presence, so raw and unreceptive, and I could practically *feel* it vibrating around his space. His eyes held a hollow soullessness and he wore sorrow like a second skin, yet his unmistakable arrogance countered any sense of sympathy I felt for him in this moment.

Despite unwittingly being drawn to this stranger, just looking at him made me grind my teeth together. I scoffed and returned his scowl while popping a hip for added sass.

"Who are you? Like, Batman or something? Because I don't believe the real Batman wears a small animal on his face."

He laughed for sure this time. A rough, contemptuous chuckle rolled over me and his scowl turned into a smirk.

"Well, aren't you just a little ray of sunshine."

Before I got the chance to reply, Mace (who was completely forgotten beside us until now) cut in with his voiced raised.

"Lil, this is my cousin, Gage Westbrook. He's just moved up from Tauranga to work with me and Dad." Mace glared and pointed the top of his bottle my way. "Play nice, Missy."

Ignoring Mace's bitchy tone, I folded my arms across my chest then darted comparative glances between the pair of them.

Despite being cousins, the physical family resemblance was non-existent. They did, however, possess the same manner of assertiveness in the way they held themselves; both standing tall with their shoulders back, showing that they not only looked powerful, they felt it. But that's where the similarities ended.

Snapping from my assessment, I turned to Mace. "I always play nice. You just can't handle all this badass," I declared and waved a hand over myself.

Mace dropped his chin slightly and raised his brows at me. "Lil Bean," he warned.

I waved him off with an irritated flick of my fingers then stepped back a pace. Batman's presence was too commandeering and suffocating for my liking.

"Yeah, yeah. Whatevs, Macey."

Ignoring Mace's growling retort about being called Macey, I turned on my uninjured heel and crouched to collect scattered bottles. As I stood, I mentally reset my mood to fun-loving and forced the sullen, party-crasher from my mind.

Taking the deck steps as fast as I dared, I made my way inside to exchange my drinks for non-shaken ones while willing myself to resist the urge to glance back at Gage. He had me unreasonably flustered and I didn't like it one bit.

The feeling of eyes boring into my back made my lungs constrict. I ignored the shit out of them, and I'd be damned if I admitted to emphasising the sway in my hips ever so slightly.

3
GAGE

FUCK. COMING AROUND here was a mistake.

I had only moved to Auckland a few days ago and every aspect of my life was in various states of disarray; being in this bullshit city just emphasised that fact. Now, standing with my cousin at some random broad's house, I regretted my decision even more.

Mace insisted I make an appearance tonight since these were his best mates, and I would apparently be seeing a lot of them. He had assured me that they were a decent group of people who would do anything for each other. 'The Crew' they called themselves.

I wasn't exactly thrilled about acquiring new 'friends', but better to hang with the devil you know than the devil you didn't. I didn't want to be part of their clique, but I trusted my cousin. He knew what had brought me here, and I couldn't blame the guy for trying take my mind off things.

Mace studied me with hope shining in his eyes. His aspiration that I would fit in here made me want to make an effort simply for his sake. Plus, I had nothing better to do tonight.

Our conversation was interrupted by some long-haired bimbo blazing across the deck before landing tits up at my feet. When she looked up at me with her big round eyes, I felt as if she stripped me bare in that single glance.

An internal battle waged within me as I tried to summon all composure and not lose my shit by laughing in her face. Laughter didn't pass my lips often, and tonight wasn't going to be the exception.

I glanced at Mace who wore a shit-eating grin while he laughed loudly. His features were alight and adoring; the girl meant something to him, that much was obvious. The least I could do was show an ounce of gentlemanliness, so I extended a hand to help her up.

The tip of her tongue darted out as I tugged her to standing, and out of nowhere I wondered what she tasted like.

Jesus Christ. Get a grip man!

I tightened my grip on her hands and waited for her to become steady on her feet. That was when I felt it; whatever the hell it was that surged between us.

I recoiled and dropped her hands like a hot fucking rock. Taking a hasty step back to see her properly, her eyes were wide and her shiny lips were parted in surprise.

Those same eyes skipped over my entire body in a way that exposed me infinitely more than it should have. I knew she was judging me based on first impressions. I drew myself to full height and held still under her scrutiny.

She was hot and intense while unintentionally drawing me in like the fucking sun. Damn, this girl was somethin' else, that was for sure. I resisted the urge to cover my crotch with my hands, opting to tuck my free hand into the pocket of my jeans.

Thank Christ Mace finally spoke up before I burst into flames. However, his introductions didn't provide any further information apart from the little spitfire's name.

Lil.

He said her name was Lil.

Despite my curiosity, I didn't want to know more. There was no point; I wasn't prepared to go down *that* road again.

Mace's introduction caused her eyes to flick back and forth between us and a crease to appear between her brows. I was aware of her having a clipped conversation with Mace, but I couldn't hear a goddamn thing as I visually drank her in.

She sauntered back into the house and my eyes dropped to her ass as she excessively swayed her hips, obviously having had a few drinks tonight. No matter how much the little voice of warning inside my head screamed, I simply couldn't tear my eyes away from her.

With much effort, I shook off my thoughts and blinked hard before turning my attention back to Mace. What I saw slammed into me like a tonne of bricks. Mace also stared after Little Miss Sunshine with his eyes glazed over. I twigged; it was like *that* between them.

I resisted the urge to rub my chest where an unexpected pang rocketed through me, then I thumbed towards the house. "Who the fuck was that?"

Mace scoffed. "That, my dear cousin, is hell on wheels in the form of Lily McMillan." A hint of pride pricked his voice before he chuckled and took a swig of beer.

"Christ," I muttered and ran a hand through my hair.

One of the guys headed for the house and offered a beer on his way past. I took a long pull from the bottle and tried to wrap my head around what just happened. That woman was one gorgeous train wreck...

Leaning forward and tilting his drink in my direction, Mace elaborated. "And that was her brother. They're both my best mates, so don't get any ideas."

I matched his patronising tone. "And you looking at her with your tongue hanging out counts for nothing?"

"Bullshit I was! She means more to me than you'll ever know, but she's family and totally off limits," he bit back.

Frustration lit his face; Lil seemed to be a sore point for him.

"Riiight," I drawled. "So, you going to be rude all night or properly introduce me to these mates of yours?"

I needed a distraction, and being scrutinised by strangers seemed the best way to go about it after meeting Sunshine.

"I've just been letting you warm into it. Little ol' Lil back there is nothing compared to the whole crew together. And it's rare that we are, because, Nico is usually away."

"Away?"

"Army," Mace explained.

He gestured towards the firepit and walked me over. "Yo guys," Mace yelled over the music and laughter. He rattled off a round of introductions, and as he spoke I exchanged bottle salutes and head nods while trying to remember everyone's name and occupation.

Nico was in the Army, Trav was a piss-head mechanic, and Kimmie liked to get her freak on with a pole between her thighs.

"You're so full of shit, Mace!" Kimmie shouted and pegged a half-eaten sausage at him.

It hit him in the chest, leaving saucy spots on his light-coloured shirt. A glare accompanied the action before she turned her pretty smile on me. "I'm a photographer. It's nice to meet you, Gage."

Mace let out a string of expletives and fingered the greasy stain. He licked his fingers before wiping them on the side of his jeans, then stabbed a finger at Kimmie.

"That'll keep, lil' Kim."

She giggled and wiggled her brows at him.

Lil and her brother strode across the lawn together, both of them scowling and ignoring each other. Mickey stopped at my side and offered his hand.

"Mickey is our pyromaniac Firefighter," Mace explained as the guy openly sized me up. Mickey said an icy, "Mate," before releasing my hand and throwing himself onto a couch.

"And last but not least, this is Lil. But you two are already acquainted," Mace chuckled, obviously thinking he was a fuckin' comedian.

Little Miss Sunshine didn't acknowledge me as she wove through her friends towards the spot Kimmie created for her. She did, however, spare me a single glance when I sat in the only seat left; a tatty old armchair directly next to her. Her focus appeared to remain firmly fixed on Mickey as if they were having some sort of silent argument.

Her being distracted gave me the perfect opportunity to study her a little closer. Initially, I thought she was a brunette, but now next to the fire I saw her hair was a stunning deep shade of red. Her ripped jeans gave me teasing glimpses of her legs, and her dark top totally exposed a smooth shoulder. A whiff of vanilla breezed my way and I bit back an involuntary groan. Usually perfume of any scent made me want to gag; it always reminded me of someone I couldn't forget.

A swift backhand to my chest jolted me from my assessment.

"Eyes up here, Batman," Lil drawled and cocked a knowing eyebrow at me.

Her teasing eyes sparkled as they danced over my face. I hid my smirk behind my bottle, analysing her as I drank. I then pointed at my chest.

It had the intended effect; her eyes dropped to the spot she just backhanded then lingered for a beat *much* too long.

I flicked my forefinger upwards and mimicked her words in a dry tone.

"Eyes up here, Sunshine."

Our gaze snagged and locked. Neither of us seemed to be able to look away. As much as I needed to break our trance, I never wanted it to end. The seconds stretched into what felt like minutes.

There was something oddly unique about her that I couldn't put my finger on. Something I had never stumbled upon before. I wasn't used to feeling like this; stumped, blindsided, perhaps mildly flirtatious, plus shit scared for what that meant.

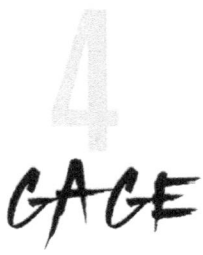

4
GAGE

OUR SPELL BROKE the instant Kimmie jumped into Lil's lap and declared that it was time to get their groove on. She tugged Lil to her feet then danced in front of the fire.

I cursed when my gaze landed on Lil's ass, making me feel like a dirty fucking cheat. Hating myself once again, I retreated into the dark place within my head—the place I came to welcome.

The girls combined high pitched noise was grating on my nerves and making my jaw tick. There was no way I would tell them to shut the fuck up, not after only being here for an hour.

Lil's giggle rose above the pandemonium, drawing my eyes back to her. Horror dawned during that same second as I realised they were now hug-dancing dangerously close to the open fire. It would only take one of them to trip and... The thought made me shudder.

I jumped to my feet as Nico launched to his. Together, we man-handled the swirling mass of arms, legs and hair away from the flames and onto the open lawn. It was like herding goddamn cats—cat's that were high on catnip. Fucking hilarious to be sitting back watching, but a right royal pain in the ass when you were the one trying to get their drunk asses to safety.

Trav and Mace were pissing themselves as I made my getaway. I vented my frustration by flipping them off as I threw myself into the couch beside Mace.

We watched as Nico tried desperately to leave the dancing duo. His efforts to escape were impeded by the death grip the girls had on all parts of his body. I swear to God their hands were everywhere all at once. I'd never heard a guy giggle before, but that's exactly what he sounded like—the kind of smart-ass laugh that made others crack up.

I rolled my head Mace's way. "So, is this what your 'low key' barbeques are normally like? A pack of raving lunatics?"

Mace barked a loud laugh. "There's been some crazy shit go down in the past, but this is pretty normal for when we hang out."

I watched Lil being tossed around on Nico's back. She raised her arms above her head and laughed loudly as her long hair whipped around her face. I was starting to see how much of a free spirit she was.

Mace chuckled again. "Aside from Trav, Lil's normally at the centre of the mayhem." Casting me a pointed look, he continued. "Thought I should give you fair warning about that."

I stiffened. My throat became tight and my heart thumped faster. "You don't need to worry about that, cuz. It's too soon."

I had no intention to pursue someone when I didn't plan on entering into a relationship.

"Gage." Mace seldom used my given name. "It's been a long while, I thought maybe—just *maybe,*" he emphasised then paused to mull over his words.

I cut him off before he could even go there. "No."

Mace scowled briefly before cracking a grin. "Bro, anyone with eyes in their head could see you two had a moment over there." He pointed back towards the house. "I could've cut that sexual tension with a knife, and it was outright fuckin' awkward to be standing around as a third wheel."

"I said NO! Jesus, I've only been up here for a few days. Enough of this conversation already!"

Christ, he was grindin' my gears by not letting it drop. I had to nip his ideas in the bud before they caused problems.

"And I'm not blind either, anyone with eyes in their head can see how into her *you* are." Bomb dropped, waiting implosion.

"Bullshit," Mace snarled and scrubbed his hand over his face. Realising he still had a drink in hand, he downed it and turned back to me. "Don't get me wrong, I love her to bits, but it's not like that." He was right up in my face now. "She's helped me through things, things that you don't know about. Hell, things that no one in our family fucking knows about. And for that, she means the world to me. End of."

Shit. That came as a surprise. Mace seemed to have his life together and under control, now though… It seemed that I wasn't the only Westbrook with skeletons in their closet.

I lowered my tone. "Everything okay, cuz?"

"Dandy," he snapped.

The conversation was now closed until another time and place.

I eyed him warily then nodded. "Okay, I get it."

"Good."

Mace stood abruptly like he was about to storm off but paused and deftly jumped over the back of the couch.

"Another?" he asked from the chilly bin.

Checking the level of my second beer, I accepted. When Mace didn't reply, I glanced over to see him standing tall and alert. Mindlessly passing me the fresh bottle, he turned and casually strode towards the house.

No sooner had he reached the steps, light raindrops began to fall. Mace folded his arms over his chest and grinned. Turning to look behind me, I found Trav standing with the garden hose at the rear of the garage and pointing it skyward. Mickey was up and moving in a flash across the yard.

Both Mace and Trav roared with laughter, thinking it was the funniest fuckin' thing since the Spice Girls. When Mickey furiously twisted the tap on the second garden hose, I realised shit was about to get real.

I was up and moving as Trav aimed the hose at Nico and the girls. Lil and Kimmie let out a delayed ear-piercing squeal, and that seemed to be the signal to unleash chaos.

Taking a running jump over the fire, I cleared the shortest distance to the house and arrived on the deck slightly puffed from my unexpected sprint—complete with beer still in hand.

Strings of expletives and roars of laughter filled the yard while bodies sprinted in all directions.

"You're an asshole, you know that right?" I growled at Mace.

"Hey, there was no way I was hanging 'round out there when I could be sitting pretty, and dry, up here."

Lunging at his shoulders, I pulled him into a grapple, inducing a minor scuffling match. Despite me being slightly taller than my cousin, his shoulders were broader. The physicality of our jobs meant that we were strong, but when it came down to it, we both knew that Mace would eventually get the upper hand; I wasn't into pumping weights like he was.

Our wrestle ended when Mickey snuck around the corner of the house and turned the hose on us.

"Shit!" was all he managed to laugh before Mace stalked towards him.

My ass was staying put. I leaned against the weatherboards and was soon joined by Nico. Together, we silently watched mayhem reign.

The two girls were crouched behind one of the couches like sitting ducks; they just didn't know it yet. I smirked knowing it was only a matter of time before they were found, and it would be sooner now that Mickey noticed me looking in their particular direction. A wicked grin spread across both our faces as he crept up on them, all the while Lil maintained her scathing glare at me.

Mickey timed his assault perfectly, turning the hose on the girls as Trav boxed them in from the opposite side. The amount of shrieking and cussing was enough to send Nico and I into fits of laughter.

Doubling over and gasping for breath, I realised I couldn't remember the last time I laughed like I meant it. The awareness sucker punched me right in the heart. I really hadn't allowed myself to relax—let alone smile—more than a dozen times over the last few years. That thought was enough to sober me immediately, leaving me overcome and overwhelmed.

With what? I wasn't sure. It may have been bitterness over the friendship they all shared, it may have been because they had accepted me without question and treated me like any other member of their crew, or it may have been guilt because for a split second, I was actually bloody enjoying myself.

Quietly slipping into the house, I searched for the bathroom. By the time I returned, the party had moved in-doors and the fire pit lay dark and smouldering outside. Kimmie handed out towels and demanded the removal of wet clothing. No way I was sticking around any longer.

"I'll catch you later, Mace, I'm off," I informed him and thumbed at the door.

Against my will, my eyes did a quick scan for one last glimpse of Lil, and I couldn't fathom if I was disappointed or relieved by her absence.

"Not on my watch," Mace declared and came at me. "We have one major rule here, and that is, if you drink, you stay."

"Pfft, yeah, I'm not staying," I scoffed, my bike keys already dangling from my forefinger.

"You're staying," Mace growled.

He matched my stance with his hands raised and looked like he was gearing up to put me on lock down. Being the stubborn fool I was, I wasn't backing down either.

"No, I'm leaving," I snapped, emphasising the 'leaving' part by opening my eyes wide and giving him a *You're a tosser* look.

Mace huffed out a breath and slapped his hands on his thighs, clearly exasperated by my total pig-headedness.

Before I could react, he lunged and grappled for my keys. I tried to regain my balance by taking a step back but two hands landed on my back and pushed against me. Glancing quickly over my shoulder as I struggled with Mace, I was met with determination blazing in Lil's big hazel eyes.

The unwelcome distraction caused a momentary lapse in concentration and Mace took full advantage of it. He tore the keys from my hand and pocketed them in his own jeans.

"There," he puffed and shot me a smug grin that my fist itched to punch off his face. "The decision has been made for you."

Without letting me argue, he spun on his heel and walked away whistling. Anger and frustration flared in me. I wasn't used to having to answer to someone or being told what to do.

Cool patches formed on my back where Lil's warm hands had been pressed. As if having her hands on me wasn't overstepping the mark enough, she then had the audacity to poke my side in a silent hint for me to move out of the goddamn doorway. I snapped my head downwards just in time to see her fingers tentatively extending towards my abdomen again, no doubt to cop a second feel.

E-fucking-*nough*.

Maybe I had more to drink than I thought, or maybe simply being around her heightened my intoxication.

Either way, I was feeling well out of my depth and it was clouding my judgment. I allowed the anger on my face to reflect my inner turmoil as I stepped into Lil's space.

I was close.

Too close.

Lil inhaled rapidly and stepped back in surprise. Her eyes flared and it was obvious she was slightly ill at ease over my sudden change in demeanour. I knew I was being an asshole, but I couldn't care less. I felt uncontrolled around her, and I had only ever felt that once before, many years ago. And as a result, my entire world broke.

A wave of guilt washed over me again, causing my irritation to spike over this entire cluster fuck of a night.

Giving her body the once over again, I balled my fists when my gaze connected with hers. I didn't look away as I rounded on her, each step guiding her further towards the darkened end of the deck. She gasped when I laid a single finger on her arm, and from that fleeting moment I was unable to hold back.

Want flared within my veins. I needed to feel, to taste her, and as soon as fucking possible. Boxing her in against the house with my arms either side of her body, I bent my head to her ear and grinned devilishly when her breath hitched.

"Playin' games with me, Sunshine, isn't wise."

"Only if you're a bad sport about it," Lil replied with a distinct edge to her voice.

My palms landed on the back of her thighs and hoisted her up. Her legs instinctively wrapped around my waist. I suppressed a growl in satisfaction knowing that when I pushed forward, I would be grinding between her legs. With her finger tips digging into my shoulders, I ducked my head again.

"Depends who I'm playing with," I growled against her lips.

When she opened her lips to respond I claimed her mouth with my own and was taken by surprise when she reciprocated with matched vigour. It wasn't my intention to be like this; rough and unpredictable, but she had awoken something feral within me that had been dormant for too long.

Lil's throaty hum gave me all the confirmation I needed, and I settled into devouring her as best I could while fully clothed.

In my greed to touch every part of her, my hand roamed up her ribs while the other pulled her hips impossibly closer. She moved with me, pulling and tugging at my hair and clothes.

The moment her fingertips flicked under my shirt and connected with my bare skin, I let out a grunt in shock. There was that feeling again—the energy between our connection, the one that stopped me in my tracks earlier tonight.

Fuck, this girl was completely undoing me and I needed to stop, but selfishly, I didn't—she was too damn responsive.

Our bubble burst the instant Trav stuck his head out the door and hollered into the night.

"Oi, you two coming in? What's the hold up?"

Sealing my lips back over Lil's so she couldn't make a single sound, I froze, fearing the barest movement would draw attention to us.

Giving a confused huff, Trav headed back inside, and judging by the tone of his voice, he was inquiring about our whereabouts.

With one last taste, I broke away with a frustrated growl. I couldn't look at her, couldn't even bring myself to help steady her when she stumbled a little.

Unable to be near Lil any longer, I jumped over the deck railing and stalked around the side of the house to move my bike.

Now in the solitude of the night, guilt rose and took hold of my heart. I couldn't fathom what the fuck just happened back there, but it wouldn't be happening again.

LIL

"WHAT THE HELL....?" I breathed, struggling to calm my racing heart and regain my breath.

Gage stole the oxygen from my entire body, leaving me lightheaded yet alight and aching. The throbbing between my legs was a lasting reminder of his presence that contrasted with the sting on my lips left behind from his beard. The prickly heat I felt under my palms when I pressed them to my face was enough for me to know what my skin *looked* like right now.

It all happened so fast, and there was no denying that the guy was as confused as I was. He had lit a whirlwind of emotions within me that no one else had even come close to kindling. As much as I tried to deny it, I liked it, a lot. Curse my treacherous body for wanting more of the delicious preview he'd just given me.

What have I gotten myself into?

After running my hands through my hair in a quick effort to tame it as best I could, I made sure all my clothes were in the appropriate spots before heading inside. My quick pace was muted on the decking timber and I prayed no one would notice me slink in. I wasn't more than two steps into the house when everyone paused and turned their attention on me. The various questions and smirks on their faces caused me to shuffle on the spot.

"Er, what's going on?" I calmly asked, my voice sounding thick and tight. Inside, my pulse hammered and the blood roared in my ears. I could feel a guilty flush rapidly rising up my neck and spreading across my cheeks.

"We could ask *you* the same question, Lil," Kimmie tittered. Her eyes twinkled and her smile dazzled my intoxicated vision. She bloody well knew exactly what had been going on.

Mace's question rolled off the back of Kimmie's comment. "And what have you done with my cousin? You didn't eat him alive, did you?" He gave me a wicked smirk, and I wanted to melt into the floorboards and die between the cracks. Mace casually stroked a hand over his chin. "You, ah, had a reaction to something there, Lil Bean?"

Oh God kill me now. I was already dying of embarrassment; it couldn't possibly get worse!

I sucked in a rapid breath, which unfortunately resulted in me coughing on my own saliva. While bending over with my hands planted on my knees, completely red faced and spluttering, Kimmie took pity on me enough to slap my back and offer a glass of water. As I caught my breath, Trav's feet appeared in my downcast line of sight, then a bottle of mouthwash was thrust into my face.

"What's that for?" I croaked.

"You know what it's for. But if you want me to spell it out for you, I can do *Storytime with Trav?*"

"Damn you, Travis!" I hissed, snatching the mouthwash and pegged it blindly in his direction.

Laugher broke out at his yell of surprise as the bottle found its mark—close to his junk—before skidding along the floor.

It was at that precise moment Gage made his reappearance. Now it was his turn to feel the wrath of their interrogative stares.

"What?" he snapped in a pissy tone. "I was moving my bike around the back so it wouldn't get stolen. What's with the awkward as fuck silence?" he challenged. Then, as an afterthought and seeing me still bent over trying to regain composure, he added, "You ok there, Sunshine?"

The son of a bitch actually had the gall to rest his hand briefly on the small of my back, sending a bolt of lightning searing up my spine. I straightened instantly, and if it had been any other moment, I would have bragged about executing a perfect 'bend and snap'. However, right now I needed a diversion and fast, and Mace was by far the easiest target.

"Is that going to stain, do you think?" I grimaced, pointing at his discarded shirt with the grease mark clearly visible.

Thank goodness the change of subject was successful. Attention turned back to Kimmie who was edging away from Mace, sensing his imminent attack.

With the festivities resuming, Gage whispered, "Nice work, Sunshine," and chuckled deeply as he walked away.

My annoyance flared and I wanted to growl because of it. I didn't know what 'this' was between us, but it was remotely nowhere near over. It was only just getting started… And it was going to be complicated.

. . .

For the rest of the night, Gage and I avoided each other like the plague. That didn't stop me from stealing glances his way, and every now and then I was positive I felt his gaze searing over my body when I least expected it.

Regardless of the distractions, it felt as if there was a gigantic flashing neon sign above our heads with the words *'Just hooked up'* blinking obnoxiously for all the world to see. I noticed Mickey giving Gage the brotherly death stare on multiple occasions, which Gage took like a man-child; returning an equally dark glower from across the room. Only Mace had the balls to question me outright—for the moment; Kimmie was simply biding her time to get the juicy details.

Mace sidled up to me, bumping my shoulder before slinging his arm around my neck. "Sooo, moving the bike, huh?"

"Nope, not me. I was picking up the empties and turning the hoses off."

My cover story was total baloney and he knew it, but it was the best I could come up with in the state I was in. Holding my gaze to ransom, Mace tilted his head towards mine and gave me an affectionate squeeze.

"You two would actually suit each other really well. Plus, I haven't seen Gage interested in *anyone* in a *long* time. Which means, he also realises that you're one of a kind."

"Aww, that's real sweet of you, Macey-Poo," I mocked before snapping to a factual tone. "But yeah, that ain't gonna happen."

Straightening to full height, Mace got serious too. Burning me with a sullen look, he grumbled, "If you ever call me Macey-Poo again, there'll be hell to pay, Missy."

Loud laughter burst from my mouth before I cooed at him like he was a tiny baby bird, all ruffled and vulnerable and scruffily cute. Mace snorted and tried to look badass despite his eyes crinkling with amusement.

Shaking his head in feigned resignation, he reached across the bench and grabbed a bread bun, which he then slapped into my palm.

"Eat that, you're a goddamn pain in the arse."

"Well, *I* happen to think I'm rather *awesome!*" I sang with over inflated self-confidence.

Ignoring Mace's snigger, I turned my attention to the bun, mauling it with exaggeration and biting off way more than I could chew. Literally.

"Jesus," Mace muttered and pointed at my bulging cheeks. "You're ridiculous! Eat. Carefully!"

Kimmie breezed past on her way into the kitchen. She danced as she filled the jug with water then moved onto placing savouries onto an oven tray.

"Aww, Kimmie, I love the shit out of you right now," I declared as I reached around her for some water to clear the bun induced cottonmouth.

"I love you, too, Lil, but quit breathing on my neck," Kimmie giggled.

I puckered and tried my hardest to lay one on her. It was true though; she was basically my sister and I loved her as such.

The same could be said for everyone in this room tonight. I loved each and every one of them, and hard. Well, apart from Gage, because that man was grinding my gears by simply being here.

We were a family, and we would fight through hell or high water for each other if we needed to. The grilling and questioning always came later, but we all knew that if anyone had a problem, we were all there for one another, no matter what.

Now that Gage was part of our group, he was automatically included. That's how we rolled. I just hoped that he would also come through for any one of us if we needed him.

. . .

It was now well after two in the morning when everyone began to slump into the living room furniture. Kimmie set about making sure everyone had a place to crash for the night.

Neek and Trav checked the outdoor couches and proclaimed them dry enough to be slept on. They lugged them onto the deck, and since Trav and Mickey were the ones spraying the water around, they were automatically relegated to sleeping on them. Luckily for those two, the nights were beginning to warm up now and they wouldn't freeze their assess off.

The master bedroom was always off limits, Neek called dibs on the spare room. Gage and Mace claimed the crazy comfortable living room couches, leaving Kimmie and I to share her bed. That was a pretty sweet deal too, even if I had to deal with *Morning Kimmie,* whom I despised deeply. Her chirpiness at the crack of dawn was something that no human should be exposed to. Waking up to her singing or declaring what a beautiful day it was made me want to rip my ears off and shove them down her throat. No guesses needed for my emotive state upon waking; a total freaking grouch!

After exchanging goodnights, I dragged my ass to Kimmie's room and flopped onto the bed. It took a huge amount of willpower to stand again and tug off my jeans and top. Making the most of being vertical again, I grabbed a pair of Kimmie's PJ shorts and singlet top from her drawer. Stumbling back towards the bed as I pulled them on, I used momentum to complete the dive between the soft welcoming sheets. Bliss! Total bliss until my bra made itself known. With a frustrated growl, I worked my way around the bed until the annoying piece of clothing was disentangled and flung on the floor. Kimmie stumbled through the door and stopped short as it landed in a crumpled heap on her carpet. Her eyes narrowed then skipped over all of my discarded clothing strewn around the room.

"Did you just get naked in my bed?"

"You-" My reply was rudely interrupted by a hiccup. "Wish."

Throwing back the top sheet, I confirmed that I did, in fact, have my lady parts covered. Kimmie shucked off her clothes then dug through her sleepwear drawer, then fell onto the bed with an exhausted sigh. My stomach pitched a little from the bed moving as she twisted and squirmed to get comfortable. Once she was settled, we rolled towards each other and talked for a little while, reminiscing about the parts of the night that were totally hilarious. As time wore on, the silence between our giggles lengthened until the lure of sleep was too great to ignore.

God, I hope tomorrow morning isn't totally awkward with Gage!

My brain instantaneously snapped awake and began to replay what transpired between us earlier. The more I reflected, the more my head worked itself into a black cloud. I couldn't fathom why I was stressing over him so much. Gage had pressed all my buttons, and half the problem was trying to work out why the hell I wanted him to do it again.

Needless to say, tomorrow morning was going to be excruciating. Uncomfortable silences and not knowing what to say were the worst. And we hadn't even *slept* together! Not that I wanted to, but still, the thought of having sex with Gage turned me on more than I cared to admit.

Tossing and turning for what seemed like hours, I finally fumbled for my phone on the bed side table and squinted at the illuminated screen. Ten to four. Gah! I hated the hour between three and four am; the 'witching hour', when everything felt too still and too quiet. It was then that most people left this world, I knew that from first-hand experience, and that knowledge created a wave of goose bumps to fan over my arms and shoulders.

The only noise was Kimmie's deep breathing and I couldn't stand to listen to it any longer. Gently slipping from bed, I silently made my way to the bathroom and then on to the kitchen for a glass of milk. Surely that would help cure hiccups that had plagued me since going to bed.

I knew this house well enough that walking through it in the dark was an easy task, and the kitchen was easily lit by the various appliances. Grabbing a clean glass from the cupboard then opening the fridge for the milk, I froze when a throat softly cleared behind me. I knew who it was without looking over my shoulder, and it drove a shiver through my entire body.

Batman.

LIL

JESUS, GAGE MUST be in stealth mode; I hadn't heard him approaching.

When I turned to confirm what I already knew, he was leaning against the doorframe, and despite me not being able to see his expression, I could feel him studying me. It was unnerving as heck.

The fridge door remained open and forgotten as Gage stole my attention. My eyes skipped over the beautiful artwork inked over one of his muscular shoulders and down his bicep. He'd obviously just pulled on his jeans before coming out to the kitchen; the zipper was done up but the button hung open, making the jeans ride precariously low on his hips and displaying the waistband of his underwear.

While I blatantly ran my gaze over his torso, he returned the favour, lazily looking over the entire length of my body. When the paths of our searing gaze finally crossed, we both startled like we hadn't been expecting to be caught staring. His line of sight dropped briefly again before his dark eyes re-locked on mine. The smirk on his lips caused self-consciousness to creep in despite my sleepwear covering me where I needed. However, I was also acutely aware of the chill in the air making my nipples hard, and the two obvious points were undoubtedly visible through the thin fabric.

My traitorous body responded to him far too easily. I fought to take a calm, full breath while squeezing the forgotten milk carton in my hand. I was torn between stepping closer and finding out why he was really here, or putting the milk back in the fridge and getting my ass out of dodge. Not to mention I was still miffed about what happened outside earlier.

Our awkwardness compounded with each long second that passed until I dumbly held up the milk as if it verified my reason for being in the kitchen in the first place—plus, it also helped hide my nipples from view. I didn't get self-conscious often, but with Gage being all mysterious and intense, my emotions were heightened and completely thrown off guard.

"I didn't mean to wake you," I whispered.

My apology snapped him back to the present and he cleared his throat again, though his voice remained gritty from sleep. "It's ok, I'm a light sleeper."

Without breaking my eye contact, he pulled out the bar stool from under the kitchen bench and sat before I could object.

I snorted softly at his audacity. "You want one?"

His reply was clipped and closed off. Just like his body language all of a sudden was. "Sure."

I pushed a full glass of milk his way then sighed as I lowered myself onto the stool next to him. My hangover was beginning to kick in despite the litre of water I powered back while eating the savouries. Resting my elbows on the bench, I picked up my glass of milk and nursed it in my hands. I halted with the glass poised by my lips.

"I feel like we've met before," Gage whispered, so low I hardly heard him.

It was as if he was reasoning to himself and I was merely overhearing his thought process. Funny thing was though, I grasped his meaning immediately; in every sense Gage was a stranger, yet, there was a charge between us that I neither of us understood.

"That's such a shit pick up line," I scoffed.

He rumbled a chuckle and leaned slightly into my space. "Wasn't a pick-up attempt."

I glared through the dim light as he tilted the glass of milk to his lips, now ignoring me.

"Maybe I was Batman to your Robin in a previous life," I taunted then took a sip. I was stirring him, wanting to see how far I could push him before he bit back. "Or maybe *Cat Woman!*" I added in a louder whisper.

Gage snorted. "Not fuckin' likely," he whisper-growled. "If anyone's being Batman, it's me. To hell with Robin."

We both chuckled quietly, acutely aware that every little sound was outrageously loud in the otherwise silent kitchen.

Truth be told, now that we were sitting in close proximity without being assholes to each other, I identified with what he alluded to; deep down, in my soul perhaps, I recognised him as someone I already knew, and well. That type of connection was rare. What I didn't understand was why the two of us shared such feelings of intimacy without knowing each other.

Thinking for a moment, Gage added, "Besides, you have to be a female character because there's no way I'm fucking Robin."

I felt my eyes flare and my mouth hung open as I processed what he'd just implied. The look on my face must have been amusing because he took one look at me then smothered a trace of laughter behind his hand.

"Oh, that's too darn bad because I have a real thing for green spandex," I deadpanned.

"Now I know you're lying," he drawled.

Smirking into his glass, Gage downed the rest of the milk then stood to set the glass in the sink behind us.

"Different folk, different strokes," I mumbled.

Gage's arm brushed mine as he returned to his stool and I couldn't stop the sharp intake of breath that escaped my lips. This time he faced me and frowned.

"Look, Sunshine, whatever 'this' is between us, I'm not in."

Offense blindsided me that in turn morphed into annoyance.

"Excuse me?" I leaned back and gave him the evils. *"You're* the one who mouth raped me earlier, so don't go putting your guilt trip on me," I hissed through clenched teeth and balled my hands into fists on the bench top.

His top lip curled ever so slightly. "Don't deny you didn't want it, or enjoy it for that matter."

I spluttered, taken aback at how quickly his mood had fluctuated. The audacity of the man was insane. I didn't tolerate being spoken to like this at work, and I sure as hell didn't tolerate it at home.

"Are you for real right now? Like, really?" I spat.

"Let's get this straight, *Sunshine...*" The way he sneered his new nickname for me made uneasiness weave through the pit of my stomach, "Just because you've got Mace dancing on a thread, doesn't mean I'll give you what he won't."

The sharp sound of a slap echoed around the kitchen, and the reverberations from the impact stung my palm. The shock on his face was priceless, and I almost laid out another just to see that look on his face again. However, it took less than a second for his features to go from astonished to furious, and by then I was on my feet and leaning right into his face, dishing out some information of my own.

"You arrogant *bastard!*" I whisper-yelled. "You come waltzing in here like you fucking own the joint, do whatever you want, don't give a shit about what you say—which couldn't be further from the truth—then try to twist it around like it's my fault. Newsflash, you're an A-class asshole and I won't stand for being treated like a piece of shit on the bottom of your shoe. Why don't you take a running jump an-"

Gage crashed his lips onto mine so hard the connection sent me flailing for balance. His movements were hurried, desperate, seemingly consumed with craving that only searing me with a kiss would satisfy. As soon as his tongue swiped against mine, a sense of déjà vu spurred through me. I reciprocated without hesitation, all irrelevant thoughts leaving my mind as I took all he gave me, my own lust igniting at a terrifying pace. The bench bit into my lower back as Gage pressed his hips into mine, the denim of his jeans rough through the thin fabric of my sleep shorts.

My knees weakened when his fingers wove through my hair and held tight.

"Need to stop," he murmured, still kissing me for all it was worth, and I groaned when his hips moved against mine again.

The guy had more mood swings than a group of ladies all PMSing together and the thought was the reminder that I was making yet another mistake.

I allowed myself one final taste of him before I reacted, yet that extra sample poured fuel on my desire. Regardless of what my body wanted, I had to snap out of it. Gage couldn't say crap like that and assume I would sit by and take it.

With the decision made, I grabbed a fistful of his hair and tugged. His contact on my lips broke, and I was both relieved but craving for it to be reinstated. Gage cursed and grabbed my wrist, jerking it free from his hair.

His glare hardened and the shadowed kitchen light made his eyes appear black and unwelcoming. Despite the dimness, I couldn't mistake the blatant look of lust in his gaze that conflicted with his expression. I forced myself to meet his eyes after my own unintentionally dropped to his lips.

"Do you like your balls?" I whisper-hissed.

"What?" he snapped.

"I said, Do. You. Like. Your. Balls?"

"I'm rather attached to them," he drawled between heavy breaths.

"Good."

Gage's steadying breath turned to a sharp inhale when I reached between us and grabbed said balls through his jeans. A smug smirk tilted my lips when he momentarily closed his eyes to my touch. I squeezed harder until I felt him begin to pull from my grasp, then added a little more pressure for good measure. When he grunted and wrapped his fingers around my wrist, I snarled with as much sass I could muster while my heart hammered so loud in my chest I was sure he could hear it.

"Because if you ever speak to me like that again, I will tear them from your body and shove them so far up your ass you'll be tasting them!"

Gage opened his mouth to reply but snapped it closed and clenched his teeth when I tightened my grip. He was learning the hard way that you didn't fuck with Lily McMillan—or any of the McMillan's, for that matter.

Without a word and any other movement, he slowly released my wrist and I kindly returned the favour by releasing my hold on his balls. As soon as he was free, he drew himself to full height. He was tall, slightly taller than Mace, and despite looking so different from his cousin, his presence was no less consuming.

Gage swiped a hand over his beard and muttered, "Fuck," under his breath. He looked at me from under his dark brows, gauging my reaction to what just went down.

I fought to calm my breathing, to steady my pulse while it thrummed in my ears, to remember the way his beard softly scratched against my skin. My fingertips trembled against my mouth as I pressed them against my tingling lips.

Gage looked like a man getting torn apart at the seams. There was a deep ache etched on his features, so profound that it was obvious he was being destroyed from the inside out.

Unable to see the hurt so loud and clear any longer, I made to move away from him. No matter how much he heightened my emotions—both good and bad—I couldn't stand to see blatant agony of any description. My sidestep was halted by his hand gently snagging my shoulder.

"Lil," he whispered softly.

I upturned my face to meet his imploring expression. The moment his hand slid up my neck to cup my head just below my ear, the butterflies in my stomach increased at a nauseous rate.

"Yeah?"

He ducked his head and his lips brushed mine, slowly this time, barely making contact but enough to send my pulse skyrocketing. My mind raced with a thousand incomprehensible thoughts as I surrendered to his touch.

What we shared was intense and unexplainably deep. Our kiss quickly escalated from apprehensive and restrained to heated as we lost ourselves in the moment of pent up passion. I hadn't been kissed like this for.... well, ever.

Gage returned my hum when I kissed him deeply and pulled his hips into mine. I was lit and wanting nothing more than to roar to life and burn so brightly I would combust.

"Fuck, I need to stop," Gage whispered hoarsely.

The urgency in his voice almost made me falter. With his hips still pinning mine in place, his actions belied his words as he grasped the hem of my singlet and tugged it upwards. The feel of his roughened knuckles grazing over my sensitive skin sent goose bumps rippling across my body. My breath hitched and quickened as I passed the point of caring about the possibility of getting caught. Despite trying to be quiet, our desire had apparently been sufficiently loud enough to get the attention of at least one person in the house.

"It sounds like a goddamn farm in there! Kimmie's gonna rip you both a new one if you two screw on her bench." A long chuckle then followed.

Mace's interruption snapped us both out of our lust filled haze, and Gage put two steps between us then clung to the edge of the bench.

I squeezed my eye lids together and squealed inside, feeling my face instantly flame with embarrassment.

"You were *listening* to us? Fucking creeper!" Gage whisper-yelled towards the lounge.

It dawned on me that I had been suckered in, again. We were back at square one where it would, no doubt, end with hurtful words being exchanged to help dull the guilt and confusion over our inability to walk away. The realisation sent me moving around the kitchen island towards the doorway without looking back at my mistake. Mace's chuckling had me shushing him angrily.

"Kind of hard not to listen when I wake up to the sounds of rutting. Now I've got a perfectly usable semi going to waste..." he trailed off.

I smothered my scandalised laugh with both palms.

"Damn right it's going to waste, and it had better be gone by the time I come back in there," Gage hissed behind me.

The distinct sound of poorly contained laughter came from the living area where Mace was having a right ol' jolly. With the break in conversation, I couldn't help but steal a departing glance over my shoulder before heading back to Kimmie's room. Gage was re-adjusting himself in his jeans but looked up as though he felt my gaze land on him. He crossed his arms across his chest then glared like I was some kind of walking felony.

I returned his glower and flipped him my middle finger as I spun on my heel and strode away from the human who possessed the knack of bringing out the worst in me. I hadn't reached Kimmie's room when his low, cynical voice found me through the darkness.

"Sleep well, Sunshine."

"Go to hell," I hissed back.

A rumble emanated from deep in his throat as I all but threw myself at Kimmie's door.

GAGE

OWNED. SHE FUCKING owned me right from the start and there wasn't a goddamn thing I could do about it apart from push her away. Fuck I wanted her. I'd never felt an ache so hard in my chest than I did around her. That feeling emphasised how much I had lost before coming here, and I resented Lil even more because of it.

After copping a ribbing from Mace when I returned to the living room, I was left with my head whirling with unstoppable and conflicting thoughts.

I still couldn't comprehend what happened with Lil. She had some kind of hold over me, one that neither of us understood, but it was fierce, it was feisty, and it was burning with passion. Whenever Lil was close, it was like I was possessed, then would wake from the hypnotic state wondering how I let my actions get out of hand—again. My balls ached in frustration while my heart bled for the feelings stirring to life within me. The worst part was, I was trying to convince myself that I didn't want more of what happened in the kitchen—aside from the ball busting. However, I couldn't bring myself to go there. I wasn't ready, and it was slowly killing me.

I woke to movement on the outside deck and footsteps shuffling through the house. Instead of getting up to see who was creeping around this time, I glanced at my phone and groaned when I saw that it wasn't yet eight in the morning.

Running on a few hours' sleep was going to slaughter me today. Not sleeping wasn't through lack of trying; no matter how much I tried, I just couldn't tear my thoughts away from Lil.

I didn't come to Auckland to hook up with women or to get laid. I came here as a last-ditch effort to make a clean start—no strings attached. It was beyond irritating that my actions last night would no doubt complicate my resolve for a drama free existence.

Murmuring voices came from the kitchen then the sound of cupboards opening and pans clanging woke me fully. I lay on my back, listening to someone make breakfast, wrapped in warm blankets that hid both my body and my secrets.

I got the prickly feeling that I was being scrutinised. With a glance over to find Mace lying on his stomach, I frowned at the daggers he glared at me.

"What?" I grumbled.

Mace huffed before answering in a whisper so we wouldn't be overheard. "I hope you're interested in Lil for the right reasons. I don't want to see her come out the other side of..." he half-heartedly waved a hand around, "...whatever the fuck is between the two of you, in a bad way. You'll have both Mickey and myself on your arse about it."

Well, straight to the point it is then. Mace was never one to mix his words; he said it like it was, and I respected him for it. At least there was no confusion.

"You know I can't guarantee that," I snapped. "Besides, there is *nothing* happening between us, trust me."

I scrubbed my hands over my face in exasperation. That was exactly what I came here to avoid. I didn't want the responsibility of having someone relying on me. History was the spiteful reminder that those people got hurt, and so did I.

"That's not why I uprooted to move here. I don't know why, but there's just something about Lil that's so...." Words failed me so I made a vague hand gesture to convey what my mind couldn't find the words for.

"Yeah, mate, I know." Mace paused for a second. "She's a spit fire when she needs to be. If you treat her wrong, you'll hear about it," he warned.

"Don't I know it," I muttered as my hand went protectively to my crotch.

Mace narrowed his eyes at me again.

"Look, I'm not one to fuck around okay. I don't even know why I'm defending myself to you about this."

"*I* know that, but she only just met you last night. And while intoxicated, might I add." He winced and moved slightly to get comfortable then chuckled to himself. "So, you gonna tell me what was going on in the kitchen?"

I planted my palms over my eyes. "I'm glad you find that funny, because I certainly do not. And that's a definite *fuck no.*"

Mace sniggered again. It came out dry and ended in a hacking cough. I wasn't even going to bother offering to get him a drink. It was karma for all the shit he'd been giving me. Standing up and stretching my arms above my head, I noticed Mace eyeing me again and I couldn't help but flex my biceps at him.

"Get a good look at how muscles are meant to be, little cuz."

"Pfft," Mace scoffed, "You haven't seen anything until you've seen these," he countered while flexing his arm that was hanging from the couch and pouting his lips in what I assumed was meant to be some kind of erotic grimace.

Whatever the fuck it was, it looked fucking stupid and I barked out a laugh because of it. His display was interrupted by Kimmie coming into the living room and her giving him a condescending once over.

"You know you like it, Kimmie. I see you perving," Mace smirked.

Kimmie scoffed and set her hands on her hips. "You wish. Once you two have finished your creepy little *mine is bigger than yours* show, brekky is ready if you're hungry."

"Show's over, lil' Kim, this power house has gotta eat."

"Ha, trust me, there ain't nothin' here to see," she drawled and raised a brow while skipping her eyes from Mace's exposed arm to his torso. "And for goodness sake, Mace, I know you're still tensing!"

One finger flipped out of Mace's tensed fist to flip her off. She left the room giggling like mad, and once she was out of ear shot, I glared my brows at my cousin.

"You're a bloody show off."

"And *you* are seeing what you want to," he retorted. With a roll and a grunt, he stood and pulled on his discarded jeans.

I didn't bother replying, not having the energy, or the care factor, to really give a shit. I was hungry, tired, and I was dropping balls at seeing Lil over breakfast.

An unwelcome flashback of having Lil pinned against that very bench slammed into my mind as soon as I stepped into the kitchen. Blinking it away, I focused on exchanging half-hearted *good mornings* with Mickey and Trav, who were leaning on the bench eating strips of bacon. I couldn't stop myself from glancing around for Lil, automatically assuming she would have risen at the same time as Kimmie.

"She's not up yet," Mace declared loudly through a mouthful of bacon. He wiggled his eyebrows at me, and if I was closer, I would have wiped the smug grin off his face.

"Who?" I asked, playing it cool as I filled a glass of water.

"Oh, Lil," Kimmie supplied, waving off the comment. "She's demonic in the morning and thankfully won't be up for a couple of hours yet."

I didn't bother answering; it would have only provoked Mace, and we were already skating on thin ice. I could feel thick hostility radiating off Mickey in waves. It was no secret that he considered Lil to be in the 'no-go zone' for me. *'Too late mate'* I thought as I met his eyes in an unwavering challenge, trying not to look too conceited.

I didn't, after all, want to cause an early morning brawl in the kitchen with someone I hardly knew. It was obvious by his clenched fists that he wouldn't hesitate to inflict some damage.

The tension was broken by Trav practically dropping the plates and cutlery onto the bench. The clatter snapped us from our awkward stand-off as Trav shot an apologetic glance at Kimmie.

"Throw them on the bench, why don't you!" she sassed.

Trav held up his palms. "It was an honest accident, Kim. I'm just a little fuzzy this morning."

She pursed her lips then went back to stirring eggs in the pan. "Can someone make coffees please?"

All eyes fell on Mickey. He looked up from licking the bacon grease off his fingers. "What?"

When no one made an attempt to move, I slapped the bench and declared that I'd do it.

"Thanks, cuz, you're a real help."

I glared at Mace over my shoulder. "Don't get used to it, I'm not your kitchen bitch."

Mace was chortling around a mouthful of bacon when Nico stumbled in.

"The fuck was that crash just before? Made my heart drop waking up to that."

"Travis dropping everything on the countertop," Kimmie snapped while tipping the eggs into a serving bowl.

"Sorry, bro," Trav supplied nonchalantly.

Nico slapped him on the back on his way past to Kimmie and plucked the bowl from her hands. He pointed to a spot at the bench for her then set the bowl in the centre. The six of us helped ourselves, and it wasn't long before Mace offhandedly directed a question at Kimmie.

"So, lil' Kim, you reckon this bench would hold the weight of two people?"

I inhaled swiftly, causing a piece of toast to lodge at the back of my throat.

"Oh, hell to the no, you did not do the dirty on my parents' bench! And who with?"

It hurt so bad my eyes burned as I coughed and sputtered, resorting to gulping scalding coffee in an effort to remove the debris. All eyes were on me as I roughly cleared my throat then wiped the sheen of sweat that had cropped up on my forehead.

I glared at Mace, clenching my jaw so damn hard my teeth creaked. I had to hand it to him; he was bloody good at keeping a straight face. The corner of his mouth, however, showed a subtle twitch as he struggled for control.

Kimmie looked between the two of us with her mouth hanging open in horror. "Please tell me one of you didn't." She pointed her fork at me. "And that only leaves one other person in this house who it could have been, because it definitely wasn't me."

Mace held up his hands in defence. "Strictly hypothetically speaking, I mean. Your bench is untainted as far as *I'm* concerned." He leaned back and tilted his head towards me with a smug grin that tested the last of my composure.

Fuck he was in for a beating! Especially after the lecture Kimmie just passionately delivered about keeping our asses off the sacred place meant only for food.

"Better pass that onto Lil as well," Mace added with a shrug then shoved another forkful of scrambled eggs into his big gob.

Internally considering what he would say next, he waved his fork around then spoke after swallowing. "You know, just so we're all on the same page. Wouldn't want her to miss the memo, aye Gage."

Everyone's eyes landed on me again, this time with various shades of sentiment; Trav was perplexed yet smirking, Mickey was pissed—no surprises there, Kimmie was suspicious as hell—I felt my balls retreat under the heat of her glower, and Mace, the fucker, was loving every second of my torture. I couldn't help but shift uncomfortably under the weight of their combined attention. I clenched my fork and jabbed it at Mace.

"You're full of shit this morning." I then turned my attention to Kimmie. "You have nothin' to worry about, your kitchen is safe from me." Giving her a forced smile, I deemed the subject closed.

We ate without conversation for a short while until Mace's phone broke the silence. Pulling it from his pocket, he checked the screen and groaned.

"What the hell does he want this early on a Sunday morning?" In answer to our unspoken question, he added, "Dad."

Stabbing the call accept button, Mace slapped the phone to his ear and excused himself. It was Trav—again—who broke the snowballing awkward hush that surrounded us.

"So, sweet ride out there, man. You had it long?"

Setting down my fork and wiping a hand across my mouth, I finally felt like this was a conversation I could confidently immerse myself in.

"Thanks, mate. Yeah, I've been riding since my late teens. Had that bike for a couple of years now. Wish I'd got a Victory sooner. There's something about American bikes that sing to me. Fuckin' love it."

Mickey's attention honed in on me as he ate, and Trav continued. "What model do you have?"

I grinned like a schoolboy. "She's a 2015 V-twin Gunner. *Mint* condition."

Trav let out a low whistle of approval.

"Bloody nice, that's for sure."

"So, you know about bikes?"

He hummed and swallowed a mouthful. "I don't ride. But I've fixed a few."

That jogged my memory; he was the mechanic.

Nodding in thought, I turned my attention to Mickey and raised a brow in question. It would be good to have at least one other shared interest with Mickey besides his sister.

Dammit, fuck. I am not interested!

"You have a bike?"

He set down his glass and shook his head. "No, I don't ride. Not often anyway. I've ridden a few motorbikes, mostly trail bikes since we grew up on a farm and all that shit."

I hid my surprise at that information, storing it away for a later time.

"Besides," Mickey continued, "I don't like riding around town, mostly because I've seen the aftermath of motorbikes versus vehicles, and that shit ain't pretty."

My stomach curdled as my blood solidified. Bile rose into my throat and formed a burning knot at the back of my mouth. I tried my hardest to stop the reaction showing on my face, but by the look Mickey gave me, my distress was obvious.

Thank fuck Trav was too busy eating to notice my anxiety. Kimmie was equally engrossed in a little conversation with Nico, so neither of them seemed to detect the halt to our discussion.

I excused myself to grab another coffee, and by the time I sat down again I had regained a little composure. Clearing my throat, I attempted to resume my chat with Mickey.

"So, Lil can ride too?"

Trav laughed loud and shook his head as he re-joined the conversation. "Mate, I bet she's already polished up her helmet and leathers."

"She has all the gear?" I couldn't keep the surprise from my voice. The girl surprised me at every turn.

Mickey's face closed off again. "Yes," he said cautiously. "She's got the gear because she pillions with Mace often enough. Though, he let her ride his bike once and came back pale as fuck. And he paled further when I threatened to rip him a new one if he ever let her ride solo again."

Mickey huffed a small laugh through his nose at the memory before his hazel eyes hit mine, issuing an immediate and blatant warning.

"She's got a real thing for bikes. She's not allowed near yours, let alone lay a fucking finger on it!" He jabbed his fork my way. *"And, while we're on the subject, you keep your hands off her."*

I internally rolled my eyes, though was thankful he had no idea that *that* rule had already been smashed out of the park.

"Trust me, there is no way in hell she's taking my baby for a ride."

Conviction brimmed in my voice; there was no mistaking just how serious I was, and I'd only just managed to bite off the next sentence before it slipped off the tip of my tongue. *I'm not making that mistake again.*

"So, what bike did you used to have before the Victory?" Kimmie asked, blushing a little after Mickey caught her ogling him.

"Harley," I snipped, not wanting to talk about it, but I knew what was coming.

"Oh nice. Why'd you change to a Victory?"

My body stiffened and my throat tightened again. This time I struggled to simply breathe let alone get words out. Preparing myself for that question never seemed to make a difference to how my body reacted. I had no control over it, and I wasn't prepared to have a full-blown panic attack in front of everyone. Mace, thank fuck, chose that moment to make his reappearance into the kitchen. He must have overheard Kimmie's question because, without missing a beat, he answered for me.

"Because he couldn't handle the fact that my Hog pulled more chicks than his did."

Walking around the group, he stood beside me and slapped me on the back as I shot him a relieved look. He slapped my back again just as Kimmie asked a question which made his back slap turn into a punch between the shoulder blades.

"Like, aren't they pretty much the same anyway?"

Mace took the comment like a bull stabbed in the ass. *"God no, woman!"* He slapped a splayed hand to his barrel chest. "You wound me! Have I taught you *nothing?*"

There was no question whatsoever as to where Mace's allegiances lay when it came to the age-old question of which chopper was the best. He'd spent a pretty penny on his Harley and would have it in his damn bed if he could get it into his house.

"So, you done here, cuz?" Mace asked and tipped back his coffee.

"Yeah, why's that? Is Dave all good?"

He waved off my unease. "He's fine. But there's an urgent job just come in and he's keen for our help."

I took a double mouthful of coffee. "When's he needing us?"

"Soon as."

I stood and patted my pockets for my keys. That triggered Mace's memory and he stuffed one hand into his jeans then tossed the keys my way. Giving him a wry look as I caught them one-handed, I headed down the hallway to the bathroom. Secretly, I also hoped to bump into Lil before I left, but by the sounds of it, those chances were slim to none.

Finishing up, I made my way back to the kitchen to find Mace waiting for me at the door. I shrugged on my jacket then grabbed my helmet. With a departing goodbye and thank you to Kimmie, I stalked over to where I'd stashed my Gunner last night. Thank Christ, it was still under the eaves of the garage where I'd parked it.

Mace was by my side without me realising it. "Gage," he said gruffly and grabbed my shoulder. "You all good after what was said in there? I didn't hear it all, but enough to know it sent you reeling."

"Fucking peachy. I don't want them knowing, Mace."

He raised his palms at my warning. I shouldn't have issued it; Mace was as loyal as they came and I had no concerns whatsoever that he wouldn't tell my story without my permission.

"You know I'm a sealed book. However, I do think there's something going on between you and Lil."

My glower made his brow rise. "There's not."

I had my helmet hovering above my head, about to squeeze it down into place, when Mace's comment stopped me in my tracks.

"Oh, there she is!"

"Where?" I said, *way* too enthusiastically, immediately wanting to punch myself in the dick.

Mace chortled. "Yep, that's what I thought," he crowed.

Mounting my bike, I glared at him through the open visor on my helmet.

"You're an asshole. *That* stunt will keep. Last one there shouts lunch."

And with that, my bike roared to life beneath me and I left a nice big gouge on the lawn as I took off. After manoeuvring past the parked vehicles in the driveway, I opened the throttle and tore down the street. A sly smile was on my lips knowing that Mace would be cursing me all names under the sun while he backed his ute out.

Lunch was on him and he bloody well knew it.

LIL

A WEEK. AN entire freaking week after our steamy encounter and I still couldn't get the feel or taste of Gage off my mind.

The last time I *saw* him was in Kimmie's kitchen at four thirty a.m. six days ago, and the memory still made me ache inside. The last time I *heard* him was the next morning as he left, hell for leather, at some ungodly hour. The racket roused me from a deep sleep, and I wasn't happy about it. The problem was, my head was telling me how infuriating he was and had slammed up the walls around my heart, but my heart was telling me to quit being so hard on the guy.

He conjured up a vast array of feelings, changing from one second to the next so fast it was giving me whiplash. Truth be told, I was both looking forward to, and dreading, seeing him again. And that wasn't a situation I was used to. It was only a matter of time before our paths crossed now that he was living and working with Mace.

At least we managed to avoid the awkward 'morning after a hook-up' situation.

Standing in my kitchen after lugging a boot full of grocery bags from the car to the bench, I paused to catch my breath. I didn't mind food shopping; it was the unpacking I hated.

Muttering under my breath and surveying the load, I cursed Mickey for weaseling his way out of shopping again. However, his absence did mean I had the house to myself tonight. When he and I decided to flat together, we had agreed to take turns and share like adults. Luckily for us, we were incredibly in-tune with each other, and living together was simple. We knew exactly how the other was programmed and, to be honest, being separated still didn't feel right even after twenty-six years.

Opening the music app on my phone and connecting to the Bluetooth speaker, I scrolled through looking for something that would get me pumped and energised. Increasing the volume until the music drowned out the world, I closed my eyes and let the melody penetrate my soul. The procrastination immediately began to subside and I soon melted into my happy place.

Shamelessly moving my body to the beat and singing at the top of my lungs, I shimmied around the kitchen, opening cupboards and chucking in items. Just as I was collecting up the empty bags, a loud voice boomed over and above the volume of the music.

"Party for one and I'm not invited?"

The ear-splitting screech that escaped my mouth didn't even come close to describing how much of a fright I got. I literally jumped as I high as I could while flapping my hands spastically in alarm. Once my feet reconnected with the floor, I stood pressing a hand to my heaving chest and panted hard.

Gage clapped his hands over his ears and ducked in reaction to my shriek. Goddamn, I was having chest pain as I turned down the music. Gage's alarm gave way to hilarity which he failed miserably at suppressing. His shoulders shook and his hand, despite being pressed over his mouth, utterly failed to disguise his laughter. Obviously, my pain and humiliation were comical to him, and the fact he caught me dancing like a maniac really did make me cringe and die a little inside.

"Jeez you scared the crap out of me!" I cried, still too shocked to be fully embarrassed at this stage. "I actually think I just had kittens. What the blazers are you doing here? And how did you find out where I live?"

He ignored my questions which caused my blood pressure to elevate further. I glared, not saying a single syllable while he filled the room with his deep, rolling laughter.

"If you've come here to mock me, you can leave," I finally snapped.

He held up his hands in surrender while his chest still vibrated. "Hey, if I get to see you dancing like *that* again, then I'm officially your stalker, Sunshine," he chuckled.

I snorted. This was preposterous. I raised my brows as he invited himself in and leaned his hip against the bench. Despite his smirk and the ghosts of his laughter not long passed, the air of sadness around Gage never seemed to leave. Something about him was foreboding, and him being in my kitchen made it hard to breathe. His scent swirled around me and my inner self clawed at the walls, desperately seeking a grip to hold onto while outwardly willing myself to remain calm. I spoke to his back as he bent and started collecting the scattered bags.

"So, speaking of stalking, how did you actually get my address? You're so lucky Mickey isn't here; any hint of an intruder and he's prowling around with his nunchucks at the ready. He hardly needs an excuse to throw them around."

Gage twisted his head to look up at me. "Are you serious?"

Seeing me nod, he raised his brows then pointed an accusatory finger at me "You're both fuckin' insane."

"Thanks. I'll take that as a compliment," I sassed.

Dammit, he's provoking me and I knew it.

Gage stood and balled the bags before tossing them onto the bench top behind me. He paused, looking me over, searching my gaze for something I wasn't sure I could give him. The moment between us stretched out until he pressed a fist to his mouth and cleared his throat.

"Can, I, uh, come in?"

I felt my eyes flare at his audacity before my unchecked burst of laughter broke free.

"Bit late for that, isn't it?"

Gage's dark-brown eyes warmed as a full and genuine grin made the corners crinkle. With that, his entire demeanour changed to show a handsome, more likeable side of the broody, scowling Gage I had become accustomed to.

I ducked my head when I realised I was staring at him. "Uh, so… Coffee?" I offered from under my lashes.

His smile was smaller this time, yet no less warm. "That'd be nice."

Thankful to have a reason to move out of his orbit, I bit back my smile once my back was turned and reached for the mugs. Mickey, damn him, had purposely shoved my favourite one right at the back of the shelf where he knew I couldn't reach it. Completely forgetting about Gage's presence for the barest of moments, I cursed Mickey as I rose on the tip of my toes and stretched my arm to full extension.

"Let me help."

Gage's body lightly pressed against my back and a tanned forearm appeared in my vision.

"This one?" he queried, holding up the mug that had Cactus pictures all over it.

"Yes," I whispered, acutely aware of his warmth seeping through my clothes.

His low chuckle reverberated around me while his smell made me want to sigh. I held my breath so it didn't come out shaky, and only let it out once he stepped back a pace.

Dayum!

I fought to calm my pulse before I turned and forced a breezy smile onto my lips.

Without asking, Gage made two coffees—both the same—and handed one to me with a nervous smile. We still hadn't exchanged a word. I mean, what the hell was there to say? Everything, yet, nothing was needed right now.

I met his eyes expectantly. Tension rolled off him in waves, emphasised when he rubbed a hand over the back of his neck then looked up at me from under his brows. Clearing his throat, Gage broke the silence.

"I confess, I blackmailed Mace into giving me your address."

Note to self; maim Mace.

"And since he agreed to tell me, I believe that speaks volumes about my non-dodgy character," he added, the cocky side of him now back.

Taking a sip of hot beverage, I countered his pretentious comment. "All that tells me about your character is that you will shamelessly use any form of persuasion to get what you want."

I rotated my hand around in a *get on with it* gesture.

Gage let out a resigned sigh and fingered the handle of his mug.

"Look, the truth is that I don't know what the fuck came over me the other night—I'm sure you felt it too—but, I apologise for how I treated you..." he trailed off and looked at me like he expected me to be able to provide those answers. "There's no excuse."

Wow, an apology was unexpected. I shrugged off his expectant gaze, weighing the responses of my heart versus my head. I knew I needed to formulate a calculated response and take this easy; I didn't want to get his back up again since I actually enjoyed seeing that softer side of him.

"Um, what happened was er..." I felt the flush rising on my cheeks.

No way was I admitting how much I enjoyed our kiss and how my body begged for a repeat. Ignoring the heat on my face, I shook my head, dismissing the treacherous thoughts from my mind. I had to stop the mixed signals, for both our sakes. Taking a deep breath and reining in my feelings, I decided to take the plunge.

"I can't explain what's between us, but, regardless of what either of us feel, I don't want to be just another notch on your belt."

The millisecond the words passed my lips I knew it was the wrong way to phrase what I wanted to express. Gage reared back like I had slapped him again, and undeniable offense darkened his expression. Guilt immediately churned in my stomach; it wasn't my intention to offend him, however, I'd done just that.

In my line of work, honesty and direct explanations were crucial, nevertheless, honesty was not the best policy in this instance. I opened my mouth to salvage the situation. "Look, Gage, that's not what I m-"

Gage took a step into my space and silenced me with his yell. "Save the *bullshit,* Sunshine. You know sweet fuck all about me, and what's on my belt is none of your goddamn business. You can stick your coffee you know where!"

Turning on his heel and storming from the kitchen, he slammed the front door back on the hinges and disappeared from sight.

I stood glued to the spot, unable to comprehend how the atmosphere had flipped on its head in an instant. The door still hung agape as I listened to the rumble of his bike accelerate down the street.

Disbelief grew into irritation. Sure, I had inadvertently touched on a highly sensitive nerve, but that was no excuse for turning up at my house uninvited, throwing around accusations then storming out without an explanation; from either of us. My day had officially turned to shit. Grabbing my phone, I fired off an SOS text to Kimmie.

L: Had a visit from Batman. It went well… NOT!!

L: Come to mine later for goss and a movie! And bring wine!!!

K: What, no hot sex?

L: KIMMIE!

K: Ok ok. I'll c u in a bit!

With that priority taken care of, I turned my attention to the root of my annoyance.
Mason Montgomery Westbrook.

L: Thanks for sending your maniac cousin my way to stalk, flirt, then dress me down before storming out. NOT APPRECIATED! *flipping you my middle finger right now*

I waited for a reply that never came. Mace's silence which meant either one of two things; one, he was working out to loud music and didn't hear my text, or two, he was hunting down Gage to put his muzzle back on.

I hoped it was the latter. Since the heat had now dissipated from my coffee and it had been tainted by Gage's bullshit, I tipped it into the sink and huffed as I wrenched open a cupboard. I needed food A.S.A.P.

LIL

KIMMIE ARRIVED IN a flurry of bags and cheery tones. The crew had a 'no knocking' policy at each other's houses, so when we arrived it really was *bowl through the door like you own the joint*. So, it didn't surprise me when she waltzed straight in and sang out, "Hey biarch," from the kitchen.

I could hear the gentle clink of wine bottles being loaded into the fridge and then the rustling of other various packaging. Snacks!

"Wassup!" I whooped coming into the room.

"Well, you know, just coming to rescue a friend in need." Kimmie pressed her lips together and eyed me. "So, spill. What happened? You really didn't get some, did you?"

Surely the answer was clearly visible on my face. To be honest, 'getting some' wasn't at the top of my priority list right now.

I pointed a finger at her. "For me to tell you about it, there must be wine."

Kimmie's eyes briefly pinged to the clock. "Midday, shmidday," she scoffed, "It's always five pm somewhere in the world so now is as good a time as any!"

"Fuck I need this. Honestly, Kimmie, that man is a walking contradiction, and he riles me simply by being in the same room."

She didn't bother hiding her grin. "You know what I'm gonna say, aye?"

"Gah, don't bother." I set my elbows on the bench and cradled my head in my hands.

"You can cut the sexual chemistry between you two with a spoon. All that pent-up lust just gagging to come out..."

"Jeez, Kimmie, you need to shut your mouth. This isn't purely for your entertainment! I can handle a lot of bullshit, but *never* has someone made me want to bludgeon them to death one second then throw myself at them the next."

Kimmie's snickering turned serious as she slid a brimming glass of wine across the bench at me.

"So, what went down this morning?"

On a huff, I ripped into a packet of chocolate favourite biscuits and plucked one out. After cramming it into my mouth and groaning in ecstasy, I motioned for Kimmie to follow me to the lounge. She was moving before she had even picked up both her glass and the bottle of wine; we were in this for the long haul.

Only once we were comfortably slouched on the couch did I give Kimmie the low-down of my run in with Gage. She sat at the opposite end with her legs tucked up and listened intently. After much demanding from her, I then went on to tell her about my dirty little secret—that also involved Gage—from the barbeque last weekend. Her light blue eyes grew comically wide as she implored for the dirty details, which I shared but skipped the finer particulars about what had stirred within me that night.

Finally satisfied that she was up to date with the goss, Kimmie leaned back, took a sip of wine then let out a long breath.

"Wow. I can see why that required alcohol. You guys are explosive, and I haven't worked out if that's a good or bad thing yet."

"I know," I grumbled and picked at my nail.

There wouldn't be an issue if I never needed to see him again, but now that he was residing at Mace's, there was no way I *wouldn't* see him.

Kimmie seemed to be contemplating something else as she swirled her glass in circles. Long seconds passed before she voiced her thoughts.

"There must be something big, like *really* big, in Gage's past for him to react like that. I mean, everyone's got baggage, right? But from what you've told me about this morning, his reaction seems a little excessive."

I ran my hand through my hair then tugged it over one shoulder. "Yeah, I guess so. And I actually feel really terrible about it. The worst part is, I was trying to not make a big deal out of telling him how I felt but it totally blew up in my face."

"Yeah," she grimaced. "That wasn't the best way to put it."

"Fuck, I *know!*"

I took a deep breath and exhaled forcefully. My life had been simple and uncomplicated for years now, right up until the point where Gage Westbrook had turned it completely upside down all over again.

I shook my head and contemplated everything while sipping wine. Kimmie silently topped us both up and I watched her as she set the wine bottle back on the ground.

"Once I hear from Mace, I'm sure he'll be able to shed some light on Gage. They're cousins after all. And honestly, how much do we know about the guy? Basically nothing."

"Yeah, I'm assuming they're reasonably close since he's up here working for the family business," Kimmie reasoned.

"You'd think so. I just don't want to make the situation worse by poking around for information. I mean, the guy makes me want to tear my hair out, but I'm sure he's not that bad. But holy shit, Kimmie, if you'd have seen how he kissed me at your party you would have *died*. It was so fucking hot."

That admission marked the point in time where the wine started to take effect and I was beginning to feel careless over the complexities of Batman.

Kimmie threw her head back and laughed. With a finger pointed my way, her eyes grew sultry. "Hey, I saw the way you looked afterwards, and holy hell, babies had practically been made orally."

"That's so terrible!" I yelled through a burst of laughter and threw a cushion at her face.

I gasped when the cushion knocked her glass and sent a mini wave of wine sloshing onto her leg. Our laughter filled the room until she used the cushion to soak up the spillage.

"Dammit, Kim, don't use that! I'll need to wash it now." I pouted and snatched it from her hands.

"Yeah yeah. You're lucky I'm wearing shorts! I hate spilling drinks when I'm wearing pants. *So uncomfortable.*"

"Tell me about it, girlfriend. Hey, pass me the shnacks," I asked, drawing out the sssshhh part. "You should totally stay the night!"

Kimmie quirked her mouth off to the side as she mulled over my suggestion; she liked to sleep in her own bed so I added some tempting crumbs to sweeten the deal.

"That means we can have more wine, order pizza and have a movie marathon. Theeeen, you can sleep in

Mickey's bed so I don't kick you all night. And don't worry, he changed his sheets this morning so they'll be jizz free."

Disgust slammed onto Kimmie's face. "Ugh! Gross, Lil! And, where's Mickey gonna sleep?"

I fended off the cushion she pegged my way while trying not to spill more alcohol on the decor.

"He honestly won't mind," I assured her. "It's not like you're some random I picked up on the way home and offered a bed for the night." To put her out of her misery wondering where my darling brother was, I added, "He's out at some rave bar and I'm not expecting him home until mid-morning. Which means, you can totally stay the night."

Despite being appalled, I could tell Kimmie felt uncomfortable at the thought of sleeping in Mickey's bed—*uninvited*. She mulled my proposal over for a short while before throwing her head back in defeat.

"As long as you're sure Mickey won't completely flip out when he finds out that I stayed in his room! Maybe I should text him to see if it's actually okay."

"He won't care. Anyone else and he would, but with you, I can guarantee he won't." I held her stare until she threw up a hand.

"Gah! Fine! Go on then, top me up!"

"Ha! Now who's got a rubber arm!" I cheered while topping up our glasses. "Promise me you won't go sniffing his underwear."

Kimmie's mouth fell wide as she laughed at me. "Gross! Now who's the creepy one!"

I fended off another wayward cushion attack while laughing hard. "Okay okay okay okaaaay," I wheezed. "I'll stop teasing now I promise."

"You suck," Kimmie muttered.

The only sound that escaped from me was a snort as I tried to keep my snickering in check. Kimmie wasn't a prude, but she was most definitely more reserved than I was. And while she was forthcoming with telling me intimate details, she still found it a bit awkward to be so open, depending on the subject.

"Right, movie or series binge?" Kimmie demanded.

"Movie!"

"Okay, how about Beau-"

"*And we watched Beauty and the Beast last time*," I cut her off. "Yes, it's good but we need something a bit more badass today."

"Amen to that."

I smirked. "Mmhmm! Anything Hemsworth or Gerard Butler—I don't care which one."

"I thought you'd never ask," Kimmie said breathlessly and swooned against the back of the couch.

Double checking that my phone was on silent, I set my glass down and crawled over to the TV. From that moment on, I did *not* want to be disturbed by anything other than hearing my glass refilling and letting my eyes feast on gorgeous, non-dickhead, men.

10
LIL

GERARD DIDN'T FAIL to deliver all our hopes and dreams, and as the movie finished, Kimmie's stomach let out a loud, angry growl.

All of a sudden, I was *famished!* Like, *needed food right now before I ate my own arm* famished. Who was I kidding; I would totally eat Kimmie's arm first!

"I'm ordering pizza before you lose an arm," I announced and fumbled with my phone.

She did a double-take my way. "What does ordering pizza have to do with my arm?"

"Taste," I shot back and, ignoring the awaiting messages, dialled for delivery. I tapped my thigh impatiently while the call connected.

"'BBQ Meat Lovers and Chicken Fajita?" I mouthed at Kimmie.

She widened her eyes and nodded. I smiled at her smirk then turned my attention to the voice in my ear as soon as he answered, stressing how urgent our order was; limbs practically hung in the balance!

"Gah, he had better be pronto. I *hate* waiting," I growled.

Kimmie tittered. "You've always been impatient, Lil. Even when we were little, you were a demanding little shit."

"Hey!" I yelled and slapped her leg.

Our laughter was halted by a knock at my door.

"No fuckin' way! That has got to be the quickest pizza delivery known to man!" she breathed when my eyes locked with hers.

We jumped to our feet and stampeded towards the front door, slamming into each other and shrieking hysterically in a drunken stupor. Swinging the door open, the smile dropped from my face and was quickly replaced with a frown deep enough to leave permanent lines.

"What are *you* doing here?" I huffed.

"Nice to see you too, Lil Bean," Mace deadpanned and folded his arms across his wide chest.

"We were expecting the pizza man, and we're raaavenous," Kimmie purred and gave him a flirty wink.

A grin split his face. "For you, ladies, I'll be God if you ask me to. But I'll settle for playing pizza boy," he chuckled and flexed his biceps unnecessarily before muscling his way past us into the house.

"Looks like my timing is impeccable since there's delicious, fatty food on its way."

I scoffed extra loud. "And just *why* are you here? You know you're welcome anytime, of course, but there's usually a reason for you to grace us with your presence." I raised one brow and waited.

Narrowing his eyes, he replied in a dry tone. "You didn't read my text, did you?"

"Nope."

I picked up my phone and saw he had, indeed, given me fair warning of his impending visit.

M: *rolling eyes* What's that dipshit done now? He came home major pissed!

10 minutes later;

M: It must be bad if you're ignoring me…

6 minutes later;

M: On my way. You can't snob me in person!

I re-read Mace's messages out loud, royally taking the piss by using a high-pitched and needy tone. By the end of the fourth read-through, Kimmie and I were crying with laughter. Our tears flowed harder when Mace wore the most ridiculous look of indignation on his face. He shook his head while frowning between the two of us.

"How much have you two loons had to drink already?"

Kimmie and I looked at each other. "Two?" I asked.

"At least… three?"

"No, definitely not three!"

"Two then" Kimmie announced with confidence.

"Glasses?" Mace questioned.

"*Bottles!*" I cheered and threw up my hands. My exclamation ended on a hiccup.

"Oh shit! You two are trouble," he declared through an amused chuckle and rubbed his hands together. "What's the occasion?"

Kimmie scoffed. "Your cousin is the occasion."

I whacked her hard on the arm, shocked that she had blabbed so quickly. Mace's face immediately darkened and he began to apologise profusely for giving out my address.

"It's fine," I sassed, well and truly not wanting to rehash things. "I don't want to down-buzz right now."

Mace held up his palms and motioned them in a placating gesture. Kimmie and I were still heckling Mace when we heard a car pull up outside. We all knew what that meant and the three of us did a happy dance on the spot before I swung the door wide for the second time in fifteen minutes.

The pizza man stood with his arm extended in a pre-knock stance. He froze to the spot when Kimmie and I rushed through the doorway and mobbed him. The poor guy all but shat himself. Mace chuckled behind us before finally putting the delivery boy out of his misery.

"Sorry, mate, my girls are ravenous right now." He gave the guy a wink that insinuated so much more than hunger. The guy paled slightly and took a step back.

Relieving the pizza man of his burden, Mace hustled Kimmie and I inside while holding the pizzas above his head. We turned our attention to the unreachable goods, jumping up and down in a hungered frenzy. Mace's composure was cracking with our relentless assault on his arms—and other parts of his body. The top box had become unstable during the scuffle and tilted precariously before plummeting towards the floor.

"Noooo," I yelled.

My clouded reactions made my actions seem way more epic than they were as I completed another of my signature slow motion dives. I *had* to save the stuffed crust circle of amazingness from impending doom.

Kimmie cheered and gave me a celebratory high-five as we laughed our way into the living room again, settling cross-legged on the floor in a circle with Mace.

"You two are fucking brutal," he chuckled, flicking an accusatory finger between the both of us.

"What can I say," I shrugged, "a girl's gotta eat. Don't get in the way of a woman and her food!" I grinned behind my hand, hiding my pizza smeared teeth.

"So, Lil told me all about her personal encounter with the sinfully hot Batman," Kimmie piped up.

She was messing with me and we both knew it. Her sweet demeanour wasn't enough to disguise the glint of mischief in her eyes.

Mace choked a little and grunted to clear the blockage.

"Was it really that bad?" Concern etched onto his gathered brows. Seeing my pursed lips, he added, "All I know is that he arrived home—leaving half the rubber from his tires on the driveway—and was in a right bitch of a mood. Got all up in my face as soon as he saw me. We're both lucky not to be sporting black eyes right now. Plus, I'm certain he broke the front door off the hinges with the force he threw it open, just like a goddamn hormonal teenager!"

That last comment lightened the mood and I felt a giggle bubble up.

"No, not *that* encounter." Kimmie burst in exasperation. "I'm talking about that of the sex-u-al kind that happened *last* weekend."

I gasped and threw a crust at her. "Bitch! Shut your mouth!"

Mace's laughter boomed around us. "Oh, I thought you were referring to their sex-u-al deviousness on your bench—also that night."

It was Kimmie's turn to gasp and savagely slam her pizza slice into the box.

"Lil! You *didn't!"*

I glared daggers at Mace as he held his stomach and guffawed like it was the funniest damn thing since *ever!*

"One of these days I'm gonna cut your balls off in your sleep, Mason!"

"Lil Bean, you're too easy," he wheezed in laughter.

"You suck! Both of you. As of this second, I'm in the market for new best friends."

Kimmie giggled, quickly forgetting her snit with me for corrupting her parent's kitchen bench.

Once Mace had finally pulled himself together, he turned serious again and I felt the weight of his words land heavily on my chest.

"Seriously, Lil, was his behaviour really that bad?"

"Well..." I waved the pizza in the air between us. "It wasn't pleasant," I concluded in a matter-of-fact way. "And are *you* okay, by the way?" I added as an afterthought to his well-being.

He waved off my concern and circled his hand, impatient for me to spill the beans. With a sigh, I set my pizza down and talked, sparing him no detail.

Mace re-positioned himself two clicks to the left so he could lean against the front of an armchair as he listened. Sprinkles of cussing came from him as I relayed the entire story from start to finish. I finished with a question, hoping he could shed light on the situation.

"So, what's up with him hating on the world, with the whole dark and broody badass thing he's got going on?"

I could see Mace waging an internal battle, wanting to tell me what I wanted to know while not crossing the line of family privacy. He came to a decision and looked at me frankly.

"Lil, Gage has had an extremely rough time in the last few years, and he's a changed man from what he went through. The tats and piercings were his way of dealing with the shit that broke him. He came up here for a fresh start, to get away from all the wallowing that was drowning him back in The Bay. It's not my place to give you the finer details, and I bet my left nut there's more to the story than I know about, but I assure you, he's a great guy. He just holds his cards very close to his chest. It's going to take time—and getting to know him—before you'll fully be able to see, and understand, that."

I looked at my hands and grumbled, "I'm hesitant to get to know him after this morning's effed up fiasco."

"Lil," Mace's tone was soft. It had me lifting my downcast gaze to meet his. "He reacted like that because you inadvertently touched on a subject that he doesn't ever want to talk about. I also know that he is incredibly confused about how he feels about you, though he hasn't told me in so many words," he added wryly. "I know him well enough to read between the lines. Gage's way to shut out the feelings is to be an asshole. And believe it or not, it means he actually cares." Mace hesitated, but decided to forge on cautiously. "You know, Lil, I don't want to drag up the past, but I totally get why you would be guarded towards a guy that you hardly know..."

His blue depths held sadness and his expression softened further, now full of affection as he searched my eyes with his. I felt myself smiling back at him in equal adoration. Mace understood how much my previous relationship destroyed me; he was one of the ones who fought hardest for me. He was right though, everyone had baggage and it wasn't fair on Gage for me to expect to know all about his past while keeping my own hidden.

As Mace's advice sunk in, I felt the slump in my spine as guilt spread through me. I'd totally jumped to conclusions, yet again, about Gage.

"You'll need to speak to him sooner or later because he's one of us now, and we'll be seeing a lot more of his handsome face in the future," Kimmie tentatively advised, leaning against my shoulder.

Looking between both of their expectant faces, I couldn't conjure up a legitimate excuse as to why I shouldn't at least try to make amends with Gage, apart from the obvious fact that both of our encounters thus far had ended in total train wrecks.

"Maybe, yes, no... Hell, I don't know right now!" Locking stares with Mace, I turned my insecurities into sass. "But one thing's for sure, he's not allowed back at my house until he's got his attitude in check."

Always one to want the last word, Mace barked out a laugh and shook his head.

"You'll be waiting until hell thaws from a deep freeze for that, Lil."

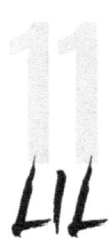

LIL

FOR THE LIFE of me, I couldn't fathom how Mace put up with our crap. As much as he looked bored to death, and no matter how many exasperated looks he cast in our direction, I knew he secretly thrived on the fact that he was privy to our girl talk. You know the kind that involved lots of juicy gossip that wouldn't be uttered around the guys.

Mace pretended to be all scandalised and shocked, but there were occasions when his guard totally fell off the wagon and he immersed himself in the conversation as much as Kimmie and I did. Those moments were the best.

Mace and Mickey had been mates since Kindergarten, so I knew Mace well growing up. We'd been good friends, but our relationship reached new depths during periods of personal crises that could never have been battled alone. We had pulled each other through those times by equal amounts of sheer willpower, determination and outright stubbornness. I battled to get him through the lowest time in his life, and he returned the favour to pull me through the darkest time in mine. Needless to say, Mace and I were connected in a way that only the strongest relationships are bound by. We trusted each other with our lives, literally. For that, I would always cherish him deeper than mere friendship. I loved him as hard as one could without wanting someone intimately.

Mace, always the protective presence when around Kimmie and I, remained sober while us girls let our hair down. We reached the point in our drinking escapade where it was late and we were falling asleep; Kimmie was on the couch propped up by the oversized cushions, and me on the floor with my feet up on the couch where Mace was lounging. Seeing us shutting down for the night, he put on his authoritative hat and stated that play time was over and it was time to get our asses upstairs to bed.

He handled our complaints like a champ, not caring that he had to help brush our hair or be bullied into helping remove or re-dress various items of our clothing. Kimmie managed to crawl up the stairs purely by willpower, fiercely declining Mace's repetitive offers of assistance. She was driven by the fact she would be sleeping in Mickey's bed tonight. I, however, was being a right pain in the butt and I knew it.

Uncontrollable giggles overcame me as Mace tried to coax me upstairs with his serious face; brows drawn together and lips slightly pouted. Coming to the end of his patience, his command ramped up a notch by snagging my wrists and dragging me semi-upright. There, he scooped an arm behind my knees and lifted me into his arms.

"Stop squirming, Lil Bean," he growled.

"Your tickly fingers are tickling me!"

Mace snorted. "I've said this before and I'll say it again, you two are fucking trouble." He chucked between grunts as he climbed the stairs, holding me tight to his chest.

"You know you love it. I'm glad we're entertaining you," I slurred and rubbed his chest playfully. "And!" I shouted as I snapped to full alert, "I love you so hard because I'm such a horrible mess and, no matter what, you're always there for me."

He nipped at my fingers when I poked at his face. "You know I love you, too. You're the little sister I never had and I can't help but sort out your sorry ass when you need it."

"Yeaaah," I sighed. "I think I'm going to officially adopt you as my brother. You're much more fun and helpful than the one I shared a womb with." I contemplated my suggestion; it was a great idea.

Mace scoffed. "You know he would do anything in the world for you, Lil. He's crazy protective of you, if you hadn't noticed. He's just got a diff-"

"It's official; I'm going to keep you!" I yelled, cutting him off then began combing his hair with my fingers, cooing at him like a cute puppy.

In my distracted state, I hadn't noticed we had made it to my bedroom. Next thing, I was sailing through the air and bounce-landing on the bed where Mace tossed me. I rolled to the edge where he sat and studied me intently. His features grew increasingly concerned the longer he stared. With a heavy sigh, he scrubbed a hand over his forehead and eyes.

"Lil, it's getting worse again."

I feigned obliviousness. "What is?"

His light blue eyes swam with disquiet as he reached for my hand and caught my gaze again. The concern etched on his face made a pang of regret shoot through my heart.

"Your drinking, Lil. It's been increasing recently and it's beginning to worry me again."

Dipping my head in shame, I knew he spoke the truth. I had felt the pull for a month or two now, I just tried to ignore it.

The truth was, six years prior, I had been madly in love with the supposed love of my life. He was caring, treated me like a queen, was confident and smart, and had effortlessly worked his way into my heart. Mickey warned me copious times that Jono was no good, but I assured him that he was. Jono was what I considered 'safe'. He wasn't wild and destructive, and he brought out a tamer version of myself that I hadn't recognised to begin with. At the time, I hadn't realised that I should never have changed who I was in order to please someone else, especially a man who I was meant to spend my life with.

I met him at the tender age of twenty, nine years his junior, but it felt like he was put on earth to make me happy. Our relationship rapidly went from non-existent to full blown within a few weeks and, despite not being able to get enough of each other at any given moment, I realised now that was mostly infatuation I felt—not being head over heels in love with him. It was as if I had been picked up in a whirlwind and all I had to do was ride it to see where it took me. Soon, Jono moved into my flat and met my parents, all the while enthusiastically making grand plans for our future. At the time I didn't find it weird that he never brought me home to meet his parents; he had told me they had passed away in a car accident years earlier. He also claimed he was an only child with no other relatives in New Zealand. He was all alone, and that made me—stupidly—think he needed someone to care for him. Looking back, the issue lay in his love of top shelf spirits. He consumed them in large quantities on a nightly basis, and naturally I developed the habit too.

After only a few short months of living together, he proposed at the end of a night spent getting pissed. In my inebriated state, I had instantly agreed. I figured the proposal was planned as he presented me with a gorgeous princess cut diamond ring. I couldn't believe my luck; he was the entire package and wanted to be with me. The love-drunk feeling began to develop minor cracks around the eight-month mark when he became increasingly preoccupied and short tempered. When I asked him about it, he would fob me off with a legitimate excuse—usually something to do with stress at work. Every now and then, our evening would be interrupted by a 'work call' which he took outside—out of politeness.

He came home one day looking extra stressed and finally confided that his employers were sending him to Sydney for an open contract position which would be at least six months. I was so disappointed to be distanced from him for such a long time and offered to put my study on hold and go with him. He shot down that suggestion instantly with another excuse that seemed totally plausible; that his work would only pay for a single hotel room and we couldn't afford to pay for the room upgrade for long term. And, stupidly, I believed every single word.

So, there it was; my fiancé was heading to another country for the foreseeable future, and I was left fumbling my way through life without him. The only thing that kept me optimistic was his daily phone calls. In my blinded state, I began to neglect the people who loved me the most—my friends and family. The crew stepped up and made an effort to keep me occupied, but when I wasn't with them, I turned to the bottle. To add insult to injury, I couldn't afford some of the spirits I was used to drinking but I always found a way to make sure I had small amounts stashed throughout the house. The alcohol began to take priority over eating, my grades plummeted, and my social life took a dive when I began opting to stay home drinking by myself. My life went from peachy to rotten overnight. Mickey wasn't at all impressed with the situation and desperately tried to convince me to ease back on the booze and open my eyes to take a real look at the situation. Evidently, he could see through the whole façade.

It wasn't until Mace and Mickey came back from a piss trip on the Gold Coast of Australia that the cracks in my love life began to tear wide open then crumble and crash around me, all within a matter of minutes.

I picked them both up from the airport with anticipation, expecting to see happiness radiating off their tanned bodies after a week away doing God knows what. My heart slammed into my gut the moment they appeared through the arrivals gate. My grin faltered further when I took in their grim expressions.

Something was wrong. Very wrong.

They weren't giddy and excited to see me; they were sombre and their welcome hugs were much more protective than the big 'great to see you' squeeze I was expecting. The drive home was filled with bullshit small talk and tension. The uneasiness in my stomach increased tenfold when Mickey refused to let me into his head, blocking me completely.

Pulling into Mace's driveway, I parked and flung the door open before they had unbuckled their belts. After storming onto the front porch, I paced like a caged animal as I tried to take my mind off the sick feeling in my stomach.

Mace came up and set his bags down to unlock the door then wrapped me in another hug and whispered in my ear, "You're amazing and beautiful, Lil. Never for a second forget it."

Then, he put this hand on my back and ushered me inside before him. Anxiousness was making me lightheaded but I refused to take a seat when Mickey came in and suggested we go sit in the lounge.

"Cut the bullshit guys. What the fuck is going on?" I urged them, unable to hold back my emotions any longer.

They cut a glance at each other before Mace cleared his throat. "Lil, we were in Brisbane and saw something unexpected. I'm just not sure how to tell you."

I was going to be sick for sure. I pleaded with Mickey to elaborate. Letting out an angry growl, he picked up where Mace left off.

"Lil, we saw Jono with another woman. They looked cosy, both wearing wedding bands, and... she was pregnant," he whispered the last three words.

I actually laughed at the absurdity of his accusations and shock my head in denial.

"Impossible, he's in Sydney, not Brisbane," I reasoned.

The devastation I saw in their eyes made my composure falter. It was at that moment, I knew in my heart of hearts that they were telling me the truth. There was no way they would pull a prank like this. No way in Hell. Mickey ventured further by fumbling in his pocket for his phone.

"We took photos, Lil. It's not a joke. I'm so fuckin' sorry for having to do this to you, it's tearing me apart."

"Tearing you apart? Tearing YOU apart?" I screamed through the tears spilling down my face. "Give me the goddamn phone, Josh!"

He hesitated for a beat then reluctantly held it out. I snatched it from his palm and started furiously flicking through the photos. With each swipe of my thumb, the more my heart broke and realisation began to hit home. It was Jono without a doubt, the birthmark on his forearm was enough to confirm that. But who the hell was the woman that he was intimately kissing and fondly touching her small rounded belly bump? I couldn't look at them anymore and dropped the phone as my breathing became quick and shallow. Within seconds, I saw the tell-tale fog gather in my peripheral vision before darkness drew in and stole my sight. My hearing went, leaving me deaf aside from high pitched ringing within the depths of my ears.

Mace was by my side in a flash as I tottered sideways. He caught me in his arms before I hit the ground. I woke up soon after with a cold cloth pressed to my forehead and Mickey gently shaking my shoulders. Realising that it wasn't a horrid dream, I willed myself back towards the darkness that wouldn't reclaim me. Seeing the tenderness in Mickey's wide eyes ignited all the anger that was boiling within. I flung myself at him, screaming and pounding my fists on his chest as hard as I could. Mickey stood there and took it like a man, taking away some of my anger and pain in the only way he knew how. He was just the messenger, and I was shooting him for it. Mace's strong arms once again surrounded me, wrapping *around my waist and dragging me back from a dazed Mickey. Mace then sat down and pulled me into his lap, engulfing me in a fierce bear hug until my struggles began to wane. At that moment my anger gave way to grief. It spilled out in ugly waves while Mace continuously rubbed my back. Mickey couldn't handle 'womanly outbursts' well, and I wasn't offended when he disappeared outside to compose himself over a ciggy. From that day on, I turned to the bottle more than ever in last-ditch desperation to forget the clusterfuck that was my life. The days that followed were an alcohol induced blur of rejecting Jono's increasingly frequent calls and texts, a never-ending river of tears, a frenzied assault on my flat—removing anything that was remotely associated with my asshole EX-fiancé, and the constant murmuring voices and hugs from my beautiful friends who stuck by me like glue.*

When the last of Jono's meaningless belongings were piled in a heap in the backyard, Mickey poured diesel over the crap and I struck the match. Satisfaction wove through me at seeing the last of Jono's presence burn from my life. The last thing I tossed into the flames was my engagement ring. It saddened me a lot that the beautiful diamond would be forever lost, but it was my final 'fuck you' to Jono.

I handed Mickey my phone and asked him to do the honours of taking my picture in front of the burning inferno. My first—and only—contact with Jono since I found out about his double life, was sending him that picture and telling him to get lost.

Needless to say, that caused a shitstorm to erupt, which I ignored and gladly let Mickey deal with. When Jono knew the game was up, he confessed on voicemail that he was only in New Zealand on a contract job and had returned home to his WIFE, who had fallen pregnant during a weekend visit—which had been roughly a month and a half before his official contract here had ended. Jono offered me a half-hearted apology and somehow thought it made up for all the deceit. Not in a million years after Hell froze over would I forgive him.

I battled hard with the booze for a long time after, and put myself in unsafe situations time and time again.

Mickey and our family did all they could to pull me back into the light. I'm there now, but every now and then the darkness reaches for me, clawing at me, calling my name, trying to drag me down once more; especially during the turbulent or unpredictable times in my life. It was at those times when I felt most unworthy. In those times, there was only one person who seemed to make a real difference to my will to get through the shit and make it out the other side again.

Mace.

"Lil Bean?" Mace gently shook my shoulder.

His intrusion to my thoughts snapped me from the trip down memory lane. My eyes automatically searched for his when he lifted my chin with his forefinger. I grimly nodded and squeezed his hand.

"I know it is. I'm so sorry," I whispered. "And I'm thankful for you, for everything… But, he… he broke me, Mace."

I let one—just *one*—tear slip from under my lashes. Mace bent until I felt his lips meet my forehead, there, they moved against my skin.

"I know he did, Lil Bean, and I could kill him because of it."

He pulled back and his thumb quickly dashed away the single tear that escaped. With exaggerated care, Mace helped me beneath the covers and tucked me in. He bent to kiss my forehead again. "We'll talk about it tomorrow," he said softly before disappearing from the room.

Minutes later, he returned and ensured that Kimmie and I both had a glass of water by our beds.

"I'll be sleeping on the couch if you need me. Goodnight, Lil," he whispered and gave me a friendly pat on the rump. I squirmed until I was propped up on one elbow.

"Go to sleep," he commanded with his voice and pointing forefinger.

"Goodnight, Macey-poo," I murmured.

He scoffed as he walked to the door. I called out once more as the light clicked off and plunged us into darkness.

"Mace?"

He sounded wary. "Yeah, Lil Bean."

"Stay with me?"

Without question, he left the door open and padded back into the room. After a minute of shuffling through the dark, I felt the bed compress and his hand found mine beneath the covers. Only then, with him by my side like so many other times previous to tonight, did I snuggle into my plush bedding and let sleep claim me.

GAGE

THE MORNING AFTER greeted me like a freight train. A big, shitty, explosive, enormous son of a bitch from Hell, thundering through the most echoic canyon in the entire motherfucking galaxy. Needless to say, I was not a happy camper, especially once I remembered the reason for getting annihilated last night.

Lil.

Fuck! I'm so screwed.

I had no idea how I managed to make it to bed, though I was forever thankful that I turned off the thumping music before passing out; this hangover was killing my head enough as it was.

Groaning as I sat up and precariously swaying on the edge of my bed, I held my pounding head in my hands and cracked an eyelid. My sight landed on the bottle of well-aged whisky that had cost me half my left nut sack, now lying empty on the floor.

Stumbling to my feet, I made the slow and arduous shuffle to the bathroom while trying not to lose my stomach contents throughout the house. The room tilted and swayed beneath my feet, making the task of standing to piss near impossible. I was torn between vomiting into the bowl while urinating on the floor, or sitting down to piss while vomiting on the floor. Surprisingly, option three became available, allowing me time to relieve my bladder before throwing myself to my knees to follow suit with my stomach contents. Abso-fuckin'-lutely awesome.

Returning to my room long enough to jam a pair of sunglasses onto my face, I peered into Mace's room on my way to the kitchen. His room was empty and appeared to be unslept in. Nothing seemed to have been moved in the kitchen either, and I was more than a bit dark to see the front door looking worse for wear. That was my job for today, then.

Sighing and setting the coffee machine to full power, it didn't take a scientist to know how much I fucked up yesterday. Which now meant I had some serious apologising to do.

My behaviour was appalling and downright embarrassing. I'd directed my anger and frustration at Lil in the first instance, then Mace copped it when I got home. We were damn close to having an all-out fist fight as we locked into an altercation that walked the thin line between shoving and brawling. Now, in my pitiful hungover state, I was pissed at myself for being a total asshole. To irritate me even more, I couldn't stop thinking about how gorgeous Lil was when all riled up. She was a little spitfire, and was beginning to unknowingly work herself into my subconscious. And, to be honest, I was beginning to crave more where that came from. She had me intrigued as hell.

Squinting at my phone screen then minimising the brightness, I procrastinated before opening my text history with Mace. He was the easiest person to start with; I knew a lame apology wouldn't cut it with Lil. Aside from the obvious grovelling, actually finding the words I wanted to tell her was the hardest—and something I wasn't yet ready to do.

I tapped out a message then deleted it since it sounded way too dumb. I typed out another but deleted that too. With a massive sigh and reminding myself that I was overthinking this, I kept it short and to the point.

G: Where you at? Sorry for being an asshole yesterday.

His reply was instant.

M: At Lil's. All g.

G: What's her number? I need it!

M: I'm not giving it to you.

I swore out loud both at Mace's reply and the painfully loud grinding sounds coming from the fucking coffee machine. This was a slow agonising death from all angles.

G: Fine, be an ass! Pass this onto her, will you...

Fuck, fuck, fuuuck, why is the backspace button so damn close to the motherfucking send button on this stupid device!

Now I had to follow through with a text that made an ounce of sense. Unable to leave that text hanging, I struggled to think of something semi decent to add.

G: Lil - Can we talk sometime?
G: Please.

I shoved a mug into the coffee machine while shaking my head—since when did I beg to talk to someone? The answer to that was *never.*

Cursing under my breath again at my stupidity, my phone buzzed in my fingertips.

M: She says no.
M: Do we need any food? I'll be back later to cook dinner.

After carelessly typing back a reply, I nursed the coffee until I had worked up enough energy to shower. Finally dressed for the remainder of the day and with another caffeine hit in my hand, I set about fixing the front door that I had so satisfyingly destroyed yesterday.

The morning after was a right bitch.

. . .

I was dozing on the front step later that afternoon when Mace pulled up looking all smug and cheery.

"You're home," I snapped.

He raised a brow but didn't bother asking me how I was—I looked as shit as I felt.

I grabbed a couple of grocery bags and followed him into the house, waiting for him to say something. The silence continued as he got out various pans and utensils then started bustling around the kitchen like Martha damn Stewart, slicing and dicing mushrooms and onions. The smell of them frying in butter made my stomach growl in hunger, which was a nice contrast to feeling it turn on itself like it had been doing all day.

Mace finally turned and glared at me from under his eyebrows. "Seriously, Gage, what the fuck?"

"Is Lil ok?" I raked my fingers through my hair. "I didn't intend to lose my shit at her..."

He waved me off with the tongs in hand. "She's fine. Confused obviously, and out for blood, and nursing a wicked hangover." He chuckled like there was some secret joke I wasn't privy to and it stirred unwelcome jealousy deep in my gut.

"Well, that makes two of us then," I grumbled, rubbing my temples and rustling around the cupboard for more painkillers.

Mace laughed and didn't bat an eyelid. "It's your own goddamn fault so suck it up." His tone then turned dark. "You're lucky Mickey wasn't there, mate, he would've lost his shit."

"So I've been told," I mumbled.

I got the distinct impression that Mickey would break anyone who laid a finger on his precious sister. Fuck, I knew I would lay a guy out if he so much as dared to break one of my sisters' hearts. I already suspected that one of them was keeping shit from me but I hadn't managed to get a confession out of her before I left.

"I get that he's doing the brotherly thing," I replied to Mace. He snorted and chewed while grinning, knowing full well how much of a goddamn handful my sisters were. "But maybe he needs to keep his focus on his own love life. Him and Kimmie aren't together, right? I sure as hell didn't miss the way he was looking at her the other night."

"They're complicated. Shit happened in high school that they can't get over." Mace frowned slightly and shook his head then snapped his eyes up to mine. "He's possessive over his women, if you hadn't figured that out already."

I pursed my lips and cursed myself for being attracted to a woman with a bloody guard dog.

"Is that gonna be an issue for me patching things up with Lil?"

Mace shrugged and chucked spaghetti pasta into a pot. "Depends how you go about it. If you go in all guns blazing again, then there's gonna be a problem. Treat her right, and you'll be all good."

I worked his advice round my head before his next statement flared the irritation and guilt within me again.

"She's worth the effort, cuz."

My eyes locked with his. "I've told you already, I can't go there. It's too soon."

Mace's relentless stare bored into mine and made me shift nervously in my seat. His next statement hit way too close to home.

"I'm not telling you to forget. I'm suggesting you forgive yourself and let yourself be happy again."

"Fuck you," I growled. Not because I was mad, but because I knew he was right and I didn't want to admit it.

Mace pointed a spoon at me. "Just sayin'."

Sensing the sudden heaviness within my heart, silence endured for a long time while Mace plated up the spag bol. I sat at the table opposite him and watched as he chased a pasta noddle around his plate with his fork. The sight left me exasperated, causing my words to came out gruffer than I intended.

"You know them well?"

His attention snapped to me.

"Lil and Mickey, I mean?"

"Yup. Since we were little. Their parents are fucking awesome too."

Surprise ran through me and I waited for him to elaborate.

"Their monthly family dinners are great."

Again with the surprise, and a little more jealousy—dammit!

"So, you've been to one before?" I asked, probing for further information while moving food around my plate.

"Yeah, bro, I pretty much go every month. Matt and Ev love entertaining, and it's basically 'the more the merrier'. All the crew gets invited."

"Huh," I breathed, stupidly feeling left out. "So, you think Lil's up for a visitor sometime? I really feel like I should apologise to her..."

"Hell no, you are *not* going tonight!" Mace clipped in alarm.

I scowled and shook my head. "No, not tonight. I can't think of anything worse than feeling like shit and trying to have a decent adult conversation with someone who doesn't want to hear it."

He agreed with me on that one.

"I was thinking you might give me her number?"

Mace swallowed then shoved more food into his mouth. "No can do, bro. I'm on strict orders not to, and if I do there'll be hell to pay. Especially after I gave you her address, and we all know how well that went down."

"You're whipped, mate. Whipped like sweetened cream and spread wherever she wants it."

Mace didn't bite as much as I was expecting, aside from a half-hearted, "Fuck you." He swallowed again then drawled words that had me choking on my own breath.

"I do, however, happen to know that Lil Bean likes whipped cream used in various ways..."

I inhaled suddenly at the unexpected revelation and spluttered uncontrollably. My fork hit my plate and bounced along the glass table top, making me wince through the clatter. I blinked away tears then pounded on my chest.

"How the fuck do you know that?" I croaked.

That provoked more laughter from Mace and his eyes shone with amusement. "I'm telling ya, there are benefits of being the BFF of those girls. And trust me," he pointed his fork at me, "they talk some utter shit when we're hanging out and think I'm not taking notice. And *that* leaves me feeling well and truly violated."

It was my turn to chuckle as Mace feigned a shudder.

"Yeah right, because you're all innocent and all that shit."

He held up his hands and smirked. "You know I am. Besides, all I'm sayin' is that those girls can talk. Sometimes, Lil even jabbers in her sleep!"

A scowl hit my face so damn hard it hurt, and it deepened when Mace's smirk carved into a shit-eating grin.

"Where did you sleep last night?" I asked slowly.

Despite him saying that they were just friends, I was still sure him and Lil were doing the dirty behind everyone's backs. Mace's comment simply fuelled that suspicion.

"In her bed," he replied casually while gauging my reaction closely—which was to pick up my fork and slam it down again, wince, then glare at him.

"Something wrong, cuz?"

"Apart from you bullshitting me and everyone else? No, there's fucking not," I snarled.

He set his fork down. "I'm not bullshitting anyone. Lil and I are mates. End of. Yeah," he raised his voice over the start of my argument, "I sleep in her bed every now and then. We talk, but we don't fuck. You've got nothin' to worry about."

My hand itched to wipe the wry expression off his face. He was baiting me and we both knew it.

I inhaled deeply, seeking composure. "Well, since you know *everything,* did you know she's got a nipple piercing?"

Mace coughed a little then barked out a laugh. "Discovered that, did you? As a matter of fact, I was there when she got it done. So was Kimmie," he added upon seeing my jaw tick.

It was stupid; I had no claim on her, yet, I felt like no-one had the right to touch her or know intimate details about her that I didn't.

"In a nutshell, last Christmas holidays, Kimmie and Lil made a bet about who could fit the most marshmallows in their mouths, and whoever lost had to get their nipple pierced."

"You're kidding?" I dead-panned. Were they ten years old?

"Nope. Discovered any other hidden piercings by chance?" he smirked.

"Fuck, you mean there's more?" I hissed, needing to know this information right fucking now.

Chortling from the intensity of my reaction, Mace shook his head. "No, I'm having you on there. As far as I'm aware, she's just got the one. After the amount of cursing and verbal abuse she gave the guy doing the job, I doubt she would've gone back for more. She swore black and blue that the rest of her lady bits were remaining unpierced indefinitely."

"Jesus. You're cruel."

I jabbed carelessly at the forgotten Bolognese in front of me as Mace chuckled.

"You think *I'm* cruel? Just wait until Lil starts keeping you on your toes, you'll be begging for mercy."

"I don't beg, I command."

Mace stood and slapped me on the back. "We'll see about that."

13

LIL

I ANSWERED THE phone and quickly mashed it between my ear and shoulder as I kept sifting through paperwork.

"Heya, Kimmie, what's up?"

There were patients waiting to be seen and I was under a hell of a lot of pressure to get them all through before a riot of monstrous proportions broke out in the waiting room.

Her voice came through muffled against the side of my head. "Just seeing if there are any updates from you-know-who."

"No, there aren't. It's only been three days, and thank God he doesn't have my number. Sorry, chick, I'm under the pump and don't have time to chatty-chat-chat-chat right now."

"Shit sorry, I thought you were on nights this week. I'm the opposite here; bored out of my mind and procrastinating hard. I'll let ya get on with it."

A pang of guilt rose after hearing the resigned note in her voice.

"I totally didn't mean to snap, but I'll need to call you later though, okay."

"Sure thing. Keep your knickers on... For now," she added with an evil cackle.

I rose my voice. "Goodbye, Kimmie."

"Ciao for now."

Jamming my phone back into my scrubs, I checked the triage list to see who was next. Plastering on a smile in the hopes that I appeared cool, calm, and collected, I pushed through the door into the waiting room. All eyes expectantly turned my way. It felt like walking into the lion's den.

"Mr Andrews?" I called.

Seeing an elderly man slowly stand, I made my way over to help him, remembering that he came in late last week for stitches on a nasty gash on his arm. Despite me advising him to see his GP for a check-up, he was back here. Before I reached his side, a tall man came to Mr Andrews aide and helped steady him on his feet.

My heart leapt into my throat and my chest squeezed.

What the hell was *he* doing here? And being all gentlemanly to boot! Greeting Mr Andrews and taking his arm, I subtly turned towards to Gage.

"What are you doing here?" I asked in a lowered tone, trying my hardest not to hiss.

Judging by the look of surprise on his face, Gage hadn't expected to see me here either.

"I brought my uncle in. He had a small incident on site involving a nail gun."

Gage winced at the memory. Sure enough, I looked around his shoulder to see Dave Westbrook sitting with his foot elevated and looking a little on the pale side.

"Hi Dave, I'll be with you soon. Stay put," I added with a point.

He chuckled and gave a two fingered salute off his brow—which I returned.

"I'm glad you reminded me, love. I was gearing up to sprint laps around the waiting room to kill some time."

"Don't make me reprimand you when I come back," I warned.

Turning my attention back to Gage—who had been watching our exchange in stunned silence—I put my figurative nurses' hat back on.

"Mr Andrews has been waiting since this morning so I'll get him sorted then be back out for Dave. Go sit, I'll be out shortly... Hopefully," I added under my breath, which made Gage chuckle softly.

After a slow shuffle with Mr Andrews, I carefully peeled off his dressing while he yakked my ears off about his week thus far. He seemed to partake in a lot of tea drinking and complaining about his neighbour's cat. I couldn't help but give him a genuine smile as he got riled up in the details.

With his wound healing well and the stitches looking nice and clean, I redressed his arm and reminded him to see his GP, not the emergency room, to have the stitches removed in a weeks' time.

Guiding Mr Andrews to the exit, I quickly checked my hair in the reflection of the one-way window that separated the clinic cubicles and the nurses' station, on my way past.

Dave looked to be in reasonably good spirits when I entered the waiting room. He was chatting with Gage but stopped when I approached.

"Ah, love, there you are."

"Ready when you are, Mr Westbrook."

Blatant relief washed over Gage's expression now that official help had arrived to alleviate him of his responsibility. He stood and pushed his uncle's wheelchair into the Emergency Department ward while I held the door open for him.

We got Dave transferred to a bed and settled comfortably before I started my interrogation. I put on my best bossy nurse face and flicked my attention between Dave and Gage. Ironically, Gage was looking paler than his injured uncle.

"You guys weren't playing silly buggers, were you?"

Gage opened his mouth to answer but Dave bet him to it.

"No, the lads had nothing to do with it, it was my own silly mistake. Accidentally bumped the nail gun trigger when I went to put it on the ground. It's not the first time either, though a good many years since it happened last," he chuckled at himself.

I pursed my lips while investigating his boot with the nail protruding from the top.

"Well, let's hope it hasn't done any nerve, ligament or bone damage. First, I need to get you pumped up on meds, then we'll get that nail out and boot off to have a look at the injury. Thank goodness you guys didn't try to remove the nail yourselves."

Dave nodded and at least tried to look as if he was taking my nurse rant seriously.

Once the painkillers were charted and signed off by the doctor, I inserted an I.V. line and watched smugly as a look of medically induced euphoria settled over Dave's features. A Cheshire Cat grin wove onto his mouth the moment the intravenous Morphine began to work its magic, and Gage and I chuckled when Dave closed his eyes and gave us a thumb up.

It was hard to predict how a patient would react to Morphine; for the most part, it was comical. There were, however, a select few times when the effects made the patient unpredictable. Despite knowing Dave well, with caution in mind, I kept a close eye on him for the first minute while I decided which way he would go.

Happy with him now being settled and sedated, I turned my full attention back to the task at hand, which was made infinitely harder by the fact Gage was watching my every move. I selected the appropriate equipment and I looked across Dave's tranquil body at Gage.

"I'll need your help to hold him still while I remove the nail."

Gage visibly blanched but stood and got into position without protest. I put my hand on his arm, trying to ignore the energy that pulsed between us, and spoke gently.

"If you're not okay with the sight of blood, I can get someone else to assist. I don't want to be picking up your carcass off the floor if you faint. You'll be way too heavy," I teased, unable to help myself.

I caught the smallest tug of a smile on his lips as he drawled, "It's all muscle, baby." Wink. "I can handle it, less talking yeah, and more doing."

A slurred voice cut in between us. "When you two have finished hooking up, can we get this show on the road?"

I burst out laughing. "Mr Westbrook, I don't think you understand what *hooking up* is, because that definitely wasn't it."

"Dave," he corrected me with a little pat on my arm. "What's it called nowadays, then? Eye-sex?" he demanded, *way* too loud for our surroundings.

"Good Lord," I muttered and ducked my head to avoid the scandalised stares from the other nurses dotted around the room.

My attempts to hush Dave were overrode by Gage cussing under his breath then telling his uncle to, "Pipe the fuck down."

That was hilarious to Dave and I intended to take full advantage of his distracted state.

"Hold him still," I hissed at Gage.

There was a brief flicker of annoyance in his eyes before he complied. Grabbing the tip of the nail with a pair of pliers, I pulled it out in one smooth movement.

"Sweet bleeding mother of Mary," Dave roared and struggled under Gage's weight that pinned him to the table.

I took a hasty step backwards, narrowly missing being hit in the chest from Dave's flailing arm. Gage's stricken eyes hit mine as he held Dave as still as he could, and all it took was one quick nod from me for Gage to let go and flop into the chair next to the bed.

Dropping the nail into a bowl then handing it to Dave, I set about unlacing his work boot and gently slipping it off. Once I had his sock peeled off, I was able to get a decent look at the wound. The nail had lodged itself *between* the tiny metatarsal bones of toes three and four. Prodding carefully, I concluded that it had indeed missed the bones—God knows how—and that nothing was broken; just punctured and bruised. After flushing the site, I carefully dressed the area while running through the care instructions that were to be strictly followed. Lastly, I handed Gage a script for antibiotics.

"The nail should have been reasonably clean since it was new, but foot infections quickly turn nasty, especially if you don't rest them properly before going back to work." I pegged Dave with a stern look. "And yes, I will be checking up on you."

He fobbed me off with a lucid flick of his hand and muttered about having it sorted already. Rolling my eyes then smiling, I turned to thank Gage for his help.

What I saw stole the air from my lungs; the unguarded look in his eyes was raw and brimming with admiration, respect, pride, plus something else I couldn't quite decipher. All it took was a single blink for him to carefully re-mask his reactions. I kept my eyes locked with Gage's as I spoke to Dave.

"You're free to go home now, Mr Westbrook."

"Dave!" he barked, startling me slightly.

I looked down and set my hand on his shoulder. "Okay then, *Dave*. You're all fixed up and it's time to go."

"That'a girl, love. I'll let you get back to saving the world."

With what sounded like a snigger, Gage helped me manoeuvre a much floppier Dave back into the wheelchair.

"Are you going to be okay with him?" I puffed.

Gage's frown of concentration eased slightly. "How hard can it be to get him home? I'll be fine."

While walking them to the door, I ran through the care instructions one last time before saying goodbye. I was checking to see who was next on the triage list when a hand carefully took hold of my elbow. I turned to see Gage standing close.

"Hey, you were amazing in there," he said, nothing by sincerely.

"Just another day at the office," I replied, realising that this was the first nice thing Gage had said to me.

"When can I see you, to uh, you know..." He rubbed a hand awkwardly over the back of his neck. "I want to right the wrongs, so to speak."

My heart soared in an instant and I tried not to let the surprise show on my face. I studied him for a few beats, wanting to say yes but cautious over giving in too easily; our short history wasn't great.

His dark eyes never left mine, imploring me to give him a chance. After a long pause, my subtle nod created a warmth within those dark depths.

"Come by this weekend sometime?"

A hint of satisfaction tilted the corners of his mouth. I felt he was about to say something when Dave's booming voice echoed throughout the crowded waiting room.

"Gage, get your ass into gear and stop chatting up Lily. I know she's gorgeous, but let's bust out of this joint already!"

"*Fucking hell!*" Gage hissed. "He'll be lucky to make it home with only a sore foot at this rate. Catch ya 'round, Sunshine."

I watched as he stalked across the waiting room and thrust Dave's chair through the automatic doors before he caused more embarrassment.

Oh, my, Lord, Kimmie was going flip over our phone call tonight.

14

GAGE

"I'M SORRY, AUNTY." I openly laughed at Aunty Sandy's scandalised expression when I dropped my uncle home, relieved to be relinquishing him from my care.

He was still high as a kite. As entertaining as it was, I drew the line and held up my hands to indicate that I was *not* going to elaborate on the so called 'double eye-sexing' incident that Dave was currently spouting about.

He was quite the handful, and there was no question who Mace had inherited that particular trait from. I only wish Mace had witnessed this stellar side of his dad in person. Despite Dave being the main source of my afternoon's entertainment, the best part by far was the chance meeting with Lil in A&E.

Thinking back to the night we first met, Mace introduced me to everyone along with their occupation, but had omitted that for Lil; whether on purpose or not, I wasn't sure.

If I was honest, seeing Lil in action impressed the fuck out of me. I was completely in awe the whole time—aside from feeling outright queasy at the sight of Dave's injury—as I watched her expertly doing what she did every single day on the job.

With a final apology and hug for my aunty, I let her know that Lil would stop in at some stage over the next few days to check up on Dave.

Peeling away in my truck, I headed for home, needing a stiff drink.

. . .

Mace's laughter boomed around the kitchen as soon as he stepped through the door.

"Looks like you had a much more entertaining afternoon than I did. Jeez, the old man was right on form!"

"That's the goddamn understatement of the century."

As Mace ripped into a packet of chips, I pulled out two beers and handed one his way.

"Jesus, I feel like I've just experienced what it's like to deal with a pain in the ass teenage son."

Mace laughed through his mouthful, ignoring the few wayward chip crumbs that flew out.

"So, anything else you care to share...?"

There was that look again; the one that told me he knew there was more to the story than I was letting on. I narrowed my eyes and studied him for a moment as I slowly chewed my mouthful.

"You sneaky bastard!" I exclaimed. "Yes, now that you mention it. What a coincidence that a certain someone just happened to be the duty nurse in A&E today, and that you just happened to be too busy to take your own father to the hospital."

Mace raised his brows. "So Lil *was* working today? Thought she might have been," he replied with a smirk.

"You fucking knew the entire time, didn't you! So much for having your dad's best interests at heart," I scoffed and tilted the beer to my lips.

"Wish I had taken him myself now, I missed out on way too much dirt."

"Why didn't you say she was a nurse?"

He set his beer down and ploughed his hand into the bag of chips again. "You didn't ask, so I didn't feel it was imperative information."

I scoffed. "She just seems so… un-nurse like." Seeing the confusion on his face, I elaborated. "She's this wild, sassy, she-devil by night, then professional and proper, dressed in scrubs with her hair tamed, by day."

The rolling chuckle from Mace's direction told me that I was bang on the money.

"Yep, but sometimes by night too. She alternates shifts."

"Do you know when she's working next?"

He flared his eyes and leaned towards me. "Do I look like her fucking pocket organiser to you?"

Flipping off his last comment, I took a final swig of beer then grabbed out another two from the fridge.

"Ev and Matt have invited the crew around this Saturday," Mace casually said to my back. *Too* casually.

"Oh yeah?" I tried to keep the interest from my tone. "What does that mean?"

"It means you're coming too."

I shook my head. "Not unless I've cleared the air with Lil. I'm not risking a showdown at her folks' place. Apparently, I give off bad first impressions," I drawled and gave him a wry look.

Mace scoffed. "And I wonder why that is."

"Fuck you. Hey, so what's Lil's number?"

Mace's joviality turned suspicious. "*Why?*"

Letting out a huff, I figured I had nothing to lose by being straight up with him.

"I'm going around there and want to give her a heads up."

"No can do, I told you that already. She'd have my ass."

He was loyal to a fault, and frustrating as hell.

"Okay, so I'm going to turn up unannounced again and hope that Mickey doesn't take exception to me," I growled before shoving a fist full of chips in my mouth.

Mace's reply was a snort.

Setting his bottle down with a decisive *'clunk'*, he pulled out his phone, scrolled a couple of times, then slapped the phone to his ear while glaring at me. I heard a muffled female voice answer and Mace barked out a laugh in response. He briefly pulled the phone away from his face and whispered to me, "Apparently I can't get enough."

I studied him as he conversed with a giddy grin. Something ached deep inside me just from seeing him so happy.

The friendship they all shared was something I hadn't been a part of since high school. I hadn't given it a moment's thought until now as I sat observing Mace's interaction with Lil.

I knew what that type of happiness felt like, and the knowledge created a ball of anxiety in the pit of my stomach. Furthermore, I was jealous of Mace's friendships, jealous of his relationship with the girl I was finding myself increasingly attracted to, and jealous of his carefree lifestyle. A part of me resented him for it, because, at that precise point in time, I wanted what he had.

"We're coming around," Mace informed Lil then raised his voice to cut off her reply. *"And,* we're bringing pizza."

More girly talking.

"Ha! I knew you couldn't resist the pizza man, *again*," he chuckled into the phone.

That must be some kind of personal joke I wasn't privy to. *Another one.* He signed off and cast a passing glance at me.

"Grab your shit. We've got a pizza order to deliver."

I shoved my wallet and phone into my jeans then followed Mace out the door. He gunned the engine of his white Holden Clubsport as I slid into the passenger seat. As he drove through the streets like we were part of Bathurst 2000, I placed a pizza order for pick up that could have filled our stomachs ten times over.

Hanging up, I glanced his way. "Do we need to bring beers?"

Alcohol seemed quite the common theme for their get-togethers.

"Nope, tonight is dry. Lil's trying to tone it back a notch."

I scoffed. "And why's that?"

Not taking his eyes off the busy road, Mace gave me the summed-up version that said enough while not saying much at all.

"A few years ago, alcohol was an issue. If we hang out on weeknights, we make an effort to have no alcohol."

"Christ." I muttered.

I wasn't expecting that. I mulled over his explanation as he ducked inside the fast-food joint to collect our order. When he slid back into the driver's seat, I wasted no time in asking further questions.

"What the hell happened? With Lil, I mean?"

"Give her time and she'll tell you, it's not my place to say. Just like it's not my place to tell her why you're a moody old fucker."

He laughed when I punched his bicep. I appreciated his honesty though.

"You realise I'm only two and a half years older than you. How is that old?"

"I'm not the one pushing thirty," Mace muttered as he backed from the parking space.

"Don't even go there, I'm in denial about the whole damn thing."

And I was, turning thirty seemed like total bullshit to me.

"It's next year, right?"

My reply was absolute silence. I could see Mace's lips moving which meant he was doing calculations in his head.

"Yip, next February if I'm not mistaken. I'm expecting a massive party."

"No bloody party," I snapped.

Mace didn't need an excuse to party and I was not going to encourage him in the slightest.

"We'll see." He paused and I knew exactly what he was doing, that scheming son of a bitch.

"I mean it, Mace. No fucking party!"

"Didn't say a word."

No, he didn't, but the stupid smirk on his face said everything that his voice didn't.

I was still scowling when he pulled to a stop out the front of Mickey and Lil's house. Reaching into the back and grabbing an armload of food, I followed Mace towards the house as he balanced the pizzas in one hand above his head.

"What the hell are you doing?" I growled.

Laughing in response, he didn't bother knocking as he flung the entrance door wide and strode in, grinning back at me over his shoulder.

"You'll see."

Hardly four steps into the house, I heard hasty footsteps on the stairs then we were accosted by a red-headed crazed maniac who apparently hadn't eaten in twenty-five million years and was so starving she could eat at least four humans.

Her caring nurse side had obviously checked itself at the door at the end of her shift.

Mace laughed while fending her off, then all but threw me to the wolves.

"Back up, Lil Bean, he's the one with your chicken nibbles and hot sauce," he yelled, pointing his thumb back at me. "Hold 'em high, Gage!"

I was confused as hell until I saw the evil glint in Lil's eye as she shoved past Mace.

"Hand 'em over, Batman."

I side stepped into the kitchen. "Hand what over?"

She strode after me, her cute appearance and small stature wasn't fooling in the slightest. This was predator versus prey, and right now, I was the prey; or messenger prey, since I was holding what she actually wanted.

Lil quickened her pace as I hastened around the kitchen island and back towards the lounge, feeling like a little kid trying to escape one of my dickhead sisters.

Having three of them to contend with, I knew competitive spirit when I saw it.

Running from the kitchen and rounding the corner into the living room, I stumbled from the unexpected force and extra weight of Lil jumping on my back. Diving for the couch, she let out an *'oomph'* as we landed heavily. As Lil lay puffing against the back of my neck, her breath sent waves of hot chills over my skin.

Unfortunately for everyone who actually wanted to *eat* the food, most of the paper bags of sides flew from my hand and scattered across the carpeted floor. The only thing left in my fist was the bag containing a box of chicken nibbles, and since my brother survival instincts had been provoked, there was no way in hell I was giving them up without a fight.

Not having had this much fun in literally *years,* I giggled—actually fucking *giggled*—as Lil increased her efforts. She clawed her way up my back while wrapping her legs around my hips. Despite my free hand wrapping around her thigh, I was unable to get enough leverage to drag her lower, but it at least slowed her progress.

She laughed hysterically as she slithered her way up my body, getting increasingly closer to her goal. I gathered my strength and heaved, managing to roll onto my back. Lil slipped from my body a little before she resumed her attack, straddling me this time and unknowingly squashing her boobs onto my face.

The position also enabled me to get a better grip around her waist, and I held on tight while struggling to keep my other hand extended above my head while she pulled on my arm with all her might.

As if it had never been there to begin with, the bag of chicken nibbles was plucked from my hand, leaving me with nothing to defend except the air between my closed fingers.

Lil slumped for a second, effectively re-squishing her boobs over my mouth. I chuckled into the valley between them, barely resisting the urge to snake out my tongue and taste her. Within that same moment, I felt her respond to my breath on her exposed skin, and my own body began to react to what that meant.

Mace's sniggered comment snapped us back to reality. "How come I never get that kind of welcome?" He grinned widely as he munched on a few fries, enjoying our little show-down.

Lil pushed off my chest and looked down at me with a mixture of shock and embarrassment. My chest shook as I struggled to contain my amusement at the absurdity of the entire situation. Her lips parted in a silent gasp right before she hastily climbed off my lap.

Now realising that Mickey was also in the room with us, my eyes locked with his hardened glare that issued a loud warning without speaking a single syllable. The only other inclination to his annoyance was the box of chicken nibbles in his hand getting the life squeezed out of it.

Mace however, thought it was a hell of a joke and didn't bother trying to tone down his laughter. Lil stalked over to Mickey and snatched her chicken nibbles back with viciousness that startled him out of his fixated glower. I flipped the lid on a pizza box, grabbed a slice without glancing up, and took a massive bite.

Realising that we were all still sitting in silence a minute later, I glanced up to see Lil sitting cross-legged on the floor, avoiding all forms of interaction with us as she devoured the chicken like it was her last meal. Mace, fuck him, was *still* chortling under his breath and shook his head with a gleam in his eye. He grinned at me as he chewed, making me long to kick the smug bastard. Mickey was perched on the arm of the chair closest to Lil and seemed too preoccupied to notice my analysis.

"They're arguing about you," Mace dead-panned as he lifted a new slice of pizza to his mouth.

"What?" I mumbled through my own mouthful.

He indicated to the siblings, sitting as still as gargoyles. "I said, they're arguing about you."

I narrowed my eyes. "No, they're fucking not. They're not even talking."

Mace grinned. "You don't know yet, do you?"

Fuck he was grinding my gears tonight!

Rolling my eyes in exasperation, my patience was running out at a great rate of knots!

"For fuck sake, Mace, you know I don't know shit about these people! Spit it out already!"

And there it was. A burst of my pent-up anger just in case everyone had forgotten how much of an asshole I could be.

Mickey turned his attention to me, his grin brimming with malice. "We were talking *about* you, not *to* you."

Lil lashed out and pinched his Achilles tendon, making Mickey yelp. For retaliation, he kicked the box of chicken nibbles from her hand, sending the last few flying in slow motion through the air and landing on the other side of the room.

"See, told ya," Mace chipped in his two cents.

He plonked himself down beside me and the two of us watched Lil and Mickey engage in a scuffle.

"Care to elaborate?" I growled.

Mace took his time to swallow before speaking. "So, you know that Mickey and Lil are twins, right?"

He rolled his eyes at my surprise.

"Well, I figured they were super close in age, but no, I didn't realise they were twins," I defended. "Though, that explains why they're close."

"More than close, mate. Those two can read each other's thoughts. And, I'll bet my left nut they weren't just *talking* about you a minute ago; they would've been *arguing* about you."

I sat there stunned, looking between the three of them to see if they were joking.

"You're bullshitting right?"

"No, Gage, he's telling the truth, on both accounts," Lil spoke softly and, for the first time since I met her, she seemed genuinely shy.

Mickey seemed wary, eyeing me closely, analysing the barest reaction that I gave. I turned to Mace for more answers, and, thank Christ, he indulged my curiosity by elaborating.

"They can communicate telepathically, and you can tell when they are having a conversation by their eyes; they glaze over slightly, like a daydream."

"You realise that we are actually in the same room as you, aye?" Mickey huffed and raised his brows at Mace.

I snorted, not giving a toss that the guy obviously didn't like me. "I take it that you didn't have anything loving to say about me then, Mickey?"

"The fuck do you think. Mace's family or not, you're not worthy of my sister."

My hackles bristled and I was on my feet within the same second as Lil stormed from the room. Mickey met me halfway, his fists clenching and unclenching at his sides. Mace used his muscle to shove us apart enough to stop me from giving Mickey a new breathing hole.

"Whoa, whoa, whoa, calm the fuck down both of you before you do major damage in more ways than one."

"What the fuck is your problem mate?" I yelled around him at Mickey.

Mickey jabbed a finger in my face. "Firstly, I'm not your fucking mate. And secondly, I don't want you near Lil."

"Oh, you know all about me, do you?" I spat over Mace's shoulder as Mickey and I put the squeeze on him.

Mace muscled us apart again then stood with his palms braced against both of our chests.

"Guys, you both seriously need to chill the fuck out. This has gotten way out of hand. Both of you sit down, shut up and hear me out."

With a final glare and shove at each other, Mickey and I reluctantly reneged and sat for Mace. He proceeded to give us both a fully-fledged dressing down that made us both shrink into our respective chairs. I wanted nothing more than to get the hell out of Guam. Mace's heated rant had me feeling like a complete ass.

"You two fuckers need to sort your shit out. "You," he pointed at Mickey. "Loose the shit attitude. Yeah, we get that you're playing your part but you need to tone it back a fuck-tonne." The smirk slid from my face when Mace pointed at me. "And you, for fuck sake, you've only been up here a fortnight yet you're stirring shit. Stop antagonising him, otherwise I'll be cheering him on when he throws down. I'm not gonna have my best mate and my cousin throw daggers at each other every time the crew gets together. Sort it out or I'll knock both your fucking heads together!"

Mace was sweating and visibly shaking with fury as his outburst came to an end. Out of the corner of my eye, I saw Lil slink out the back door, wrapped in a towel. Mace threw himself into an armchair and ran his hand through his hair.

I needed to say my piece before Mickey spoke first and got me riled up again. Clearing my throat, I began.

"Look, Mickey, I apologise and regret that we've got off on the wrong foot. Straight up though, for reasons *I* don't even understand, I'm drawn to Lil, and I really want to get to know her, and you, better. Especially since I've moved here trying to put my life back together." I held up my hand to stop him interrupting. "I'm not a player, even though my tats, piercing and beard apparently suggest otherwise, and I'm going to do everything in my power to not hurt her. And I think everyone is getting way to ahead of themselves because Lil and I have hardly spoken and aren't even remotely near a relationship," I finished with a shout as my anger crept up again. "I'm going outside for fresh air."

I stalked through the back door before anyone, namely Mickey, could protest.

GAGE

THE SIGHT OF Lil—head back, eyes closed, reclined in the spa—stopped me in my tracks. She was so different from everything I knew, yet so damn alluring.

The more I stared, the tighter the neck of my shirt felt, even though the top two buttons were open. She looked so goddamn beautiful with her long hair piled on the top of her head. Even in the fading evening light and her body being under the water, I could still make out the contrast between her dark bikini and her pale skin. Her eyes flickered open briefly and she smiled.

"You can come closer you know, I don't bite… much," she whispered, and giggled quietly to herself.

I approached the spa and braced my arms on the side as I leaned against it.

"Lil," I started. Effing hell, I felt like a walking apology. "I'm sorry for what happened in there, and I'm sorry for flipping out at you last week."

Taking a deep breath, I paused and stared into the welcoming water. She seemed to ignore my confession.

"Jump in if you want. This bad boy can fit at least seven people, so there's plenty of room just for two."

She moved her legs to the side in invitation. It was the smallest hint of a peace offering, and I chose to grab it before it slipped away.

"Yeah, righto, um, I don't have my boardies with me though."

A snort of amusement came from Lil. "Just wear your underwear, I won't judge. That is if you're even wearing any..." she trailed off and gave me the side-eye that made me feel as if I was strung up ass-butt naked in front of her.

Lil maintained eye contact in what seemed like a challenge to see if I was going to chicken out.

As if.

I shucked items of clothing, starting with my boots, socks and shirt and glanced up to find that Lil still hadn't taken her eyes off me. Her darkened hazel gaze now smouldered as she examined my every move. Her eyes lingered on the spot where tattoos snaked across my shoulder and bicep. I paused at my jeans, casually fingering the button and watching her reaction closely. Her pupils dilated like a goddamn owl, and, Jesus, my blood ignited at the sight.

"Remember what Dave said about eye-sexing?" I drawled in an attempt to ease the heightening lust between us. Seeing her nod in response, I continued, "You're doing it now and it's fucking intense, Sunshine."

Her light snicker had me smiling as I stepped out of my jeans and tossed them in the pile with my other discarded clothes. Ignoring her scrutiny, I climbed over the edge of the spa and let out a breath as I lowered myself into the hot water.

"Fuck, that's bliss."

"It is," Lil murmured, her voice low and dreamy.

Our conversation had to happen now; I needed to clear the air before it got any harder. I growled the tension in my throat then watched her reaction carefully.

"I need to tell you something personal because it might help you understand my reaction last weekend."

Lil's eyelids flew open and she sat higher, the water lapping over her shoulders as she gave me her undivided attention.

Taking a deep breath, I began. "Just over three years ago, I was in a relationship that... ended... very abruptly. It wasn't expected and some days I feel like I haven't gotten over it at all. But what you need to know is that I haven't been in a relationship of *any* sort since then. Even the mere thought used to make me physically sick. I never wanted to have a relationship again. *Ever* again. I just, I don't know what it is about you, but you... *Fuck.* For whatever reason, I'm drawn to you no matter how much I don't want to be. You're like the dawn of a new day after a thousand years spent in darkness; the very place I've become accustomed to living in. You would never be 'just another notch on my belt', as you put it, and it's hard to ignore what naturally seems to be between us. Plus, it's baffling the hell out of me. What's even more confusing is that I'm not even sure I *want* to ignore it. I just don't fucking know." I finished in an audible whisper then waited for her reaction.

It was out in the open now—well, *some* of my skeletons at least.

Despite Lil's expression remaining relatively blank, there was sadness in her eyes and an underlying hint of understanding that she knew all she needed to for the moment.

"That's really heart-breaking to hear. And I'm sorry too for jumping to conclusions about your past. I'm also confused as hell about what I feel for you. I don't know you, yet it feels like déjà vu on steroids."

"How do you mean?" I questioned, concerned that I had triggered something that was going to backfire on me.

Moving a corner closer, I gave her hand a reassuring squeeze. Her lips curved in a whisper of a smile. Despite the hint of reassurance, her sigh was bitter. That was when I noticed her eyes held a certain kind of pain that made my stomach drop.

"Gage, when I was twenty, I fell madly in love—or, what I *thought* was love—with a guy who screwed me over and discarded me out of nowhere." The hurt in her voice made my heart ache for her, and I got the unfamiliar sense of wanting to move heaven and earth to make it better for her—even by just the tiniest piece.

I sat, utterly dumbfounded and speechless as her story spilled out, weighing me down as it eased some of Lil's burden. She gave me everything, blow by blow, even answering the unspoken question that I didn't dare let pass my lips.

"Mace and I don't have anything going on together. He is the one who dropped everything to help me through. He was relentless even when the others didn't know what else to do; even Kimmie or Mickey couldn't drag me out of the funk I was stuck in. Mace gave all of himself to me to make sure I made it out the other side. He made sure I kicked the booze, went back to finish my nursing quals, and to be honest, I can't help but think that he partly blames himself for what happened. It was him and Mickey who had to break the news to me, and it wasn't pretty. Mace is there for me, and I for him, always, without question."

Raking my fingers through my hair, I tried to get my head around everything she just told me. So many things made sense now; her accusations, Mickey's over protective behaviour, the booze embargo... The special connection she had with Mace.

"How could anyone ever do that to you, Lil? You are such a beautiful person inside and out. What I saw of you today at work just emphasises that. Your asshole ex wasn't remotely good enough for you and it's bullshit what he put you through."

I slid closer and reached for her. Lil let me pull her onto my lap and leaned her shoulder against my chest when I wrapped my arms around her waist. In this moment, I wanted to protect her and fix everything broken in her world. Not just because I had been jealous of her connection with Mace, but because she was a strong woman with a heart of gold. However, I of all people, knew it was never that simple.

"If I ever see him anywhere in the world, I will punch him off the face of this earth, just for you," I rumbled in complete seriousness.

Lil giggled and squeezed my bicep. "I don't doubt that for a second. Thank you."

I cupped the back of her neck and drew her mouth closer to mine, so close that with each breath our lips all but brushed together.

"Let me see you again. Just us," I whispered while flicking my gaze between her pretty eyes and sexy as hell mouth.

"What, no please?" she breathed back.

"Batman doesn't beg, he commands," I drawled in a deep tone.

Lil pulled back, feigning regret. "Seems we've reached an impasse then."

I slid one hand up the bumpy path of her spine as the other wove around her hip. I used both holds to gently tug her closer. So close that her breasts pressed against my chest when she twisted in my lap. Her hands smoothed up my arms and wrapped around my neck where her fingers could weave through my hair.

I sighed unintentionally from her touch, realising how much I'd missed the feel of a woman beneath my hands. It had literally been years since I welcomed and craved the intimacy that Lil so easily lit within me. My desire for her burned low in my belly, consuming my thoughts, lacing through my veins to the point I began to struggle holding back. I wanted, *needed*, to take this slow, savouring her, devouring her, absorbing everything about her over time until I knew her mind, body and soul as well as I did the back of my hand.

However, my head and heart still battled with my body's reaction as Lil grazed her lips over mine, gently teasing my resolve. The cracks in my already broken heart tore wider as guilt began to rise. Vibrations of restraint coursed through me as I fought off the wave of self-condemnation while running my tongue along her bottom lip.

My breath was barely a whisper. "One chance, Sunshine, that's all I ask."

She tightened her grip on my neck and moved to straddle me, her thighs squeezing the outside of mine.

"So, Batman doesn't beg, but he dates?" she murmured against my lips.

I scoffed under my breath; I didn't bloody date either, but for Lil, I would try to change that.

"What does your heart say?" she whispered on the passing breeze.

My head fell back and I cursed softly into the darkening sky. "I'm a broken man, Lil. I've been through hell and am still nowhere close to emerging out the other side. The side of me you've only seen so far? That's not the real me. Well, the *old* real me. Fuck, I don't know if I can ever be that man again."

Lil gently lifted my head so she could look at me closely. The amber flecks in her eyes sparkled in the last of the setting sun. Despite their beauty, I saw pain and sadness lingering within them.

The moment was indescribable and my internal reaction caught me off guard. I wanted to pause us, right here, right now, and lock it away forever in the deepest place within me where only I knew where to find it. I returned her tentative smile then lowered my sight to her lips as she licked them nervously. I couldn't tear my eyes away, nor could I prevent the rumble of approval from my throat when she moved in my lap. I knew she felt how much I wanted her; the two thin layers between us did sweet fuck all to hide it.

Cupping her face in my hands, I guided her face towards mine and ran my nose down hers until our lips finally made contact. Softly and slowly to begin with, I kissed her with a tenderness that was in complete contrast to what we shared previously. I felt her relax against my touch, opening her lips more, granting me access to her mouth. Slowly our urgency heightened and our movements increased in hunger.

Each pass of her fingertips against my skin left a blazing trail of desire in their wake. I let my hands wander, enjoying every little moan or sigh she made against my mouth, then smiled against her lips when my thumb found her piercing.

Fuck, she tasted and felt good, too good. Tightening my grip, I stilled her and held her hips hard against me as I slowly tore my lips from hers. When I pulled back, Lil's vision stole my breath. Her eyes were wide and shone with recklessness I hadn't seen since Kimmie's party. They pegged me to the spot as she looked down at me like I was all she ever needed.

I didn't know how she did this to me; I wasn't meant to want, to *crave*, to *feel* ever again. Yet, despite how much I tried to deny it, I wanted all those things and so much more.

I used this moment to study her face. The mascara on her lashes had slipped, leaving black smudges under her lower lashes. Wisps of loose hair were dampened and plastered to her flushed neck and forehead. Her lips were pouted and her chin was reddened from where my beard had made contact with her sensitive skin, and the combination of all of the above teased the hell out of me.

As much as I wanted to have more of her, it was my subconsciousness that set me back.

Fuck. What was I DOING!

I no longer saw Lil as my mind turned against itself. It took me back to happier times; ones when I thought everything in the world was so fucking perfect and looked forward to my life filled with love and wholeness.

Trust wasn't an issue for me, but the guilt. The guilt fucking devastated me at every turn. Now, with Lil in my arms, it systematically clawed its way through my mind, tainting even the freshest of memories.

Lil and I had confided in each other, shared a small, blemished snippet from our past, to a point where trust and understanding began to form between us; both of which were incredibly important to the two of us.

Lil began to squirm under my gaze and rubbed at her mouth and chin. "What? Do I have beard rash?"

I forced a chuckle, brushing off the burden that gave me heartburn. She looked gorgeous all worried.

"Just enjoying the view, Sunshine. But we need to stop."

It came out gruffer than I intended and I immediately felt like an ass when hurt flicked across her face. I wanted her, of course I did, but when—*if*—we even went there, it was definitely not going to be in *here*. I looked at the water surrounding us. God knows what kind of crap was in the spa water right now.

Lil jerked her head and began to slide off my lap. Digging my fingers into her hips again, I stopped her then wrapped a hand around the back of her neck. I needed one last taste, and I took her lips hard and fast, claiming them for a few frenzied seconds before pulling back, allowing her to move into the deeper groove of the corner seat.

Her chest heaved as much as mine did. What I was feeling confused me so bad, and I didn't know what to do about it. I was torn.

"This leaves you in somewhat of a predicament." Lil cocked her head to indicate at my crotch with a devious smirk.

I scoffed and ran a hand through my mussed hair. "Keep lookin' at me like that, Sunshine, and it won't ever go down. I'll sort it out later."

"Alone?" Again with her devilish smile.

"Jesus Lil, you might just be the death of me."

Quietly cursing my 'predicament', I tilted my head back against the side and closed my eyes in an attempt to regain some goddamn self-control.

"Just as well I'm a medical professional. I know how to keep you alive if needs be."

"At this rate, there *will* be a needs be," I grumbled.

She giggled and laid her head back against the side, mirroring my own position.

Night had fallen during our intimacy, and now in the dark, Lil appeared soothed and relaxed. The tension had eased from her shoulders and the crease had disappeared from between her eyebrows. And just like that, everything seemed okay between us. A shiver racked over her body and I wouldn't have noticed unless I was watching her intently.

"Cold? We should probably get out."

Lil rolled her head my way as a playful smile tipped the corners of her lips. She stilled for a second and I stopped to try and focus on whatever she heard. Half a minute later, heavy footsteps stomped within the house and the window closest to the spa swung open. To my surprise, a towel was dropped onto the lawn beside us before the window slammed closed again.

"That was you, wasn't it?" It was safe to say that I found the whole telepathic thing more than weird. "So, Mace wasn't bullshitting? You and Mickey really can read each other's thoughts?"

"Only when it's wanted. And for the most part it comes in handy."

When I realised she wasn't going to look away, I angled my body so she copped an eyeful of my ass and the ink on my back as I climbed out. I glanced over my shoulder with a smirk and I picked up the towel. Sure enough, Lil hadn't torn her eyes off my body.

My smirk faltered as I struggled to shake off the feeling of familiarity; no woman had looked at me like I meant that much to them in a long time.

Quickly drying, I waited until Lil was out and wrapped in a towel before I tossed my towel at her.

"I suggest you hold this up, Sunshine, if you don't want to cop more of an eyeful."

Lil's mouth parted in confusion then dropped with a gasp as I pushed my underwear down. I chuckled as she scrambled to hold the towel up and shield me from view. After pulling on my jeans and zipping them, I turned to her and ran my thumb over her jaw.

"Thank you, Lil. For more than you know."

She snagged my hand and smiled. "It's nothing."

"It's not nothing. Now get your ass inside."

She led the way with a giggle, and I would be lying if I said my eyes weren't glued to her ass.

Inside, we found Mace and Mickey watching a movie. Seeing us come in, Mace jumped up and gave Lil a tight hug before suggesting we get going.

Mickey, surprising the hell out of me, shuffled over and stopped just shy of my personal bubble. Since we were roughly the same height, he met my suspicious glare with ease.

"I overreacted and was out of line. I take it you now understand why?"

Seeing me nod stiffly, he offered a hand in the small space between us. I accepted by slapping my palm onto his in a handshake that was a silent battle of strength. It communicated that neither of us was particularly fond of the other, but we were willing to make allowances for Lil's sake.

Lil coughed discreetly and moved into my arms when I opened them for a hug.

"See you at dinner on Saturday? If you're up to it?"

"I'll be there," I confirmed.

As Mace and I walked out the door, he chuckled. "Ha, told you it wouldn't be long until she had you begging for it."

My answer was to flip him off, slide into the passenger seat of his car and slam the door closed.

GAGE

WITH THE AIR cleared between me and Lil, and somewhat settled between her brother and me, I was cautiously looking forward to the get-together at their parent's place this evening. First though, Mace and I stopped by his folks' house to see how Dave was recovering.

Lil's car—a metallic blue Mazda 3 with tinted windows and a set of decent mags—was visible as soon as we pulled up on our bikes. And Lil was the first person I saw inside the house. Our eyes locked and neither of us moved until Aunty Sandy spoke.

"There are my boys! How are you both?" She hugged Mace then myself. "Someone is feeling rather silly after his outbursts the other day," she murmured and raised an eyebrow in Dave's direction.

Mace barked a loud laugh. "I wish I was first hand witness to your shenanigans, oh wise father of mine. The Snapchats didn't quite cut it."

"What!" Uncle Dave stared at me, feigning disbelief while I cracked up at his expense. "You sent my son pictures of me? Jesus, talk about kick a man when he's down."

"They were short videos, Uncle, and how could I not? Besides the fact that you were in fine form, your outbursts were bloody embarrassing."

He leant forward in his chair so he was closer to where Lil crouched over his wounded foot. There, he gently set his large hand on her forearm.

"I *am* sorry for my outbursts and embarrassing you, love. It's not as if you don't have enough troublesome patients to deal with, but add my behaviour..."

Lil laid her hand over his and smiled warmly. "Honestly, it's absolutely fine, Dave. Most people react to harder drugs in a similar fashion, and you were tame compared to some behaviour I've had to work with," she shrugged. "You didn't cause any physical harm, so that's a pass in my book."

That last comment reignited the fire in my belly. Knowing that she has had hands raised upon her while doing her *job,* made me want to hunt down those individuals and give them a taste of their own medicine.

"Huh?" I said, snapped from my darkening thoughts to see Aunty Sandy talking to me.

"Are you on your way to the McMillan's too?"

"Yep. We're heading there after this." Anxiety crept in. "Do I need to be worried?"

"Of course not," Aunty waved off my concern while Dave chuckled.

"What?" I asked while narrowing my eyes at him.

He winked. "You'll see, son."

Lil stood, making the cute little sundress swish around her toned thighs.

"It's looking good so far, Dave. Keep it elevated for a little longer yet. I'll stop by again in a few days to recheck it. I start nights tomorrow, so it'll be before my shift on Wednesday."

Uncle Dave smiled up at her. "That'll be perfect, thanks, love."

"You're welcome. Not everyone gets special treatment, so count yourself lucky," she teased and bent down to give him a goodbye hug.

The hem of her dress rode precariously high where I got an eyeful of her toned muscles flexing as she held her balance. Goddamn best show in town. Seemed I wasn't the only one to be noticing either; Mace was also transfixed on the view.

Giving him a backhand to the stomach, his reaction was to grin and wiggle his eyebrows. Lil stood and absentmindedly ran a palm over her ass, ensuring it was decently covered. The action gave me a fleeting glimpse of her figure. I blinked away the daydream as Aunty walked us to the door.

Mace kissed her cheek. "Have a good day, Ma."

Lil and Sandy embraced and hugged tight for a few moments.

"Great to see you, love, thanks for stopping by."

"Anytime, Sandy. Thanks for the cuppa. See you both on Wednesday."

I followed Lil down the garden path, thoroughly distracted by her dress flowing around her thighs. Her deep-red hair reflected the sun, making the rays reflect off each glossy strand.

In my inattentive state, I crashed into her back when she halted at the edge of the parking spaces. Panic rose in my gut. Stepping around her with Mace hot on my heels, we both let out a collective sigh of relief then turned back to Lil.

"Shit, I thought my Hog had been stolen!" Mace hissed, running a hand through his hair.

I couldn't find a single word. The intense stare Lil pegged me with stole all my ability to breathe. Desire and lust emanated from her entire posture as her eyes flicked between me and my Gunner.

"What?" I demanded again, becoming damn uneasy.

She strode over to me as I swung a leg over my ride and picked up my helmet. Much to my surprise, Lil started running her hands over my chopper like it was the sexiest fucking thing she had ever laid eyes on. And goddammit, her reaction alone was getting me hot under the collar.

A breath whispered past her lips. "I need to ride this."

"And here I thought you liked me for me, not what I've got between my legs."

Lil's eyes snapped to mine. "I never said I liked you, but I do a little now," she replied coyly.

Cussing came from Mace's direction. "Don't tell me you're about to commit the foul act of treason too, Missy! You'll never sit your ass on my Hog again if that's the case. Harley for life!" he declared and hit his fist against his chest.

There he goes again, being loyal as fuck. Though, I had to admit, I missed my Harley. My Victory, however, was the next best thing. Nothing could beat the sound of pure horse power roaring to life as soon as I opened the throttle. It was an addiction.

I would never own another Harley after what happened. Mace knew why too. For me, from here on out, I was a converted Victory fan and had chosen the Victory because it was American made (like Harley Davidson) and was comparable to all the aspects of my Hog that I used to love.

"Don't kid yourself, you'll let me ride behind you any day," Lil sassed at Mace.

He grinned while shoving his helmet over his big-ass head, knowing full well that she was right.

Lil turned back to me. "Like I say, I need to be on this."

I pointed a finger at her ass. "Your sweet ass can perch behind me anytime, Sunshine."

And I meant it. The thought of her wedged against my back had all my blood rushing south.

Lil laid a swift, flirty whack on my arm. "Tease!"

"You are," I mumbled back, somewhat darkly, because damn, she was!

I winked while fastening my helmet then grinned when her cheeks flushed. Kicking up the stand, I revved my Gunner to life and felt the reciprocating soul run through my veins.

"See you there, Lil."

"Ride safe," she yelled and pointed a forefinger at each of us.

I watched her ass again as she walked to her car and slid behind the wheel. With a final wave though the open window, she peeled out of the driveway in the direction of her parents' house.

Mace smirked at me as he sat waiting on his idling Harley. I flipped him off as I drew up beside him.

He yelled over the combined rumble of our motorbikes. "Race you there, loser shouts lunch this week."

And with that, he peeled out onto the street in the same direction as Lil turned before I could shout that I didn't know the fuckin' way. My race was lost before it had even begun, but that didn't mean I was gonna let him win easily.

17
LIL

CRUISING DOWN THE motorway with the window down and the music pumping was freeing and uplifting. I loved the air whipping my hair around my face, and the permanent smile on my face was testimony to that.

And, oh my Lord, I was pretty sure I drooled on the spot from seeing both Mace and Gage straddling their muscle bikes. They were too goddamn sexy for their own good, and my panties all but removed themselves.

Mace always looked great—especially all kitted up; he had the whole muscle-man physique to go with the attitude his Hog evoked. Gage however... That man was on a whole other level with his dark broodiness and bold words, not to mention his sinfully hot ride. I had been surprised to discover a sweetness to him this week; the way he held my face in his roughened hands, and looked into my eyes had every romantic part of me swooning.

And the tenderness I felt when he kissed me in the spa before it turned heated…

My daydream slipped back to reality when the song began to fade, making way for the unmistakable rumbling of muscle bikes tracking at speed down the motorway behind me.

Glancing at the rear-view mirror, I saw two bikers in the distance, one ahead of the other, weaving in and out of traffic at an alarming speed. The sight made my heart skip more than a few beats as a surge of adrenaline filled my veins. Not to mention my panties were reduced to rubble again. Mace was in the lead, and close behind him was Gage. The only way it could have been better was if I was riding pillion.

Mace gave me the 'rock on' salute as he smoked past, then seconds later Gage followed suit.

The drive time from Albany to Whangaparaoa was roughly thirty to forty minutes, depending on traffic, and from their pace I knew they would arrive long before I did.

Pulling off the highway and cruising around the smooth streets on the peninsula, I checked on the whereabouts of the rest of the gang, through Mickey.

<Where you guys at, brother?>
<Stuck behind a dooshbag driver, still twenty minutes out>
<Sweet. I've pretty much arrived, see yous soon>
<Roger>

His sign off made me smile as I parked up outside Mum and Dad's beach house. Unsurprisingly, there were already two bikes stood neatly side by side in front of the closed garage doors.

Grabbing the bowl of salad off the floor in the backseat, I hastened towards the front door, worried about what I would find.

"Hi," I called into the empty foyer as I flicked off my jandals.

"Out the back, hun," came Mum's voice.

Going via the kitchen to put the food in the fridge, I grabbed a beer on a whim, then headed out onto the back deck. Dad had Mace and Gage bailed up and immersed in deep, manly conversion that stopped when I appeared.

"Hey, Lil. I love that dress on you!"

"Thanks, Ma," I replied and I returned her hug. "The others will be here soon."

"Joshy driving?" she asked.

"Yup. They're carpooling today."

Mum's wide smile crinkled the corners of her eyes. "I'm going to get more snacks ready," she declared then made her way inside.

According to my mum, one could never have enough snacks! I walked over to Dad who planted a kiss on my cheek when we ended our squeeze.

"You're looking well, bud."

"Thanks, Daddyo, so are you. And looks like you've met Gage already?"

I was curious to know just how much information he had interrogated out of the two guys. Dad was a first-class interrogation officer, which meant whatever he wanted to know he would eventually find out using any technique he deemed necessary. He always looked like he meant business too.

Outside of work hours, Dad's personality was the opposite of serious and the only thing that conveyed that was the occasional twitch of his lips.

"Oh, you mean this guy? He was introduced to me as Batman."

Mace snorted a laugh and Gage raised his beer in salute. "The one and only."

At least he wasn't letting Dad get to him; both men were intimidating in their own right, and I figured that Gage should be fine from here on out. I took a sip of beer then turned a suspicious expression on Mace and Gage.

"How long have you two been here?"

"Oh, I'd say around fifteen minutes." Mace winked as my jaw fell open.

I couldn't bloody believe it. I was all for driving in the fast lane, but *that* was pushing it.

"And just how many tickets did you collect along the way?"

"Here's hoping none," Mace dead-panned.

He knew full well that blatantly admitting to *breaking* the law would earn him a lecture from Dad at some stage during the night. As with all Police Officers, Dad took his duty to *uphold* the law extremely seriously.

"You two are a bad influence on each other," I sassed then shrugged sheepishly when Mace pointed at the beer in my hand. "It's just *one,* I promise!"

Dad excused himself to grab another round from inside, and Gage seized his opportunity to get me alone. A marvellous wash of his scent rolled over me and I bit back a hum when he bent his lips to my ear.

"So, your dad eyeballed my brow, then questioned how many tats I had before asking me how much jail time I had under my belt."

I gasped loudly, totally appalled that Dad had even gone there. Gage chuckled within his chest as I apologised profusely.

"Don't worry about it, Sunshine. He sure as fuck didn't have a comeback when I told him I'd done seven years and was finally released on probation, and that my crime was being too good looking."

"You *didn't!* Please tell me you're joking?"

More chuckling came from Gage as a rare, full grin graced me with a view of his straight, white teeth.

"Nope, not kidding. All he did was look at me weird like he was trying to figure me out, then raised his beer and said, "Well, I'll cheers to that." Your mum looked well impressed though, I must say. I'm sure she was checking me out..."

I playfully slapped his bicep. "Oh my *God*, she didn't." When Gage laughed louder, I threw up my hand. "You're all fucked I tell ya. Fucked! I'm surrounded by special people," I declared through my own laughter.

There was never a dull moment to be had at 'de casa McMillan'.

It wasn't long before new rowdy voices sounded within the house, and Mickey, Neek, Trav and Kimmie soon appeared. Mickey had spent the day with Neek and Trav—something about helping with Trav's car restoration project—so it made sense that they carpooled. What didn't make sense at all was why they had all squished into Kimmie's beat up old Mini, which was affectionately named *The Crab Bucket*. The poor wee mustard coloured Mini would have been sacked out, and by the sounds of their complaints, Nico and Trav had crammed into the back, 'balls to balls', as they put it.

Trav totally had a 'thing' for my mum. Actually, I suspected he had a thing for older women—and to be honest, Mum enjoyed his attentions, as innocent as they were.

"Thanks for having us around again, Mrs Mick," Trav grinned as he engulfed Mum in a massive hug.

"You know to call me Ev," she playfully scolded. "It's lovely to see you again, Travis."

"Pa-leese! You know to call me Trav."

"Touché." Mum pointed at him. "And you still owe me that dance later."

"Noted, just holler when you're ready."

I didn't know how Trav did it. He was all boyish charm and grins, and could talk his way into panties with his mouth taped shut. The buddy-buddy banter between him and Mum still weirded me out a little at times, though it had been going on for as long as I could remember, starting the very first time Trav had called around to check out something on Mickey's old car.

Mum had taken a shining to his mischievous streak and enjoyed hearing about his outrageous adventures. However, she made it crystal clear that if he ever got Mickey in the shit, there would be hell to pay.

As per usual, us girls gathered in the kitchen to make sure all the food was in order. We all quietened when a loud conversation broke out amongst the guys outside.

"Hey, Mr Mick, I know for a fact Lil doesn't like her sausage burnt," Mace's voice boomed, followed by a string of laughter.

"Christ, Mason, how many times have I told you to call me Matt? Mr Mick makes me sound old."

More rapturous laughter broke out before Mace continued, knowing how to give as good as he got from my father.

"I wouldn't worry about age, Matt, according to the latest Womens Day, fifty is the new thirty."

Mum and I burst with laughter; they were both still in their forties.

Dad's bewildered voice rose. "Bloody Nora, you're in for an asswhooping, boy. I'm not pushing fifty yet!"

Mum, Kimmie and I were cracking up to the point of tears, and when any one of us so much as squeaked or snorted or went to say something, it set us all off again.

"Er," Gage stuck his head around the door frame, looking perplexed at the scene before him. "Party for three and I'm not invited?"

He hesitantly stepped into the kitchen like he was about to be chewed up and spat out purely for sport. I waved him in and turned to the bench to select a plate of food to pass him. The moment his hand landed on my lower back, I gasped, totally unexpecting the intimate touch around my family and friends. It was fleeting but I felt it throughout my entire body; every cell now hummed in response.

"Pass me something, Sunshine," Gage murmured when I remained paused for a little too long.

"Oh, ah, here." I shoved two bowls of salad his way then ushered him from my space.

I hadn't expected him to return, so was surprised when he came back, not even a minute later, and plucked the bowls from Mum's hands without asking if she wanted help. I received an impressed look from her, who seemed a little dazzled by Gage using his initiative.

"He's gorgeous, Lil," she whispered once Gage had disappeared again.

"You don't need to tell me that, Mum, I have eyes. Which happen to be working exceptionally fine, might I add. But, he's not actually mine, so don't look at me like that," I pointed at her face and raised a brow in return.

"I see the way he's looked at you in the short time you've been here."

I rolled my eyes. "It's not like that."

"That's not what he told us. Gage introduced himself as your other half," she replied with a cheeky glint in her eyes.

I felt my brows hit my hairline and a little pang wove through my heart.

Play it cool, dammit. Play. It. Cool!

"Did he now?"

Kimmie grinned behind Mum's back, and Mum made an amused hum in her throat as I gathered as many condiments as I could carry. Then I got my butt out of the room before she could make any more borderline observations about whatever the heck was going on between me and Gage.

Finally seated with Dad at the head of the table, we prepared to say a quick Grace. Faith wasn't an everyday occurrence in our family, but when Mum and Dad entertained a large group of people, we made an extra effort to be thankful for the loved ones in our lives.

As soon as my hand slid into Gage's palm, the jolt of energy caused us to look at each other. Neither of us had come to terms with our connection yet.

Mickey popped into my head.

<No eye-sexing at the table>

He'd evidently heard the now infamous story of Dave's visit to A&E. I snorted while trying to swallow the urge to crack up. Kimmie—on my other side—gave my hand a warning squeeze.

<Speak for yourself, I've seen your eyes all over Kimmie like a rash>

I was delighted to see a grin straining Mickey's pursed lips as his body shuddered, trying his hardest to suppress his own laughter.

"Amen," we all said as one.

Our voices combined as bowls and platters of food were passed from person to person. I almost squealed when my eyes landed on Kimmie's famous crab and pasta salad. I piled a generous serving onto my plate and stabbed as much as I could onto my fork. Cramming the load into my mouth, my taste buds erupted in euphoria. I swear to God they banded together and sang *hallelujah* at the top of their tiny lungs. I tilted my head back to savour every last morsel as it slid down my throat.

Unbeknown to myself, my foodgasm caused quite the stir; Gage stared at me with dilated pupils and looked like he was about to devour me instead of his meal. His hand landed heavily on my knee then slipped upwards until his fingertips applied pressure to my inner thigh—the soft part I always considered a little flabby. My breath hitched when he leaned close and murmured into my ear.

"You moaning like that is thoroughly distracting during my meal, Sunshine. It's hard enough keeping my hands off you without you making noises like *that*, but now, you've got me planning all the ways I can get you to make those sounds while not eating food."

Heat pooled between my legs and I felt heat creep over my cheeks. I utterly failed to regain composure as Gage strummed every cord in my body—starting with the one his thumb was coaxing where it flicked back and forth on my inner thigh. I put my body on lock down as I suppressed a shiver. If I wasn't careful, I was going to make a right spectacle out of myself.

As it was, our exchange hadn't gone completely unnoticed; Neek didn't tend to say much, however he was incredibly perceptive. What he didn't say, he made up for in observation skills. He was one of those guys that looked like he would have all the girls hanging off him with his smooth, tanned skin and dark hair clipped short in true Army fashion. Combine that with his emerald green eyes and cheeky grin, he was irresistible. Neek smirked across the table as he watched the interaction between me and Gage, knowing full well what was going down between the pair of us.

Gage chuckled softly when I subtly slapped his hand off my leg and attempted to give him my best 'behave yourself' eyes.

"How's the pasta?" Kimmie innocently asked, her timing impeccable as always.

Gage barked out a loud laugh and I blushed furiously while avoiding her eye contact—wishing I could contact the Star Ship Enterprise and get Scotty to beam me the fuck up.

"Amazing as always, Kimmie," I coughed.

Enough said.

She offered me the bowl. "More?"

Glancing at Gage and seeing him wink at me, I cursed Scotty for his delay with the teleportation beam. I backhanded Batman's bicep while throwing a, "No thanks," to Kimmie.

"Your loss," she sang.

I wasn't the only one losing out; Gage would have to be content with eating his meal without the added sexual innuendos.

As the evening wore on, our banter and laughter were swallowed up by the waning light as the sky darkened.

"Cocktail time," Mum declared. "Who wants one?"

Kimmie and I chorused 'yes' in response, and I added, "But make mine minus the fun, please Mumzie."

She gave me a thumbs up and entered the house with a renewed sense of purpose. I smiled happily to myself; Mum was so full of life and, now that I was an adult, she felt like more of a friend instead of a parent—*most* of the time.

Dad spied her when she returned with a tray of cocktails. He hastened towards her to help and plucked up the last pretty drink with a flourish. He took a sip before handing it to Mum with a cheeky smile. I grinned when she playfully slapped him on the arm then pouted her lips to receive his kiss.

Seeing them happy together after all these years made me wistful about my own future. I wanted to grow old with someone who I'd spent almost my entire life loving, and be loved just as hard in return. Maybe that was why I had jumped headfirst into engagement with Jono without truly thinking it through. My parents had been together since High School, so it seemed natural for me to follow the same pattern.

I scanned over the group until my gaze landed on Gage. Running my eyes over his body, I couldn't get over my instant attraction for him—albeit, I had mistaken that for annoyance at the time. There was never that breathless spark with Jono. Looking back in hindsight, he had simply been what I thought was a failsafe option.

Sure, Gage *looked* on the rough side and could cuss like a sailor, but there was something about him that felt like he was specifically made for me. Behind the arrogant façade, I caught glimpses of a reverent and unpretentious personality that I respected greatly. Gage being here, amongst my nearest and dearest, made all the bullshit in my past irrelevant now that he was in my present.

I watched him from where I danced with Kimmie, Trav and Mum. He looked at ease interacting with the guys and Dad, as if he felt he belonged with us—with me.

The angel on my shoulder told me to proceed with extreme caution because we hadn't even dated *once* yet and I was getting ahead of myself. The devil on the other shoulder told me to drag him to the nearest unoccupied room and jump his bones—which right now was the laundry. Obviously, my devilish side severely lacked all romantic notions.

. . .

It was nearing midnight when Dad turned down the stereo and informed us that party time was over, and to piss off home.

Since Mickey was sober driving the Crab Bucket back to Kimmie's then going clubbing with Trav, Dad insisted that someone accompany me home to make sure I got there safely. I rolled my eyes at his over protectiveness but truth be told, I really didn't like arriving home late at night when Mickey was out or on shift at the station.

Since Mickey and the rest of the crew were going in a slightly different direction than me, Mace offered to tail me home on his bike. For that I was grateful.

We all went through the goodbye process then made our way to our various modes of transport.

I hadn't even taken two steps when a scuffle broke out between Trav and Neek calling shotgun over the front seat of Kimmie's mini. Kimmie didn't even get a shoe in the passenger door before she was manhandled into the back of the tiny car. Trav lucked out, again, since Nico was bigger in strength and stubbornness.

We convoyed down the road then peeled out onto the highway where I tooted a tune as I sailed past the four of them squashed into the Crab Bucket. I was graced with their middle fingers and crude gestures. I chuckled out loud, envisioning Mickey with his foot flat to the floor and cursing the shitty little car to pick up speed.

As soon as I had pulled back into the left lane, the rumbling of motorbikes thundered past me at a much more sedate speed than earlier.

GAGE

I HAD ONLY been waiting for a few minutes before Lil's little Mazda pulled into her driveway and cruised to a stop. She slipped out moments later.

"You drew the short straw, huh?"

I sniffed a smile. "So to speak."

I wasn't going to admit that I had been locked in a battle of wills with Mace over who would see her home safe. And over my dead body would she find out that I resorted to bribery to get my own way; I now owed Mace lunch every day next week, and that's not including the bet I lost earlier in the afternoon.

I followed Lil around the side of the house and noted the location of the spare key despite being thoroughly distracted by her bare legs. Turning the key in the lock, she gave me a thankful smile and pushed the door inwards.

I halted her then brushed past to enter the house first. Flicking on lights as I went, I did a quick walk through, checking each room like I was on Magnum P.I.

Lil was leaning against the bench with her arms folded across her chest when I wandered back into the kitchen.

She raised her brows. "Finished?"

"Yes. I take my responsibilities very seriously."

Coming to rest against the bench beside her, I noticed for the first time the various photos that peppered the walls. My eyes were drawn to the selection of candid shots on a pin board. I stepped forward to look at them closer as she spoke to my back.

"From what I just witnessed, I don't doubt it."

The selection of photos was much like Mace had on his fridge—random snaps of the crew. I stared for longer than I should have, trying to absorb everything there was to Lil.

Hearing the jug fill, I spun to see her looking over her shoulder at me. Her hair was wild from dancing the night away, and her mascara had slipped from her lower lashes again. It took all I had to hold myself back from running a finger over the dark smudges.

"Do you need to get going, or would you like to stay for a hot drink?" she asked and worried her lower lip with her teeth.

"Coffee would be great, thanks."

"You sure you want a caffeine hit this late? You'll be up all night."

"That's the plan, Sunshine."

Her eyes lit when I called her that. To see if I could add to her disposure, I winked and raked a smouldering gaze over her body. She took my meaning loud and clear, and I chuckled when a cute as hell blush hit her cheeks.

Lil turned quickly and mindlessly busied herself. Having been here once before, I walked over to the mug cupboard and grabbed two out.

We made small talk while making the drinks then settled at opposite ends of the couch. I couldn't tear my eyes away as she tucked her legs under herself. I relaxed into the comfy cushions and took a sip of coffee.

"So, did you have a nice time tonight?" she ventured.

My brows raised in surprise. "I did actually. You're a clone of your mum, all wild and crazy, dark red hair and sparkly hazel eyes to boot. And Mickey is like your Dad, that's for sure. A fucking hard ass."

I could totally see what Uncle Dave had been getting at. What I didn't tell her was how unexpectedly welcome I had felt; definitely not like the outsider I was.

Lil nodded while giggling at my description. "That about sums them up."

I saw the real Lily tonight; spirited and free, loving and fierce. I couldn't take my eyes off her as she danced—I was fucking mesmerised. She had roused more dead and buried feelings from the bottom of my soul, and she ignited a lust in me that was extremely hard to ignore. The way she had moaned while eating left me fisting my hands under the table in a tremendous effort to stop myself from touching her. In my heart I already knew she was mine, I just had to convince my head.

I felt a small nudge on my leg which broke my thoughts. My hand found Lil's ankle and squeezed lightly before she pulled it away again.

"They're younger than I was expecting, too. Fucking funny when Mace gave your dad jip about pushing fifty."

Lil slapped a hand over her eyes and groaned. "Oh my *God!* One of these days someone is going to take the banter too far and actually offend someone. Like Dad grilling you about your tats and jail time. I'm still really sorry about that by the way."

I waved off her apology and indicated for her to carry on her story.

"My parents have been together since they were sixteen; they met at High School and Mum fell pregnant at eighteen. So, Dad's parents said that since he would be responsible for a child, he had to get a decent job. He completed his Police Recruit Training before Mickey and I were born. Family has always been important to them. They've had their ups and downs, just like anyone does, but really are meant for each other. You can see how they light up when they're together. They are definitely role models for the relationship I want for myself."

At the last sentence, Lil gave me a shy smile and smoothed a hand over her dress. This shyer side of Lil intrigued me; I'd really only experienced her being outgoing and sassy. She gave me a glimpse of her inner insecurities while in the spa, and this was another peek at her on a different level. She was beginning to trust me enough to let her guard down a little, thus letting me in.

"Well, we had better get to know each other better then, hadn't we?" I stated, and saw her raise a brow. "Not like *that*... *yet*."

I checked her reaction and was pleased to see her cheeks pinken as she hid her smile behind the mug.

"How about twenty questions?"

"This should be interesting," I chuckled and bent my knee in the space between us on the couch.

"Rules are simple. Either of us can ask a question, but we both must answer."

I nodded while she took a slow sip of milo. A slight furrow between her eyebrows appeared, making my finger itch to smooth it away.

"Ok," Lil declared. "How about favourite animal?"

"Velociraptor, without a doubt."

She gave me a condescending look. "Is that even an animal?"

"Do bears shit in the woods?"

Lil snorted. "You're ridiculous. For me, I would definitely say pygmy goats."

"You're bullshitting me, right?"

Christ, this girl was all over the place; so much for a 'one size fits all' approach to females.

"What's so great about a goat?" I demanded.

"They are freaking hilarious," she grinned. "What about pet hates?"

"Flannelette pajamas," I countered without hesitation. That was met with disbelief.

"What's so wrong with flannel PJs?" Lil exclaimed.

I leaned towards her. "Everything."

My comment lit a little spark of attitude in her gaze and I smirked knowing I had provoked it.

"Yeah, well, my pet hates include arrogant men."

"I wouldn't expect anything less from you, Sunshine," I drawled and set down my mug.

Aware of the time, I decided to push my luck and shoved my phone at her.

"Add your number."

Lil raised her brows at my demand.

"Please," I added.

She scoffed. "I thought Batman didn't beg," she said in a stupid-ass voice while her fingers tapped against the screen. "I'm only going to do it because you have a hot ride."

"You have no idea."

Her eyes hit mine, brimming with lust that burned so brightly I had to force myself not to look away. Blood roared in my ears as I recognised exactly what it meant.

"How presumptuous of you," Lil whispered, barely loud enough for me to hear. She studied me from under her lashes. "Text me."

"I will," I whispered back gravelly. "I should get going."

"You should." Again, with her whisper.

Lil locked her gaze onto mine before making a move to take our empty mugs to the kitchen. I followed closely behind, practically being pulled along by her wake.

She set them in the sink then went to breeze past me again. My hand flew out on its own accord and snagged her wrist. Before I could register what was happening, my lips were on hers and her tongue was meeting mine.

Desire roared through my veins so fast that it was impossible to stop, even if I wanted to. Lil's hunger took me by surprise and her tenacity added to my already heightened craving. Everything around me faded, all other thoughts vanished purely from tasting Lil.

"Got to go," I mumbled against her mouth as my hands gathered the hem of her dress.

"I know," she whispered back.

I picked her up by the back of her thighs and found the nearest wall. "Goodnight," I growled between kisses.

She giggled into my ear and squirmed against the scratch of my beard on her neck.

"I had fun."

"Want tucked in, Sunshine?" My lips sought hers again.

I hissed as she bit my lower lip and pulled back without releasing it. "Only if you're good at it."

My breath came out as a grunt as I ground my dick between her legs.

"The fucking best. Where's your room?" I demanded while tightening my grip on her ass.

"Upstairs on the left."

Pinning Lil in place with my hips, I tugged her arms above her head. She took my hint and kept them there as I peeled her dress up and over her head. Chucking it over my shoulder, I ignored the noise of something clattering to the ground; I was too busy focussing on her breasts filling my hands.

"Hold on," I rumbled.

No further words where needed. I all but ran up the stairs with her body locked against mine, her fingers working at the buttons of my shirt. My hand dragged along the wall as I kissed her, instinctively feeling for her room. We fell onto the bed where her body became pinned under my large one. Her hands resumed frantically tearing at my clothes.

"Light," I demanded, wanting to see all of her.

"Scared of the dark, Batman?" she giggled, which turned to a gasp when I ground my erection into her again.

Lil's body turned under mine and I felt her stretch for the bedside light. Once the temporary blindness subsided, I couldn't help the rumble that resonated from my chest... That ass!

Making the most of her on her stomach, I flicked the clip of her bra then wasted no time in running my hands down the backs of her legs and up again. The hum she made when I grabbed a handful of her rounded ass evaporated all moisture in my mouth. Rolling her so she now lay on her back beneath me, the sight of her took away what oxygen my body had left.

Lil's unsure voice swam through my senses. "What's wrong?"

"Fuck, you're even more beautiful out of your clothes. Don't cover yourself," I said, batting her hands away from her chest.

It wasn't until Lil tugged off my shirt that the hunger in her eyes blindsided me. I fucking faltered because I recognised that look and it brought everything flooding back in the worst way possible.

Without warning, we weren't alone; Lotte was in the room with us, watching us, surrounding me with her presence that had me flashing back to when she was beneath me, not Lil.

Lil immediately noticed my change in demeanour. "Gage?" Concern laced her voice as her hands reached for my face. "Seriously, what's wrong?"

I realised I had frozen in place, not moving, barely daring to breathe as I fought my conscience on every level.

I reared back from her touch as panic clawed through my chest. My breath became ragged as I grappled to regain control, struggling to become grounded again.

"Fuck. I... I'm so fucking sorry, Lil. I can't do this. It's not you, I swear. But I just can't fucking do this."

I was up and moving before I could think, zipping my jeans and grabbing my shirt off the floor. The single glance I dared to cast back at her when I reached the doorway sent me spiralling even more. Lil had the cover pulled around her and sat hugging her knees. The hurt etched deep on her face smashed what remained of my heart to smithereens.

Her wavering voice halted me to the spot. "What did I do?"

With a heavy sigh that did nothing to ease the agonising ache in my soul, I turned to face her. She flinched at the sight of me, and it sickened me that I was doing this to her. It wasn't intentional, but that didn't make a shred of difference to how badly I'd just offended her.

"Nothing, Lil, I promise. I wanted to. *Fuck,* Lord knows I do. I just can't right now... It's me, Sunshine, not you. Don't ever think it's you."

I'm the one who can't let go of the past.

She eyed me until moisture began to spring along her bottom eyelids. It was when she dropped her head to her knees that my knees weakened. She was fighting for composure, and it killed me that I was the cause of her tears.

"I'll sleep on the couch," I croaked.

Without looking up, Lil sniffed. "Give me a minute and I'll grab you some sheets."

I nodded despite her being unable to look at me, feeling like an absolute bastard for what I had just done. Despite the fact that I knew I should probably go for her sake, I couldn't bring myself to leave her alone and upset. Seemed like every time I was around her, shit got stirred up and people ended up getting hurt.

Wordlessly trudging from her room, I finished dressing in the bathroom. I couldn't even look at my own fucking reflection. The amount of self-loathing I felt was crippling.

I was standing in the kitchen with a bottle of vodka hanging from my fingers when Lil shuffled past a short while later with an armload of linen. I did a double take and couldn't help but scoff under my breath when I saw she dressed herself in flannelette PJs. Message received loud and clear.

Lil stilled from making the couch when I stepped up behind her and softly touched her arm. She froze.

"Lil," I murmured. "Stand up for a sec and listen."

She stood as requested but looked everywhere around the room to avoid me.

"I wasn't leading you on."

Her eyes snapped to mine, rejection confronting me in her hazel depths so plain to see that I had to look away to gain a moments reprieve.

"I think I understand and you don't need to explain, Gage. You're not ready."

When I didn't react, Lil ran her hands through her hair and turned back to my makeshift bed.

"I just…"

I gently clasped her elbow and squeezed. "What, Sunshine?"

She looked at me now with unmistakable determination. "I won't let myself be broken in order for you to heal."

Anguish slammed into me at full force. Fuck! Seeing her hurting because of me immediately negated all the progress I'd made over the last three years.

"I'll always be broken, Lil. No matter how much I heal on the outside, I'll forever be broken on the inside."

It was true. What wasn't true was Lil's assumption that women were my outlet; they weren't. Riding hard and long, and whisky, were the only things that helped numb the gnawing pain that held my heart in a constant state of arrest.

In fact, I had only had sex once in the last three years, and that was during the initial weeks where I swam, unfeeling and disorientated, through a grief so merciless I wished I was dead.

The woman involved was a close friend of mine—of ours—and we had blindly fucked each other in desperation to dull the desolation that we both struggled to come to terms with. It was a mistake. As soon as the lust faded, we knew it instantly. Neither of us had spoken about it since then, and we never would.

Lil laid a warm hand on my forearm, her touch bringing me back to the present and somehow settling some of my inner turmoil.

"Sometimes, we need to be broken so bad to realise just how whole we were to begin with. Then, *that* memory becomes the very thing we need to focus on and fight hard to restore. But you can't do that until you want to be at the starting point. Only once rock bottom is reached, and only once you want to *try,* only then can you begin the arduous journey of clawing your way back towards the light."

Her words spoke truth that slammed home. She spoke them as though she knew exactly what each of those words meant. She bent to continue making the couch but I stopped her again, this time speaking barely above a whisper.

"Go back to bed, babe. I'll sort this."

Lil nodded without a word and left me standing and feeling isolated once again. The stairs creaked every now and then as she ascended them. Only once the house had settled again did I move. I grabbed the bottle of vodka and quietly slipped out the back door.

Leaning against my motorbike, I poured a shot into the bottle lid. Throwing it back then opening my mouth through the burn, I promptly poured another and downed that just as fast. The heat helped dull the discomfort in my chest, but failed to wash away the residual guilt.

Whatever there was between Lil and I, was something greater than the two of us could control, and it scared the shit right out of me. It didn't seem right. However, after my fuck up inside, I had to face facts; I had to get my shit sorted before I ruined what little friendship I'd forged with Lil thus far.

As if it wasn't confusing enough, my dick decided to make itself known. In that moment, with three vodkas under my belt, being alone with darkness surrounding me, and sitting pretty on my chopper while my dick filled my jeans, there was only one thing that would help me forget, if only for a little while.

I let the zipper down and reached into my jeans.

GAGE

WADING THROUGH THE dark undertows of slumber, I fought against the awareness that threatened to drag me to consciousness. I stopped fighting the pull when slaps began to sting my cheek.

Lil was in a right panic when I woke up and was frantically shaking me.

"What, babe, *what?*" Now I was fucking panicking.

"He's in jail, Gage. We have to go, now!"

"Lil," I shushed her and rose to gather her into my arms with the intention of taking her back to her bed; being roused during a sleepwalking episode could be really traumatic.

"For fuck sake, I'm already awake!" she exclaimed and batted my hands away.

I squinted at her face while she glared back then clicked her fingers, causing me to blink and shake fully awake.

"Okay, tell me what's happened. And who the hell is in jail?"

Lil started pacing, her agitation obvious. "Mickey! He's in jail with Trav."

I almost, *almost*, fucking laughed. "How do you know that?"

She gave me an exasperated look and gesticulated wildly about her body that was now dressed in clothes instead of PJs.

"What? He told you in your sleep?" I scoffed. That shit was way the hell weird!

I grabbed my jeans and shirt and shoved them on as fast as I could while Lil took deep breaths. Crossing the room, I gathered her into my arms in an attempt to soothe some of her worries away.

"Give me your keys, I'll drive. Just tell me where to go, okay?"

She looked up with worry creasing her forehead and a silent plea showing in her expression. With a quick nod, we headed outside. The few moments in the fresh night air helped her regain a little composure. While I backed down the driveway, Lil spoke.

"I'm sorry for the horrible wake up call, I was in a state of full-blown panic. I can't *believe* they got *arrested!*"

"It'll be alright, Lil, I promise. I'm sure it's just a misunderstanding that got them locked up. Coppers tend to get a bit trigger happy." A sudden thought hit me. "Won't your dad find out?"

She pinched the bridge of her nose and hung onto the handle above her head as I took the corners without slowing down.

"I really hope not. If Mum finds out, she's gonna ream out Trav big time."

I did let a chuckle through then. It was only a matter of time before it came back to bite Trav on the arse.

When we reached the local police station Lil practically jumped out of the car before I had the chance to park.

Jogging to catch up with her hasty footsteps, I held the door open and followed her inside. I felt bad for the officer at the front desk; Lil gave him a dressing down, demanding that he release her brother this instant before the fury of hell was unleashed.

Managing to calm her down for a second while I spoke to the guy, I organised the release of the two dip-shits that had dragged us from the house at four forty-five in the morning! If it was up to me, I would have left them to stew overnight then strolled in at a more leisurely hour—after midday sometime—to bail out their sorry asses.

We sat and waited until the two shamefaced guys shuffled out of the lock down area.

Lil beat me to the interrogation. "What the *hell* are you two playing at? And why the heck were you *arrested*?"

Trav looked guilty as hell and avoided all eye contact. He was the instigator then, and Mickey was a willing accomplice.

"I'm really sorry, Lil, please don't tell Mrs Mick," Trav begged, actually begged, with his palms pressed together.

Mickey fought a smile. If he didn't compose himself and fast, Lil was going to blow her stack.

"Do you want the first reason or the second reason?" Mickey asked.

"You mean there's more than *one*?" Lil's eyebrows met her hairline as her voice pitched.

"We, ahh, got arrested for being drunk and disorderly..." Mickey was stalling big time.

Lil and I gave him matching gestures to hurry the hell up and elaborate on the second reason. Trav decided it was time that he took one for the team.

"And for resisting arrest."

"Oh, for Christ sake guys, how old are you? What did you do and *why* were you resisting arrest?" Lil's voice dropped as she clarified her questions. "And, do *not* let your answer for resisting arrest be 'because we were being arrested', or I swear to God..."

She pinched the bridge of her nose again like it was going to grant her unlimited patience. It was the final straw for me; I couldn't help but crack out a laugh that I quickly converted into a discrete cough under Lil's ice queen glare.

Mickey blew out his admission as fast as he could, as if saying it faster would lessen the after burn.

"We thought it would be funny to chuckpiesaroundatthegasstationonthewayhome."

"You *what!*" Lil's voice actually cracked with disbelief. "Please tell me you *fools* are taking the piss right now? You woke me up, causing me to panic thinking you had been in a horrible fight, and I come down here to find out that you were arrested for chucking *pies around a gas station!*"

The three of us guys couldn't take it anymore. Our laughter burst out the floodgates that had held strong right up until Lil's recap. It was bloody hilarious and such a ridiculous reason to be arrested.

Unfortunately, the lack of sleep began to catch up on Lil and she could not, or would not, even acknowledge that it was more than a little bit funny.

Seething, she shoved her hand into the front pocket of my jeans and extracted her car keys with such ferocity it left me concerned for the safety of my junk. I clapped a protective hand over the area before I lost a nut. Her shoes made an aggressive clapping sound as she headed towards the exit without a backwards glare to see if we were following or not.

We all needed to get our shit together before we reached the car, otherwise, there wasn't a doubt in my mind that the three of us would be walking home.

Lil sat with the car revving impatiently like it was going to speed up our urge to enter the capsule of tension. Silence reigned for most of the ride back until Mickey finally realised that something was amiss.

"Hey, how come you two arrived together?" He leaned forward from the back seat and flicked a forefinger between us as if it was unclear who he was referring to.

"You aren't in the position to be asking the questions, so shut the hell up," Lil snapped, not taking her eyes off the road.

Honestly trying to be helpful, I suggested, "Why don't you ask her internally?"

"She's blocking me," he replied dryly.

Both Trav and I let out an amused snort.

"You guys did it, didn't you?" Mickey questioned.

Seriously, the guy had a death wish and was jumping on wafer thin ice.

Lil sassed out an unexpected answer. "Yes Mickey, we fucked, on the couch. Twice."

I bit back my shout of laughter as Trav let his free. Jeez, I was in over my head with this lot. Mickey, however, lost his shit.

"Bullshit! Please tell me she's bullshitting me, Gage? On the *couch? Seriously!* I'll never be able to sit there again."

"Sorry, mate, I don't kiss and tell."

Lil and I shared a knowing, albeit strained, glance as Mickey huffed in the backseat, cursing me all manner of names under the sun.

20

LIL

DAWN WAS BREAKING as I pulled into my driveway after picking up my moronic brother and our stupid-ass friend.

I strode around the side of the house without a word to look back at the three of them still in the car. I already knew they weren't coming just yet; Mickey and Gage were taking lame selfies with Trav while he slept. If I wasn't in such a bitch mood, I would've joined in, but running on minimal sleep with a night shift ahead of me, my patience was wearing thin.

I let myself into the house and left the door open. The laughter coming from the car began to increase and Trav's alarmed voice rang out. Shortly after, car doors slammed and I was graced with the presence of three people who were not in my good books right now.

I was still highly embarrassed about what had—or hadn't—happened with Gage last night. I could tell he hadn't been ready, but was unable to resist in the heat of the moment.

Speak of the devil. Gage's hands landed on my waist in a way that was both intimate and intended to keep distance.

"About last night..." he spoke in a low tone against my ear.

"What the fuck is this!"

Both Gage and I snapped apart and saw Mickey—with the fires of Hell burning in his eyes—holding up my discarded dress and toeing the strewn pens that had clattered to the ground last night.

"My dress."

"Lilianne!"

"Don't call me that!" I yelled as my anger spiked unexpectedly. I literally saw red after hearing my full name—the one I never let anyone call me—pass his lips.

Mickey at least had the sense to look apologetic, though voiced his disapproval regardless while glowering between me and Gage.

"You weren't joking, were you?"

I sneered at my shithead brother while distancing myself from Gage. "You're such a fucking hypocrite, Josh! But I don't rub it in your stupid face!"

Mickey spluttered as I took flight, taking the stairs two at a time. As I reached the doorway of my room, unhurried footsteps followed my ascent. Mickey's furious warning from downstairs had a sadistic smirk forming on my lips.

"You're a fucking dead man, Gage Westbrook. Right after I've had some fucking sleep!"

Gage was chuckling under his breath when he entered my room, and stopped short as I rounded on him.

"Thanks for helping me out back there," I said, not meaning a damn word.

He looked at the floor while running a hand over his beard. His eyes were filled with remorse when he finally flicked them to mine, putting an abrupt end to me checking him out while he wasn't looking.

"Lil, about last night-"

I held up a hand, totally exasperated about everything that happened during the last six hours.

"It's fine. Honestly. Probably for the best anyway," I muttered while trying to quash the lingering sting of rejection. It hurt more than it should have.

The guy had baggage—*huge* baggage—and I needed to tread cautiously. Hell, even Mace had warned me about it.

Gage reached for me and this time I let him, unable to remain staunch as he ran a finger across my jawline then down my neck. The barest hint of a smile tugged his lips when he saw goose bumps prickle my arms.

"It's not fine. I should never have started something I couldn't finish. It was shit of me."

I huffed a laugh. "You're right. It was shit. But... I know there's more to the story than you're telling me. I can feel it."

My heart actually panged for the guy when he looked at the floor again and cursed.

"Batman?"

He looked up at me from under his brows. "Yeah, Sunshine?"

I extended a hand and cringed internally as a single word slipped from my lips.

"Friends?"

With a smirk, he accepted my peace offering. "Friends."

"Okay, cool. Now it's time to hit the road."

"Did you just kick me out?" he scoffed. "It's not what a good friend would do."

"Yes, it is. I'm on nights as of tonight and I need to catch up on sleep."

Gage's dark-brown gaze studied me for the barest of moments before he gave a subtle nod.

"I'll walk myself out. You," he turned me towards my bed, "in you get. I'll see you later."

I didn't bother protesting as I slipped beneath my bed covers and did a little wave when Gage looked back from the doorway.

As the door softly clicked shut behind him, I rubbed the bruised spot on my chest where Batman resided within my heart. It was obvious that he was consumed by something greater than confused feelings for me, and whatever it was, it was something he needed to work through at his own pace.

...

Trav was still passed out on the couch amongst the bedding Gage had used when I rose for the second time that day.

Mickey, however, sat in an armchair, drinking a coffee and scrolling through his phone with a smirk on his face. As soon as I stepped through the doorway, the smirk morphed to a scowl and he chucked his phone down beside him.

"Lil," he hissed in a whisper, "we need to talk."

I rolled my eyes and turned, heading back to the kitchen knowing he'd follow me.

Sure enough, the sound of the dining table chair being pulled out then a heavy sigh hit my ears.

"Lil," Mickey started again, this time his voice was full of resignation.

"Joshy, I know what you're gonna say, okay, and Gage and I aren't a 'thing'." The pang in my stomach caused me to snap, "We're friends."

"He's working through some serious fucking baggage, Lil. Mace filled me in on the vague details and I just don't want to see you get hurt again. Last time was fucking horrible and you almost didn't fucking make it." I sniffed hard as the prickle of tears stung the back of my nose. My brother was right. I almost hadn't made it, and at the time, I didn't see how I could.

"I know," I whispered. "But you've got to realise, I'm a different person since then. That was six years ago." I slid onto the dining seat across from him. "I wish I could help him."

I didn't add that Gage's broken state of mind and soul was part of the reason I felt so drawn to him.

"You can't fix everyone, Lil."

"I know," I murmured.

There was a hunger within me that wanted to fix everyone I came across, and I made it my mission to try my very best to do that during each shift I worked at the hospital. It was what I felt compelled to do, and that would never change.

Mickey leaned forward and grabbed my hand. "I understand, Lil, I really do. I wish I could save everyone too, but some days it's simply impossible."

I returned his squeeze, my heart feeling heavy with the knowledge that we both have been witness to injury and death more than either of us cared to remember. It came hand in hand with our choice of occupations, though it didn't make it any easier to deal with, or accept.

"He's different, Joshy, I can feel it."

Mickey pegged me with a look that never failed to make me stop and think. "The deepest injuries are the hardest to cure, Lil. Remember that."

Silence surrounded us as his words sunk in. He was one hundred percent right, and no one could help those who weren't ready or willing to accept it.

With a final tap on my hand, Mickey rose and murmured about showering. After he had left the room, I texted Kimmie.

L: Shit went down last night. Are you up?

Her reply was almost instant.

K: Let me pee. Then we talk.

Sure enough, I was making my way upstairs when my phone vibrated with her call.

"Morning," I grumbled.

"Afternoon. Oh my God I am *so* hungover!" Kimmie exclaimed. I imagined her throwing herself back amongst her bed covers. "What the hell has happened now?"

I pulled out a fresh set of scrubs and switched my phone to speaker.

"It'll need to be the condensed version because I've just started getting ready for work."

"Hit me," Kimmie declared while munching on something crunchy.

The next fifteen minutes were spent with me speaking as I dressed and did my hair, elaborating when Kimmie needed more information. By the time I was finished, I needed a stiff drink, and I said as much.

"Okay, okay, firstly, you definitely do not need a drink right now," Kimmie assured me.

I looked at my reflection in the mirror and nodded in agreement.

"But you know what, Lil? I've known you all our lives, and this is me telling you straight up that straightforward and simple aren't your style. You know, like, boring doesn't rev your engine or give you something worth fighting for. Likewise, the guy for you will fight for you no matter what it costs them, and when he does, you'll know. You'll know so damn hard just how much you mean to him and there will be no doubt in your mind. Yes, you and Gage are messy, but for whatever reason, and even though neither of you can see it, you both need each other. Give him time, I'm positive that if he wants you, he'll come out swinging sooner or later."

My pulse raced as she finished her speech; Kimmie was so fucking right. Straightforward and simple were never my style. Her pep-talk re-ignited my determination to, first and foremost, do right by me.

"And that is why I love you, Kimmie. I'm sorry to have dumped this all on you."

"That's what friends are for. God knows I've relied on you over the years. Love your face."

"Yours is better," I countered and grinned when I heard her scoff. "Seriously though, thank you, chick."

"All good. Now go save the world while I watch Beauty and the Beast."

I giggled through our goodbye and was still smiling when I made my way back downstairs to where Mickey and Trav were also watching a movie.

I headed for the kitchen to raid the pantry for snacks to see me through my shift.

"Yo, Lil!" Trav cheered right behind my back.

I squealed a little and jumped in the air as I whirled. He was all grinning face and mussed hair.

"Shit, Trav! Back it up a pace will ya. I almost shat myself," I sassed then resumed my foraging.

I loaded my arms with food and turned to the bench. Trav's eyes snapped from my ass to my eyes as I narrowed mine.

"Um, are you needing something specific or just wanting to stare at my ass? I'm on my way out the door."

Trav frowned while his gaze skipped over my scrubs and sneakers.

"What?" I demanded, looking down at myself.

He chuckled. "Nothing, Lil. Scrubs aren't made to be sexy, are they?"

"Oh, for fuck sake, Travis. Don't start with me, you're still in my bad books after last night, so don't go making it worse for yourself!"

He grinned again, knowing full well that I couldn't stay mad at him. By tomorrow, my snit would be forgotten.

"I actually wanted to apologise. Last night was fucked up, Lil, and I can't believe we ended up in the slammer. Thanks so much for coming to bail us." He threw his arms wide and stepped closer.

I backed up a pace. "Trav," I warned, crouching slightly and getting ready to run.

He snagged the back of my shirt as I took off. He was the rough one in the crew, and I wasn't at all surprised when he boisterously engulfed me with his arms and squeezed the ever-loving shit out of me.

"I should've left you there like Gage wanted," I muffled into his chest.

"But you didn't, because you love us," he declared, already weaseling his way back into my good books.

I scoffed. "Yeah, for some reason, I do."

As abruptly as it began, Trav released me from his hold and enthusiastically smoothed down my hair.

"So, you and the new guy, huh?"

I slugged him on the arm then started shoving food into my bag.

"Dog house, Travie, that's where you are. The only way to fix it now is with M&M's," I called to Trav's chuckling back as he headed back into the lounge.

GAGE

"OVERNIGHTER, EH?" MACE'S smug-ass grin greeted me the moment I got in the door.

"Fuck you."

He raised his hands and backed off before coming at it from a different angle.

"Haven't received any complaints from Lil Bean this morning…"

I flipped my middle finger over my shoulder as I angrily jabbed buttons on his stupid coffee machine.

"Whoa, go the fuck easy, bro. Don't take your bleed out on my woman!"

I added another jab just to get my non-existent point across and grinned when I heard his pissy growl behind me.

"Thought you'd be in a better mood today?" he ventured.

The urge to rant climbed through my veins and Mace must have realised he was walking a fine line. I turned to face him while my coffee made itself, and my expression alone must have been enough for him to work out that shit went down.

"Please tell me you didn't."

"Didn't what?" I bit.

"Leave on bad terms."

Fuck he was annoying me. Taking my time to sip the scalding coffee then run my fingers through my hair, I leaned on the bench and looked him square in the eye.

"I didn't. I left in the fucking friend zone."

And it was my own goddamn fault.

I was being held back and didn't know how to break the cycle.

Mace scoffed a laugh then slapped his palms on the bench. "Is that what they're calling it these days?"

"Fuck you." I took another sip. "You really wanna know what happened?"

"Yup."

"Nothing, that's what. I had her laid out on her back and, fuck, I was all but *in* her, then I freaked out. A huge block came over me and when I looked down at Lil, I fucking saw..." Telling him this was killing me. "...I fucking saw Lot, and, and..."

And it fucking killed me and broke my heart further than it already was.

Mace's hand came down on my shoulder and squeezed hard. "Mate."

"It's fucked up, cuz. How is it even possible to not be able to have sex with someone I want to for the first time in three fucking years! As soon as I touch Lil it's like she lights fireworks under my skin and all rational thought goes out the window. I practically want to fucking *eat* her!" I yelled, much to my horror when Mace started pissing himself laughing. "You know what I mean, asshole. And I all but did before an overwhelming sense of guilt consumed me. I ended up on the goddamn couch," I mumbled, so deflated I couldn't even look at Mace.

"You ever... you know, fucked the grief from your system?"

I winced at his words, remembering that single time with Heidi.

"There was one, a mutual friend, not long after, and it was a *colossal* mistake for both of us!" I admitted. My anger swiftly followed the memory; it was such a desecration on Lotte.

"And since?"

"Nothin'," I confessed, the words leaving a bitter aftertaste in my mouth.

"You need to sort your shit out before even contemplating taking things further with Lil. My guess is that she accepted it for what it was, after your talk with her this week?"

I nodded.

"Good. A word of warning though, she won't tolerate being fucked around. Then you'll have Mickey raining down on your ass and I'll be next in line."

"You think I don't know that?"

Mace sniggered. His eyes grew wide when I added, "We picked him and Trav up from the slammer last night."

"Bull-fucking-shit!" Mace boomed then pointed at me while pulling up a stool. "Details, *now.*"

His enthusiasm got a smile out of me as I relayed the previous night's events in between sips of coffee and his laughter. I allowed the recap to overshadow the not so great details of last night.

One thing was for sure, I had only been here for a few weeks and I had more fire in my soul than I'd had over the last three years combined. It was an odd feeling to feel half-alive again. There was a small part of myself that loathed to perceive again, but there was a growing part of me that was welcoming it more with each passing day.

. . .

Lil constantly played on my mind, ensuring that what should have been a restorative sleep, was broken and fitful. I hadn't long got back from the lunch run when Uncle Dave came limping into the on-site office and threw himself into a chair.

"What the hell are you doing here?" Mace demanded through his mouthful of pie.

"You sound just like your mother. I needed to get out of the house," Dave grumbled, reaching for the unclaimed brown paper bag in the middle of the table.

Mace snatched it out of his reach then smirked at his father. "You're getting slow old man."

There was a flurry of movement as Dave lunged across the table and grabbed the bag from Mace's hand. Dave and I pissed ourselves laughing while Mace flipped his father off while chewing savagely.

"Did Mum not feed you before letting you lose?"

Dave's reply was cut off by a sharp wolf-whistle slicing through the air outside. A round of roaring laughter followed a short pause then the office door swung open, revealing a slightly flustered Lil.

"Love! What are you doing to my boys out there?" Dave chuckled.

Lil scoffed and cocked a brow. "Giving them something to look at aside from my ass. More to the point, what are *you* doing here?" she accused.

Mace chuckled and continued eating, and as Lil gave Dave the once over, I gave *her* a twice over.

Her legs painted in tight blue jeans stole the moisture from my mouth. My tongue darted out to wet my lips as I studied hers, looking all pink and shiny. My gaze dropped to her chest while she handed my uncle a box. I was doing another skim over her hips and legs when the brown paper bag was thrown across the table and Mace shouted a curse when it landed in his lap.

The movement snapped me from my hungry thoughts, and my eyes locked with Lil's. A pretty little blush began to snake its way over her cheekbones.

"Both of you shut your mouths," Mace muttered, now eating the rejected cream bun and getting icing sugar everywhere.

"Er, uh... Hi, Lil."

Dammit. Now she was stealing my ability to form a decent fucking sentence!

Lil sounded as breathless as I felt. "Hi, Gage, how's it going?"

"Good," I snipped and focused on eating my sausage roll.

Dave's brow furrowed as his eyes ping-ponged between me and Lil. "Am I missing something?"

"Nothing, Uncle."

"I'll tell you if you give me one of them donuts," Mace smirked, wiping his mouth on the back of his hand.

Dave flipped open the box Lil just handed him and pushed it into the middle of the table.

"David Westbrook! Who knew you had such a rubber arm!" Lil exclaimed, sounding a little bewildered. "At least wait until I leave," she sassed at Mace before turning her attention back to Dave. "As for you, boot off."

"How come you never bring me donuts?" Mace bitched.

"Because you never bring me M&M's," she retorted without looking up from examining Dave's healing injury.

Mace looked indignant at her accusation. "I do bloody so!"

"Yeah, when I *ask* for them."

Mace turned to me. "Hear that, cuz? Don't bother sending Lil flowers as a random act of romance, pick her up a five-dollar bag of M&M's and she's all yours."

"You're an asshole," I snapped.

Dave's chuckling broke the silence. "You boys still bicker like you did as kids. Some things never change."

Mace—the fat bastard—ignored his father's dig and shoved a donut into his mouth.

I used his momentary distraction to visually drink Lil in again, unsatisfied with my last stolen skims over her body. Her concentration face made me stifle a smile; it was cute as hell when her lips pouted ever so slightly. At least this time, watching her as she worked, I wasn't fighting the urge not to pass out.

"How are you not the size of a house?" Lil asked Mace, her facials thoroughly dismayed at how much crap food he consumed within one meal.

Mace stood and flexed. "I work it all off, baby."

"Goddammit, I've raised a show pony," Dave muttered while re-booting.

Lil scoffed at Mace then laughed heartily at my uncle's comment. When she turned to me, the grin slid from her lips where it was replaced with unusual shyness.

"I'll see you guys later," she said without breaking my eye contact.

Her gaze briefly dropped as I licked moisture back onto my lips. I managed a nod while Mace and Dave said their goodbyes. Not a word was spoken after she slipped from the office, then my uncle turned to me.

"You're smitten with that girl, son."

Mace choked on his drink and coughed violently while Dave studied my reaction; which was to completely ignore them both and curse the entire situation.

22
LIL

I SHOULD HAVE melted from the way Gage looked at me when I turned up at their job site on my way to work earlier in the week. The hunger brewing in his dark depths almost flattened me. It was obvious that our awkward intimate situation had done little to dampen his desires; if anything, it had heightened them.

Bloody Mace though! I made a mental note to maim him out next time I caught him alone, which would be tomorrow since the crew was meeting up again. This time it was at our house since we were the only ones with a spa.

By the time my night shift was done, I was beat. My feet ached and my muscles complained as I drove home in the early hours with dangerously heavy eyelids.

Pulling into our drive behind Mickey's ute, I locked the car then started for the back door. That's when I felt it. Ripples of ice wove across my shoulders and down my spine. Without a doubt, I knew someone was watching me.

I spun in alarm, expecting to see, or at least hear, someone lurking in the shadows close by, but there was nothing. No movement, no sound, *nothing*.

<*You home at the mo?*>

Mickey's reply was instant. <*Asleep*>

Knowing he was in the house, I wasted no further time loitering on the driveway. Unlocking the door then slamming it closed behind me, I engaged the lock. I was still leaning against it with my heart hammering when Mickey shuffled down the stairs in his boxers.

"What's with all the fucking noise?" he muttered, palming his eye socket and lazily rubbing them.

"I think someone was watching me."

His eyes snapped open and he was at the window a second later, peering in all directions.

"You sure?"

"I felt it, Mick," I replied warily. My bed was calling my name and I wanted nothing more than to comply with its orders.

"The doors are locked, aye?" Mickey asked, continuing his investigation.

"Yup."

"Go on up to bed, Lil. I'll check it out." He reached for his nunchucks then looked back from the door.

"I'll wait here," I countered.

He slipped through the front door and into the night, leaving me anxiously waiting for a few long minutes.

"Nothin'," he puffed, slamming the door closed again. "Go to bed, Lil. You're dead on your feet."

There was no point in arguing. Mickey waited as I summoned the last of my energy to climb the stairs, then followed me after turning out the lights.

Despite Mickey being in the house and knowing we were locked up tight, I still couldn't shake the residual creep that lingered at the tip of my spine. I hardly slept a wink before first hints of daylight began to weave through the curtains. With it came the reassurance I needed to fall asleep.

. . .

I was up and still kicking around in my PJs early the next afternoon, when rumbling reverberated through the house. Skipping downstairs when a knock sounded at the door, I swung it open to see Gage standing there in full leathers and his hair mussed like he had just ran his fingers through it.

His gaze drank me in and lingered on my bare legs where the tiny sleep shorts failed to cover. In that same moment, I wished I wasn't wearing a hoody; the temperature in the house just skyrocketed at least ten degrees.

"Gage! Uh, good morn- afternoon," I managed.

His dark eyes snapped up from their leisurely stroll. "Suit up, Sunshine. We leave in five."

It took me all of two seconds to decipher what he meant, and after that, he didn't need to tell me twice. Hell, I left him standing at the door in my haste.

Stepping into my protective pants as fast as humanly possible, I pulled on a long-sleeve, braided my hair then grabbed my jacket, boots, gloves and helmet. Gage was sitting on the front steps in the sun with his bent legs spread wide and his forearms casually propped on them. I sat beside him and pulled on my boots.

"So, what's the occasion?"

He looked at me then. "There is none. I just felt like going for a ride and thought you might wanna come."

"Sure do." I confirmed, zipping my jacket.

Gage stood and gave me a crooked smile.

<*Where you going?*> came Mickey's question from the bathroom.

<*For a ride with Gage*>

<*Lil!*>

<*See you this afternoon. I'll be home in time for the barbeque*>

I blocked his reply as I fastened my helmet. Stopping at Gage's side, I waited for him to swing his leg over then give me a nod. I effortlessly settled behind him and grabbed his jacket. Gage reached for my thigh and tugged me impossibly closer. I took the hint; plastering myself to his back and holding on to either sides of his jacket as he opened the throttle and took off down the street.

No matter how many times I rode, the euphoria never got old or waned. The roar of the motor, the vibrations, the wind whipping past and the speed were freeing in a way that only motorcycle enthusiasts would understand.

Gage slowed for a red light and the backs of his thighs pressed against my knees when he set his feet on the ground. He turned his head enough to be heard over the rumbling.

"All good?"

Giving him a thumbs up, I grinned to myself when he grabbed my hand after I set it on his waist again, briefly linking our fingers and squeezing. I liked this part of him; quietly commanding yet sweetly concerned.

I don't know how long we rode for, and I didn't care. Eventually, Gage pulled into a reserve and leisurely followed the sealed lane that wound its way through large oak trees. I sat back a little from his body and took in more of our surroundings. He pulled up at a clearing and waited for me to get off before he killed his bike. The sound of birds and cicadas engulfed us. After removing my helmet, I stared up at the bright green canopy above that protected us from the direct sunlight.

I looked back at Gage when I felt his stare. He didn't look away as he removed his helmet and tugged down his face shield. Wordlessly, he swung his leg over his bike then took my hand, leading me to a wooden park bench near the stream.

"I got you something," he said with a smirk once we were sitting.

I laughed loudly when he pulled out a large bag of M&M's from his internal jacket pocket and shook them up and down.

"You shouldn't have!" I said, accepting the bag and holding it up. "Some?"

"Hit me," he replied and held out his hand.

I put one in his hand then poured a whole lot into my own, throwing them all into my mouth in one go.

"Fucking stinge!" He grabbed the bag back and chuckled at my shout of indignation.

"Hit me," I threw his words back at him then giggled when he placed a single yellow M&M in the centre of my palm.

"Like the sun," he mumbled.

Gage searched out a black one for himself then watched as I nibbled at the yellow shell, his gaze continuously flicking between my eyes and my lips. He crunched the brown M&M down without looking away. Just as I leaned in to reach for the bag, he grabbed the back of my head and set his lips on mine in one smooth movement. There, we both stilled with his upper lip between mine and my lower lip between his. When Gage eventually re-instigated the kiss, it was slow and soft, no tongue, and simply sweet.

My fingers lazily ran through his beard, the other hand forgotten entirely as the bag of M&M's fell from my fingertips.

Gage hoisted me onto his lap. With my face captured gently in his hands, he continued to tease me with his drawn-out approach to savouring my taste. I hummed when his tongue finally ran across my lip, but still he remained unhurried. We paused, breathing in the same air, lips parted yet barely touching.

"What was that for?" I whispered. "Friends don't kiss friends like that."

The torture swimming in his eyes made my heart ache.

"I like you Lil, and as much as I need to keep my distance from you, I can't. Besides," he grinned cheekily, "I wanted to see what yellow tasted like."

I giggled. "And? How does it taste?"

"Like fucking gold," he growled.

I swear I blushed hard at his words. No matter what he said, whether good or bad, his words were always filled with emotion and conviction.

"Hmm, interesting, because you taste sinfully dark," I teased.

He emitted an amused snort despite the ghosts resurfacing in his eyes. "That about sums me up."

Climbing from his lap, I rescued the bag of discarded M&M's from amongst the grass. Finding a blue one from the bag, I sat beside Gage and sat it in his palm.

"Where there's a tiny bit of light, the darkness has an opportunity to fade to blue."

Pain. I could see him visibly struggling with what I just said. He was filled with deeply set affliction that visibly etched on both his emotions and body. My fingers lingered on his palm and I only pulled away once his fingers closed to encase the M&M I'd placed there. He didn't eat this one, just held it while he studied me with a furrow on his brow and wonderment now in his gaze.

We hardly spoke the rest of the hour we spent at the reserve, purely happy to be in each other's presence. I did, however, spend most of that time in Gage's arms, or, at the very least, with my hand in his. By the time we left, he seemed to have an air of resolution about him. He felt more settled, more accepting of our connection, just… more.

23
LIL

WE TOOK THE long way home, and I made the most of my arms wrapped around Gage's torso, feeling his stomach move with each breath he took.

Weaving around the two utes and my car that filled the driveway, Gage parked up on the back lawn. Trav was already at my house, beer in hand and spinning a yarn to Mickey as my brother casually smoked.

I jumped off the bike before Gage cut the engine and strode over to Mickey, plucking the fag from his lips and stubbing it out on the grass—barely refraining from stubbing it out on his leg.

His bitchy reply was muffled as I tugged off my helmet.

"You know it's bad for you," I sassed, hugging Trav, who shook me from side-to-side.

"Whatever," Mickey mumbled back, his lips already connecting with the top of his beer.

Gage came to my side, now stripped of his helmet and jacket, and ran a hand through his hair. The tight black t-shirt drew my attention and encouraged it to linger, greedily looking over every hint of muscle on his torso and arms.

"Lil!" Mickey barked. "Stop staring at the poor fucker. It's awkward for everyone."

"Not for me," I called over my shoulder as I made my way towards the house.

Now that we didn't have cool air rushing around us, standing around in the afternoon sun in leathers was hot as Hell.

Gage's footsteps followed me through the house and up the stairs. He walked close, too close, and when I stopped abruptly and turned to face him, he stopped short where the toes of his boots connected with mine.

"Are you following me?"

His low chuckle came from within his chest. "It would appear that way, but I'm actually heading for the bathroom."

"Oh," I said on a laugh, feeling silly for thinking he was up here because I was. I waved him off. "Of course you are. It's in there."

I rushed to my room, shut the door then held my face in my hands because that was freaking embarrassing! I cursed myself the entire time I undressed and slipped into a bikini. By the time I pulled a cute little sundress over top, I heard a knock at my door.

"Come in," I called, brushing out my hair in front of the mirror.

The door slowly swung open to reveal Gage's large form. His eyes landed on my bed where he stared for a moment before clicking the door shut behind him. He'd been surprisingly non-talkative today and it was beginning to unsettle me.

"Gage, is something wrong? You've been... different... today."

He didn't say a word as he slowly prowled my way, but took the hairbrush from my hands and turned me back to face the mirror. I watched him as my heart hammered so loud in my chest, I was sure he could hear it.

Our eyes connected in the reflection as he lifted the brush and gently swiped it through the length of my hair. I didn't know whether to feel awkward or at ease; no guy had ever brushed my hair before—apart from Mace—and the air had definitely *not* been charged with sexual tension like it was right now.

"I enjoyed today," Gage murmured, his focus remaining on the brush strokes.

"Same."

The silence drew out, and my eyes drifted closed from the continuous rhythm through my hair.

"I liked it more than I wanted to," Gage admitted, almost sounding pained.

My eyes reopened the same time he stepped a fraction closer. The breath snagged in my throat when his fingers skimmed down my back, lower than where my hair stopped.

Gage brushed my hair over my shoulder then pressed a kiss below my ear. My head tilted to the side on its own accord, and the hairbrush made a dull thud when it dropped to the floor. Gage's hands found my hips and tugged me back against him. I linked my fingers with his and relaxed against him as he wove his arms around my waist then smoothed up my stomach.

"Same," I breathed again.

As soon as my head fell back against his shoulder, his lips landed on mine and quickly turned urgent. Spinning me in his arms, I held on as Gage lifted me by the backs of my thighs and sat on the bed with me straddled on his lap. His warm hands held my exposed neck where his thumb could work over my jaw as he kissed me. Our movements synced and I quickly fell into a state of heightened need.

A tortured groan escaped my mouth when Gage pulled far enough away for his eyes to flick from my lips to my eyes. His fingers dug harder into my ass and his voice grew hoarse.

"Come home with me tonight."

I studied him at close range, searching for the answer in his eyes; the same answer my mind wanted to give him.

"Mace is working later," he clarified, assuming my hesitation was due to Mace potentially being home with us.

"I want to, I'm just not sure if it's wise…"

"You're right, it's not wise," Gage replied, still eyeing my lips. I licked them nervously and smiled when he mimicked the action. "Not wise at all," he whispered while trailing his fingers up my inner thigh.

My breathing grew heavy and heat pooled between my legs. "You're distracting me, Batman."

Gage smirked, knowing full well what he was doing.

"There'll be Hell to pay if you move an inch higher," I warned despite my body demanding that he hurry up and touch me how I wanted.

Gage rumbled another deep chuckle. "Hell is where I roll, baby," he drawled with a smoulder that had me second guessing my restraint.

He held my gaze in challenge as he inched higher. I watched his daring expression until my eyelids fell closed.

"You're playing with fire," I hissed as my body involuntarily ground against his fingers.

"Don't I fucking know it," he bit back.

Another knock sounded at my door.

"No," I instinctively yelled which brought on Mace's chuckling from the other side.

"Tell Gage I've got his gear here… I'm assuming he's in there with you?"

"Fuck you!" Gage called and threw himself backwards onto my bed.

More of Mace's laughter sounded through the wood as I climbed off Gage's waist.

"Well, you may as well come in," I sassed, whipping the door open to find him casually leaning against the door frame, holding a bottle of mouthwash, and grinning.

He tossed bottle at me then held out a pair of Gage's black jeans, which I snatched from his hand. Mace followed me into the room and sniggered at Gage sitting on the edge of my bed looking dark as fuck.

"Was I interrupting something?" Mace scoffed.

I backhanded his chest. "Your time will come, and I'll be the first leading the charge into your bedroom." He flinched slightly from my sudden lash-out. "And yes, you were interrupting. We were in the middle of a conversation."

"Is that what they call it these days. I've been doing it all wrong."

Gage unlaced his boots while Mace and I continued our bitchy tête-à-tête.

"You've never done it right to begin with," I teased.

Mock outrage crossed over Mace's face. "I'm a fucking conversation *God*. It's a good thing you haven't had a piece of this, Lil Bean, because I would have ruined you for my cousin here. On that note, go easy on him, he's out of practice."

I smothered a gasp behind my hand at Mace's brazen pot-shot at Gage, who cussed Mace out.

"You know I won't go easy on him. Oh actually, you don't know, because you haven't had the pleasure of getting this," I declared and whacked my ass.

Mace barked a loud laugh. "Jesus, Lil Bean. Doin' you would be like doin' my sister, if I had one. And that shit I don't need to see," Mace called over my shoulder.

I turned to see Gage kicking off his leather pants and bending to pull on the jeans. I froze and blatantly stared at his toned thighs as the muscles flexed with his movements.

Words.

No words.

No w…

"Close your mouth," Mace sniggered close to my ear. "Catch yas out back," he added with a slap to my ass that jolted me back to reality.

Absolutely mortified at my reaction, and Mace calling me out for perving, I declared that I, too, would wait outside. However, Mace slammed the door shut before I could follow him through it, then held it closed.

With a final curse at him through the wood, I risked a glance back at Gage. He now faced me, slowly zipping his jeans with a smirk. I snapped back around and studied the light switch.

"Lil?"

"Mmm?"

"You can look now. I didn't mean to make you uncomfortable."

I snorted and turned. I seldom got uncomfortable or bashful around anyone; Gage was the exception. It also meant that I was crushing on him harder than a school girl crushing on the latest boy band.

"You didn't," I lied. "You just keep on confusing me and it's, well... *confusing!*"

Gage stepped close. "Story of my month," he rumbled.

He used his large body to walk me to the wall. With his forearms braced on the wall either side of my head, he brushed his body against mine. An unchecked groan slipped from both of our mouths. The moment my fingers flicked under his shirt and landed on his lower back, the weight of his body increased.

"Fuck, I can't stop touching you," he mumbled, pulling my leg up around his waist and grinding harder against me. "I don't know what you're doing to me, Sunshine, but I can't fucking help myself."

"You don't need to fight it. I'm not going to hurt you."

"It's not me I'm worried about, Lil. You deserve someone who's whole, who's not going to drag you down into the dark."

I looked up to see his brown depths trained on me, boring so deep into my soul where no one had ever reached before. His gaze became more intense with each word I spoke.

"I deserve someone who's going to accept me for who I am and not try to change me. I deserve someone who can give them self to me in a way that scares them to the centre of their being. Someone who's gonna fight for me as hard and as fiercely as they can, because to them, I would be worth the battle. And I deserve to be loved so hard it hurts in every way imaginable."

Gage rested his forehead against mine where the tip of our noses met.

"We need to go downstairs."

Disappointment washed through me.

I took a risk by opening my heart and speaking my mind, and it appeared to have backfired. I nodded, because if I talked my voice would have held a definite waver. I took comfort in the fact that he took my hand and didn't let go until I was sitting in a deckchair outside.

24
GAGE

I KNEW WHEN she spoke those words they came directly from her heart and were intended to ignite a passion within me that couldn't be falsified. And you know what? They fucking hit home like a sledgehammer.

Lil deserved all those things and so much more, and it killed me right now that I couldn't be the man to give everything she needed, and more.

As much as she tried to hide it, I felt her body deflate the moment I changed the subject, suggesting we head downstairs. The longer we stayed in her room, the further my resolve slipped. I wanted her more than anything, and that scared the living shit out of me.

I didn't drink during the party, conscious that I needed to ride home later. Also, Lil hadn't given me an answer to my question.

We sat around the outdoor fire and I was more than aware of Kimmie and Lil across the flames, talking and stealing glances my way. Likewise, I was aware of Mickey sitting to my right and glaring in my direction while I had a yarn to Neek.

"I gotta get going," Mace announced. He was bouncing tonight at one of the local clubs. "Am I gonna see you two later?" he questioned, pointing at Mickey and Trav.

"Probably, most definitely," Trav yahooed.

"Fuck. Just don't give me a reason to kick your arses out."

Mickey scoffed and flipped Mace the bird as Trav, again, replied for them both, "You can sober drive us home after shut down."

"I *can,* as long as you let me do my job without being dipshits."

That was where I joined the conversation. "Well, if you're bringing those two home, then don't expect me to be there."

"Why? Where you gonna be?" Mace smirked.

I took a sip of coke. "Dunno yet."

My attention couldn't help be drawn across the fire to Lil, who was playing slaps with a rolling drunk Kimmie. Mace clapped me on the shoulder and gave me a look I couldn't quite decipher.

"I'll see you tomorrow," he murmured on his way past.

Ignoring the jests being hurled at his back, Mace disappeared around the side of the house.

It was another three hours before Neek gave everyone the bums rush to finish their drinks and get in the car if they wanted a ride to town. I glanced down at Lil where she was snuggled against my side, and caught her and Mickey glaring daggers at each other.

I was beginning to get used to their way of communicating now, so I didn't think anything of it until her hand landed on my thigh, suggestively close to my crotch.

Drawing her closer, I stooped to speak against the shell of her ear. "Now who's the one playing with fire?"

She turned her wide eyes on me and my heart skipped a fucking beat. When I licked my lips, it drew her sight downwards.

"Not sure yet," she crooned.

I flicked a look across the fire to find Neek watching us with a knowing smirk. Holding his eye contact, I dropped my head to speak in undertones to Lil again.

"You coming home with me or am I staying here?"

I felt her shift then her face became level with mine. Looking me square in the eye, she issued a statement I was sure held deeper meaning.

"If you want me, all of me, you'll know where to find me."

In other words; don't waste your time if you aren't going to man up and take a risk. And, if she had been anyone else, I would have walked away at that very moment. With Lil, however, that wasn't happening.

She got up and collected an armful of empties then disappeared around the side of the garage where the bin was kept. Mickey straightened and sprinted after her moments later.

Filled with alarm, I followed. Lil ran into my chest as Mickey stalked off down the driveway.

"What the fuck just happened?" I demanded.

"I think someone was watching us," Lil puffed.

With a sharp shove that propelled Lil back into the back yard, I took off after Mickey and together we methodically searched the front yard and street. Coming up frustratingly empty, Mickey and I exchanged a look that didn't need words to explain what we both thought.

Once the crew—minus Mace—were all gathered around the fire again, Mickey turned to me.

"You're staying with her tonight, right?"

Seeing his clenched fists, I cautiously answered. "I am now."

Mickey looked at Lil and she nodded.

"Keep her safe while I'm out. Who knows who the fuck that was. Hopefully it was just a one off."

Him and Lil shared a moment again.

I darted my glare between them. "What am I missing?"

Lil hesitated a beat, glancing at Mickey before she spoke. "When I got home from night shift the other night, I'm positive someone was watching me. Mickey checked it out but there was nothing." She shivered. "Gah, it's giving me the creeps!"

"Pack an overnight bag. You're coming back to mine tonight."

She stared at me long and hard, not arguing, yet not agreeing. Eventually, her subtle nod was all the approval I needed.

Lil made her way upstairs to pack while Trav doused the fire. Mickey was by my side within the same instant, and I cut in before he spoke.

"When I arrived this morning, there was a green Holden station wagon parked across the street. It took off as soon as I got close. I didn't think anything of it at the time, but now it seems odd. Might be nothing though."

Mickey cursed and scrubbed a hand through his hair, leaving it wild and unruly.

"Why didn't you say earlier? Fuck. Maybe I need to rain check on town and hang out with Lil."

"Mate, I didn't think anything of it. Besides, I've got it sorted." I tried not to snap while throwing one arm wide and gesturing to myself. "I'll be with her."

Mickey eyed me, his jaw twitching. "I can't say I'm over the fucking moon about this, and I appreciate you watching out for Lil, but I'm gonna say this nonetheless; don't fuck with her. She's not as hard-ass as she appears. Underneath her tough exterior, she never fully recovered from her last relationship. I don't want it to happen again."

"Demons are demons, that doesn't mean I want to dance with them."

Mickey's lip curled. "What the fuck does that even mean?"

Not bothering to hide my smirk, I clarified for him. "It means, I fucking know how it feels to be broken inside and I've seriously considered my options when it comes to Lil, not wanting to dredge hers up all over again. I'm an all-in or nothin' kind of guy."

"So, which one are you with her?" he challenged.

I glared at him for a moment, fucked off that he was cornering me into making admissions I wasn't yet ready to voice out loud.

"All in," I growled into his face.

He grabbed the front of my shirt and fisted it roughly. "You'd better fucking mean it."

"How about you watch where your own piss is landing instead of focusing on everyone else's."

His eyes flared at my insinuation then he stilled. I looked over his shoulder to see Lil, with hands on her hips standing next to Kimmie on the deck. Lil was leaning into the glare she aimed at the back of Mickey's head. She then gasped as her eyes snapped to me.

"What did you say to her?" I demanded, fisting his shirt in return.

"You'll need to ask Lil for yourself."

"You know what? It's a pity Kimmie doesn't have a big brother to stick up for her, because if I was her brother, I would beat the *fuck* out of you. Like I said, focus on where *you* are pissing."

"You're an asshole," Mickey spat, giving a little shove before he stepped away.

I headed to my motorbike. "I know," I snapped.

Mickey gave Lil a quick lecture about staying safe then aimed a final glare at me before he climbed into the backseat of Neek's car, with Trav and Kimmie in tow.

Trav hollered out the window as they peeled down the street, headed for town.

I waited until Lil climbed on behind me and pressed her breasts against my back before I started my bike and followed in the same direction as the crew.

The ride to mine passed too quickly; I could have ridden all night with Lil sitting pretty behind me. Riding with her today had been fucking amazing. The ease we now had together, not needing to say a single word to communicate, was refreshing to say the least.

Arriving home, I locked my Victory in the garage next to Mace's Hog and headed for the house.

"C'mon, Sunshine."

Lil stepped up to the side door and unlocked it.

"You have a key?"

She turned at my surprise. "Sure I have a key. Why?"

I floundered, not wanting to get possessive over the fact she had a key to Mace's house.

"No reason."

"Uh huh," she drawled.

Flicking on a couple of lights, I grabbed her hand and tugged her towards my room, practically catapulting her over the threshold in some sort of fucked up display of alpha rivalry.

I tossed her bag in the corner then stalked towards her, blindsided by a primal instinct I had long since forgotten. I needed this, I needed Lil, and I needed her right fucking now.

"PJs time?" Lil asked, her breathing already growing shallow.

"If you packed flannelette, then hell no."

Her laughter bubbled freely and she stepped away half a pace. I countered the distance by taking a step towards her, scrutinising her every reaction. The barest hint of a smile tugged her lips.

"Maybe I'll have to sleep naked then."

Christ.

"You provoking me, Sunshine?"

Lil scoffed. "Says the person who all but threw me into their room."

I took another stalk forward. "Do you want to leave?"

And another step to counter the small pace she took around the corner of my bed.

She snorted. "As if you would listen if I said yes."

"That doesn't answer my question, Lil. Do you want to leave?"

I rounded the corner, still stalking towards her as she stepped onto my bed and bent her knees for balance. Her eyes flickered with glee as she tormented me.

"Do *you* want me to?"

"You're in my room, aren't you?" I countered.

"Doesn't answer my question, Batman."

Not caring that I was still wearing boots, I stepped onto my bed and managed to snag Lil's wrist as she made to jump off the other side. The unexpected tug sent her bouncing onto the mattress with a shout of surprise. I fell to my knees beside her and held her arms outstretched either side of her body while she giggled and squirmed.

There, in that moment, I could hand on heart say I was happy and Lil was the sole reason for that.

I waited until her laughter petered out. It was then that I looked down at her with utmost sincerity.

"No, I don't want you to leave."

Her softened reply matched her concerned expression. "Gage, after what happened last time, I shouldn't stay in here with you. I can use the office."

Although there was minor relief that she hadn't suggested she sleep in Mace's room, I was angry at myself from putting those doubts in her head in the first place. Last time was a one off; I wasn't going to let that happen again. Not for my sake, but for Lil's.

"I haven't stopped wanting you, Lil. In fact, not being able to have you makes me want you even more."

Her sight dropped to my lips as she issued a whispered challenge. "Prove it."

I lowered myself until my dick pressed between her legs.

"Feel this? I haven't been this hard over a woman for years, Lil. You fucking do this to me. Every goddamn day for weeks, you've given my dick a mind of its own. Only thing now is, I want what he wants."

The way she bit into her lower lip had me smirking with satisfaction.

"And what's that?" she asked coyly.

My voice dropped low as I forced out one word. "You,"

Lil's mouth parted in an invitation I wasn't passing up. I sealed mine over hers, my tongue immediately seeking hers, unable to wait a moment longer to get a taste of her. She was sweet from the lemonade she'd been drinking all night long, and it was her drawn out hum that was the catalyst for our kiss turning heated and filled with untameable desire.

Riding leathers got removed with urgency that left us both reeling and breathing hard. There wasn't a pause until she was under me again, completely naked and looking so fucking delectable.

With my hand splayed wide, I smoothed it up the back of her thigh until her ass filled my palm. Her fingers weaving through my hair brought our mouths back together, and the sharp tug on my scalp super-charged my lust. Each movement, every sensation and sound, fuelled my hunger for her.

I groaned as soon as my dick slid through the wetness between her legs. "We're so fucking doing this."

Before Lil could reply, my lips were back on hers in a frantic, wild, uncontrolled kiss that was both punishing and demanding.

Reaching back to tug Lil's legs until her knee was bent by her shoulder, I kept my hold on her ankles as I ducked, needing at have at least one taste of her before my dick did. She gasped as my tongue made contact between her legs, and fuck me if I didn't go back for seconds.

So goddamn sweet, so goddamn perfect.

The squeeze Lil had around my dick when I finally slipped inside her had me clenching my jaw and all but praying I could keep my shit together for more than a single minute.

Lil's body, so smooth and soft under my calloused palms, was faultless. Each of her curves, her blemishes, her imperfections, were goddamn perfect.

The whirlwind of lust that followed was a blur of panting, moaning, cursing, hair pulling, begging, and demanding right before pushing her over the edge, was everything I hoped for and more than I ever imagined it would be with her.

With a final hard thrust, I shuddered and groaned my way through one hell of an orgasm. Lil's legs fell wide, fully relaxed either side of my thighs, as I lay panting into her dampened neck.

"Holy shit, that was one hundred times better than I'd imagined," I confessed, my lips coming to rest where her pulse raced against my lips.

Her hands lazily grazed up and down my back, leaving goose bumps in their wake.

There was a smile to her voice. "So, you've imagined doing me?"

"*Fucking* you. And yeah, every night since you seared me with a look of pure disgust like I was the Devil's own spawn."

Lil's body vibrated in laughter. "Well, I hope I lived up to expectations."

"Exceeded them, babe."

"And it wasn't disgust. It was rage."

I pulled back and questioned her with a single look.

"I can't explain it. Just that you infuriated me from the moment you opened your mouth and I looked up to see you glaring down at me."

"I bet that's changed," I drawled.

Lil scoffed softly. "I bet it hasn't."

"I bet I can make you come again, and just as quickly."

A wicked grin spread across her lips. "I bet you can't."

"I'll prove it. Just gimme ten to recharge."

I rolled and tucked her into my side, holding her close as she settled with her head on my chest.

Despite the maelstrom of emotions and turmoil ebbing and flowing within me, I was surprised to find that regret and guilt weren't one of them this time. And, for the first time in a long time, I was okay with that.

An hour later, I had Lil sleeping beside me with her ass nestled in my crotch. My arm remained under her head as she breathed heavily into my inner elbow.

A tiny broken part of me was pieced back together tonight, and having Lil sleeping in my arms was healing yet another fragment.

25

GAGE

RUMBLING TO A stop in Lil and Mickey's backyard a week later, I'm borderline desperate to get my hands on Lil again. Mickey had better leave pronto because, after a full day at work, I now had plans.

I knocked on the door and turned the knob without waiting for someone to let me in.

Locked.

What the? They locked me out?

I was mid-turn to go around the front when I heard hasty footsteps inside jogging in my direction. Mickey opened the door as little as possible and darted a suspicious look through the gap. Taking in my scowl with an eye roll, he swung the door wider and ushered me in like we were part of an undercover operation of the highest security.

"What's all that about? You would've heard my bike when I arrived..."

He looked worried and his frown was more prominent than usual.

"We're being extra careful at the moment."

Lil came bounding down the stairs with a spring in her step, apparently not burdened with the same dilemma as her brother.

"Hey, Sunshine, how are you?" I hugged her and kissed her briefly while Mickey huffed in impatience.

I spun Lil so her back was to my front, then got down to business. "What's going on guys?"

I wasn't all intuitive and shit, but something in the air felt off.

Mickey folded his arms and leaned his ass against the bench. "That car was hanging around and it's making me chary as hell. I've noticed it parked in a few different places up and down the street now, but always facing our direction. Describe the car you noticed."

I rested my chin on Lil's head as I gave him the description. "Dark green Holden Commodore station wagon, older model, tinted windows. Other than that, it was run of the mill, factory wheels et cetera, no other mods that I noticed."

Mickey started pacing. "It has to be the same car without a doubt. It's fucking weird I tell you, and I don't have a good feeling. You sure you have no idea who this could be?" he asked Lil, who simply shook her head.

Mickey huffed as he snatched up his keys, phone and wallet.

"Well, I've got places to be and people to see." He aimed a finger at me. "I'm leaving you in charge."

"Like there was ever any question about that," I drawled.

I ignored Lil's cry of indignation; Mickey's comment was vague, plus his body language was shifty as hell.

"Where you off to?"

Mickey ignored my question, which only fuelled my suspicions.

"Well, seeing as I'm 'in charge'," I air quoted, "we won't be climbing out of bed before the crack of dawn to bail your ass out of jail this time."

Mickey's nostrils flared as he inhaled deeply. "And likewise, I don't want our couch to be tainted any more than it already is."

Despite his warning, I got the feeling it was issued purely to keep up appearances.

"No promises either way," I replied.

"Hold your tongue mate, that shit I don't need to know about. I'm outties."

Lil and I sniggered as he made his way to the door. He halted and spun on his heel, holding up a hand while listing off the 'rules' for the night.

"I'll be back late tonight so don't wait up, don't leave Lil alone in the house, don't leave the doors unlocked, don't put the lights on without closing the curtains first, and for fucks sake, *don't fuck on the couch*."

"Trust me mate, we will *not* be waiting up."

He flipped me off as Lil pushed him out the door and closed it on his mutterings about how he doesn't know how he puts up with this bullshit. Lil giggled and securely locked the door then gave Mickey one last wave from the window.

I needed to feel her body in my hands again, wasting no time in wrapping my arms around her waist, pulling her back to my chest and peppering kisses along the curve of her neck. Her body relaxed for a few moments then tensed again. She spun in my arms and tugged on the zipper of my leather jacket.

"You'd better take this off, Batman."

"Layer for layer, Sunshine. What are you going to remove?" I skipped my sight over her singlet top and tiny shorts, my mouth already salivating either way.

She snorted. "I'm not cooking while naked. The risk of burns is real."

I chuckled against her forehead and dropped my hands to cup her ass. "No, that's not wise. However, I think you'd cook a hell of a lot better with your shorts off."

"Hey, if I'm removing my shorts, you're removing your entire top half."

"Deal!" I declared without a pause and flicked the button of her shorts.

Lil threw her head back and laughed when I tugged them down and removed them with a growl. When I remained crouched, highly distracted by her underwear,

Lil grabbed the collar of my jacket and hauled me to standing. She stepped back a pace and clicked her fingers.

"Remove it, now."

"Damn, you're feisty. I like it," I drawled.

"Just focus on taking your gear off," she feigned seriousness.

I muttered under my breath about getting *her* off as I shucked my jacket then tugged my shirt over my head. I threw them both at the stairs where I'd tossed her shorts then smirked when I turned back to Lil.

If eyes could fuck, then that's exactly what hers were doing.

"Hungry, Sunshine?"

Lil snorted and smiled coyly. "Always." Her eyes snapped to clarity. "Seriously though, I need to get dinner on, then, we can do…" She waved her arm around. "Stuff."

I chuckled and stepped into her space, planting a kiss on her lips that lasted longer than I intended.

"Let me help."

"Okay," Lil breathed then pointed at the knife rack. "Cut the veges?"

"Now that I can do." Grabbing a knife and deftly flicking it through my fingers, I made light work of my allotted task.

"What *are* you? A sous chef?" she exclaimed.

I glanced at Lil's astonished expression and grinned. "Impressed much?"

"Yeah, I'm impressed! I haven't even cut up half the chicken breast." She slapped the side of her knife on said chicken. "You know how to cook?"

"Weeell, cook no, not really, but when I was at high school I had a part time job as a kitchen hand at a local restaurant. Part of my job was prep. It's amazing how fast you learn to chop properly when your fingers are on the line; getting sliced up gets old real fast."

"Well, no bloodshed tonight, I'm off the clock," she joked. "I hope you like curry?"

"The spicier the better."

I side-smiled at her while I continued to slice, dice and be fuckin' awesome.

Our arms bumped a little as we worked, and I caught whiffs of her perfume as she moved around me. So many questions raced through my mind as we worked; there was still a huge amount I didn't know about her, and I wanted to find out everything all at once. Sure, I knew *of* things and how important her friends and family were to her, but she kept me guessing at every turn. Just when I thought I had part of her figured out, she would surprise me all over again.

As it was, Lil was first to cautiously voice her own questions.

"Do you ever wonder why we are so drawn to each other?"

Jesus, could she read my mine too?

The thought caused momentary panic within me. Seeing me startle, she hastily added, "Like, you can feel the crazy energy when we touch, aye? And the fact that you just happened to move up here and Mace just happened to invite you round, and..." she frowned looking for the right words. "It seems too coincidental, don't you think?"

I nodded slowly, letting her words sink in while trying to formulate a response.

Carefully setting down the knife then leaning against the bench, I took her in. The mere fact that I had *wanted* to be around her after all the heartbreak in my life meant that Lil was as rare as they came.

"That is something I ask myself multiple times a day. I find you in my thoughts more and more when I work, when I ride, and when I sleep. The more I try to resist, the more you pull me in. It just feels... right."

That's the best way I could explain what I didn't understand. Putting feelings into words was bloody hard and something I'd always struggled with.

"Gage...?"

When she didn't continue, I hummed in response.

"Who's Lotte?"

I felt the blood drain from my face and all rational thought left my mind. Gripping the bench as I fought against the spots appearing in the outskirts of my vision, I focused on forcing the air in and out of my lungs.

I was snapped back to reality by Lil's warm touch on my forearm. "I'm sorry," she whispered. "I didn't want to ask, but I know she means a lot to you."

I couldn't meet her eyes; I just hung my head as I uttered the most incredulous words. "Can you read my mind?"

She startled and shifted her weight slightly.

"Er, no. Mickey is the only one I share that ability with."

The relief from her response was short lived. She had asked about Lotte, and hearing her voice Lot's name sent me spiralling as bitterness pitched and rolled within my gut.

"What do you know about Lotte?" My voice was rough, demanding, unforgiving.

It took every ounce of willpower not to yell at Lil, not to storm from the room and lose my shit. I needed to hear what Lil had to say, and since she had broached the subject using Lotte's name, the very name neither Mace nor I had given her, I needed to find out how Lil discovered her name.

Sensing my distress, Lil tugged at the hem of her t-shirt. "I don't want to upset you, Gage."

"Too late. Tell me."

I had to strain to receive her hesitant reply over the white noise drowning out my hearing. "Okay. Not long after we first meet, I dreamt of her. Then, when you approached me in the spa that night, I knew she was attached to you somehow."

Letting out the breath I'd been holding, I fought hard to find my voice.

"Remember how I told you about my serious relationship that ended a few years ago?"

Lil nodded.

"Lotte."

"I'm really sorry, Gage. I really didn't mean to pry..."

I forced myself to reassure her, to fob off how much she had rocked me with that one question. "It's okay, Lil, you weren't to know. Now let's get this cooking before you resort to cannibalism."

She cast me a small smile that was marred with sadness. When her hand reached for the pan, I snagged it and squeezed gently. We didn't talk for a long while after that, instinctively working around each other as we cooked dinner.

"So..." Lil broke the silence. "Moira's all that and a bag of chips."

I paused, and frowned because I legit had zero idea of what she was referring to. "Moira?"

Lil turned a stellar grin on me. "Your bike."

"Since when the fuck is her name Moira?" I boomed through a laugh.

"Since I named her when we went for a ride the other day."

"You can't call her Moira," I deadpanned.

"And why not?" Lil sassed.

I gawked at her like she was fucking crazy and spread my arms wide.

"Why the fuck do you think? Moira is not a suitable name for a badass muscle bike."

"Wow. I'm sure all the Moira's in the world are disappointed right now," Lil mumbled.

"I'd rather call her Blanche!" I scoffed.

Lil's jaw dropped. "You definitely cannot call her Blanche."

"And why not?"

Lil rolled her eyes like I should know the answer already.

"Because, Blanche is a Vesper name, not a muscle bike name."

I shook my head while stirring the curry. "This conversation is so fucked up. Heaven forbid we have babies and you name them," I sniggered.

My heart dropped as soon as I heard what I'd just said. Lil gasped and tried to cover it as a covert cough. Acutely aware of what I insinuated, I cleared my throat and shrugged like it was no biggy; even though it was a *huge* fucking deal.

"Hypothetically speaking, don't freak out."

Lil avoided eye contact as she grabbed plates and cutlery. "So, when you gonna let me take Moira for a spin?"

I choked on an inhale and pounded my chest. "It's not fucking *Moira!*" I spluttered then added, "And that shit ain't happening, Sunshine, so don't ask again."

Lil feigned a pout. "And why not?"

"Because, only gu-"

"Don't you dare say that only guys can ride or I swear I will steal Moira in the night."

I swiped a hand over my beard, praying for some goddamn sanity.

"Christ, you're going to be the end of me. What I meant to say was, it's a big bike, Lil, and, well, you're *not* big."

She snorted and poured two glasses of wine. "That's a backhanded compliment if ever I've heard one. Besides, I've ridden Mace's before."

I glared as she beamed me with a wide grin. Regardless of how many beats that look made my heart skip, that shit wasn't happening.

"Answer's still no."

"Your loss," she sang and turned to the fridge, swinging the door wide. Lil bent at the waist (despite not needing to) and graced me with an eyeful of ass and panties that had my jeans growing tighter by the second.

"I know what you're doing, Sunshine, and it ain't gonna work," I growled without diverting my eyes for a goddamn second.

"I don't know what you mean," she snickered.

With a little bum wiggle that had me hiding my shit-eating grin behind my palm, I continued to watch the spectacle as Lil moved around the kitchen to set the table.

"Like what you see, Batman?"

A rumble climbed up my throat. "Don't tease me, Lil."

She motioned for me to sit on a dining chair then straddled my lap. Her lips brushed against my lips, causing my hands to slip to her ass.

"Make you a bet."

"No."

Lil nipped at my neck, and fuck me if it wasn't working.

"Let me ride Moira."

My grip tightened as I summoned as much conviction to my voice as I could under the circumstances.

"The only way your ass is touching the seat of my bike is while you're behind me with your thighs squeezing mine."

LIL

"THE ONLY WAY *your ass is touching that seat is while you're behind me with your thighs squeezing mine.*"

Gah, his words just obliterated my will to ever wear panties again. I hid my smile by ducking my head and gently biting Gage's neck again, secretly smiling when his breath grew ragged and strained.

His hands moved from my ass, smoothing their way up my back in a way that had me arching into his touch before they wove through my untamed long hair. With a gentle tug, he tilted my head to meet his gaze. Despite the jovial twinkle in his eyes, there was an unmistakable edge of warning blackening those same depths.

"You're not gonna seduce me into agreement, Lil."

I climbed off his lap while offering a proposal. "If I can touch Moira before you stop me, then I can take her for a spin."

He shook his head and stood, making me feel much smaller than I was. "It's not Moira. You're a shit stirrer, Sunshine!" he leered. "And my answer remains no."

I couldn't stop the devilish smile forming on my lips. "I'll stop calling your bike Moira if you win."

His eyes snapped from my legs to my eyes. "You're on."

Gage moved a mere split second after I ran for the door. Blindly grabbing at the dining chair as I pass, I tipped it into his path. It hit the floor with a loud bang and I heard Gage curse loudly as he jumped over it. That small moment of distraction bought me enough time to unlock the door and leg it across the deck.

A sinuous forearm snaked around my waist just as I reached out and slapped Moira's handgrip. Gage let out a grunt then a string of expletives as he swung me with the momentum I'd gathered, holding my back tightly against his front when we came to a stop. We both puffed heavily from the excursion, then a giddy giggle escaped my lips. I'd just nailed his ass.

Gage's low growl vibrated against my back before I felt his teeth nip my neck.

"Dirty tactics. I'm gonna have to teach you a lesson."

"I thought you'd be more onto it after growing up with three sisters," I teased, tilting my head to grin up at him.

He set his chin on my cheek and scratched the shit out of my skin with his beard. As I laughed and struggled in his arms, he spun me so our chests bumped together. That's when I caught the pain in his gaze. The twisted torment that transported him a million miles away while physically remaining present with me. The suffering I saw had the playful smile slipping from my face.

"Hey," I said softly and reached up to touch his face. "Are you okay?"

He forced the misery from his features, however, the detachment in his eyes persisted. His voice was flat, void of all feeling and emotion while he locked eyes with me.

"Just figuring out how to tell you, you ain't riding my bike."

"Na uh, deals a deal, Batman."

The nickname accompanied with the little slap to his chest roused the smallest of smiles to his lips before the frown resumed.

"Some deals are made to be broken."

I scoffed. "The only people who say that are the ones who lose!"

"Sweet baby Jesus," Gage muttered and slipped a hand from the small of my back to scrub it over his face. "Why the *hell* did I agree to that," he reprimanded himself.

When his attention fell back to me, the intensity and conviction radiating from his expression caught my breath. "You've got me doing all kinds of crazy shit, and I'm torn between loving you and hating you for it."

I froze.

Did he mean *loving me* loving me? Or was he just saying that to emphasise his irritation. My feelings for him were growing stronger each day, much past the liking stage, but had definitely not reached the *loving* stage yet.

"Hey, Lil! Where'd you go?"

"Huh? What?"

From the look on his face, he knew exactly where my mind had wandered, and that he also realised how his words had come across.

"Were you talking to Mickey?"

I frowned until comprehension took hold. I smiled shyly and made light of the situation by flicking his nipple.

"Not just then. I uh, just had a silly moment. Ignore me," I added, waving him off. "Now, more importantly, back to Moira."

Gage was visibly relieved for the change in subject, however he strode over to stand protectively in front of Moira with his arms crossed over his chest. His shirtless physique drew me in; the arms, biceps, pecs, broody scowl, penetrating eyes, the tats…

"When you've finished eye-fucking me, I'm gonna reiterate that you ain't riding my goddamn bike."

27

GAGE

I STAYED THE entire night, uninterrupted, at Lil's. The more I consumed her, the more I craved.

It was as she lay asleep in my arms, still holding me tight in her sleep, that the nagging voice in my head reminded me that I needed to make a major decision; one that would lead me back to The Bay for a short while. I had apologies and goodbyes to make.

After internally debating back and forth, my head finally caught up to where my heart was, recognising that the time had come to put my past respectfully to the side so I could wholeheartedly move forward with Lil. Never in a thousand years did I think for a second that I would ever consider a future with another woman. Not when Lotte would always own a large portion of my heart.

Lately I had discovered that love changes as time passes, but it would never be forgotten.

Lil's scent brought me back to the present as she snuggled closer. I was still fuming inside over what she had me agreeing to do. I still couldn't believe that my judgement had been so clouded that I had agreed in the first place. There was no way in hell I was caving. No fucking way.

On the flip side, Lil's spontaneity and enthusiasm were parts that I loved about her. As infuriating as it was, it was refreshing in the most unexpected way.

The thing that miffed me the most was that I usually *never* let people talk me into things I was dead against. I don't know how Lil did it. The profound affection and fondness I felt for Lil had me by the balls. Those feelings weren't going to go away; they were real and growing stronger each day.

I slowly peeled myself up to peer at the clock on her nightstand. Just after six a.m. It was too goddamn early on a Sunday morning to be awake.

Lil turned in her sleep once I settled on my side and buried her face into my chest. Her legs intertwined with mine in an effortless move to have as much skin contact as possible.

God it felt good to have a woman in my arms again. One that I wanted. Craved. And, dare I say it, *needed*.

A tickling sensation on my nipple made me startle then smile. I linked our fingers together then slit one eye open. Lil's big morning eyes looked back at me. I lazily set my fingers above her eyes then dragged them downwards, closing her lids with my touch.

"Not gonna lie, it's fucking creepy you watching me while I sleep. And since when are you such a morning person?"

She turned her smile on me. "Since I got laid last night."

I sniggered and rolled close, setting my chin on her stomach. "I'll keep that in mind."

"So, have you reconsidered?"

I groaned loudly. I was kidding myself in hoping that overnight she would have developed amnesia of our bet.

"I knew I should have slipped you some roofies last night," I joked then hummed when she pulled me on top of her. "Now this is more like it."

Her fingers danced their way up and down my back.

"Answer's still no, Lil."

Her hand slipped lower, teasing me without touching my dick. "Still, shall we get up and go for an early ride together?"

"And *how* is this going to get me *out* of bed earlier?" I demanded.

Lil gave me a hefty shove off her body then moved to the edge of her bed. Lying on my back and watching her stand up, I bit back a frustrated growl at seeing her bare skin but no longer feeling it against mine.

A pair of underwear sailed over her shoulder and landed beside me.

"Get your ass dressed."

I scoffed. "Jesus, you're relentless."

"Would you prefer me meek?"

"Fuck no. Where's the fun in that."

"Exactly," Lil sassed over her shoulder.

Her eyes dropped to my dick where it let the world know just how much it appreciated her naked body. She walked across the room without taking her eyes off it.

"For once you're lost for words," I smirked.

Her eyes snapped to mine and a blush slammed onto her cheeks. She turned away, muttering about clothes, but came up woefully empty handed aside from a scrap of cloth hanging from her finger.

"You owe me new underwear since you hulked out and ripped these last night."

The dark blue scrap of lace was tossed in my direction where I plucked it from mid-air.

"Babe, if I get to rip them off you every time, I will buy you a truck load of every kind of sexy underwear known to mankind."

"Well that's, reassuring, I guess..." Lil's eye roll turned into a look of blatant shock as I picked up my jeans.

"Did you just pocket my *worn* underwear?"

I didn't bother hiding my devilish grin. "Fuck yeah I did."

"That's just creepy."

I stalked towards her and pulled her body flush with mine, letting my fingers roam over her back and ass.

"Still want to go for a ride?"

"Yes! Stop distracting me, Batman!"

Lil went to her wardrobe in a hurry to find her gear while I pulled on my jeans. Her wearing clothes didn't help ease my throbbing erection that I strategically adjusted while doing up the zipper.

We ate breakfast at breakneck speed—purely at Lil's insistence after I insisted that we actually eat in the first place. Before I could do a quick security check, she swung the back door open and headed outside. My lecture about complacency dissipated off the tip of my tongue when I glanced over her shoulder at my motorbike.

"Are you *fucking serious!*" I roared and shoved past her.

"Ouch, batman, what the hell?"

I crossed the lawn in a matter of split seconds and smoothed my hand over the huge gouge that ran the entire length of Moira's gas tank.

I couldn't believe my eyes. The more I examined the damage, the more my vision clouded with anger so fierce I wanted to punch the fuck out of something.

Lil came to my side and gasped. "Someone *keyed* your bike? What the fuck!"

I couldn't answer, I was too busy tearing at my hair and eyeballing the deep scratch, as if glaring hard enough would magically make it disappear. To say I was livid didn't even cut it. I was fucking ropable to the point if I ever laid hands on the asshole who did it, it would be to squeeze the ever-loving life out of them. There were two things you didn't fuck with; one was a man's missus, and the other was his ride.

Mickey's footsteps stomped across the deck.

"Mate!" he yelled then clapped eyes on the damage. "Jesus fucking Christ."

"When did you get home?" I demanded.

He held up his palms. "Early hours. No one was out here; I had a look around to make sure."

Mickey and Lil shared a look that I didn't need to be a mind reader to know what was said. The random shit that kept happening over the last few weeks was beginning to increase.

"Fuck, a custom paint job isn't cheap, mate."

"You think I don't know that already?" I roared, my attention back on the damage.

"I'll ask Trav to hook you up with a guy he knows; he owes me big time after the other weekend," Mickey deadpanned.

I would have chuckled at the memory of them getting locked up if I wasn't sickened to the pit of my stomach.

"Poor Moira," Lil muttered.

"Who the hell is Moira?" Mickey exclaimed, eyes wild.

I scoffed a humourless laugh as Lil explained. As soon as my eyes hit the damage again, I wanted to fucking cry!

"So, what did you get up to last night?" I asked Mickey in an attempt to take my mind off what was killing me more with each passing second.

"None of your business. And, by the way, *why* is there a pair of Lil's shorts on the stairs?" He shot me a dirty look.

"I need to call Kimmie," Lil mumbled.

Mickey stiffened and his eyes flared briefly before he composed his face to appear carefully nonchalant. Lil didn't notice the flash of alarm; her attention was still on the motherfucking scratch, but I sure as hell noticed.

"Er, why?" Mickey asked suspiciously.

I smirked at him, wondering whether his odd behaviour at the mention of Kimmie had something to do with where he was last night. And he knew what I was thinking too by the 'shut your mouth' glare he aimed my way.

"*Because*," Lil emphasised her exasperation. "Kimmie and I are meant to be going shopping this afternoon."

Mickey paled a shade. He was a big dude but right now he was shuffling like a nervous teenager. His demeanour changed instantly when he saw me grinning despite my inner turmoil. Mickey's eyes narrowed on me and his jaw clenched. I knew that look and I understood it completely; the instinctual need to defend thy sister's honour was strong for any brother. And I also knew the type of comment that would drive any brother batshit crazy.

"We fucked," I mouthed and my smirk grew. Holding up three fingers where Lil couldn't see, I continued our soundless conversation. "Three times."

Mickey pressed his lips together as his nostrils flared again. I had hit right on the nerve. He threaded both hands through his hair, no doubt trying to erase the vision from his mind. There was no denying that I found it bloody hilarious being on the giving end instead of the receiving end.

"Goddammit, Lil!"

"*What!*" She jumped at the sudden shout from Mickey. "Jeez, you obviously didn't get laid last night, you're in a right ass of a mood."

"Or maybe he did and that's why he's..."

Lil savagely interrupted me. "Whatever! Josh, go ring Trav. She stepped up and squeezed my forearm. "You ready to go?"

Mickey's voice cut through the early morning air. "You're not letting her ride, are you?"

"No!" I growled over a muttered complaint coming from Lil's mouth.

"Break her and I'll break you, you know that, aye?"

I turned and met his challenge. "Mickey, I have three sisters, I know *exactly* what you mean."

He gave me a quick nod. As rocky as our 'friendship'—or whatever our relationship could be called—that was one part of the guy code that we both understood loud and clear. Our man to man conversation ended with Lil rolling her eyes and stepping closer to Mickey.

"I think we need to let Dad know about this." She didn't sound happy, and he didn't look happy.

"I know," Mickey murmured. "Fuck, I seriously can't deal with this today."

"First things' first; get Trav to ring me after you've called in your favour," Lil called over her shoulder as she led me towards my ride.

I swung a leg over Moira then winked at Lil before she climbed on. The bone deep rumbling thrummed through my body as soon as I hit the start switch. It served to take the edge off my anger over the gouge across the tank.

Once Lil was settled, I did a circuit of the backyard while Mickey stood with his arms folded over his chest, glaring.

Life lit within my soul when we peeled out onto the street. The exhilarating speed combined with the woman I wanted sitting behind me made me one smug son of a bitch.

28

LIL

AFTER A FULL-ON day at work tending to injured and sick people, I desperately sought the relaxation that could only be achieved by lounging on the couch while watching a movie. My phone ringing caused me to jump a little. Saying that I'd been edgy over the last couple of days was an understatement. At work it was fine, but as soon as I was home alone, the paranoia crept in.

Pressing a hand to my chest, I answered breathlessly.

"Hey, Trav. Wassup."

"Hey yol, Lil. Mickey said something about Gage's bike getting keyed? What the fuck?"

I sighed and turned the TV volume down. "Tell me about it. Mickey's on night's this week and I'm jumping at every little sound."

"Just say the word and I'll come hang out. But only if you make cookies," he added, munching on something while speaking.

I scoffed. "That'll be the day. You go through a whole freaking batch at once! You're a pig, Trav."

He munched more in my ear before he deadpanned, "I'm frowning at you right now."

A smile appeared on my mouth. "Well, if you bring me those M&M's you still owe me, I might think about getting my bake on."

"Deal. Hey, I actually rang because I've got a contact for you to pass onto your personal magic stick." There was an obvious grin in his voice.

"Travis! That's none of your business. And just message me the deets."

More munching then the sound of drinking graced my ears. I rolled my eyes as I waited impatiently.

"Keep your panties on, if you're wearing any," Trav chuckled.

"Yes, because I sit around at home, by myself, and enjoy being naked from the waist down," I sassed.

Trav shouted a laugh. "Whatever floats your boat. Just make sure you've got the curtains closed. Seriously though, this guy is the best in the biz for custom paint jobs. His name is Connor, and just a heads up, he's a little rough around the edges but he knows his shit, okay."

"Okay, as long as he's not dodgy…"

Trav hummed as he swallowed. "He's done time, right, but he's all good now. He's the only guy I trust not to stuff up my paint jobs."

"Well, if he's up to your standards then he must be good."

"He is. It's all about *who* you know, baby."

I giggled as I listened to the fridge at Trav's house whoosh open then a bottle clink.

"I'm surprised you aren't at the garage still."

"Hit a snag," Trav replied simply. "I know it's gonna take years to restore her, but I want it done now, you know what I mean?"

Trav bought a Chevrolet Impala a couple of years ago with grand plans to restore it to its former glory. Obviously, that task was no mean feat.

"Sure do."

"Just messaged through Connor's contact details. Get Gage to ring him asap—he's a busy man but I've given him a heads up to expect a call from Gage."

My phone beeped.

"Thanks, Trav, you're awesome and you know it!"

I meant it too. If there was anything needing fixed or people needing contacted, Trav was our man.

He chuckled. "Damn right I know it. And anytime, Lil. I'll catch ya later."

I signed off then opened his message.

No matter how shit the situation was, Trav was always the one to add a joke to take the heat off. His *looking on the bright side* approach to life always made him a joy to be around. There hadn't yet been a situation that he couldn't handle.

I read through the information in Trav's text then realised my hands had turned sweaty at the thought of calling Gage.

My finger hovered over his name for what seemed like minutes. Finally deciding I was being stupid, I stabbed the connect button and waited.

"Sunshine," Gage answered my call as I pleaded with my heart to calm down and give me back my breath.

"H-" I had to stop and clear my throat. "Hey. I um..."

Completely thrown by his voice, all rational thought left my brain as I rallied to pull myself together.

His low chuckling came through the phone. "Are we doing phone sex, because I need to move if we are."

I choked, literally choked, at his question then blushed furiously when I heard Mace crack out a laugh in the background.

"No, that's not why I'm calling! I've got a contact from Trav to sort out Moira."

"It's not Moira."

"It is."

Before Gage could complain again, I relayed the information from Trav about Connor but assured him he was all above board, according to Trav. Gage didn't say much afterwards and I knew he was spewing about what had happened. Hell, I was and it wasn't even my bike!

"So…?"

"So, what?" Gage drawled.

"You gonna let me ride Moira?"

He cursed under his breath which ended in what sounded like a growl. I heard Mace ask what his problem was and I stayed quiet as they had a quick conversation.

"Lil," he explained to Mace.

Mace laughed. "Told you, mate."

"Fuck you."

"Hey! I'm still here you realise!" I yelled into the phone then heard Mace laugh a second time.

Gage's voice was low when he replied after a few beats of silence.

"Look, Lil, you're not riding my bike. End of."

"Why?" I challenged, irritated that he was still holding back from me.

He huffed then spoke quietly. "It's complicated."

"Try me."

"You're just gonna have to take my word for it."

I scoffed, hating that he was fobbing me off without an explanation. "Will I?"

"Yeah, you will," he countered, easily matching my stubbornness.

With a deep sigh, I pushed down the frustration. "It's been a crazy long day, Gage. I need to go. Goodbye, Batman."

I cut off his reply and tossed my phone onto the couch.

Sure, I could be headstrong when I wanted to be, and I know it annoyed the shit out of Mickey, but the thing was, up until now I was reasonably unchallenged. Gage was the only one who seriously tested my sanity.

Now completely uninterested in the movie, I clicked it off, messaged Gage Connor's contact details, double checked all the doors and windows downstairs, then made my way upstairs to run a bath. I started nights tomorrow and had to make the most of the uninterrupted bathroom time while Mickey was on shift.

29

GAGE

I FINISHED SAYING goodbye to the dial tone after Lil disconnected. Agitated by her dismissal, I chucked my phone on the coffee table and glared at it.

Sniggering came from my left. Turning my glare his way, Mace's wide grin instantly pissed me off.

"What?" I snapped.

Mace chortled through his explanation. "She won't back down, mate. Prepare yourself, because once Lil's mind is set to something, she's bloody relentless. And I'm going to go ahead and assume that you've had at it already, so that means you've already made the decision to commit to her."

"Quit with the assumptions and conclusions. I'm not gonna say that I regret my decision, but hell, she's gonna have to rein it in!"

Mace scoffed. "She won't change for anyone. And you don't want her to either. I can see how she comes alight around you, and it's obvious you dig that shit, regardless of your current mood."

"I'm dark as hell about my bike. How would you feel if anything happened to Monica?"

Mace's face darkened at my question.

"Exactly," I emphasised.

"Question, who's Moira?" he asked and cocked a brow.

"Fuck, don't you start too."

His laughter filled the room as he leaned forward and pointed at me. "She's named your Victory, hasn't she!"

I flipped him off with both hands. "Don't wanna talk about it."

Raking a hand through my hair then along my jaw, I struggled to get a grip. The darkness was heavy today, and the only good thing about the last twelve hours just hung up on me.

I cursed myself for not being honest with her, but I wasn't ready to share that part of myself. I really didn't know if I ever would be ready to say out loud what I went through. Also, I was worried that it would scare Lil off. I couldn't lose her, not now that I'd opened my heart again.

The thought gave me indigestion. I swallowed the rising bile then reached for my phone when it beeped. There was a pang beneath my ribs when I saw Lil's name. I felt an odd sense of disappointed relief when I saw it was nothing more than a quick text detailing Connor's phone number.

Giving Mace a final glare—which he ignored in favour of the TV—I slapped the phone to my ear and made my way out of the lounge. I had a bike to get fixed.

. . .

Arriving at Lil's place just after lunch, two days later, I pulled to a stop in the driveway and peered up at her window. She had her curtains still closed, presumably still asleep after a graveyard shift last night.

Knowing where the key was kept, I let myself in, sat the biscuit container on the bench then toed off my boots. I wasn't sure whether to call out, ring her, or creep upstairs.

After re-locking the door, I did two of the three; tentatively calling Lil's name as I made my way to her room. The bedroom door opened silently, and the only sound in the room was Lil's rhythmic breathing as she slept.

Shit, now I didn't want to wake her; she looked too damn peaceful and sweet. There was no way I could leave without saying goodbye, though.

"Lil," I whispered, a little louder.

Nothing. Not even a hint of rousing. I bent to see her up close, smiling while I looked over her wild dark-red hair splayed across the pillow, and the freckles on her sleep-pinkened cheeks.

"Sunshine," I murmured, softly touching her shoulder.

She snuffled a little, creating an adoring smile on my lips.

"Sunshine," I repeated with a slight shake of her shoulder.

The soft sweetness on her features instantly turned to alarm and fright. She lashed out as she woke to someone—me—standing beside her bed, uninvited, and apologising profusely for scaring the shit out of her.

"Gage! What the hell? Oh my God, I'm having heart palpitations," Lil wheezed and pressed both hands to her heaving chest.

As she sat up, her bewildered stare pegged me to the spot while the untamed storm of fright slowly receded from her hazel irises.

"Fuck, I'm really sorry to have scared you so bad."

She scoffed and rubbed her eyes, then finger combed through her hair.

"What did you expect was going to happen? I didn't hear you arrive." Her eyes narrowed. "Did you break in?"

"No, I used the outside key. And I really was trying to wake you slowly, I promise."

Lil huffed and pouted her lips, thoroughly unimpressed.

"Been asleep for long?"

"Oh, you mean before you broke into my house and woke me up?" she grumbled, leaning over to see the bedside clock. "A little over six hours."

"Here," I said, lifting the blankets and sliding into bed beside her. "Snuggle into me and sleep some more."

Her body didn't move while her eyes followed my movements, and there was a slight crease on her brow.

"Bathroom stop first."

My eyes were glued to her ass as she moved across the room and out of sight. I lay back with a stupid-ass grin on my face and waited with absolutely no intention to get naked. Lil was still in my thoughts when she re-appeared and slid against my body when I lifted the sheet for her.

"So, I know you didn't come here for lunch-break sex because you've kept your clothes on. What are you up to?"

My pulse quickened as I looked at her, wanting so bad to run my hand under her top, to feel her smooth stomach and peaked nipples. Instead, I cupped her cheek.

"I need to head back down to Tauranga for a short while, like a week or so. I've got a couple of people I need to visit and some loose ends to tie up."

"Oh." Lil said softly. "When do you leave? You're not on Moira, are you? I would have woken up when you arrived."

"I leave this afternoon, after this. But I couldn't go without saying goodbye to you in person. And no, my *Victory* is with Connor getting fixed while I'm gone."

She breathed a smile. "I'll miss you."

I kissed the tip of her nose. "I'll miss you too."

"Did Connor seem okay?"

I wrapped my arms around Lil and pulled her on top of me. "Yeah. He's patched, though. I saw the tat on his forearm. Hades' Horsemen. However, that doesn't mean he's not good at his job, and first impressions aside, he showed me his current work and Trav's right; the guy knows his shit."

Worry swam in her eyes. "You sure it's okay if he's part of a gang?"

"Babe, have you seen the asshole, tattooed man lying beneath you right now? People assume I'm one of those guys to stay away from, and you know as well as I do that I'm not a fucking crim. I chose to give the guy the benefit of the doubt."

"I didn't mean to offend you, Gage. I was just making sure you're okay with Trav's recommendation."

I nodded and trailed my hands down her back until her ass filled my palms. Squeezing as a groan came from my mouth, there was no secret that now I wanted sex before I left too. Lil rolled her hips against my hard-on then wiggled a little.

"Fuck, do that again," I murmured, already pulling her hips harder against mine.

Lil's smile was mischievous as she flicked her long hair to the side and held it off my face.

"What? This?"

My chest rumbled with another groan. "Yep, that. We're doing this," I declared and shoved her singlet up until her tits were in my hands.

Lil tugged it off and tossed it aside. Her body was gone from under my hands a moment later and my growl of protest turned into a hum of satisfaction when she worked my jeans undone and stood to pull them off.

My shirt was removed with one quick tug at the back of the collar, and my underwear was gone and kicked aside. Lil slid her panties down her legs then crawled up the bed until she was straddling my hips again.

I shook my head. "I want to kiss you while I fuck you, so this position ain't gonna work."

She didn't move. "Sit up."

Her hands braced on my chest as I sat with my back against the headboard. Wrapping my hands around the back of her neck, I guided her lips to mine.

"Now this is more like it."

My murmured words were cut off by Lil's tongue seeking mine before our lips had made the barest of contact. With my tongue sweeping against hers and her hands weaving through my hair, I gripped her by the hips and lifted her high enough to line up with her entrance. My low hum mixed with Lil's breathy exhale as she eased onto me, her fingers demanding my mouth back to hers.

Our movements were urgent, needy, blinded by lust that heightened then unexpectedly faded into something else. Lil's kiss slowed, deepened, sweeping me to a place where I knew she was showing me how she felt. My hands smoothed over her skin, my fingers exploring every part of her body I could reach while she took me slow and deep.

Gradually, our desire heightened again. I gripped Lil by the back of her neck and hip, my fingers anchoring her against me to sync our movements. It took all my willpower to tear her lips from mine and put a little distance between our chests when my orgasm climbed; she needed to see how easily she brought me to my knees.

"Jesus, Lil."

My growled words held the weight of a thousand unsaid thoughts. They contained every single emotion that my heart was ready for her to hear.

She slumped against me and held my head to her chest, my ear directly above where her heart raced within. I fought for breath, eventually holding her away from me again and grinning with satisfaction to see the aftermath on her face left behind from my beard.

"You're beautiful."

"Thanks," she said breathlessly. "Wow, that was good."

I hummed in agreement before realisation dawned on me.

"Lil, shit, I was unprepared. Do, uh, would you like me to take you to get the morning after pill?"

Her eyes locked with mine and didn't waver in the slightest. "I'm on the pill, Gage. And I take it religiously so you won't get any nasty little surprises."

I cupped her cheek. "Those surprises aren't nasty, Lil. You'll agree we're both not ready for that, but worse things could happen."

When Lil's mouth fell open, I used my thumb to guide it closed again. "It's not a slip of the tongue, Sunshine. I love you," I murmured, watching her reaction closely.

"Gage..." Her eyebrows pulled together as she searched my face.

"Shit, let me document this," I pretended to reach for her phone. "For once you're lost for fucking words."

I chuckled when she threw back her head and laughed to the ceiling. She was breathing back composure when her stomach rumbled.

"Worked up an appetite, eh?"

She flung the pillow at me. "Yeah, I did."

"Biscuits?"

"You brought me biscuits?"

"Uh huh. Aunty Sandy made them for you."

Lil's eyes lit and darted around the room. "Where are they?"

"Downstairs. Want me to grab them?"

"C'mon, Batman, what are you waiting for?" she exclaimed, already climbing from my lap and shoving me towards the edge of the bed.

I paused long enough to tug on my boxers then threw a, "Back in a sec," over my shoulder as I made my way downstairs.

"You've got ten!"

Challenge accepted. I jogged into the kitchen, snatched up the container and ran back up the stairs, diving for the bed just as Lil yelled, "One!"

She grabbed the container and tore off the lid. "Just in time, Batman!"

I chuckled. "Or what?"

"You'd get none," she mumbled through crumbs.

"There's no way you'd be able to enforce that. I'd overpower you with my little finger."

Lil scoffed. "I'll let you think that."

Snagging a cookie before she slammed the lid closed on my fingers, I shoved the entire thing into my mouth then sat with my back against the headboard. Needing Lil to be as close as possible, I tugged her to sit between my legs, her back to my chest.

I wouldn't deny that I was disheartened about telling her I loved her and not hearing those words returned, but at that precise moment with Lil in my arms, I realised my life was beyond fulfilled, and I wanted her with me every spare moment we got. Hence my reason for leaving her for a week to go home. Something had clicked within me. I simply knew without a doubt that I loved Lil with my entire heart. The only exception was the special place Lotte still owned; that part of me would forever belong to her.

Right now, with Lil leaning against my chest and biscuit crumbs gathering between us, I was so fucking happy. It was the first time in over three years that I was one hundred percent certain that I had made the right decision. Lil was never going to be the one that got away; right from the start she was meant to be the one to capture me—*all* of me—and reignite my desire to live hard and love even harder.

I kissed the back of her head, burying my nose amongst her untamed hair, filling my lungs with her scent. Her hum of contentment was music to my ears.

"Gage?"

"Mmm?"

"I think I love you too," she whispered, so quietly I barely heard.

Jesus fuck, my heart swelled so fast it all but burst, and I hadn't grinned so widely in thousands of days. She fucking broke me at the very same time as making me the happiest man in the world.

Setting my fingers on her chin, I tilted her head back to meet my lips. The biscuits lay forgotten, as did the crumbs that further crumbled between us. They were the last concern either of us had in that moment. We wordlessly fell into each other's orbit, joining, devouring, savouring every damn thing we could in that moment.

If I had known that the next time I saw Lil she would be shrieking at me to not fucking touch her ever again and screaming that we were so fucking done, I never would have left that afternoon until she understood just how much she meant to me and how hard I fucking loved her.

30
LIL

GAGE HAD BEEN away for a week, and I was having serious withdrawals as I went about my job, now back on days again.

The thrill that wove through me each time I thought about him telling me he loved me, left me equally as breathless as the actual moment did. It sent butterflies spiralling throughout my stomach, leaving me giddy and grinning. The moment was every bit the way I'd imagined it would feel hearing those words coming from someone I absolutely adored and was falling in love with. Even though it was early days, what I felt for Gage already surpassed what I ever felt for Jono. My only regret was leaving Gage hanging before I professed my own love in return. However, he took the lag on the chin and never once made me feel bad for the delay. He was the man who had begun to steal my heart, and the more I got to know Gage, the more I wanted to give it all to him.

I'd already learned the hard way from saying *I love you* too early, but with Gage I was positive I wouldn't live to regret it. Despite it being obvious that he owned a broken, battered soul, he was a caring, genuine guy who didn't bestow his love lightly.

I wanted to heal him, to show him that he wasn't the dark lord he viewed himself as, that he was making me realise that a love so fierce exists within me, for him. A love so compelling that once you're under its spell, there was no way you'd willingly leave.

Right now, my emotional state was somewhat frazzled, which magnified the shitstorm at work. Most days I honestly loved my job, but today, no matter how many times I chanted *I love my job,* there was no fooling myself into believing it. There were only so many times one could be puked on before the joke became old. My thigh throbbed painfully after copping a flailing elbow from a distressed patient. Add being spat on to the list and being totally run off my feet, the *second* my shift was over I walked out the door and didn't look back.

Opening the backdoor to my house with a sigh, I dumped my handbag and keys on the bench. After sorting the laundry, I was scrubbing my hands under almost scalding water when I heard the door handle of the back door being jiggled.

Mickey wasn't due to finish his shift and fear started rising from the pit of my stomach. Immediately converting to my alter ego—badass bitch—I grabbed the nearest weapon... A bottle of stain remover.

Yeah, that wasn't going to cut it.

Tossing it in the tub and wincing as it loudly clattered, I frantically searched for something, *anything,* that could be used for self-protection in the face of an emergency.

Nothing.

With my heart in my throat and my breath refusing to budge from my lungs, I made my way into the kitchen as silently as I could while avoiding the windows.

My eyes landed on Mickey's nunchucks casually strewn on the hallway table as I internalised to him.

<*I've just got home and someone is stalking around the house!!!!*>

Moving like Jackie freaking Chan into a better attack position, I focused on calming my breathing as the booted footsteps returned. A loud knock sounded, making me flinch.

"Lil, it's me. Let me in."

I instantly recognised his voice, and I was both relieved and furious at him for almost causing a full-blown panic attack.

"Hmm, let me think about it." I casually swung the nunchucks at my side, wincing when they bumped into the bruise on my thigh.

"Hurry up, Lil," Mickey bitched.

"Come on in," I said sweetly as I unlatched the door lock.

He hesitated, suspicious of my pleasant tone and giving in too easily. As soon as he stepped into the room I unleashed my fiercest war cry and launched at him, nunchucks poised to inflict serious damage. Thank goodness for his lightning fast reactions, or he would have ended up in a world of pain. In an instant, Mickey ducked and rolled while neatly plucking the chucks from my hand.

Damn he was fast!

I jumped out of pure reaction as his booted foot kicked out at my ankles, and then leapt onto the bench. Mickey puffed and gave me a wide eyed *What the hell* look.

"Welcome home, little bro, that's for scaring the shit out of me."

"Me? I almost lost a nut thanks to you."

"Well, since I wasn't expecting you home yet—and the fact that you didn't use the key *or* internalise me—I naturally jumped to the most extreme scenario of home invasion."

"And you were going to kick some ass by *trying* to use my chucks?" Mickey scoffed, tossing them back onto the little junk table. "Besides, the key wasn't where it's supposed to be."

I glanced at the key sitting pretty beside me. "We need to get another key made up for the door."

"I know. Now, go put the key back before I unleash some asswhooping of my own. It's been a fuck of a day."

Mickey rolled his shoulders, stretching his neck from side to side.

"Tell me about it," I mumbled.

Grabbing the key, I went outside and re-hid the key as exhaustion hit hard. All I wanted to do was soak in the bath then be served a home cooked meal before passing out in bed.

I found Mickey in the lounge, watching TV with his feet kicked up on the coffee table.

"Can you cook dinner tonight? Don't think I won't stoop to begging, because I will if I have to."

The beer paused halfway to his mouth. "Again?"

"Please, Joshy, I'm so freaking beat. Today was a shit one."

He looked as shattered as I was, and we shared a moment of understanding. I could tell that something serious had happened.

"Is everything okay?" I murmured.

He took a long pull of beer then huffed to his feet. "Everything's fine, Lil, same ol' shit making me question why the fuck I do what I do."

"Hey," I stopped him with a hand on his arm. "Talk to me, Joshy."

Mickey's expression closed off and hardened. "Not when you cop it at the other end of the emergency services line. Just wish there was more I could do."

"You do all that you can, we both do, and we do it because a, deep down we love it, and b, we're both damn good at what we do."

He breathed a smile and slung his arms around me as he made for the kitchen, not saying another word about the burdens of our career choices.

"Dinner's not gonna be fancy. We need to do shopping again."

"You!" I pointed at him and sassed. *"You need to do shopping for once!"*

"Pfft. Just go relax or something while I sort this."

I headed for the stairs where I stopped on the first step and half-turned.

"Josh?"

"What?" he asked without facing me.

"Thank you."

He looked at me then and his features softened with sibling affection. "You're welcome."

. . .

Lowering myself into the steaming water, I panted as the hot water claimed my body. The heat immediately soothed the ache in my legs and feet, and my eyelids fell closed with a deep sigh of relief.

I was dozing when a muffled but swift knock sounded on the front door below me. It can't have been one of the crew; we didn't knock.

<You're on door duty, I'm in the bath>

<Just let me find my vagina while I pause making dinner to go to the door> Mickey internalised before he called out, "Coming," to the visitor.

I scoffed and held my breath while I strained to hear who it was. I'd be lying if I said I didn't want it to be Gage coming back early to surprise me.

Hearing nothing but the door slam, I sank low in the bath water and exhaled a long, blissful breath. Blocking out footsteps on the stairs, which rhythmically sounded like Mickey's, I focused on recapturing my relaxed bodily state.

The bathroom door flung open, slamming hard against the shower frame and causing the glass to rattle precariously.

Pure reaction caused me to sit up, sending a wave of water sloshing onto the floor. I hastily sank back and rearranged the bubbles to ensure I was decently covered.

"Mickey what the fuck! *Get out!*"

He slapped a hand over his eyes while the other gripped the door frame with a piece of paper pinched between his fingers.

"Fuck, Lil, some things can't be unseen you know."

"Says the person who barged into *my* bathroom time. I told you I was in here! Why didn't you just psycho message me like normal? That's twice in one afternoon!" I exclaimed in irritation.

"This..." Mickey hissed waving the paper around while still imposing self-blindness, "...was attached to the door and no-one was there."

Huffing at his vagueness, I held out a wet hand and waved it impatiently. "Give it here already!"

Mickey shuffled forward with his arm outstretched and I pushed back a frustrated scream as he inched his way across the room. Snatching the paper the second it became reachable, my blood chilled in an instant. Fear pooled in the pit of my stomach as I read the scrawl.

I'LL BE SEEING YOU SOON WHORE.

I wheezed as I struggled to suck in the oxygen I so desperately needed.

"What the hell? Mickey, look at me, dammit!"

He cautiously cracked an eye then opened the other once he established I was fully covered. Pacing back and forth across the tiles, he ran his hands over his face and looked as freaked as I felt.

"I don't know, Lil, but I'm not getting a good feeling about this. It's gotta have something to do with that random car and the guy you caught lurking around."

"All the doors are locked aye?"

"Sure are, I did a quick check before coming up here."

"I have a stalker?" My voice quivered. I was so fucking scared.

"I dunno, Lil, but it appears that way. Any ideas of who it could be?"

"No idea," I cried. "I mean, sure I've had the odd run in here and there but nothing that would warrant a threat of violence!"

"Fuck, I'm glad I'm here with you right now, but what happens when our shifts don't align?"

I paled and swallowed painfully. "I've two more day shifts then two days off before I'm on nights again."

It didn't help answer his question, but it was what he needed to know. Mickey resumed his pacing, now with his hands on his hips. "I'm on days until Sunday then start nights on Wednesday, so at least I'll be here at night with you until then. I'm sure Gage won't mind hanging out either," he drawled, tone heavy with irony before he pressed his lips together.

"We gotta tell Dad," I whispered, knowing full well Mum would absolutely flip and Dad would enforce a crackdown of epic proportions.

It had almost come to that a couple of weeks ago just from mentioning the prowler. Dad was going to lose his shit over this. Mickey stopped pacing and met my eyes.

"Without a doubt," he replied quietly. "I would never forgive myself if anything happened..."

"Don't, because it won't," I snapped. "Before you ring him, I'll need a glass of wine the size of a soup pot."

I knew Dad would be here like a bat out of hell with Mum hot on his heels once the call was made, and I needed every minute I got to prepare myself. Mickey nodded and cursed, sounding as morbid as I felt.

LIL

THE FOLLOWING TWO days passed in usual fashion with nothing out of the ordinary occurring. As a bonus, my scrubs remained unsoiled, which made for a great day.

I received a message from Gage telling me he was heading back to Auckland after lunch and was looking forward to getting his hands on me tonight. I couldn't stop the goofy grin becoming a permanent fixture on my face as I went about my final day shift before a couple of days off.

"Someone's looking like she's gonna get some later," Jess—my good friend and colleague—sniggered as I passed her with a hand full of dressings.

"I hope so, it's been *forever.*" I shoved the dressings into the holder then playfully kicked her leg.

Jess laughed and flicked my ass. "Wow, he must be good if a week seems like forever. Where can I get me one of those guys?"

Her big, dark-brown eyes turned dreamy for a moment, then her long blonde hair swayed in its ponytail when she shook off the fantasy. Jess was gorgeous inside and out, and she had curves. Her life hadn't been an easy road; growing up rough meant that she didn't take shit and had to work her ass off to get to where she was today—a highly respected doctor of an Emergency Department.

"Does he have a brother?"

I giggled. "Sorry, chick, he's got three sisters."

The hope faded from her eyes but lit a little when I added, "He's got a hot cousin though. You've heard me speak of Mace before. He can pull the ladies without even trying."

"Hmm." Jess pursed her lips. "That's not my style. Besides, I don't have time to attempt a relationship."

Her statement was tainted with bitterness. With a sigh, she turned her attention back to the patient notes in her hand.

"Who said anything about relationships? Maybe you just need your egg scrambled."

"Jeez, Lil!" Jess hissed and quickly glanced around then backhanded my bicep. "Get your ass back to work."

I threw a sarcastic salute off my brow. "Yes boss."

Jess rolled her eyes; she really *was* my boss.

With a grin and a feigned kick aimed at my ass, she waved me off and got back to handover prep.

Driving home, I psycho messaged Mickey to let him know I was detouring to Mace and Gage's place instead of going straight home.

<*Let me know when you leave and if Gage is gagging for it bad enough to follow you home.*>

<*You're an ass!*>

<*Thanks.*>

I scoffed and eyerolled despite being in the car by myself. <*Wasn't a compliment. You going out tonight?*>

<*If you've got company, I'll head out for drinks with the work boys.*>

<*Okay. Be safe.*>

<*Pfft, take your own advice, sis.*>

Our meeting with Dad and Mum the other night went as expected—finishing on a lecture from Dad that someone was to be with me at all times of the day or night. I ignored how my cheeks heated from Mickey's glare as he internally bitched that he was sure Gage would willingly take one for the crew.

Mickey and I were taking Dad's advice seriously though, each of us making an effort to be extra vigilant.

I pulled up at the curb outside Mace's house and became instantly nervous. The excitement and apprehension over seeing Gage again was making my stomach churn.

Taking a deep breath before exiting the car, I got out and breezed past both Mace and Gage's utes in the driveway.

The side door of the house was open, and as per the crew's code, I walked in without knocking. My pulse spiked when I heard their voices casually conversing in the kitchen. I paused briefly to try and regain control over my breathless state, and that was when I caught words that made my heart plummet.

Gage had his back to me with his hands tucked in the front pockets of his jeans, while Mace leaned his ass against the bench with his folded over his chest.

"So, did you go see her?" Mace asked, a worry crease deep between his brows.

Gage nodded then raked a hand through his hair. "Yeah, I did. I had to see her again. It had been too long and I promised I would be back sooner than that. I've missed her..." he added in a whisper that was barely audible to my ears.

I was in the wrong, *wrong, wrong* place right now and my legs refused to remove me from the situation. I was stuck, frozen to the spot, as my heart tore to pieces. With every one of their exchanged words, the painful lump in my throat grew, and I barely contained a sob when I realised I'd been totally played, yet again. Played by a guy who had snuck his way into my heart without my permission and took a piece for himself.

I palmed my mouth in the hopes to hold in the gasps as I fought to catch my breath. I had to get out of there A.S.A.P and back to my car where I could let my heart shatter in private.

My sneakers were silent as I took a step backwards, not taking my attention off the guys despite them blurring through the sheen of moisture gathering in my eyes.

Mace caught my movement in his peripheral vision and snapped his head my way. The look of horror on his face when he realised I had inadvertently overheard their private conversation was enough to confirm my assumptions. Noticing Mace's reaction, Gage spun.

"Shit, Sunshine! I didn't hear you arrive. How are y-"

Gage took a step closer but halted as his eyes skipped over my expression. It was then he knew I overheard something that I shouldn't have.

I couldn't speak, just stood there shaking my head in disbelief, desperately searching for something to say to the two men I loved, yet hated in this moment.

Mace came towards me with his arms outstretched but all I could do was inch towards the door, torn between the desire to fall into the safety of his arms and not wanting him to touch me.

"Lil Bean," he whispered.

"Don't, Mace." I could hear the tremble in my voice and I forced myself to swallow the lump that blocked my throat. "I wasn't sneaking in to spy, I swear. But... I, I heard..."

Unable to finish my sentence, I looked between Mace and Gage, hoping like hell that one of them would provide some form of logical explanation to clear up the misconception; to tell me I'd heard incorrectly.

In that moment of halted time, Mace snagged my arms and pulled me against him. I resisted the urge to melt into his familiar body that had provided endless comfort through the darkest of my days.

I pushed against Mace's chest, feeling how hard his heart was beating beneath my palms. We engaged in a silent struggle, one where I refused to look at his face out of fear it would leave me in tears. Instead, I craned my neck to peer around his body at Gage.

He stood with his eyes closed, pinching the bridge of his nose between forefinger and thumb, while his chest heaved like he was on the verge of losing control. I couldn't even bring myself to ask if he was cheating on me, and from what I'd just overheard, I didn't want further details

"You!" I hissed, the vehemence in my tone surprising my own ears. "How could you?"

Gage's head snapped up and his stricken gaze found mine. They blazed with all kinds of fury, angst, regret and hurt. Seeing how broken he was made my heart ache for him, and that in turn fuelled my resentment. Despite knowing my efforts were futile, I began struggling hard in Mace's arms.

With instantaneous decision, Gage strode over to us and pushed Mace firmly out of the way. He then stood before me with my forearms firmly captured by his strong hands. His fingers squeezed as I thrashed in his hold, fighting against Gage's physicality as much as the energised charge his contact evoked under my skin.

"It's not what you think, Lil. I promise," Gage clenched his teeth and growled.

My heart and head were at war, and my gut was screaming at me to flee.

"Don't touch me! Don't *ever fucking touch me,*" I yelled at the top of my lungs, losing control further by the second. I sought out Mace; he also lay at the root of my pain. "How could *you! You of all people, Mace!* After all that we've been through. How could you keep something like this from me? I love you both and *you've both fucking destroyed me!*"

"It's not what you think, Lil. I didn't fucking cheat!" Gage roared.

"That's exactly what cheaters say, Gage. I even *told* you that my fiancé cheated on me, and what do you know, here I am again, a walking, talking, fucking joke!"

My head snapped on my shoulders as Gage shook me a little, frustration rolling off him in palatable waves.

"You gotta hear what I'm saying. I didn't fucking cheat," he yelled again, well past breaking point with his tone exuding the heartbreak I felt within.

A sob tore from my mouth and Mace looked like he was shattering as much as I was. I blinked through my tears and leaned towards Gage, making sure I had his full attention.

"We are *done. We are SO FUCKING DONE! Don't come near me ever again!"*

Gage seethed, anger and desperation combining into a frightening expression. "Not happening!"

"Goddammit, just fucking listen, Lil Bean," Mace yelled and forcefully grabbed one of my arms as if I was his last dying hope.

I felt like a puppet. A stuffed and battered rag doll that two people were tugging over, both wanting to have, but in reality, neither could.

"Let go of me! Let go, let go, *let fucking go."* I thrashed wildly against them both.

Gage clenched his teeth and growled, "For fucks sake, Lil, stop thrashing and hear me out. Calm down and I'll explain exactly what's going on."

"I'm not sticking around to listen to your bullshit. *Let. Me. Go!"*

Gage wore the brunt of my fist when his grasp faltered. It connected with his eye, making it water on impact. Mace released my other arm, and the three of us stood glaring, heaving for breath, and burning from desolation from the inside out.

"Shit, Lil. Please!" Gage pleaded.

"Nothing you can say will ever fix this, either of you," I said quietly, trying to keep the tremor from my words. I utterly failed.

Turning on my heel, I took off running while frantically digging the car keys from my pocket.

Mace and Gage were arguing as they followed me. Mace stopped at the letterbox and slapped his phone to his ear, whereas Gage didn't halt until he reached my car.

With a quick twist of my wrist, the engine sparked to life. I scrambled for the internal door locking switch, cursing myself for not doing it sooner when Gage wrenched the door open. His eyes were full of hurt and despair, and his voice broke with conviction as the softly spoken words flowed from his lips and stabbed at my heart.

"She's dead, Lil."

I shook my head, not wanting to believe a single word that came from his mouth even though I knew full well that it was more than likely the truth. You simply didn't say things like that without them being factual.

"I don't know what to believe anymore. I hate secrets, Gage. And I hate lies even more. Do you honestly think that now you're back in Auckland we can just pick up like everything was so damn peachy?" My tone pitched, heightened by the suffocating distress that bounced between us. "I refuse to be second best."

Gage's features contorted with pain as the full impact of my words slammed into him and penetrated deep. The quiet confession that came slipped from his lips next made my soul shatter.

"Lotte was my *everything,* my entire goddamn world, and she fucking *died.*"

His face was red from yelling and his breath was hot on my face with each ragged breath he took. Gage looked into my eyes, breaking me apart impossibly further with a whisper so raw and agonising that it made my entire body ache.

"*Lotte died!* Do you have any idea how fucked up I feel to love two women?" His quiet words grew in volume until he was bellowing in my face. "To love and pine for a woman I can never have again, the very one that broke my fucking life apart while loving another, which a huge fucking part of me resents for making me feel those feelings again?"

Seeing the devastation and anguish on the face of the man whom I loved was too much to bear. Tears streamed down my face. It was too much to process in my current state of mind and I was unable to stand it a moment longer. So, I did what I did best; I shut down, automatically slipping into self-preservation mode. I needed to escape, and I did just that.

"I can't fucking do this."

Ramming into first gear and not caring if I ran over Gage's toes, I peeled into the street without checking for traffic. The force of my haste was enough to snib the door when Gage stepped back.

Through the tears clouding my vision, I glanced in the rear vision mirror to see him standing in the middle of the road, fisting his hair like he was doing all he could to prevent himself falling to his knees. In the next moment, he was sprinting into the driveway and out of my sight.

With every metre I drove, more of my heart bled out on the road behind me. The shards scattered painfully onto the tar seal as the distance increased between myself and the man who I wanted more than anyone else.

By the time I got home, my anger had subsided. Unfortunately, that reprieve gave way to grief and loss.

I should have stuck around for a proper explanation—I owed it to us both. Instead, my bruised pride got in the way and I bolted.

In his devastation, Gage opened up about his loss and all I did was shove it back in his face like it didn't matter. And all the hurtful things I had said to him and Mace...

I hung my head in shame the moment I pulled into my driveway and guilt swept through me, extinguishing what little spirit I had left.

My eyes were red and puffy from constantly wiping them. I rummaged through my bag for my phone, only now picking it up to check the continuous barrage of calls I had ignored. Seven missed calls from Mace, five from Mickey, three voice messages, and three waiting text messages. I dealt with the texts first, quickly skimming Mace's messages. My alarm grew as each text increased in urgency.

.

M: Fuck Lil! I'm so sorry you found out like that. But there's more to the story, he wasn't cheating on you! I swear.

Three minutes later.

M: You need to wait for one of us to catch up.

Sixteen seconds later.

M: We're on our way.

Shit! In my haste to leave, I'd completely forgot to let Mickey know I was leaving.

<Home now. Things turned to shit. Left early.>

Shoving my phone back into my handbag, I got out of the car, slammed the door shut and trudged towards the back door.

<I know, Mace rang me. I'm already on my way. Wait in the car until I get there!>

I scoffed, already in the act of unlocking the door. It opened silently and I wasted no time in kicking off my shoes and dumping my bag on the bench. Today could go fuck itself, and it could do that from the comfort of my own bed.

<I'm already in. Locking the door right behind me.>
<I've got a real bad feeling, Lil. Seriously, wait outside!>

I hesitated, feeling the urgency Mickey transferred to me though his thoughts. An unease settled at the base of my neck. He was right, something didn't feel right. I spun on my heel and ran for the door.

That's when I heard them; footsteps on the floorboards behind me.

<*Mickey, someone's in the house with me.*>

<*Fuck! Get the fuck out, Lil. Now!*>

Fumbling with the lock, I felt a presence step close, well into my space. Goose bumps rippled over my shoulders, spreading like wildfire over the entire surface of my body. The moment he spoke I knew exactly who it was.

"Hello, Lilianne. So glad you could finally join me."

There was a reason why the use of my full name sickened me to the pit of my stomach, and *he* was that reason.

Terror paralysed me and I choked on the gasp where it lodged in my throat. Swallowing the rising bile, I slowly turned to face the man who discarded me all those years ago. If I thought I would be okay coming face to face with Jono, I was completely kidding myself.

He didn't back up, instead set his hand on the door beside my head as if it was the most natural place in the world for him to be. Seeing him in the flesh tore my wounds open again despite them being as healed as they would ever get.

Jono's lips curled and fear curdled my stomach. The blue eyes that I once found alluring were bloodshot and as cold as stone. He looked unhinged and terrifyingly unpredictable. What I saw in his eyes was enough for me to know that he had come for one thing and one thing only; *me*.

The smell of stale cigarettes hung in the air and his hair was greasy and unkempt. His image was a stark contrast to how immaculate he used to present himself. Even though he had aged ten times over in the last six years, his underlying features were still those of the man I thought I once loved.

I set my jaw and squared my shoulders, my stance contradicting the vulnerability I felt inside.

"It's *Lil*," I sneered. "What are you doing here? You're not welcome and you need to leave. *Now!*"

He clicked his tongue as he slowly looked me over.

"I've come for my fiancée. Or have you forgotten? I must say you look a little worse for wear, my darling..."

He snagged my hand and held tight as I frantically tried to tug it from his grasp. Revolt surged through me as he pressed his lips to my ring finger.

"Fuck you, Jono. We're not engaged anymore, or have *you* forgotten?" I taunted, not caring about the repercussions the man could inflict.

I knew I had backup on the way, I just prayed they got here in time.

The backhand across my face caught me off guard. It made my head swim and my legs fight to remain balanced.

"Don't fuck with me, Lilianne. You are mine and I'm going to take back what belongs to me!"

He used his body to pin me against the door. I struggled against a male body for the second time in one afternoon; the first occurrence I was fighting for my feelings, now I was fighting for my life.

Fear ricocheted throughout my body when he forced a cloth over my mouth and nose. A smell assaulted my senses that could only be one thing.

Chloroform was my last thought before the world disappeared.

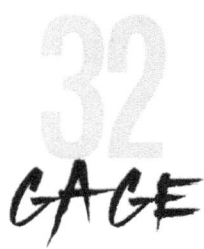

GAGE

THERE WAS NO way in hell I was letting this slide. Lil hadn't heard the full story and she was gonna sit down and hear it whether she wanted to or not. I hated that she drove away before I had the chance to explain properly.

This wasn't over. I wasn't one to walk away easily once I set my heart on something, and I sure as fuck wasn't going to stop until she had heard me out.

I all but assaulted Mace for the keys to his Harley—my Gunner still being in the panel shop. In my haste, I didn't bother with a helmet, but that didn't stop me riding hard through the streets. Assholes seemed to be in abundance and I cursed every red light and Sunday driver that slowed my progress.

I left the Harley idling and ran through the open back door. "Lily? Babe, where are you!"

Methodically searching each room, my panic crept higher with each empty room I encountered.

Nothing. She wasn't fucking there.

Her shoes, keys and bag were, but she wasn't.

The lingering smell of cigarette that hung in the air made my gut turn. My mind jumped to the worst possible conclusions before I could find a rational explanation—*any* explanation—that could fit.

Prior to Lil walking in on our conversation, Mace had informed me that she had received a threatening note and they believed it was linked to the odd behaviour of the car and mysterious presence over the last few weeks. We were all under strict orders from her father to *not* let her arrive home by herself.

The look on Lil's face when she incorrectly assumed I was cheating was utterly devastating. It tore my soul to pieces to watch her heart break in front of my eyes. To not be able to hold her together in my arms fucking destroyed me. The tender spot under my eye was worth it if it took the smallest sliver of her pain away, but I needed to clear up the misunderstanding without delay before it became irreparable.

I told her that Lotte had died, and in return she looked at me like there was a tiny unicorn tap-dancing on my forehead. As much as Lil tried to hide her feelings, I caught a fleeting spike of surprise pass through her eyes before they shone with hurt. The next instant, she was speeding away from me.

I strode back outside to switch off Mace's Hog and turned in time to him swinging wide in my ute and hitting the driveway without slowing down. He was out of the vehicle and gunning for me a moment later.

"She's home? Tell me she's fucking home!"

His entire body reflected the dread I was struggling to keep at bay. Shaking my head, I couldn't utter the words he loathed to hear. Mace turned and swore in frustration before sprinting into the house with me hot on his heels.

"Are you sure? Are you abso-fucking-lutely sure she's not here?" he yelled while repeating the house search I'd completed minutes ago.

"Yes goddammit, I'm sure! Her shoes and bag are here, but she's not!"

I tugged at my hair repetitively and looked through each room again, needing to be doing something—*anything*—to feel like I was doing everything within my power to find her.

A second set of screaming tyres was heard as Mickey pulled hell for leather into the driveway. Slamming on the brakes and leaving rubber behind him, he narrowly stopped before tailgating my ute. Like Mace, Mickey was still in his work gear, and if I thought we had looked rattled, Mickey took alarm to a whole new level.

"She with you?" I yelled as Mace came running down the stairs and stopped Mickey by holding his shoulders at arm's length.

"No! She said that someone was in the house when she got home but she was meant to be with you!" Mickey jabbed an angry finger at me.

I knew that look; the need to inflict a massive amount of beat down on the nearest object or the person who fucked up.

Mace did his best to explain. "She was, but she left in a hurry and wouldn't answer her goddamn phone. I swear to God, bro, we tried to stop her, short of assaulting her."

"What did you do?" Mickey spat. He balled my shirt in his fists and shoved me with every word. "You haven't even been back for half a day and you've already fucking hurt her."

"You have no *idea* what you're talking about, so back the fuck off," I roared and fisted his collar, repaying the favour by slamming my fists into his collar bones.

"Enough!" Mace boomed as he grappled with our arms then wedged himself between us.

Our scuffle continued momentarily until Mace managed to roughly shove us apart with surprising strength. The effort left us all panting and snarling at each other.

"This isn't helping. Both of you get a fucking grip."

He gave us both one last shove when we stepped towards each other again.

"Can you reach her?" Mace snapped.

"No! She's completely blank. She's not even that blank when she's asleep." Horror dawned on Mickey's face. "You don't think she's unconscious, do you? Or, or...?"

Oh god no, please, not again.

"Shut up! Shut the *fuck* up!" I yelled at the top of my lungs so I didn't have to hear that single word every loved one dreaded. If the unspeakable happened, I wasn't going to make it out this time around.

I needed to get out of the house; the air was suffocating me. I tuned out Mace and Mickey talking urgently behind me as they tried to piece together every minute hint of information to Lil's whereabouts.

Mace soon came outside talking on his phone with my keys clenched in his hand.

He eyed me as he disconnected. "We're going to Matt and Ev's house. You need a lift or you riding?"

I itched to ride but wasn't in the right headspace. "Lift. You drive."

Mace nodded once then was on the move. After shoving Lil's shoes into her bag and tossing it onto the back seat of my ute, I balled my fists on my thighs as we waited for Mickey to reverse out first.

. . .

It was dusk when we arrived at the McMillan's house. Weaving through the evening traffic in a large vehicle was beyond frustrating. Both Mickey and Mace had a heavy foot and found the smallest gaps to manoeuvre into, but it wasn't bloody good enough. I took out some of my frustration by flipping off slow drivers as we steamed past them.

"Move your asses. Who the fuck does a hundred in a hundred zone anyway?" I shouted through the windshield at cars in front of us and planted my hands on the dash when Mace made another quick swerve into a non-existent gap. Mickey snaked his way in and out of vehicles in a similar fashion, and both our utes were the recipients of blaring horns and multiple middle fingers.

"Christ," Mace muttered to himself. "Grab my phone and call Kimmie will you. Maybe there's an off chance she's heard from Lil. Right jean pocket."

I reached across his body as he swerved to the left again, sending my body lurching into his lap.

"Yeah, it wouldn't be in the closest fucking pocket, would it?" I grumbled while reaching across his thighs.

Mace cracked a crude-ass joke and my urge to castrate him on the spot had never been so intense.

"If we get pulled up, I can use the excuse that I was getting some afternoon head."

He burst out laughing at his sick-ass joke before sobering quickly as he focused on performing another quick lane change.

"If you need to resort to head from your own cousin then you need to get some serious fucking help."

My thumb worked overtime opening his contacts list and scrolling for Kimmie's name. Pressing the phone to my ear, I held my breath and willed her to pick up and tell us Lil was with her.

"What's up, hot stuff?"

"Hot stuff?" I raised an eyebrow at Mace who smirked. "It's Gage."

"I stand by my comment."

Dammit, I didn't have time for bullshit right now.

"Listen, Kimmie, this is important. Is Lil with you? Yes or No?"

Her voice instantly changed from playful to alarmed. "No. No, she's not. What's going on?"

I punched the dashboard and let out a long line of expletives that served to make me feel better by piss-all-to-none.

"She's missing and it looks like someone took her just after she arrived home this evening. We missed her by mere fucking minutes," I growled and sunk my head into my hand, wrenching on my hair again. It had become a stress habit.

"Where are you now? I'm on my way." I could hear shuffling in the background and her breathing changed, indicating that she was already on the move.

"Heading to her parents."

"Who is?"

"Me, Mace and Mickey."

"Okay. I'm already out the door and I'll ring Trav on the way."

She ended the call and I tossed his phone onto the dash.

"She's gonna be alright, Gage. Lil's one tough little cookie."

I shook my head. Despite wanting to believe Mace's reassurance, I couldn't bring myself to trust in that.

"It's not the same situation as Lotte, mate..." he trailed off, not needing to elaborate.

Nausea rolled in my stomach as the same helplessness washed over me that I had spent years trying to run from. No matter what I did, no matter where I went or who I was with, I couldn't escape its clutches. I couldn't even deal with thinking about Lotte right now, and as if to prove a point, a deep defeated breath tore from my chest.

"I never for the life of me thought I would be in this situation twice!"

Mace pursed his lips. He knew exactly what I meant.

"Once Mickey hears from her, we'll be able to form a better plan. The fact that we were so close to crossing paths at the house means she can't be too far from here." Mace purposely left the *'yet'* unsaid even though we were both thinking it.

His grip on the steering wheel tightened. "We'll find her soon."

I pressed my palms into my eye sockets until it hurt. Anything to ease the pain in my chest.

"I fucking hope so."

GAGE

MICKEY PARKED HIS ute on a fucked-up angle in the driveway so Mace rode up the curb to park on the grass verge outside the McMillian residence.

I peered through the driver's window of Mickey's truck and studied him. He sat still and clutched the steering wheel, his knuckles white from the clench. His head was tilted back against the headrest and eyes squeezed closed. He jumped when I rapped a knuckle on the glass. Mace took one look at him, shoved me out of the way and wrenched the door open.

"Tell me!" he demanded. "Tell me she's okay. She's awake, right?"

Mickey nodded through the sheen of moisture that brimmed in his eyes. I had to look away and swallow around the lump that formed in my own throat. Mace reached into the vehicle, grabbed Mickey by the shoulders and shook him hard.

"Dammit, Josh, tell me!"

Mickey sucked in a big breath and gripped Mace's forearms. "She's awake and okay at the moment. She said that she's in the back of a station wagon, gagged and bound at the wrists and ankles." Mickey's lips curled in disgust and he looked as sick as I felt.

I weighed in, muscling Mace to the side so I could commandeer Mickey's full attention. "Where is she?"

He met my eyes and whispered. "She doesn't know."

I turned my back and fisted my hair, hardly feeling the shove on my back as Mickey pushed past and stalked towards the house. Mace planted his hand on my shoulder and propelled me after Mickey. Matt met us at the door and led the way to the dining room. It now resembled a special ops planning room; maps, phone, contacts list, stationary and whisky were sprawled across the table.

Pressing his palms on the table, Matt set his sights on his son and glared.

"Firstly, Joshua, don't think I don't know about the shenanigans you and that dipshit Travis have been up to recently. We'll discuss that later."

Mickey winced. "Er, does Ma-"

"Nope," Matt cut in, raising his hand to order silence. He then pointed his forefinger at each of us. "And she won't, not yet anyway. This also puts me in the dog box for withholding information, so there's mutual interest in keeping our goddamn mouths shut."

Mickey rolled his eyes and muttered something about covering asses just as his mum came in from outside. She set an empty wine glass on the kitchen counter as she walked our way. Ev greeted us with hugs, starting with Mickey. I followed Mace and Mickey's example of kissing her cheek and squeezing her tight. Her return smile was jaded, a stark contrast to the ones that lit up her face the last time we were here.

"Tell me what you know, son," Matt commanded.

Mickey dutifully repeated the information he'd received from Lil. "But she keeps fuzzing in and out, so I think she's slipping in and out of consciousness."

Worried looks were exchanged and Mickey's face became pained when he glanced at his mum, who was pressing a shaking hand over her mouth. Matt's large hand landed on her shoulder and he pulled her into a side hug. A furrow marred his brow as he thought.

The amount of information we had at the minute was extremely limited, though more than what we would have if Lil and Mickey weren't mindfully connected. We discussed various options and Matt made a couple of calls to colleagues to make sure they were on standby to jump into action if, and when, required.

Options and opinions were thrown back and forth until Mickey halted and raised a hand, signalling for us to quieten.

"She must be up north somewhere because she reckons they've just passed that massive tree at the T-intersection up towards our old place."

Some of the tension slipped from Matt and Ev's shoulders upon hearing of Lil's general location.

"Good," Matt gruffly barked. "Now we have a general idea on where they're heading. Our focus area will keep shifting, however, for now, we can narrow the search area slightly."

We pored over the map, adding little dots and times of when and where she had been in contact with Mickey. It fucking killed me that the limited information was also vague, but something was better than nothing.

Kimmie made an entrance that resembled a panicked wildebeest. Her breathless demands were silenced by Mickey's arms when they reached for her and pulled her against him. Our eyes snagged over the top of her head. Understanding passed between the two of us. He just confirmed everything I suspected about him and Kimmie without saying a goddamn word.

Matt's phone rang, breaking my stare with Mickey. Every call that rolled in dampened each glimmer of hope when each one ended with no further leads.

Trav arrived amidst the mayhem, eyes wide with worry and his jaw set tight. He went straight to Ev and hugged her for a long while before wedging himself between Kimmie and Mickey and pulling them both into his arms. I heard Trav mumble that Neek couldn't make it before

Mace relayed all the information to him. Trav followed Mace's finger as it traced over the map without saying a word. This side of Trav was unsettling; gone was the prankster with jokes on tap, here was the fighter who was ready to get down to business.

. . .

The hours crawled by in a blur of conversation, whisky and coffee; as the minutes mounted, the helplessness multiplied, desolation intensified and frustrations escalated.

It was just going midnight when Mickey stilled. I held my breath until I felt light-headed, praying to a God that had failed so far in this life to throw me a fucking bone.

"Lil says the car drove up a long, bumpy, gravel road that was uphill. They've stopped inside some kind of massive empty shed or building, perhaps an aircraft hangar. He's got her tied up and...." He jolted and staggered backwards as if he'd taken a shot at point blank.

Trav steadied him and jerked him back and forth. "What? Jesus, Mick, spill it already."

"Oh, hell *the fuck no*. He took her."

"Who?" The demand came from at least four of us.

Mickey pressed his palms on the table and raised his eyes to meet his parents before uttering a name that instantaneously froze all the fire in Hell.

"Jono."

The time warp broke when Matt punching the table and roared, "Bastard!"

The blood drained from Ev's face as she sunk her fingernails into Matt's arm. Mickey looked like he was about to copy his father's actions. Kimmie gaped at Mickey in horror, Trav was fisting his hair, and Mace was digging his fingers into my shoulder like he was a fucking Pterodactyl on crack.

Heartburn seared its way throughout my chest and rubbing my knuckles against the spot proved to be useless to ease the ache. I had no idea who Jono was or what he meant to Lil's family, though the ominous squeeze in the pit of my stomach continued to increase.

"Can someone tell me who the fuck Jono is?" I exclaimed, not at all worried that I was in bad form by cursing in my girl's parent's house.

Mace turned to me and dropped his tone. "Her ex-fiancé."

Red. It was all I saw in burning, blinding rage. I smacked a hand down on Mace's shoulder, locking us together.

The distress on his features was confronting; what I saw in Mace's face scared the shit out of me. The fear and terror I saw punched the wind from my lungs. He swallowed thickly and winced when my fingers dug harder into his shoulder joint. Awareness of a deep burn lacing above my collarbone cut through the haze where Mace fingertips were no doubt also creating deep-set bruises.

I broke away, running a hand through my hair and pacing the back wall of the dining room. "So, what do we do? Call the cops?"

"Son, *I am the cops,* and I know damn well that, legally, we can't do shit until she's been missing for twenty-four hours. Having said that, I've called in some favours and this will be handled in-house." Matt pressed his thumb and middle finger into his eye sockets. "I'll run the plates if you know them, Josh?"

It was tearing me up not knowing where the hell Lil was or if she was ever going to get the chance to come back to us... To me.

I halted and faced the wall, tugging hard at my hair, creating a sting to mask the agony within. A warm hand landed on my arm. Keeping my eyes closed for a moment, I exhaled slowly then looked down into wide eyes that matched Lil's.

Ev cupped my hands in hers and squeezed gently. "Our Lil is blessed to finally have someone who loves her for who she is without trying to mould her into something she's not." Ev's voice hitched as she drew a deep breath. "You love her, that much is obvious, and that makes you part of our family. It's time to fight for her, and I have no doubt that you will move Heaven and Earth to find my baby girl."

Her statement rang in my ears and stole the words from my mouth. I folded her hands within my own and clasped them with the gratitude I couldn't find words for.

A throat quietly cleared behind me. Glancing up, I found five other pairs of eyes trained on us with expressions ranging from smug (Mace), to scowling (Matt), teary (Kimmie), confused (Trav) and something I couldn't place from Mickey.

In the few beats that passed, I was hit with sudden clarity. I had a plan of attack—probably a shit one, but it was worth a shot.

Giving Ev's hands a final squeeze, I turned back to the table and took charge. "We head north tonight. She was in the car for approximately two hours, right? So, where would that put them, roughly?"

Everyone leaned over the map and followed Matt's finger as he pointed out the general area; it was fucking huge.

"We used to own a farm up that way, but I highly doubt he would have taken her there."

"Plus, she would have recognised the shed if it was our old one," Mickey added.

"Then he hasn't taken this route. Most likely he's headed this way." Mace followed a probable route with his forefinger. "My bet is that he's heading as rural as possible."

Matt was already scrolling through his phone for the appropriate contacts in that area to give them an update. Standing around chatting wasn't getting us any closer—physically—to Lil, and I wanted to get on the road already. Once Matt's call was concluded and before he could start another, I announced that we were leaving.

"Mickey, I'm with you in your truck. Mace, you follow in mine."

I ignored the incredulous look on Matt's face like I was undermining his authority; I *was,* but still. Clearly he was used to *giving,* not receiving orders from people who shouldn't be giving them.

"We'll head to your old place first, just on the off chance that he took her there. We'll be in touch with any developments along the way, and you let us know of any new information when it comes to light. From there, we'll play it by ear. When we get to that tree intersection, I'll call regardless of the information status."

The finality to my statement made it clear that I meant business and wouldn't back down. Ev spun on her heel and left the room. Matt gave us an assertive nod after he thought over the plan. Kimmie made a move to come with us but was stopped by Mickey. He bent and spoke to her in hushed tones, and when she started to protest, he captured her chin with his thumb and forefinger. No words were exchanged, just an unwavering look between them. Once satisfied, Mickey turned to Trav.

"Mate, stay here." Mickey tilted his head subtly towards Kimmie, and, despite his frown, Trav nodded in understanding and re-pocketed his keys.

Ev returned with an armload of blankets and water bottles. I hardly paused to thank her as I lifted them from her arms and followed Mace and Mickey out the door.

34

LIL

I SEMI-ROUSED FOR a few moments before being lulled back to sleep by the gentle rocking motion of the car travelling along a highway.

I didn't know how long I was out that time, but I woke again with a lurch that sent my head crashing into the inside of the boot. Curses were muttered from the front of the car.

Peeling my weighted and irritated eyelids open was a major mission, and it wasn't until I went to rub at my eyes that I found my arms were bound behind my back.

What the...?

Oh shit; it all started coming back to me.

Jono!

That horrible excuse for a human.

My heart dropped painfully and my gasp was smothered by the tape that adhered to my lips. *That* was going to hurt like a bitch coming off. I went to move my legs and my pulse spiked at seeing my ankles bound with duct-tape. Panic induced a sob and, for a split second, I was thankful for the horrible tasting tape plastered across my lips. There was no way I wanted to give Jono the twisted satisfaction of hearing me distressed.

Thank goodness I was in a station wagon where I could see out of the tinted windows, and not in a sedan boot. It looked like dusk outside but that didn't help me figure out just how much time had passed since I was abducted from my own house.

The constant throb within my skull was interrupted by zinging.

<*Mickey! Oh my God, thank God!*>

He proceeded to bombard me with a million questions that made my head spin even more.

<*Can you tell Gage that...*>

<*Shut up, you can tell him yourself when we find you. We've just arrived at Mum and Dad's to formulate a plan. Shit, Lil. I thought... I fucking thought...*>

<*Don't, Joshy. I'm okay. It's gonna be okay...*>

Intense relief settled within me knowing that I was still connected to my family and that they would do all they could to find me.

The drug haze tugged at me again. I fought for the smallest moment before it devoured me without having to try.

Sometime later, I felt the car slowing, almost to a stop, then accelerate at what felt like an intersection. That had me curious. Craning my head as much as possible with my limited range of motion, I tried to see a distinguishing feature; anything to help identify where I was. The sight created a wave of both relief and apprehension; Jono was taking me rural, and we were now North of the city.

<We're turning left at the major T-intersection with the huge misshapen tree—the one we used to want to climb when we were kids. You know? Up towards our old place. It's lit by a street lamp.>

I was beginning to feel motion sick and the side of my body I was cast on ached terribly. The pounding in my head was brutal from the sedative and no doubt being roughly tossed into the boot, and my mouth held a foul taste that teased my gag reflex. This time I willed myself back into the state where I was neither awake nor asleep, but unfortunately never fully reaching either.

The miles stretched out before I was jolted fully awake by the car erratically bumping through potholes. The smooth whining sound of tyres on the open highway was gone and replaced with tinging from stones hitting the underside of the car. I knew what that meant; we had left the tar seal and were heading down a gravel side-road.

There was no doubt that Jono was heading deep into the countryside where the chances of anyone finding me were slim-to-none. The probabilities of ending up murdered in a forestry block, never to be seen again, were high. I breathed hard through my flared nostrils, willed away the panic before it snaked to the surface. I couldn't afford to freak out right now.

Forcing myself to take hold of my sensibilities, I craned my head again in the hopes of making sense of my surroundings. From my prone viewpoint, it didn't appear that we were surrounded by trees, so I mentally scratched off the forestry option from my list of worries.

My relief was short lived as the car climbed higher. We were going uphill, and a *long* way uphill.

The car eventually rocked to a stop and Jono opened the driver's door then slammed it shut without saying a word. I strained my ears to hear something—*anything*—and it wasn't long before loud rumbling met my ears. My pulse and breath quickened, knowing that I was about to be hidden away from the world. I may as well have been trapped underground with the Devil himself.

An involuntary squeak came out my nose when the car jolted over a quick bump before gliding smoothly forward. My centre of gravity tilted as Jono swung the car in a wide arc. Through the rear window I could see the high roof of the large dark building looming above us. I waited on bated breath, trying to piece together what laid in wait for me.

Jono's shadow briefly passed by the car. It scared me being with him, though it terrified me more not knowing where he was or what he was up to. I blinked hard and pressed my forehead to the carpeted boot lining to wipe away the sheen of fear induced sweat as it sprang up.

There was a muffled pop, then a searing bright light blinded me the moment it lit the building. Slamming my eyelids shut then cracking them against the dazzle, I gasped when I saw Jono's figure looming at the back of the vehicle. He popped the boot latch and lifted the rear door at an intentionally slow pace. I dreaded what was to come. No good was going to come from this. None whatsoever.

The leer on Jono's face was sinister and sadistic. He had plans for me, there was no doubt about that, and it made me sick to my stomach. He wasn't the man I once thought I knew; the man I had *wanted* to marry. I now saw a side of him that I would never have thought possible six years ago.

I savagely kicked at his arms with my bound legs when he reached to pull me from the car. My self-defence was promptly punished with a harsh slap to my cheek. Jono used that moment to grab my legs and drag me to the opening.

All oxygen left my body when he pulled a knife with a large curved blade and carelessly slashed the tape around my ankles. The bastard smirked at my rapid inhale of breath when the blade caught my skin.

With one hand in my hair and the other wrapped around my bicep, he roughly yanked me until my bare feet touched the cold concrete floor. I bit back a cry of pain when he lifted my bound arms high behind my back, forcing me onto tiptoes. I knew I didn't have a hope in Hell to fight my way out, not yet anyway. I was well and truly at his mercy.

Jono frog-marched me towards a lone chair in the far corner of this building, still without uttering a word.

Thrusting me roughly into the seat, he used more tape to secure each of my ankles to the front chair legs, flashing the knife in warning when I started kicking out at him. Standing back and admiring his work, I wished I could kick the twisted smirk off his face.

"I'm going to take the tape off your mouth. If you spit at me, bite me, or fuck me off enough by talking, there will be consequences. Understand?"

I glared hard, not wanting to give him the satisfaction of agreeing. He continued to leer as he bent forward and slowly tore the tape from my sensitive lips. Tears stung my eyes as the sting increased with each pull, ripping what felt like layers of skin off with it. I blinked rapidly to dispel the sudden moisture and grimaced against his fingers when he touched them to my lips. His breath breezed across my face as he leaned closer.

"Such a pretty mouth. Too bad the last time I saw it there wasn't anything nice coming out of it."

"Fuck you, Jono, you sicko. They'll find me soon, then you'll be sorry you set your hands on me."

I flinched involuntarily, steeling myself for the impact when he snapped back his hand. The strike didn't come. Instead, he traced the contours of my cheeks with his knuckles in a tender gesture that made my skin crawl.

"Lilianne, my darling," Jono whispered, his voice now adoring like I remembered. Nausea rolled in my gut as I repressed the memories. "That's no way to talk to your fiancé, don't you think?"

"I'm. Not. Your. Fiancée. You'll never be anything to me *ever* again. You made me love you, then discarded me to go back to the perfect little family you had hidden in Aussie. I hate every cell in your body."

The slap came out of nowhere. The world around me swam as I fought off the dizzy spin behind my eyelids.

"You bitch!" he shouted in my face and grabbed my jaw. "If it wasn't for the picture you sent, my wife never would have found out about you and lost her shit. She wears the scars of her insecurities, and I'm here to seek retribution."

Jono stepped back and studied me while casually tossing the knife from hand to hand. I felt the blood drain from my face as he maintained his relentless appraisal but I'd be damned if I let it show how much that information freaked me out. I knew there was pain heading my way, and a lot of it. I just hoped I could hold on until my family found me. The constant connection with Mickey was the only thing keeping my hopes of surviving alive.

I had to bide my time, get Jono talking, tell him what he wanted to hear. I summoned the strength I needed to lie through my teeth.

"I'm sure it wasn't your fault that it happened that way, but-"

"It's not my fuckin' fault, it's *yours!*" he spat, sending little droplets of spittle onto my face that I longed to wipe away.

The knife blade glinted against the bright overhead light as he raised it. My blood ran cold. My chest squeezed and burned as I desperately tried to breathe without showing the horror I felt within.

"I really don't see how it's m-"

"Bullshit, Lilianne. You ruined all that was good in my life and now it's time to pay for it. It's time for you to wear the same scars my wife does. It's time for you to feel what it's like to have to look at them every single day and be reminded of all the things that *are your fault.*"

Oh my *God!* Jono was even more deranged than I'd realised! I could hear it in the way he said my name, the look in his eyes, the way they burned with deep seated hatred. He wasn't here for me per se. No. He was here for revenge. To inflict merciless, twisted pain, purely for pleasure.

Jono went from shouting in my face to calm and quiet, and I sure as hell found his second persona infinitely more unsettling.

"It's time, my darling." The vindictive undertones in the way he said *Darling* made my skin break out in an icy sweat.

The knife blade felt cold against my forearm for a split second before it sliced into my flesh. I hissed through my teeth, determined to not give him the satisfaction of crying out. The initial sharp sting turned into a burn when the blood started to well.

There wasn't much fat on a forearm, and I didn't need my medical training to know that a cut didn't have to go overly deep before it connected with bone. I silently prayed that, in the worst-case scenario aside from death, I wouldn't be left with permanent nerve or ligament damage. I did, however, resign myself to the fact that I would most likely be left with scars—just like Jono intended.

I ducked my cheek to my shoulder to rid the single tear that escaped. I had to prepare Mickey for what they were likely to find.

<Bring your Med Kit. He has a knife.>

"One slice down, many more to come, Lilianne. You'll be a proper masterpiece once I'm finished with you. What do you have to say for yourself?"

Frustration and anger boiled to the surface. "Are you on crack right now?"

That earned me another backhand to my already swollen cheek. That one connected close to my mouth and I felt my lip split open.

"Okay, *okay*," I heaved trying to catch my breath while swallowing the tell-tale iron tang of blood.

"I really don't know what you want me to say. But Hell will freeze over before I give you an apology. I've never owed you one. *You* made a choice to leave me, and I've moved on."

Slice.

I bit the inside of my lips to make them stay shut through the sting.

"Oh yes, my sweet darling, I've noticed that mongrel of a man hanging around you." Jono tsked. He ran his fingers through the blood welling on my arm, mindlessly spreading it around. "I must say, I don't like him one bit, especially since he's taken a particular interest in my girl."

"I'm not your fucking girl! Why can't you get that into your thick head?"

Jono's lips curled in deranged satisfaction.

Slice.

Slice.

My composure broke. An infuriated, pain-laced shriek broke free, echoing around the building as I screamed for all it was worth. I screamed until my throat turned raw and my chest burned. It was pointless, futile, but helped release some of the tightly woven fear coiled inside.

Jono stared, patiently waiting for my outburst to be over.

"You were mine first, Lilianne, and he will never have you again. Do you understand me? *Do you?*"

Slice.

I squeezed my eyes shut and sunk my teeth deeper into my lips, forcing them to remain tightly sealed until the initial sting receded a little.

"You realise that they're coming for me. *He's* coming for me. And when they do, you'll be so fucking *fucked!*"

"They don't know where we are, my darling, and you have no way of contacting them. So, no, no one is coming for you. And if they do, it'll be too late."

He looked at my arm and cocked his head to the side like he was contemplating how he could add to his masterpiece.

I was forever grateful he had no idea about the secret connection I shared with Mickey. That part of me I kept to myself when I was younger out of worry I would be shipped off to the mental ward if I talked openly about our ability. For some reason, despite me thinking that I loved Jono back then, it was a part of me I didn't feel ready to share with him.

Jono clicked his tongue before adding another slice. My teeth clamped together as he smeared his hand through the welling blood, sweeping his fingers up my arm then through my hair, leaving a scarlet trail in the wake of his touch. I tensed when he rounded to my right side where he left dotted finger prints over the virgin skin of my untouched forearm.

Without warning, Jono pressed a savage kiss to my raw, tender lips. The impact snapped my head backward and sent me reeling as he stalked off without a word, leaving me alone and unable to apply the needed pressure to the multiple wounds on my arm.

The adrenaline that coursed through my veins began to subside, giving way to heightened pain and uncontrollable shaking as the shock of the trauma began to sink in.

I closed my eyes, only too happy to follow the torment into the darkness, hoping it would hide me from what was yet to come.

. . .

Cold metal trailed under my chin and along my jawline. I flinched, trying to move away from the chill, only to freeze a second later when I felt the prick of the tip of the knife press against my neck.

My eyes were drawn to the high windows where the first pink signs of dawn were beginning to break through the dark outside world. My bladder screamed for release, reminding me of the countless hours I'd been tied to the chair.

The blade grazed my swollen cheek bone, pressing briefly before easing again.

"No," Jono murmured to himself. "Not on this beautiful face. I'm not that cruel."

His lips curled as he laughed at his own sick joke, then a flash of decision passed over his features. He stepped around my legs to loom in front of me.

"Not that anyone will ever see this beautiful face again. Such a waste..." he trailed off and shook his head slowly, raking his lifeless blue eyes over my body.

I turned my head away from his stare. I couldn't stand the sight of him. Even the idea of looking at him repulsed me.

Judging by the large, rolling doors and the convex roof of the expansive building, we had to be in some kind of aircraft hangar. Tucked away in the far corner, I spotted a large buggy that resembled a golf cart. I could possibly use that to escape…

"Look at me. Look at me when I tell you to!"

"No."

My whisper turned into a gasp when his hands wove through my hair and snapped my head back. Now I had no choice but to look up at his seething face. The painful movement momentarily held my attention until I felt the familiar sharp burn of the blade piercing the unmarked skin of my right arm. Jono wasn't quick about it this time. Nor the second, or third. The slow, deliberate movements contrasted the anger filled slashes of his movements earlier in the night. He took his time, relishing every reaction my features unintentionally gave away.

It was now time to break me, to see what it took to crack me apart, to push the limits of my body's tolerance. It was beginning to work too.

Unable to hold the pain at bay, I let my tears flow freely as I felt my inner core begin to buckle under the weight of Jono's emotional and physical abuse. My teeth clenched to the point where my jaw ached, and I mustered the energy to hiss the one thing that would never change.

"I. Hate. You."

"You disappointment me, Lilianne. What cruel words from such a beautiful mouth. Too bad you're a little whore otherwise I would have made love to you."

I gagged on the bile that burned its way up my oesophagus. "Thank God for small mercies then." I choked through the blur of hate laced tears.

Never had I felt so vile towards another human being. I was trained to *save* lives, to find a way to maintain life against all odds. It was what I did on a daily basis and it was my passion. But right now, if the opportunity arose to end Jono's life, I hoped I could wholeheartedly find the courage to follow through.

"That's enough!" he yelled, his words echoing around the large, empty expanse. "I'm going to teach you a little thing called *respect*. And it'll be one of the last things you'll remember."

The point of his knife bit into my skin again. I felt a small pop as it broke the surface. There, Jono stilled and tilted his head as if listening.

Surprise then anger lit his features, and I expected another blow to my face. In complete contrast, he jerked away from me and sprinted towards the hangar doors.

I then heard a sound in the distance that breathed life into my almost extinguished soul.

GAGE

MICKEY AND I drove in silence as we breached the city limits. It was a comfort knowing that Mace was right there with us and that Mickey was a direct link to Lil.

He shifted in his seat and grunted. I look over to see him grimacing.

"Problem?"

"Yes and no. My arm is aching like fuck for no reason."

Taking his left arm off the wheel, he flexed it a few times and shook it out.

I scoffed. "That to me screams too much wanking, mate."

He shot me a glance and smirked. "I'm right handed, not left."

"No harm in mixing it up."

"I don't give a shit about what *you* do to get off, all I know is that it's insanely sore."

I let out a reluctant chuckle which served to ease the tension in my chest somewhat, silently thankful to have my worry over Lil lessened for a few very short seconds.

"Want me to drive?"

"No," Mickey snapped and planted his foot when the road lead further from the suburbs.

As it was, I didn't need to call Matt; he called us before we reached the major intersection with the tree. Mickey fumbled for the phone in is his pocket as he focused on the road ahead. I snatched it from his hand and jabbed the accept button, putting the call on speaker.

"Any new info?" I demanded.

Glancing at the clock, it was after two in the morning. The last few hours had flown by yet dragged at the same time, and it frustrated me to no end that we weren't any closer to finding Lil.

"Not on their whereabouts," Matt informed us. "However, more information about Jono Thompson has come to light. He somehow managed to slip out of Australia undetected. Talk about a bloody joke. Heads will roll for this, I can assure you. He's got multiple arrest records for minor to serious charges ranging from causing public disturbance to domestic violence. Needless to say, the sooner we find my little girl, the better."

"He's gonna fucking pay for taking her," I growled through my teeth.

"Not a doubt in my mind, son. Maim, yes, but no further. Got it? We don't need a bloody murder-manslaughter charge to deal with as well."

I huffed and glowered at the phone without replying. The weight of Matt's expectant silence was unavoidable as he waited for us to answer. Mickey's expression was as angry as mine felt.

"Josh!" Matt barked.

Mickey pursed his lips. "I'm not gonna make promises I may not be able to keep."

I interjected. "We! *We* are not going to make promises *we* may not be able to keep."

A look of approval swept across Mickey's face. He knew I had his back, and now, I was sure he had mine.

Matt cursed and swore under his breath. "Don't let the heat of the moment cause actions you can't take back. You don't want a lifetime with that on your hands. And I'm talking to both of you. That includes Mace, for that matter."

The edge in Matt's voice didn't hide the undertones of knowledge in his statement. Mickey and I shared a look before he spoke.

"Dad, we're just about at that intersection now. Next update will be from our old place."

"Roger. And for the love of God, don't get too close to the house."

Mickey huffed. "We won't."

As soon as I disconnected the call, I turned to Mickey. "You know I'm gonna beat him to a pulp, right?"

Mickey's gaze didn't deviate off the road. *"We* are."

Our conversation ceased until we pulled to a stop at the end of a driveway that led to the McMillan's old family home. Mickey squinted through the windshield as if reacquainting himself with his old surroundings.

The driveway was lined with tall trees that stood still and silent in the night. The driveway curved slightly, making the house invisible from the road where it was shrouded amongst established shrubbery.

Mace parked behind us and waited for us to form a huddle in the beam of Mickey's headlights. We mutually agreed that the property needed to be checked out, but we needed to be wary of getting too close; rural properties often had dogs who would alert their owners to people walking around in the dead of night. The plan: check it out then get the fuck out as quickly and as quietly as possible.

"She's not here," Mickey murmured while staring into the darkness. He absentmindedly flexed and rubbed his arm again.

Mace thumbed over his shoulder towards the house. "Wanna check it out anyway just to be doubly sure? You know, like, to see if there's a single light on or a car matching the description of the one lurking around the last few weeks."

"Yeah briefly, but stay the fuck quiet!" Mickey hissed.

We avoided the crunching gravel underfoot, picking our way through the grass at the edges and centre of the driveway.

As it turned out, Mickey's hunch was right; the house held no secrets that would help unlock Lil's unknown location. We were returning to our vehicles when Mickey's phone rang out loud. Thank Christ we were a distance from the house. He slapped the phone to his ear and waited.

"Really?" he whisper-yelled into the phone. "Message me the address. We're just leaving our old place now. Needless to say, nothing out of the ordinary here. I'll call you later with what we find."

Mace and I matched Mickey's pace when he broke into a run while continuing to talk to his father. "*No, we* will handle it and call for backup if needed."

He pocketed his phone and relayed the updated information between breaths.

"There's been a tip off from an old guy called 'Jones' whose neighbour is away for a week and asked him to keep an eye on his property. The old guy apparently got up to take a piss and noticed lights on in a private helicopter hangar on the neighbouring property. Lights that shouldn't be on, nor were they on earlier."

I was already wrenching open the ute door and throwing myself into the passenger seat as Mickey said a couple extra words to Mace. Mickey slid into the driver's seat and I heard the engine of my ute roar to life behind us.

Mickey tossed his phone my way when a text alert sounded. I snatched it from my lap and clicked on the map link Matt sent through. Bracing my hands on the dash, I yelled the first set of directions as Mickey conducted a hasty three-point-turn then sped down the narrow rural road with Mace tailgating us, heading the direction we came from.

"Let Lil know, will you," I demanded.

"I've already told her we have a lead, but I don't want to get her hopes up just in case it's a cop out." Mickey paused before continuing with caution in his voice. "She didn't sound good, mate, and I don't have a good feeling." He held up his arm again. "I'm not sure what we're gonna find because she wouldn't tell me anything apart from that she's bleeding, but otherwise okay. Knowing her though, that means that she's probably *not* okay."

My fists curl in rage, digging them into my thighs to try and quell the urge to hit something.

Plenty of time for that later.

The directions to the address led further into the rural abyss, somewhere between Boondocks and Fuck-knows-where. We ended up in a completely different area of Northland. The drive dragged from minutes to over an hour, and I grew increasingly anxious with each passing kilometre.

"Here. Fuck, right here!" I frantically pointed to a batted sign post with a singular tattered post-box underneath.

Mickey slammed on the brakes and gritted his teeth, glancing in the rear vision mirror as Mace's slightly delayed reaction had him braking hard behind us. I clung to the overhead handle as Mickey took the turn hard and fast, accelerating as soon as we'd juddered across the cattle stop.

The narrow gravel road followed the natural curve of a creek before it forked. Right led to a rundown farmhouse nestled against the outer edges of a small pine plantation, and left led over a precarious looking wooden farm bridge before snaking out of sight behind a small hill.

Mickey dropped down a gear. "It's gotta be this way. We'll check if it's the correct guy. If this is Jones' property, it's likely he's still awake."

The headlights of my ute bounced in the wing mirror as Mace followed us along the pot-holed driveway. We pulled up at the house and I was out and knocking on the door before Mickey and Mace stepped up beside me. It immediately inched open.

"You the police?" The old man barked. His bushy eyebrows drew together as he looked the three of us over. "If you're here to raid my place, I ain't got shit. So, do us all a favour and fuck off."

He moved his arm out from behind the door to discreetly show us a shotgun. "Loaded," he added and drew himself up to full height; which came level with my chin.

In my impatience, I took a step forward and laid a hand on the doorframe. "Goddammit, we're not here to plunder the place. You called in about suspicious activity on your neighbour's property. We need more info."

His faded blue eyes narrowed at me.

"Please," I added quickly.

"Come," he commanded and stepped into my space.

I moved aside to let him shuffle past us, and he gestured around the side of his house before disappearing into the darkness. Acutely aware that he had taken his shotgun with him, I threw a hesitant glance at Mace and Mickey. Mace tilted his head in the unknown direction in silent question while Mickey scowled into the night.

"You boys coming or not?" Old man Jones barked, his voice gritty with age. "I ain't gonna shoot you, but your dilly-dallying is pissing me off."

Mace snorted as he made his way around the corner first, thus becoming our sacrificial lamb. Shrugging at Mickey, we both followed and came to stand beside Jones again. The silence drew out as we waited for him to explain what we were doing around the back of his house, at four-thirty in the morning.

"This is where my bathroom is..." Jones indicated behind him then pointed over our shoulders, "...and that is the helicopter hangar that should be dark as the night. Harry is away at an air show, and I know for sure he ain't back yet."

Looking in the direction he indicated, I squinted to make out the smallest light in the distance. It wouldn't seem out of the ordinary unless you knew what to look for.

Mickey turned back to the old man. "That hardly looks like a hangar, Mr Jones. Maybe it's a security light of a house?"

"Not a chance, lad. Not if I can see it from here. There's someone up there who shouldn't be. I would've gone up there myself but I'm not as quick as I used to be." He chuckled to himself and lifted his shotgun to communicate his usual method of self-defence.

Mickey took the lead. "Thank you, Mr Jones. Go back inside and stay there," he called over his shoulder, already making his way back to the vehicles.

"Wait, you guys ain't cops, are you?"

"Not directly," Mace informed him. "They'll be in contact during the day to tie up loose ends."

"Fucking cowboys," Jones mumbled before he slammed the door shut and flicked the lock.

GAGE

THE GRAVEL ROAD was surprisingly long. It snaked deeper into the countryside as it wove up a large hill, cutting back and forth on itself frequently, taking us higher and higher. At the top of the ascent, the land flattened into a large grassed terrace before the road disappeared again behind another smaller rise. The drive was rough, precarious at times, and stretched on for longer than expected.

I was on the verge of another outburst about how bullshit the hill was when the curved roof of a building became visible.

Mickey glanced at me, his eyes wide and round. "She can hear us," he whispered.

Adrenaline speared through my veins. My pulse spiked and my hands itched to find her, to make sure she was okay. Then reality hit. We were heading into the unknown. We didn't know what was waiting for us, and that scared the shit out of me.

Bright, incandescent ceiling lights shone into the early morning light through the high windows. Those must have been the ones we saw from Old Man Jones' place and he was right; no security light would ever be that bright.

Driving slowly and parking a short distance from the main doors was our only option if we were going to keep the element of surprise. However, if Lil had already heard us, chances are that Jono had as well.

Mickey leaned over to rummage through the glove box, muttering something to himself as he pulled out his nunchucks.

"Just in case."

"You'll poke an eye out with those."

"Trust me, mate, I intend to. Here take this." He shoved a pistol into my lap. "You know how to use one?"

"Yes," I snapped, not liking his condescending tone.

With a wry backwards glance at me, he slid from the vehicle and headed towards the tailgate. I joined Mace and Mickey and crouched to talk strategy.

Mace pointed at the two of us. "You two go back, I've got front."

"Bullshit you've got front. *I've* got front, you two go back," I whisper-yelled, jabbing two fingers in the air between them.

"Fine, whatever. But this ain't Gotham city, shit's about to get real," Mace hissed. "Also, I reckon Jono expects you two to turn up, right?" His eyes cut to me.

"I'm taking a punt by saying that he's already sussed out that you and Lil are a thing so that leaves me as a floater, the third wheel he won't expect."

Seeing the logic in Mace's explanation, Mickey nodded then made a move to stand. "Sounds good, but I'm taking front."

"Like fuck you are," I growled. "Let's go."

I didn't stick around for more pointless arguing. There was no vegetation to provide shadows to hide in, so I took the straight up approach by jogging for the front doors. Mickey and Mace veered towards the corner of the building. There, after a brief wordless conversation, they disappeared around the side in search of a back door.

I wasn't surprised to find the large double doors to the hangar locked, so I rounded the corner to continue my search for an entry point along the far wall. There wasn't a door, but the office window was definitely large enough to fit through. However, the noise of breaking the glass would draw attention to our presence. I deliberated for a few seconds until I heard two male voices yelling inside.

Shielding my face in the crook of my elbow, I smashed out the glass pane with the butt of the pistol Mickey shoved at me. Creating a big enough hole and knocking off the sharp edges, I hauled ass up and over the edge and fell unceremoniously onto the floor.

That was when I heard the worry in Lil's voice. "*Oh my God, Mickey! Jono, please, let him go!*"

I was at the doorway in a heartbeat and my blood turned to lead in that same instant.

Lil was taped to a chair near the back corner of the building. My chest ached as I took in her ashen complexion and blood coating her arms, face and perhaps even hair. Her jaw was set strong, yet, she appeared so goddamn broken. Love and hate welled within me as I flicked my eyes between Lil and Jono. Seeing her completely at the mercy of the man brought back all the memories I longed to forget. It also lit a fire within me, and I knew I would die trying to stop history repeating.

My eyes snapped to Mickey, standing stiff with a gun pressed against his temple.

"Oh, I don't think so, not when I've caught the pigeon pair," Jono snarled and viciously kicked out Mickey's knees so he had no choice but to land heavily on the concrete floor.

There was no way Mickey would have stood for being easily pushed around without it being a ploy. His nunchucks were hidden somewhere on his body where he could quickly access them. There was no doubt in my mind that he was acting as the decoy to give Mace and I time to get into position. Regardless, I was not okay with him being held at gunpoint to do so.

Jono approached Lil, awkwardly dragging Mickey with him. Picking up a knife from the floor, he casually placed the tip against Lil's throat while keeping the gun trained on her brother.

"One move and I'll make a cut there's no coming back from," Jono spat.

Where he stood, Jono had his back to me and it made sense to make my move now. After a quick check of the pistol's safety catch, I was about to slip from the office when I heard, "psst," from behind me.

Mace's frame filled the broken window space. I savagely gestured for him to get in here right-the-fuck-now and follow my lead. Once he had his big ass squeezed through the shattered hole and stopped glaring at me when his shirt got ripped, I made a few frantic hand gestures then slipped into the open expanse of the hangar.

The unmistakable trace of stale cigarette smoke hung in the air—just like I noticed at Lil and Mickey's house yesterday. Fuck, yesterday seemed like a lifetime ago. It wasn't *that* smell that made my stomach curdle though; it was the iron tang of fresh blood mixed with old blood hanging in the air that hit me the hardest. Flashbacks of blood covering my hands, dried and caked into the fibres of my clothes, the smell I couldn't rid from my nostrils for weeks, tore through my memory before I could halt them.

Forcefully shaking off the unwanted recollection of Lotte's death, I inched closer to where Jono held the knife to Lil's throat. I wasn't going to let her die in my arms like the last love of my life did.

"I know you're here. Come out, come out wherever you are," Jono taunted, his sinister voice echoing around the empty hangar.

There was no point in trying to hide, yet I continued my silent approach from behind him. He didn't flinch, both knowing I was there and expecting me to come at him from this angle.

I jammed the gun into the base of his skull where his spine disappeared into his deranged head. "Don't move, motherfucker."

"Well, well, well, I was wondering when you'd show up. *You* must be the new play thing that my darling Lilianne has acquired. I regret to inform you that your services are no longer needed," he chuckled like he was loving every fucking minute of his power trip.

In amongst all the ranging emotions coursing through me, it was his use of her full name that sickened me most. I hadn't heard anyone ever call her that apart from Mickey, once, and she lost her shit at him. Now, I completely understood why.

"Shut. The. *Fuck*. Up! You don't know anything about me. And Lil sure as fuck is *not* your *darling*." The words seared over my tongue. "She never deserved a piece of shit like you in the first place."

Jono's shoulders stiffened and I caught Lil wince as the knife pressed a little harder against her throat.

From the corner of my eye, I caught Mace's movement silently inching in our direction. He made sure to remain behind me where Jono wouldn't spot him. I kept Jono talking to ensure Mace could approach undetected.

"What do you truly want from this? I mean, either way you lose. You won't walk out of here, and you sure as fuck won't have the girl at the end of all this," I growled.

"Like you'll want her again now that she's partly butchered. No amount of beauty can hide the fact that she's damaged goods," he spat.

The gun trained on Mickey wavered slightly as Jono's temper heightened. I heard Lil gasp and her fingers squeezed the arm of the chair as the blade breached the skin on her neck. Nausea rolled in my gut again and my nostrils flared as I sucked in deep breaths after I saw the tiniest hint of blood well around the tip.

Mace's fingertips landed on my left shoulder and broke my thoughts. His touch swept across my shoulder blades to the right, covertly informing me of his position.

"You've got two options," I levelled into Jono's ear. "The easy way, or the hard way."

"Fuck you," he yelled venomously.

Mace tapped a count on my shoulder.

One tap.

Two taps.

I grinned devilishly. "Hard way it is then."

Three taps.

All hell broke loose.

Mace slammed his elbow into Jono's extended arm with the gun. From pure reflex, Jono's finger squeezed on the trigger and the loud *crack* of a round leaving the chamber was momentarily deafening. As soon as the pistol clattered to the ground Mace kicked the gun across the hangar floor.

Simultaneously, I rammed the butt of my pistol into the back of Jono's skull and wrenched his arm backwards to break the knife's connection on Lil's throat.

Mickey launched himself from kneeling into a barrel roll, drawing the nunchucks from his waistband. I caught the look of pure vengeance in his eyes as he drew them back and slammed the chucks across Jono's thighs with all his might.

Jono crumpled pitifully to the ground, landing heavily.

Mace's eyes locked with mine for the briefest of moments before I thrust my pistol at him and snatched the knife off the floor, already standing over Lil, using my body to shield her from the scene behind me.

Mace dragged Jono to his feet then Mickey helped drag his dazed body across the hangar.

Despite working fast to release Lil from her bindings, it wasn't fucking fast enough for my liking.

The moment she became free, Lil launched herself into my arms. I gathered her against my chest and pulled her tight, hardly giving her space to breathe out of fear she would be ripped from my arms again. Burying my nose in her hair as my hands ran over her body, I became desperate to touch every single part of her all at once to make sure she was okay—all except for her arms. Those needed medical attention right fucking now.

The relief, oh God, the relief of holding her again, and her being alive, consumed my heart and hurt so goddamn bad. The alleviation of my greatest fear made my knees weak. I stumbled and hugged Lil to my body impossibly further, muffling her sobs in my shirt, utterly overwhelmed with gratitude that I hadn't lost her when I had only just found her.

Mace was beside us, his presence instantly reassuring as always. He murmured to her, telling her it was okay now, as he checked her over.

"Turn her around for me, bro. I need to check her front."

Without a word from either of us, I gently handled Lil until her back was to my front where Mace could resume his assessment. The hasty movements after Lil became released from the chair caused her arm wounds to re-open and start bleeding again. The ruby trickle made contact with my arms where they wrapped around her waist and chest, and the feel of the thick liquid staining my skin made my world faint. I fought against the light-headedness, yet it became increasingly harder to ignore. I grunted as I sought clarity, choosing to focus on Mace instead of his actions.

Mace met my eyes once he was satisfied Lil had no other obvious injuries. He knew what I had been through with Lotte. Though, he didn't know the finer details; those I kept locked to myself.

I followed his line of sight when he flicked his eyes downwards. Bile rose in my throat when I realised just how messy Lil and I we were. I turned her in my arms again so she couldn't see my exchange with Mace. His eyes instantly intensified as I forced myself to swallow down the wave of vomit creeping higher in my throat. He reached for my shoulder, tacitly offering his help. Barely shaking my head, Mace interpreted my meaning and stepped back a pace. Lil needed me. She needed me to be present for her. And, she needed *us*, collectively.

Occasional grunts were heard from Jono as Mickey dished out his comeuppance. Lil whimpered and clung to my shirt each time a blow landed. I flicked my head towards the main doors and Mace jogged ahead to open one for us. Lil didn't need to be here—I intended to take her outside and away from the scene. We had almost reached daylight when Jono started running his mouth.

"You bitch! I'll come back for you and then you'll wish I'd finished the job I started!"

That was the final straw that broke my last sliver of restraint. Passing Lil into Mace's awaiting arms, I strode across the hangar and grabbed his scrawny neck.

"You piece of *shit*. You'll never touch her again!"

Mickey gave me space as I cocked my arm back and punched Jono in the face as hard as I could. That single punch unleashed everything that was held pent up inside of me. I roared in anger and didn't stop punching until my entire arm ached from the countless blows I landed on Jono. It was at that point Mickey stepped beside me and murmured three words that immediately melted away my need for revenge.

"She needs you."

GAGE

MY BACK ACHED as I stood upright, tearing my eyes away from the scumbag at my feet and searching out Lil.

One look at her broke my heart all over again.

She sat on the concrete floor, hunched between Mace's open legs as he assessed her arms. Mickey followed me and stayed standing when I slid to my knees in front of Lil, desperately wanting to touch her, but fearful to lay a hand on her in case it caused her more hurt. She looked too fragile, so depleted, as if one touch might make her disintegrate before my eyes.

Mace eased from behind her and indicated for me to take up his position.

"I'll get the med kit and ring Dad," Mickey muttered and strode to where the vehicles were parked with Mace following.

With my legs either side of Lil's and her weight against my chest, all I wanted to do was protect her and take away her pain. The broken vision of the once vivacious woman repetitively stabbed at my heart. Now that we had found Lil, it was clear that the shock from her ordeal was catching up on her.

Her eyes were reddened and puffy. Her pale face was bruised and swollen, marred with wet tears running down her cheeks. The blood in her hair had become matted and crusty. Her arms—her gorgeous, slender, smooth arms— were now marked with the Devil's own handy work. The right one was in better condition than the left, though the blood smeared everywhere made it hard to determine the extent of the damage. The amount of lacerations on her left arm made me dizzy. My heart ached for the amount of agony she must be in.

I carefully tilted her face with my palm, wiping away her tears with gentle swipes of my thumb. I wanted nothing more than to kiss her pain away and take it as my own burden so she didn't have to carry it any longer. Lil's eyes met mine, and the light that normally shone in them was barely recognisable. I recognised that she was sore and beaten, yet above all else, I saw relief.

"You came for me," she whispered and closed her eyes to my touch.

"Always. There's nothing in the world that would have stopped me."

Lil winced as a small smile tugged her lips, and she placed a hand over mine where it cupped her face.

"You really are a real-life Batman."

"I thought Batman didn't rock a beard? Or an eyebrow piercing for that matter."

What I thought was an attempt to laugh sounded in her throat. "Well, apparently, *this* Batman does. Thank you," she whispered then downcast her eyes. "Gage, about yesterday, I'm so sorry, I really didn't mean to..."

I cut her off by whispering into her ear. "It's not you who should be apologising, Sunshine. Don't even think that for a second. I'm the one who should be sorry, and trust me, I am. I wasn't ready to tell you the real reason I moved here, but that didn't mean I had to keep my reason for going back to Tauranga a secret. But that's a story for another day. Once we have you sorted, I'll tell you the full story, I promise."

She nodded and sighed, deflating against my chest and closing her heavy eyelids.

There was no coming back from what I felt for Lil. I knew I loved her with all my heart, I just hadn't voiced it enough. Second chances didn't come along often in life, not ones like Lil anyway. After the terror of last night's ordeal, I had to let her know exactly how I felt about her. I wanted to be her goddamn hero for the rest of her life.

"I love you, Lily. You mean the entire world to me."

She gasped and when her eyes hit mine again, they shone with renewed intensity through the disbelief. Her chin quivered as my unexpected confession sank in.

"You can't be serious, look at the state of me!"

I leaned closer, cocking a brow as if I was letting her in on my own little secret – which I was. "Trust me, babe, you could look a whole lot worse and you'd still own my heart and soul."

Renewed tears tumbled down her cheeks. The silence between us drew out while I held her protectively yet as gently as I possibly could.

Her whisper spoke the words I once swore I would never allow myself to hear again. "I love you too, Gage."

"Fuck, Lil. I thought I'd lost you, beautiful." My voice broke. "I thought I'd fucking lost everything all over again."

Mace pulled up then dropped the tailgate on my ute while Mickey continued his phone conversation with his father.

"Bring her out here, cuz."

I stood and easily lifted Lil into my arms, transporting her into the dawn of the new day. Last time I had carried her, she was clinging to me and tearing at my clothes. This time she was barely able to keep her eyelids open and her arms against her chest.

I sat sideways on the tailgate with Lil while Mace unfolded blankets. On request, Lil lifted her arms so he could wrap them around her and I tucked them between us to make her as warm as possible. Her body trembled violently and I knew we had to work fast. Thank fuck for Mickey's experience in emergency services; his first aid certificate was up to date and he always carried a huge medical kit in his ute.

Without a word being exchanged, Mickey pocketed his phone and tugged open the kit then set about carefully cleansing her wounds. Mace disappeared as I soothed Lil as best I could despite feeling utterly inadequate when she whimpered in pain. After applying an antiseptic, Mickey gently wrapped her arms with large sterile dressings. He finished by winding crepe bandages around the pads to keep them in place then packed away the kit.

"Need help getting her into the cab?"

"Nope." I slid out from behind Lil and stood in front of her.

Mickey opened the passenger door of his ute and I stopped in my tracks.

"We go in mine, with Mace."

"No, she goes with me."

I rolled my eyes. Here we go; we're going to have a battle of wills over this. I was protective as hell right now, as well as absurdly possessive, but I didn't want to get into a verbal disagreement with the guy in this instance.

"You've got shit all over the backseat. There won't be room for you both in there." Mickey explained slowly as if I was thick.

"And we both won't fit in yours."

He glared, nostrils flaring, letting me know that he was pissed. I glared back just as hard, neither of us willing to give in. Finally, he huffed and stalked over to where I still stood between Lil's legs. I scowled as he pulled the rear door open and shoved all the shit off the back seat of my ute. He stepped back and left the door wide.

"We'll go in yours, Mace can drive mine back."

Keeping my mouth shut, I helped Lil into the back seat then wrapped her in the blankets once more. Shutting her inside the cab, I turned to Mickey.

"Go inside and help Mace with whatever he's doing. I'll wait with Lil."

Mickey took my hint and cracked his knuckles. "Don't need to ask me twice."

I rounded the vehicle and slid into the backseat next to Lil. Mickey was right; I had shit for Africa in here. I focused on finding leg room so I didn't need to face the dilemma of not knowing where I could safely touch Lil.

As if she sensed my hesitation, she reached for my hand and guided it around her waist. Fuck, it felt good to hold her; especially after fearing that I would never get another chance to feel her heart beating under my palm again. I bit the inside of my cheek, willing the wad of emotion away. My attention was drawn back to Lil squirming against me.

"You okay down there, Sunshine?"

"No, not really." She sounded embarrassed.

Alarm coursed through me. "Lil?"

"I just really need the bathroom. I've been holding for hours and my bladder is seriously about to burst."

"Should have put you in your brother's ute then, eh?" I chuckled a little. It made my heart soar when she also let out a small snicker. "I'll help you," I stated as I slid from the cab.

"No! There's no way in hell you're watching me pee."

"Dammit, Lil, I ain't gonna *watch*. You need help, so I'll be helping."

She yielded easily, and it quickly became apparent that she would need my help after all. After assisting her without a single word passing between us, I carried her back to the ute.

Mace and Mickey appeared from the hangar, strolling towards us like their business was completed for the day.

Mace made a beeline for Lil and engulfed her in an enormous bear hug. She seemed so much smaller and fragile in his arms; not that her frame is tiny, but Mace is one hell of a tank. His tenderness towards her in the moment threw me. There was a deep connection between them that was hard for me to witness.

My hand itched to smack his away when he smoothed down her hair and tenderly brushed his fingers across her jaw. Lil nodded in response to his soft murmur, then accepted his help into the backseat.

After he clicked the door shut, I flicked a thumb over my shoulder. "So, what's the deal in there?"

"Bastard is tied to the chair and gagged, waiting for the Police to arrive. It's time for us to get the hell out of here," Mickey snapped, tossing his keys at Mace.

"I hope you served him dessert," I growled.

Mickey's reply was vague yet left little to the imagination, and it made the dark side of me *very* happy indeed.

Lil's knock on the window got our attention. Mace re-opened the rear door and stuck his head into the cab with concern deep on his features.

"Lil Bean?"

"I'm okay, Mace. Just, before we go... Do you have my phone?"

He nodded and rummaged through her bag. With it in hand, he waited for instructions.

"Can you please ring a doctor friend of mine? I don't want to be taken to A&E, but need these wounds checked, and probably stitched, when we get back to Mum and Dad's."

Mace flicked his thumb over the screen. "What's his name?"

Lil scoffed and rolled her eyes at his assumption that it was a *male* doctor.

"Her name is Jess. Doctor Jess Rivers."

38

LIL

THE JOURNEY BACK to my parent's house was a pain-induced blur. Each time I stirred, I found myself safely embraced in Gage's arms and the sense of protection lulled me back into slumber. He held me like I was the most precious thing in the entire world. It was exactly what I needed, and wanted.

When Gage told me he loved me the first time I wanted to squeal with excitement. The second time, this morning, I wanted to cry so hard. I was overwhelmed and crushed, and his confession hit my tender heart with full force.

I was nervous to learn about his past; I already knew it wasn't great, but his admission about losing everything all over again was hard to ignore. To be honest, it troubled me deeply.

Now, lying in my childhood bed, propped up by pillows, I watched Mum flap about like a hysterical canary, making sure I wasn't too hot or too cold. When she wasn't fussing, she was trying to force copious amounts of herbal tea down my throat. Mum was pretty lax, but when it came to one of her babies being sick or hurt, her over-protectiveness made you want to get better pretty darn quick.

Mace relayed the events of last night to Dad, Kimmie and Trav. It was the most distressed I had ever seen Trav. When he sat on the edge of my bed and hugged me for minutes afterwards, I realised just how worried he'd been for me. Thankfully Kimmie had stopped clutching at my waist while crying in borderline hysteria. She only calmed down after Mickey pulled her into him and spread his big hand over her head, holding her tight against his chest. He wouldn't admit it out loud, but I knew he loved her.

Dad and Mace were murmuring in the kitchen—no doubt making further plans, and Gage sat on the side of my bed like a loyal guard dog. In the aftermath of my ordeal, I felt completely overwhelmed by their love, and also a little claustrophobic at the amount of people around me. Enough was enough—I needed something stronger than scuzzy herbal tea!

"Dad!" I yelled then waited a couple of seconds.

His footsteps came closer and he appeared in the doorway with a raised brow. "What can I do for you, bud?"

"I'm in desperate need of something a little stronger." I held up my teacup in disdain.

Dad chuckled quietly. "What's your poison?"

"Whisky, please."

Mum tried to exercise what was left of her parental authority. "Matt! No, Lily, you are *not* having alcohol, of all things," she tutted.

"Yeah, I am. Everyone else is having some and I'm stuck with tea that smells like swamp water."

I pointedly flicked my eyes over everyone in attendance to highlight the fact that they all, indeed, had amber liquid in a crystal tumbler cradled in their fingers. Well, all apart from Mum—and I'm sure Kimmie had vodka in that orange juice of hers—but that was beside the point.

Mum came at me with the teapot. "It's restorative tea, hon. It's good for shock."

"So is whisky, that's why the Scots use it. *Dad!*"

I peered past the stupid green teapot Mum hovered in-front of me and silently begged at him. He gave a wink before he disappeared.

Whoever said it was too early for drinking at nine in the morning had never been sliced up like salami during the night. I couldn't wait for Jess to get here and administer some harder pain meds; the paracetamol wasn't taking the edge off the throbbing at all. Unfortunately, Mum wasn't letting the tea go cold, so to speak.

"You can have whisky after you finish that cup of herbal."

I couldn't hold back the shudder and knew that the tea got nastier the colder it became. On a deep breath, I raised it towards my lips, mentally preparing myself to down it as quickly as possible.

Gage, bless him, came to my rescue, yet again. Once Mum departed the room, he plucked the mug from my hand and quickly tossed it down his throat before she returned.

He grimaced. *"Je-sus!* I see what you mean."

I couldn't help the giggle behind my lips when he shuddered in revolt.

Gage spread his forefinger and middle finger to point at Mickey and Kimmie where they leaned against my dresser, grinning at us.

"If she comes back with more, you both have to take one for the team." Gage then muttered something about 'death juice' as someone knocked on the front door.

"Oh, that'll be Jess." I sat up straighter in bed, smoothing down the duvet, suddenly clammy and nervous.

Despite Jess having seen medical emergencies far worse than mine, I was anxious about her reaction. I was a friend and colleague, not a stranger seeking help from someone viewed as a miracle worker. From what Mace had told me of their phone call, Jess roughly knew what to expect.

Gage took my hand and squeezed, adding a small smile when I pursed my lips together. His smile was meant to reassure me, but it was belied by the turmoil swirling in his dark eyes. There I saw great concern.

Introductions were being exchanged at the front door as I heard Dad welcoming Jess then Mum leading her my way.

"Oh, Lil, honey!" Jess exclaimed the moment she stepped into my room and her eyes found me.

She hurried to my side with a medical bag slung over her shoulder, already exuding the confidence and command of a competent medical professional. Only I knew that she would have recently rolled out of bed—always leaving it until the very last minute—chucked on a pair of leggings and an oversized knitted sweater, then shoved her long blonde hair up into a messy bun on the top of her head. And, damn her eyes, she still looked absolutely gorgeous!

Dumping the med kit on the floor at her feet, Jess bent down to hug me and I got a whiff of her perfume.

Gingerly returning her squeeze, I snickered, "Are you wearing makeup and perfume?"

"You know I don't go anywhere without at least mascara and bronzer on, *ever*," she whispered into my ear.

Pulling back, she glanced around the room. Time for more introductions. I gestured towards Gage.

"Jess, this is Gage, my um..."

"Boyfriend," he finished for me and stood to shake her hand. "Thanks so much for coming out this early."

She smiled back and set her hand in his. "Not a problem. It's nice to meet you finally—despite the circumstances, obviously."

Jess turned to me and cocked a brow, giving me a *'dayum'* look of approval at finally seeing Gage in the flesh. Grinning when I glared in warning, she spun back to Gage.

"So, you're the infamous Batman, huh?"

Gage snorted then shrugged. "Can't help if the ladies think that."

Rolling my eyes and scoffing at his ridiculous claim, I directed Jess' attention to Kimmie and Mickey across the room.

"That's Kimmie, my bestie, and my brother, Mickey. Or Josh. Basically call him whatever you like, he answers to anything."

He scoffed before saying hi.

"Hey guys," Jess replied to their greetings then turned back to me.

Jess gave me the once over without speaking, visually assessing my face without touching the swelling. Mickey watched her every move. I knew what he was doing; evaluating the way she worked to make sure she was doing it correctly. All attention was on Jess' movements until Mace appeared in the doorway. The glass of whisky in his hand was all but forgotten when he clapped sight on Jess. His eyes flared as his jaw dropped slightly. I'd never seen him react to a female like that before and was completely gobsmacked when he drank Jess in like the fine piece of ass she was.

"Mace." I hissed.

He gave a small jerk as he snapped out of his stupor. He slid on a mask of cool when Jess looked over her shoulder at him. My brows rose on their own accord when Jess' movements halted for the barest of moments before resuming. Anyone else would have missed her falter, but I sure as hell didn't.

"Mace, this is Jess. I work with her in A&E. Mace was the one who rang you earlier," I explained to Jess after seeing a slight perplexed look pass over her face.

Mickey zinged in my head. *<You seeing what I'm seeing?>*

<Uh huh. Very interesting...>

<Say that again!>

"Sorry to wake you," Mace said lightly while openly skipping his gaze over her curves.

"Honestly, don't worry about it." Jess waved her hand in dismissal. "I'm used to getting woken all hours when I'm on call. Just another day at the office," she added nonchalantly then turned back to me. "Right, hon, let's take a look at these arms."

"Let me get that under my belt first." I beckoned Mace, reminding him of the glass he held for me.

He stepped forward and planted a hand on the bed as he reached across to hand me the whisky. My fingers touched his and held until he snapped his eyes up to meet mine. There, I openly smirked then all out grinned when

Mace's bright blue eyes flashed me a silent warning to not say a damn thing. Yeah, exactly what I thought; he fancied her—and I got the impression the feeling was mutual.

I released Mace's fingers and tilted the tumbler to my lips, hissing down two small swigs then handing the glass off to Gage. Only once I had caught my breath did I hold out my arms for Jess to start unwrapping them.

It stung as she peeled the sterile pads away from the dried blood, making my eyes water. Jess examined both arms briefly then rattled off a string of commands to Gage and Mace. I couldn't help but snigger to myself as they listened carefully, both standing with their legs slightly apart, arms crossed over their chest, shoulders back, and drawn to full height. The only difference was the reverse of what I usually saw; Gage was smugly grinning and Mace had his jaw set in utmost seriousness. Gage shot me a look before he followed Mace from the room, and Mickey immediately strode after them.

"Bitch, where have you been hiding *him,* you sneaky hold out!" Jess hissed and widened her eyes at me as soon as the guys were out of ear shot.

"Who? Gage?"

"Ha-ha. Although, he's hot, don't get me wrong. I'm talking about *Mace*. Holy shitballs, he's next level hot!" Jess' big brown doe eyes stared up at me from where she knelt at the medical bag.

Kimmie and I shared a giggle. "I've talked about him before, he's not a secret at all. I think he likes you though,

I don't think I've ever seen him listen to commands the first time without making some kind of comment or joke."

"She's right," Kimmie added. "Mace normally does things when *he's* ready, not when told."

We tittered and Jess blushed ever so slightly, which surprised me too. *She* isn't the kind of girl to get 'guy shy'.

"Yeah you've talked about him, but never has it passed your lips that he's smokin'-"

She abruptly cut off when I cleared my throat, indicating that they were back. Kimmie promptly succumbed to a fit of giggles, which left the guys shuffling awkwardly as Jess and I furiously concentrated on my damaged arms.

Mace set the towels and cloths within reach for Jess, while Gage manoeuvred around her to put the large bowl of steaming water on the bedside table. He leaned over and kissed my forehead before pointing a suspicious finger at each of us.

"You girls are weirding me out right now, so we'll be in the lounge doing guy stuff."

They departed the room again, but not before I caught the final glance that Mace seared over Jess. We waited a few beats to make sure they were fully gone before resuming our conversation.

"He isn't really a 'serious about dating' kind of guy, Jess, so I figured there was no point in giving you crumbs when the cake wasn't on offer."

She let out a wistful sigh as she gently sponged my cuts. "Yeah, that wouldn't do. What's he do?"

"Like job wise?" I asked then elaborated at her nod. "He's in construction, works for his Dad's business, the one Gage came up here to work for. And he also casually moonlights as a bouncer at Totem."

"I've never been there, though I've heard it's the place to party."

"It totally is, and the best part is that when you know the bouncer, you don't have to queue," Kimmie piped up. "Plus, there's always heaps of bar staff so you don't have to wait *forever* for drinks."

Our jovial chat soon turned serious. Jess clicked her tongue and told me to brace myself because flushing the wounds with antiseptic was going to hurt like a bitch. I wished she'd have used stronger words, because 'hurting like a bitch' didn't cut it—even with the whisky and low-level pain relief onboard my system. I managed to clamp off some of the screams as she worked quickly and as best as she could, but once she started on my left arm, the pain became unbearable. Kimmie swiftly left the room and was almost immediately replaced with Gage. He held my arm still in an iron grip with one hand while clapping the other across my chest.

Jess' demeanour was professional as always, but her eyes told me that she was finding this task almost as excruciating as I was.

"Sorry, hon, we're almost done. You're doing awesome."

I could only get out pants of breath but nodded shortly in acknowledgment.

Gage's low voice spoke softly in my ear. "Lil, look at me and listen, I'll tell you a story." Instantly, the agitation within my head subsided a little. "When I was about nine, my family went on holiday to Cooks Beach one Christmas. My three asshole sisters dug a hole, held me down and buried me up to my neck. The worst part wasn't not being able to breathe or the sand in my togs, it was the fucking sand hopper bites that flared up hours later over my entire body—like *everywhere*. Do you have any idea how embarrassing it is for a nine-year-old to have his mother inspect bites in places no kid wants his mum to look? Let me tell you, it's embarrassing as fuck. I gave Immi the beat down when I was able to move without ending up itchy as shit. It was her idea to begin with."

He finished with a growl which sustained our amusement long enough for the worst of wound cleansing to be completed.

"I need to meet these sisters of yours," I slurred through the pain.

Gage chuckled then put on a solemn pout. "All in good time, Sunshine. I'm going to put that off for as long as possible because I have a feeling my sisters will embrace you too quickly, and it will turn into *four* against one. The odds are already heavily stacked against me!"

"Aww, someone sounds scared of his big, bad sisters," I mocked, which won me a cheeky thigh squeeze from Gage and a snort from Jess.

She finished reapplying clean dressings while idly chatting with Gage about her job. I tuned out, relaxed back against the pillows, and let the buzz of the whisky take over.

39
LIL

THE EDGE OF the bed depressed and my weight shifted when someone sat beside me. I opened my eyes to see Mace's chin hovering at eye level, then felt a tender kiss be pressed to my forehead.

"Oh, hey, I didn't mean to wake you. How are you holding up?" he asked softly.

I managed a small smile, but truth be told, I was sore. My face throbbed and my arms stung. My smile must have looked more like a wince because he patted my leg then disappeared for a moment, returning with a glass of water and a sheet of decent painkillers. Perching beside me again, he handed me a dose and relayed instructions. It didn't escape my notice that he kept his face carefully composed as he spoke a certain person's name.

"Jess left these for you, two now, then another two in six hours."

I gratefully accepted them. "Has she left?"

Mace nodded. "Yeah, she has work later. She said that she'll get the roster reworked so you've got time off to recover, so you don't need to rush back. She also left a script for antibiotics for you. Ev's nipped out to pick them up before you go home."

"Oh, you all are just too good to me. Thank you, Mace, for everything," I said sincerely and gave his hand a squeeze. Tears threatened to spring up, and I blinked hard to keep them from welling.

"Hey, that's what friends and family are for, right? And I know you'd do the same for me, Lil Bean."

I smiled and handed him back the empty glass, but Mace's expression looked pained and forlorn.

"Fuck, Lil. I thought we'd lost you. You have no idea how bad that was killing us. I was hurting, but seeing Gage… He was in a bad way when we couldn't find you at your house. He loves you, you know."

I smiled and gripped Mace's hand. He squeezed back with both of his engulfing mine.

"I know, he told me."

Mace's brows rose. "This morning?"

I nodded. "And last week, before he left."

"Did that go down okay?" he asked, studying my reaction.

"It did. I, ah, I said it back," I confessed and felt the blush creep onto my cheeks.

"Well I'll be damned," Mace chuckled. "I must say that I predicted you two getting together. I haven't seen him hot under the collar over a woman in a very long time."

"Since Lotte?" I whispered.

Mace's eyes flared then narrowed. "Since Lotte," he confirmed.

We remained silent for a couple of seconds as the memory of Lotte was acknowledged then filed. Mace dashed a shy glance at me before speaking.

"So... Jess is, er... nice."

His eyes narrowed at the sound of me holding in a giggle.

"Jess is gorgeous, both inside and out, which I couldn't help but notice *you* noticing." I leaned forward to fist bump his bicep. "Mason Westbrook, I do believe you have a bit of a crush for my boss."

He fought the smile tugging at his lips and tilted the glass in my direction.

"I do believe I like you better when you are asleep, Lil Bean. Anyway, I actually came in because I need to get going. I'll visit soon, okay."

I nodded and thanked him again, then watched his retreating back leave the room.

. . .

"Yol, Lil, I know you're awake, I can fucking see your lips twitching. Plus, I bought M&Ms."

At those words, my eyes flew open. "Get your ass in here, Travis," I called.

It was day three of my recovery, and I needed some of Trav's personality to boost my mood. My back was killing me from being horizontal for most of the days and nights, but I was simply too exhausted and depleted to gather the strength to move downstairs. Gage had been by my side the last couple of days, and today Kimmie was here to look after my sorry ass for a day or two.

"Kimmie said it would be okay to come say hi...?"

I smiled. "You know it is. Just don't get too close, I haven't showered today."

Trav chuckled and shook the bag of M&Ms as he made his way across the room. He perched beside me and bent his knee on the bed to face me better. The joviality in his expression faltered when his eyes skipped over my black and blue face before dropping to my bandaged arms resting on top of the blankets. The crease between his brows deepened before his mouth parted to speak.

"Don't, Trav."

His eyes snapped to mine, and a beat passed before his grin returned.

"Oh, I was gonna open these, but since you've just said no..."

I tried to kick him from beneath the blankets.

He chuckled. "Good to see you're getting some of your pep back." Trav ripped the bag open and flicked the discarded top over his shoulder. "Kimmie can pick that up. Make her earn her keep," he winked.

I scoffed and held out my hand so he could pour the candy-coated chocolate into my palm.

"Pick what up?" Kimmie asked as she entered with hot drinks.

"The mess I make here instead of in my own home."

"Typical! Here, drink this and get out," she teased, thrusting a mug his way.

"So, what's the occasion?" I asked after gratefully accepting painkillers and coffee from Kimmie.

Trav's expression darkened a little again and his brows pulled in as he took a sip of hot beverage.

"There is none, just stopping by to say hi to my girls."

Both Kimmie and I snorted, causing Trav's scowl to deepen.

"You scared me, Lil. Scared the shit out of all of us."

"I know, Travie…"

He refilled my hand and offered M&Ms to Kimmie. After crunching his down, he reached for my hand and hooked the top of his fingers over mine. The caring touch was an unusual display of affection from Trav. Sure, he was handsy and physical most of the time, but his soft and intimate side seldom came through; and only did when he was truly worried.

"No, Lil, you don't. You have no idea how hard it was to sit on my hands while the others were out looking for you. It killed me and Kimmie to have to sit around waiting for information to trickle in, not knowing how long it would take to find you, or if they'd even be able to..."

My voice was tight and it was painful to speak. "Trav. I'm so sorr-"

He pressed an M&M against the non-swollen side of my lips to shush me. "All I'm saying is that I'm so fucking glad we got you back."

I focused on his tattooed arms and got an idea. "Well, I guess I can always get tattoos to cover the scars…"

Trav beamed a smile again. "Shit yeah you can, 'bout time you got some ink on that virgin skin of yours."

"I honestly don't know if I could handle the pain. I almost knocked a guy out when he pierced my nipple!"

Kimmie laughed at the memory. I glared at her, still mildly resentful over losing our bet.

"Ha!" Trav crunched. "It's not anywhere near as painful as that. In saying that, the pain from a tattoo gun can either be hell, or euphoric. For me…" he held up his arm in explanation.

"Tat whore," I mumbled through a mouthful.

He nodded with a cheeky grin. "Tat whore."

"More than a tat whore," Kimmie muttered under her breath.

Trav pegged an M&M at her. "Hoy! Whoa back, lil' Kim, ain't nothing wrong with appreciating a woman or two." He wiggled his brows and munched with his mouth open, making me laugh.

"Oh, Trav, don't ever change for anyone. Even the woman that will one day steal your heart when you least expect it."

Trav scoffed. "Uh huh, I doubt that."

The three of us paused and listened as someone entered the house.

"Lil? Kimmie?"

"Upstairs," Kimmie called.

"There's a party in Lil's bed and you're invited," Trav added.

Footsteps sounded on the stars along with a cheeky chuckle before Nico appeared in the doorway. He was in uniform and had his beret tucked into the waistband of his pants.

"Hey guys. I finished early for the day so detoured on my way home. Sorry I couldn't get here sooner, pre-deployment is insane," he said, coming into the room.

I met his green eyes as he sat on the end corner opposite Trav.

"It's okay, Neek, we understand. When do you leave?"

"Couple of days, all going well. Couldn't leave without saying goodbye to my homies."

"Damn right you couldn't. But seriously, what the heck is up with everyone hanging out on my bed?"

A shout came from downstairs then two sets of footsteps stomped up the stairs. "Have you guys not learned to keep the fucking door locked?"

"Party in Lil's bed and you're invited!" Trav hollered back, earning a growl and a chuckle from the latest arrivals.

Gage stormed into the room holding a large glass bowl and glared before being jostled to the side by Mace, who took a running jump and slammed onto the bed beside me.

"Gah! Jeez, Mace! Seriously, why is everyone here? Wait! Do I hear Mickey?"

Sure enough, Mickey appeared in my doorway within beats.

Mace clapped his hands. "Now that we're all in attendance, Gage, do the honours."

Gage slapped the bowl down on the bed and pulled out a massive bag of M&Ms from his jacket pocket. They dinged against the glass as he poured them in. Mace shuffled beside me and extracted a bag from his jeans then tossed them at Gage. Everyone else followed suit—apart from Trav.

"Mine have been consumed already." He cast his blame-laced eyes my way.

Flipping him off, I smiled when Gage picked out a couple of yellow ones and tossed them into his mouth. Seeing me catch his action, he gave me a smouldering smirk that instantly heated my cheeks.

"This is the last time the entire crew will be together for at least six months. We can't have a party to farewell Neek, given Lil Bean's state of affairs, so we decided to come here today to let you know how much we all love you, Lil, and also put the hard word on Neek that he'd better fucking come home in one piece." Mace leaned towards me and spoke under his breath. "Those M&Ms should last you at least a week!"

I poked my tongue at him in an effort to hide how overwhelmed I was by them all being here. Tears blurred my vision of the people who meant the most to me, and I focused on the lone M&M between my fingertips as I fought for composure.

"Right," Gage barked. "Everyone down stairs so I can help Lil get sorted. We'll be down in a few."

The crew filed from the room without a single murmur of complaint. When the door clicked closed, Gage rounded the bed and kissed me tenderly.

"Hey, beautiful, you look like you've got a bit more energy, but are you up for this?"

I dashed away a tear. "I'm always up for spending time with the people who matter the most."

He halted my movement as I flung back the covers. "One exception."

Confusion had me frowning, and Gage's features softened slightly. "I carry you downstairs, Sunshine."

I scoffed despite agreeing without hesitation. "You've got yourself a deal, Batman.

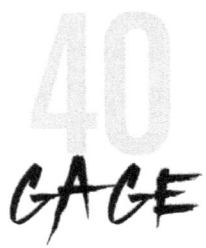

GAGE

THE EVENTS OF last week rocked me to the core and had me questioning my entire life the way it was. Why was it that it always took a crisis to realise just how precious life was and just how much people meant to you? I still felt physically ill thinking about how close I had come to losing Lil. I wasn't yet one hundred percent over losing Lotte—I didn't know if I would ever be—so to lose another woman I loved would have decimated me completely.

For the second time in my life, my heart and soul were owned by someone who deserved every second of happiness. Before Lil crashed into my existence, I had resigned myself to living out the rest of my days on my own.

Now that I'd been given a second chance, I was going to take it and hold on tighter than ever before. It was time to man up and tell Lil my story, the *entire* story, of why I came to Auckland and why I needed to briefly return to Tauranga.

It was something I didn't want to relive, however, I had to set the last of my skeletons free in order for us to wholeheartedly move forward.

Lil tried to broach the subject of our misunderstanding on the afternoon after her abduction as I drove her home, but I refused to say one word about it—for both our sakes. She was in pain, sleep deprived, and hopped up on painkillers. Likewise, I was lacking sleep and, in all honesty, only cared about the fact that she was there beside me, although harmed, still *alive*.

Kimmie had hung out with Lil for a few days after the crew's farewell for Neek, and I returned to work at the girls' insistence. Today being the weekend, I had woken beside Lil in her bed and knew we had the house to ourselves with nowhere to be for the next two days. It was the perfect opportunity to sit down with Lil and clear the slate.

I was up early cooking pancakes with bacon, bananas, maple syrup, blueberries and ice-cream. My heart skipped a goddamn beat when I felt Lil's bandaged arms weave around my waist and carefully pull me into her. I closed my eyes and smiled, just like every other time I did when she did this.

"Mornin', Sunshine. How's the pain?"

"It's okay at the moment, I just took more meds."

"I wasn't expecting you up already."

The tip of her nose pressed into my bare back. "I missed you," she murmured after a deep inhale.

A content chuckle rumbled in my chest. "I missed you too. Hungry?"

"Ravenous."

My eyes flew open at a new sensation. "Er, babe, did you just *lick* me?"

Her giggle made me smile again. "I licked it, so now it's mine."

"I was always yours, right from the moment you swooned at my feet."

Lil's laughter grew louder. "I didn't freaking swoon. I tripped!"

"Uh huh, that's what they all say."

She scoffed and buried her nose between my shoulder blades again. Setting the spatula on the bench and turning in her arms, I idly ran my chin back and forth over her forehead.

"Ugh, beard hair in my eyes!"

"Close them then, Lil. Or better yet, go sit at the table and let me wait on you."

She complied, sitting then twisting sideways, looking all cute as fuck with a grin on her lips.

"You do spoil me."

"You..." I landed a kiss on her lips, "...are more than worth it. I love you."

Telling her that I loved her was the best feeling ever, especially when she said it back. She blushed and looked up at me from under her lashes then pulled me closer by the backs of my thighs.

"I love you, too."

I cupped her head when she rested against my lower stomach. We paused in this moment, simply happy and content in each other's company. The sweet smell of vanilla wafted up from her, making my mouth water even more. But first...

"There's something I need to tell you." The words barely made it past my lips and they came out more as a breath than a whisper.

When Lil focused her hazel eyes solely on me, I melted all over again. She tried to lighten the mood, but I heard the waver of uncertainty in her voice.

"Of course, what's up?"

I sat across from her and held out a hand for her plate. After she passed it, I focused on placing pancakes onto it before handing it back. It was totally a stall tactic because I had no idea where to start. Closing my eyes, I took a deep breath and bit the bullet.

"It's about why I went back to Tauranga the week before last..." I couldn't look Lil in the eye, not yet. "I went to say goodbye to Lotte, and ask her forgiveness."

When I looked up, there was confusion in Lil's gaze. "But I thought you said she passed away?"

It was a touchy subject for both of us, and we were both trying to take it easy.

"She did, Lil. I visited her at the cemetery. I just sat and talked to her about whatever was in my head at the time, about moving to Auckland... About you..." I trailed off and glanced up.

Surprise lit Lil's face. "Me?"

"Yes. I just… I felt compelled to ask Lott to forgive me for moving on. It sounds fucking weird now that I say it out loud, but I felt like it needed to be done."

Lil shook her head slightly then focused on drizzling the maple syrup over her loaded pancakes.

"I saw her you know," Lil murmured, lifting her eyes to meet my astonished stare.

Her admission stole my breath. "You… you, *saw* her? Lotte?" I stuttered. "When?"

"Not long after I met you." Seeing my confusion, Lil set her knife down and elaborated. "I told you I dreamt of her, right? And how it wasn't until you came out to the spa that I realised she was attached to you."

I nodded and Lil continued. "What I didn't tell you was that I saw her so clearly, like she was standing before me in real life. She emitted an overwhelming feeling of pure love for you, or, more like *fierce* love…"

Lil paused while I chuckled, then her eyebrows pulled together as she picked her words. "But she felt so incredibly sad, so… broken, and full of regret. And my God, she was *so* beautiful—completely the opposite to me…"

I smiled wryly at Lil. "Yes, she was a lot different to you in looks, but similar in the fact that she was as stubborn as a fucking ox. Apparently, I like feisty women who are a pain in my ass."

Lil scoffed and giggled nonetheless.

We ate in silence, mulling over our individual thoughts until Lil gulped a large mouthful of juice and set down her glass. She reached for my hand and locked me in place with her unwavering stare.

"What happened to her, Gage? The full story. I know the overall situation, but I know there's more. So, tell me. I'm not here to judge you, either of you for that matter."

"I know. I've just never actually told anyone the whole story before, not even Mace. Talking about what happened makes it real, if that makes sense?"

She nodded and reached for her drink again. While she was distracted, I took a deep breath of courage and tore off the first band aid.

"Lotte was my wife," I blurted, thankfully before Lil took another sip because she gasped and jerked her hand.

She ignored the spilt juice and locked her wide eyes on mine. "You've... You've been married before?"

Hurt flashed across her features a second before she looked away to compose her reaction. She restlessly played with her fork and blinked rapidly before meeting my eyes again.

"I'm sorry, I wasn't expecting that." Lil cleared her throat. "How long?"

"Together for nine years, married for six. We met at college and were inseparable, then married when we were twenty."

"Wow... that's crazy."

"Yeah, it felt right at the time. She died when we were twenty-six."

The sadness increased in Lil's eyes as I continued.

"Lotte battled with depression on and off. When she was up, she was the most joyful, outgoing woman I'd ever met. She was always one for spontaneity. When she was her true self, she would leave those around her feeling happy and uplifted. However, when she was down..."

I dropped my head and swallowed. Rehashing the best and worst years of my life was fucking killing me. I forced myself to talk around the restriction jammed in my throat.

"When she was down, she was a mere shell of the women I married. So dark, so hateful... Violent. It became harder and harder convincing her that her life was worthwhile. Everything came to a head three years ago, when she had a miscarriage. *Another* miscarriage—it was the third one. The first two were devastating for us both, but the third broke her, throwing her into the deepest depression she'd had."

Pausing, I tried to expand my tightening lungs. The memory always triggered that response and I hadn't yet found a way to counter the effects before I grew breathless. I dug my fingers into my thighs to take my mind off the ever-present grief. There was no other way I could continue.

"I got home from work one afternoon and I just knew. I *knew* that something bad was going to happen as soon as I walked through the door. Lott had been drinking, and instead of lying on the couch where I normally found her during a low, she greeted me at the door with a hug that felt like a fucking goodbye. The only way I can explain it was that her eyes just looked... empty. She offered me a beer, which I accepted but went to the bathroom first. In those two minutes before I returned, I heard my bike start. I ran to the door just in time to see her tearing out onto the street, narrowly avoiding a passing car. She hadn't bothered to put on her jacket or helmet. Where she was going, she wasn't going to need them."

Tears prickled my eyes and I was aware of sniffles coming from Lil. A chair scraped as it pushed back, and a moment later she sank to her knees beside me and squeezed my hands in hers.

"I, of course, grabbed my ute keys and took off after her, only able to guess the general direction she headed. I figured she would be heading for the motorway where she could ride hard and fast. My instinct proved right. I found her, but, but... *Fuck!* She..."

"Jesus, Gage, stop, please stop. This is hurting you too much. You don't need to relive this in order to tell me. I understand."

Lil tugged my hands, and begged, fucking begged me to leave it be. But I couldn't, not now that the memories were already rolling off my tongue. I couldn't stop even if I wanted to. The words burned uncontrollably from my mouth, needing to be set free for the first time since I'd lost my wife.

My swallow sounded as painful as it felt. I didn't bother pulling away from Lil's grasp as my tears began to fall. There was no hiding from this agony, no possible escape other than to push through the anguish until I came out the other side; the side where I knew Lil would be ready and waiting.

"She had ridden into the path of an oncoming vehicle at over 120km/h, leaving no doubt in everyone's mind that it was intentional. I clung to her and fucking begged her to stay with me, to not die in my arms, even though I already knew it was too late. She died instantly on impact but was still warm, as if she was simply sleeping in my arms. But the blood... Fuck. That's something that will always haunt me. When the paramedic delivered the news I didn't want to accept, I screamed at Lotte, shouted the most hurtful words at her all the while shattering so fucking hard I wished I was dead as well. I was numb. Frozen to the spot with Lotte's body in my arms while people bustled around me, talking and trying to take her from me. I only let go when I was forcefully removed by a couple of cops. The paramedics put her into a body bag without even *trying* to save her. Seeing them give up on my wife while all I could do was watch destroyed me at a level I never thought I'd be able to recover from."

Lil let out a strangled sob as she climbed onto my lap. I welcomed her arms wrapping around my neck, giving me the comfort I needed despite having been through so much herself. I didn't resist when she pressed my face to the fabric of her t-shirt. Her scent was my saviour, and her heartbeat was my grounding. When I continued, it was nothing more than a remorseful whisper.

"I hated her for such a long time. For leaving me. For so long I thought she was selfish, but I now think that she was trying to be selfless. To save *me* from *herself* in some fucked up way... I really don't know to be honest."

I pulled back, needing to look Lil in the eyes as I spoke the next part.

"However, I can now hand-on-heart say that I've made peace with her. I'll never truly understand why she chose to ride away from me that day, but I feel like it's okay now, that it's okay to move on, to be happy again... with you."

Lil cupped my cheeks, running her fingers through my beard while her tears silently fell.

"How could you possibly ever be whole again after going through such tragedy, such loss. The pain of losing someone that way..." She shook her head slowly as she processed everything I'd just spilled, sharing the burden that hung heavily around my neck.

"I didn't want to make it for two years afterwards. I didn't want to try and move on. I wanted the past back, the one where Lotte and I were happy. This last year has been slightly better. Moving up here was a last chance type of thing, to get completely away from the Bay, that motorway, and the wallowing that I'd become accustomed to. I couldn't see the positive when Dave and my dad staged the intervention, but now I'm forever thankful they did."

"Well, that does explain the scowling beast I first met four months ago..."

I pressed my ear to Lil's chest, instantly soothed by her heartbeat. "That bad, huh?"

"Mmm, not really. Not now that I know why. It was confusing though, and I'm sure you'll agree."

I did. I remembered going from feeling numb to feeling outright pissed that the little spit fire stirred feelings deep inside me from the moment we met; feelings I was determined to keep locked away, secured and forgotten for all of eternity, forbidden to be felt again. That way there was no way I could open myself up to being hurt again.

"Did you have a beard back then?"

I leaned my head back to look at her. "No. Why?"

Comprehension lit her gaze. "It was a Harley, wasn't it? The bike she rode. That's why you have a Victory now?"

My heart skipped a series of painful beats. I nodded through a slightly stunned state of mind. "How very perceptive of you. You're right though."

Lil hugged me tight. "Thank you," she whispered into my ear.

"For what?" I whispered back.

"For trusting me, for sharing your burden, and for making me realise just how much I mean to you."

"How do you mean?"

It was her turn to pull away with regret clear on her features. "I harassed you and tried to blackmail you into letting me ride your bike, but you stood your ground and wouldn't change your mind no matter what. No wonder you were so against it. The fact that you didn't cave to my demands, speaks volumes."

"I don't know how you're doing it, Sunshine, but you're piecing me back together, one lost part at a time."

"Well, it's a good thing for you that I'm a complete sucker for people that need fixing."

I chuckled as she kissed the tip of my nose before seeking her lips. I kissed her sweetly, melting into the warmth that radiated through the thin fabric of her shirt and onto my bare chest. My hands planed over the smooth skin on her back before coming to rest on her ass as her fingers ran through my beard.

"I love you, Gage Westbrook," Lil murmured against my mouth, smiling when I growled a little under my breath.

"I love you too, Lily McMillan. Now eat something before I have a half-crazed starving woman on my hands."

Lil giggled lightly. Now *that,* was by far, the sweetest music I'd ever heard. Lil remained straddling my lap but twisted to pick up a piece of pancake off my plate.

"I think I'm going to eat breakfast right here," she declared and bit off half then shoved the other in my mouth. A full, genuine grin broke out on my face as I chewed.

I don't know what I did to deserve her, but I wasn't complaining. Lil had shown me what it was to live again, to open my heart again and love passionately like I used to.

For the first time in over three years, while sharing breakfast with Lil while her ass filled my hands, I gave myself permission to be unconditionally happy.

LIL

AS IT TURNED out, both Gage and I were both exceptional at healing broken people; namely, each other.

After spilling his heart out to me over breakfast weeks ago, our relationship had grown to reach a deeper level of understanding and appreciation. I knew he was broken and tormented when I first met him; the sheer deep-seated rawness and undisguised heartbreak that became exposed when he opened up about losing Lotte absolutely tore my heart in half. The dark, broody asshole was a ghost of the Gage I knew and loved today.

There was a fine line between being unable to stand the sight of someone and falling head over heels for them. Despite seeing red every time I clapped eyes on him to begin with, there was always an intuitive feeling inside me that knew he was meant to come into my life at the time he did. Not just for my sake, but likewise, for his.

One thing was for sure; there were no 'takesies-backsies'. He belonged to me now, and I to him, and that's the way we intended to remain.

We spent the majority of our spare time together, and it goes without saying that there were toothbrushes and clothes now permanently at each other's place. There were sleepovers and snide comments from the third wheels—Mace and Mickey.

I had worried for a long time that Jono would eventually come back to finish what he started. The dreaded thought relentlessly drilled holes in my stomach, even after Dad assured that the situation had been 'taken care of'. I knew enough about his job and code talk to know I wasn't to ask further questions; Jono wouldn't be back and I needed to trust in that knowledge to find the peace of mind I needed. It was early days, but being surrounded by my family and crew definitely helped me through the mental recovery process.

With Christmas only days away, the crew gathered at my parent's house for a pre-Christmas lunch. We were all here apart from Nico, who had deployed to Afghanistan last month with the Army.

Kimmie and Trav were beside me under the massive tree in Mum and Dad's backyard, giving each other shit about god-knows what; I wasn't listening. My eyes were glued to the sexy-ass man crossing the deck dressed wearing dark aviators, a singlet and boardshorts that hung low on his hips, emphasising his broad shoulders, toned torso, and those legs... Enough said! Just looking at him had me all gaga.

The change in him blew my mind. He had gone from being closed and withdrawn, usually wearing a scowl deep enough to part a sea of people, to exuding a genuine air of contentment that made him so darn irresistible. There were still dark days of course—for both of us—but we had a knack for giving one another space to breathe and simply understanding that hearts didn't heal overnight. It literally took years. Gage hadn't spent a Christmas with his family for three of those, and he confided that the mere thought of trying to be happy on a day where happiness and joy was expected made him sick to his stomach. Up until now, he had always spent Christmas sitting at Lotte's gravesite.

When he told me that, my heart burst with grief for him, yet, I was incredibly thankful I could bring some light to his life again.

In saying that, I was terrified of following in Lotte's footsteps because of how much Gage had loved her. Every now and then I caught him slipping into auto pilot and doing little things he had obviously done for her. Instead of getting upset or holding it against him when he added pickles to my burger, or not adding milk to my coffee, we'd both acknowledged his actions for what they were then found the humour in the situation.

When Gage loved, he loved with all his heart, and it left no doubt in my mind that I wasn't replacing Lotte, but simply filling the large space he had made for me.

This Christmas, Gage did something that made me cry; he rang his mum and asked what the plans were this year and if she would mind if he brought me home to meet their family.

I was so taken aback that I burst into tears. That step wasn't just huge—it was monumental. So tomorrow, he was taking me home to Tauranga to meet his mum, dad and sisters. If they were anything like Mace and his family, I would be welcomed with open arms.

"What are you grinning about?" Gage's question snapped me back to the present.

I looked up from my sprawled position on the grass to see him smirking down at me.

"You." I accepted the drink he offered. "Thank you."

A satisfied sigh slipped out as the *non-alcoholic* ginger beer slid down my throat. "Ahh, dayum that's good."

He chuckled and dropped down to sit beside me. His nearness had me biting my lip as he ran a hand through his hair then over his jaw. Gage still looked like a total badass without the beard, but I was still adjusting to his new look. I got the fright of my life when he came up behind me and ran his smooth chin over my exposed shoulder one night. He looked so different; yet, the same dark eyes sparkled back at me as I took in the change, unable to resist repetitively running my hands over his jaw and cheeks.

Reaching for him now, my fingers itched to touch his smooth face again. They smoothed over his jaw until finding the small scar under his chin that was hidden by his beard. It gave me a little thrill to uncover another little hidden part of Gage that otherwise remained hidden.

"I still can't believe you shaved it off."

Gage's brows rose over the top of his sunglasses. "You liked my beard?"

"Much to my surprise, I actually did. I can't stop looking at you now," I giggled.

"It's good to have it gone to be honest, it gets itchy as shit in summer." He ran a hand over his smooth chin.

"I bet. I'm finding it hot enough in this." I held up my covered arms.

The wounds had healed and the bruising and swelling on my face had long passed, but the scarring on my left arm was bad. The marks were still red and raised, and I was extremely self-conscious of them. I felt bad that I couldn't bring myself to wear short sleeved tops around my family and crew, and I saw the regret and sadness in their eyes, even if they tried to hide it. I simply didn't want everyone to look at me and be reminded of how Jono almost tore us apart.

Gage was the only one I felt comfortable around with my arms exposed. He saw the wounds on a daily basis and had helped me bathe and reapply the dressings during the initial few weeks. The scars were no longer a block that remained between us, and they went largely unnoticed when it was just us together.

"You know you can always take your top off. No one is going to judge you," Gage murmured.

"I know, and it's silly. I'm just not there yet. With you I am, but not everyone all at once." I sighed and lay down with my head resting in his lap.

"It's not silly at all. And we'd never pressure you, Lil. You'll be ready when you're ready." He hummed suggestively when his fingers slid onto my chest and dipped without hesitation into my cleavage. "Besides, it's not your arms I'm interested in right now."

"Seriously!" I startled at the unexpected intrusion from Trav. "It's awkward as fuck when you two get handsy in public!"

Trav leaned forward in the nearby sun lounger and lifted his sunglasses so we could clearly see his glare. Verbal agreement came from Kimmie where she lay between Trav and I.

"Jealous much!" I sassed and planted Gage's hand back on my boob. He did a double squeeze for added effect.

Trav barked a laugh then took a swig of beer. "Lil, trust me when I say I'm gettin' plenty when I need it. But I know someone who's not..." He sniggered and tilted his beer across the yard in Mace's direction.

We all turned to watch Mace dig through the chilly bin as he goofed off with Mickey. Their combined laughter reached us at the same moment.

"What? Mace? I don't believe you," Kimmie said dubiously.

"Oh yeah? Trust me, Kim, he's on a self-imposed dry spell. Watch this!" Trav leaned forward in the chair again and yelled. "Yo, Mace!"

Mace cut his attention our way and Trav pointed towards the back door of the house.

"Jess is here,"

The change in Mace was hilarious; he snapped up straight and spun towards the door, expecting to see her walk out. The moment he realised Trav was taking the piss, he thrust his beer bottle at Mickey and locked eyes on Trav. Striding across the deck, he jabbed a finger towards our mate.

"You'd better start fucking running, Travis."

Our laughter increased when Trav jumped to his feet. "Oh shit."

Mace broke into an intimidating jog and Gage's deep laughter was loud above my head. "Paybacks a bitch, isn't it, cuz!"

Mace flipped us off as he ran past with Trav locked in his sights. Gage laughed harder, his entire body shaking. "Fuck, that is so much better than I imagined it would be."

I tilted my head back to look at Gage. "Payback for what?"

He looked down at me and smirked. "For him being an asshole the morning after we met."

"I don't even want to know," I scoffed.

My man tugged me until I was sitting on his lap, still chortling at Mace and Trav grappling on the lawn.

"You really don't. But let's just say, if my reaction remotely resembled Mace's just now, he's already well and truly screwed."

"Yup, he totally is."

My snicker turned to a yelp of alarm as Gage tipped me off balance and claimed my lips.

"Worth it," he growled.

"For all the yellow M&Ms in the world?"

"Every single one."

EPILOGUE
LIL

~Two years later~

GAGE AND I stood, hand in hand, after the most gorgeous beach wedding imaginable. The day was perfect in every single way.

I dug my bare feet into the soft, heated sand and tilted my head towards the warm, spring sun. Bliss wove the smile on my lips, fully content and happy surrounded by the people we loved the most.

I smiled widely as I scanned the wedding guests. There weren't many—which was perfect in my opinion. It was a beautifully small affair with family only, and by family, I mean blood relatives and closest friends.

The crew had been through hell over the last two years, more than any of us could ever have imagined. Lives were put in jeopardy, relationships had been tested and friendships were solidified during our time of need.

Coming out the other side of the turbulent time as a complete unit gave today even more significance than it otherwise would have.

The Westbrook family Bach along Cooks Beach had become the crew's favourite place to holiday together. Hence the reason for having the wedding here.

Gage squeezed my hand and let go to peck his mum, Caroline, on the cheek. She smiled widely then reached for me, hugging me tight.

Seeing Gage relaxed and happy still sent butterflies spiralling to my stomach. Feeling giddy with love was something I never felt with Jono. With Gage, however, it was constant.

I ran my eyes over him again, loving the wedding attire the guys wore. White linen sleeves were rolled to the elbows, fabric was pulled taut over wide shoulders, and muscular calves were on display. All six of them—Gage, Mace, Liam (Mace's younger brother), Mickey, Trav and Nico—were various shades of God's gift to women, and they bloody knew it too judging by the way their stride held swagger and their loud laughter drew attention.

Gage, however, was next level swoon-worthy. *Literally* swoon-worthy. I had been feeling odd for the last few days and put it down to pre-wedding jitters—not that today was a stressful event; we'd planned it to be as casual and relaxed as humanly possible.

I stood beside Gage as he talked to his mum, leaning against his side after he pulled me close again. When his fingers danced over my exposed shoulder, the look in Caroline's eyes told me everything I needed to know; she was immensely proud of him, and blessed to see that I made him happy after his past heartbreak.

Gage landed a kiss on the top of my head. "You okay, Sunshine?"

"Yeah, just thirsty, I think. I'm going to grab a water."

"I'll get it, be right back. You want anything, Mum?"

"Water would be lovely thanks, Gage."

Caroline and I watched in silence as he made his way across the sand and up a small dune to where the chilli bins lay in wait under a Pohutukawa tree.

Caroline linked her arm with mine and laughed quietly. "I know all parents think this about their children, but I've got to say that I've got one good-looking son."

Our heads came together as we shared a giggle.

"You certainly do, Mumma Caz. And I'm one lucky woman to get a second chance like him."

"I'd say he's the lucky one for getting a second chance with *you,*" she emphasised and raised a knowing brow at me. "We're forever grateful for you bringing our son back to us. I hope that someday he'll make an honest woman out of you, too."

"I'm not sure if he will ever be ready to re-marry," I replied honestly. "And I really am okay with that. I understand why."

I had gotten to know Caroline and Russ (Gage's Dad) well over the last two years. They'd welcomed me into their lives from the very first time I'd walked through the front door that Christmas. Caroline and I had hit it off right away, much like the way his sisters and I had, and I was over the moon to say that I was lucky enough to be part of two awesome families.

Gage came striding back with two bottles of water and cracked each lid before passing one to me and his mum. He then resumed his place behind me so I could lean against his sturdy chest. After having a drink, I let myself be lulled by his voice vibrating against my back while he spoke to his mum. My daydream was broken when Mickey invaded my thoughts.

<Sis...>

Searching him out through the small crowd, I found him standing nearby, talking to Liam.

<Whatsup, brother?>

<Don't drink tonight.>

My eyes narrowed despite him not looking at me.

<I've been dry for months. What makes you think I'd suddenly go back now?>

<Just in case you're thinking about having champagne at the toast later.>

<Why?>

<I'm not sure I should say.>

<Mickey! Now you're just killing my buzz. Tell me!>

<You're pregnant.>

Gage felt me startle. His automatic response was to run a hand up across my chest to rest on my opposite shoulder and pull me closer.

<*Nice try. I'm not.*>

<*Lil, I'm not kidding around. I can feel it. You're pregnant.*>

<*Even if I was, it's too early to tell.*>

<*I've never been surer about anything in my life. You're brewing Westbrook spawn in there.*>

The gasp escaped my mouth before I could think to stop it. My hand settled over my womb before I realised it was moving. In my assumption that pre-wedding nerves were the cause of my constant nausea, I'd completely overlooked the possibility of being pregnant. Besides, like I said to Mickey, it was still too early to tell.

The conversation between Gage and his mum stopped and their eyes landed on me. Worry marred Gage's face when he moved in front of me and touched my cheek.

"Lil? What's wrong?" His voice was soft but I heard the edge of caution he was trying to hide.

I dropped the water bottle as a wave of dizziness washed over me. By instinct, I seized his forearm and held tight, fearful that I would cause a scene by fainting.

"Lil," he implored, shaking my shoulder slightly. "Tell me, what's going on?"

I removed my hand from my lower abdomen and claimed his wrist, guiding his hand until his palm rested against my stomach. The warmth of his touch radiated through my dress and sank deep within me.

Gage startled, the war within his eyes obvious as he fought against the dawning realisation.

"Nothing's wrong," I said quietly. A weak smile touched my lips when he shook his head in uncertainty. "Just..."

I couldn't get the words past my lips.

"Tell me, say it straight up," he urged. "No bullshit."

"You're going to be a daddy," I whispered, so quietly that I wasn't sure if he even heard me.

Beside us, Caroline gasped and dropped the bottle of water onto the sand beside my forgotten one. She palmed her chest and stared with her mouth agape.

The look on Gage's face almost broke me. It was filled with emotion so deep that I wasn't surprised to see tears welling in his eyes before he blinked them away.

"I'm going to be a dad?" he asked, making sure he'd heard me correctly before doing anything else.

"Yes," I smiled through my own blurred vision.

"But, how do you know?"

My eyes flicked to Mickey to see he had moved closer.

"I just know."

"Fuck," Gage growled before his mouth parted in a wide grin.

He took my face in his hands and kissed a path from my eyes to my lips. His kiss melted me into his embrace, so full of love and happiness.

"I love you, Lily McMillan," he murmured against my mouth.

"I love you too, Gage Westbrook."

Gage clung to me, holding me against him, knowing that a beautiful life was budding within me.

A life we created together.

Thank you for reading Ride For Me!
This is the first novel I ever wrote—almost two years ago—and it will always be my first book baby despite being released fourth in line.
I hope you enjoyed every part of Lil and Gage's story!

As an Indie Author, I rely on super awesome people like yourself to help share the word about my books.
Word of mouth is priceless and important for the authors you love.
Please consider taking a few moments to leave a review.
I'd be incredibly grateful!

V xx

ALSO BY VR BAUCKE

<u>STANDALONES</u>
Accidentally Entangled

<u>THE SEVEN THOUSAND MILES DUET</u>
1. Living for Today
2. Dreaming of Tomorrow

<u>THE NORTH SHORE CREW SERIES</u>
2. Break For Me

ACKNOWLEDGEMENTS

My readers—THANK YOU! I wouldn't be here without you guys. Each time I write a new book, I flip flop between being so fired up that I've nailed it then freaking out that it doesn't compare with other books out there. One thing I know is, you'll either like my style or you won't, and that's okay. For those that stick around, fist bumps are aimed your way and I'm forever grateful that you're part of this journey with me!

Hubby—I am ALWAYS giving you shit (keeping you on your toes) and you aren't safe from me here either. I'm freaking out while you read this book. It's 100% different from the one you started reading two years ago and frowned through the first six chapters, lol. That was when you didn't have a beard and I disliked them. Oh, how things have changed, hehe.

Badass—two words; fucking BOOM! YEARS we have talked about the crew, laughed over what they get up to and loved them so damn hard despite them being fictional figments of our imagination—with hints of our craziness sneaking through. And I know you're freaking grinning right now by the way, lol!!! It feels like I can never say this enough, but you freaking rock. Here's to finally publishing the series that first gave us both the bug!

B-licious Betas—Josey, Milissa and Laura—You guys are awesome and without your willingness to read what I've written, this book wouldn't be what it is today! I am forever grateful to you all for all the hard work each of you put in to edit my scrappy writing, haha!

Bloggers—Thank each and every one of you for being eager to read Ride for Me! It's scary has hell clicking the send button on the ARC emails, yet your excitement for this book fuels my excitement! I appreciate you all!

B-licious Babes Reader Group—Though we are still small and finding our feet, you are all so important. I love the feedback, the interaction and the general sense of awesomeness you guys all have. Thank you!

'Til next time, V xx

ABOUT THE AUTHOR

VR Baucke writes from the bottom of the world, New Zealand, and drinks copious amounts of tea, eats way too many crackers and laughs at all things ridiculous.

Connect with her here:

www.authorvrbaucke.com

Goodreads
BookBub
Facebook
Instagram

Made in the USA
Monee, IL
02 July 2020